EVIL
YOURSELVES

By Bill Hiatt

With cover art by Peter O'Connor, Bespoke Book Covers

Dedication

This novel is dedicated to Beverly Hills High School, where I taught English for thirty-four wonderful years.

What Has Gone Before

Evil within Yourselves is the fourth book in the Spell Weaver series. If you are interested in reading the previous books first, you can find their titles "The Adventure Isn't Over." However, if you can't wait to read this book, I have tried to include in the text enough information about earlier events in the Spell Weaver series to make it possible for someone new to the series to understand and enjoy the adventures in this book without having read the earlier ones.

CONTENTS

CHAPTER 1: Prelude (Titania) 1

CHAPTER 2: My Heart is Yours (Tal) 8

CHAPTER 3: Faerie Fiasco (Carla) 30

CHAPTER 4: Faerie Fracas (Tal) 37

CHAPTER 5: Ghost of a Chance (Jimmie) 52

CHAPTER 6: Cold Hands, Warm Heart (Tal) 60

CHAPTER 7: Saint Sebastian Does His Stuff (Jimmie) 70

CHAPTER 8: Justice? (Tal) 80

CHAPTER 9: Surprise Attack (Tal) 93

CHAPTER 10: Runaway Djinni (Shar) 107

CHAPTER 11: Calling the Order to Order (Tal) 128

CHAPTER 12: Strategizing for Armageddon (Vanora) 152

CHAPTER 13: Speak of the Devil (Tal) 161

CHAPTER 14: Finding a Way to Hy-Brasil (Tal) 168

CHAPTER 15: Always Expect the Unexpected (Shar) 199

CHAPTER 16: The Song of Creation (Tal) 208

CHAPTER 17: Love Hurts (Shar) 217

CHAPTER 18: You Have To Be Taller To Take This Ride

(Khalid) 223

CHAPTER 19: Unexpected Rescue (Tal) 238

CHAPTER 20: Hanging with an Archangel (Khalid) 245

CHAPTER 21: Making the Team (Alex) 250

CHAPTER 22: Working the Con (New Dark Me) 270

CHAPTER 23: Poison (Vanora) 281

CHAPTER 24: Destiny Calls (a watcher upon Snowdon) 283

CHAPTER 25: Unpleasant Surprises (Tal) 285

CHAPTER 26: Unexpected Castle (Tal) 326

CHAPTER 27: Saint Jimmie (Jimmie) 340

CHAPTER 28: Change of Heart (Tal) 347

CHAPTER 29: Surprise Attacks and Reinforcements (Tal) 362

CHAPTER 30: Repentance or Hellfire (Carla) 380

CHAPTER 31: Demons and Darkness (Jimmie) 395

CHAPTER 32: Captured (Tal) 408

CHAPTER 33: That Plan Could Have Gone Better! (Tal) 416

CHAPTER 34: Deus Ex Machina…Sort of (Tal) 423

CHAPTER 35: Last Things (Tal) 444

THE ADVENTURE ISN"T OVER 454

ABOUT THE AUTHOR 463

Chapter 1: Prelude (Titania)

William Shakespeare had been dust for centuries, but I still remembered watching unseen as an actor spoke for the very first time those now famous lines from *Henry IV Part II*: "Uneasy lies the head that wears the crown."

I had not suggested those lines to Will. Frankly, I was so put out about the way he handled the secrets I had whispered to him before that I would hardly have given him the time of day, much less suggestions for another one of his plays. Even now I still resented the way he twisted my tales, making me look ridiculous in *Midsummer Night's Dream*. I still from time to time sneaked into the theater during performances, however, and that particular line was carved indelibly into my mind. At the time I did not understand why. Now, as I stood at risk of losing both crown and head, I wondered if that moment had been prophetic, if Will had somehow known I would be in the audience and that one day I would experience the kind of suffering human monarchs did.

Uneasy? Henry IV had never faced quite the trauma I now endured. Oberon, my husband, languished in prison, accused of deeds I would scarcely have believed had I not witnessed some of them myself, yet in my heart I knew that they were somehow not his, that an as yet unknown evil force had led him down a darker path than he would ever have trod on his own. I had no proof, though, and I was met everywhere with ill-concealed scorn if I tried to suggest he might be innocent. Not only that, but my once loyal subjects looked at me with mistrust, for if my husband had done such evil, how could I have been as ignorant of his vile purposes as I claimed? Even the members of my court were no better, whispering that perhaps I too belonged in prison. I lay awake each night, fancying I heard my rivals sharpening the daggers that would assassinate me. No, assassination was too risky for those cowards to attempt. It was the executioner's axe they sharpened, for the time when I would be condemned as my husband's co-conspirator.

It was not cold in the room where I hid myself, but I shivered as much as if a chilling wind were knifing through me like the very daggers of my imagination. With difficulty I silenced my fears and focused on the task at hand.

I knew the dangers of entering the mortal world, far greater now than they had been when I had tried to make a friend of Will Shakespeare. Nonetheless, I had no choice: I needed to reach Taliesin Weaver, and I had no way to do that except to seek him out in person. I hardly knew him, having only met him once, and then under circumstances unlikely to win his trust. Still, I had to have his aid; whether he trusted me or not, I had to trust him. There was almost no one else I could turn to.

Despite the urgency of my need, I dared not appear randomly in his world. Allowing myself to be seen by other humans would simply feed the flames of the funeral pyre my enemies were building. Before venturing from my realm to his, I had to locate him. Peering into his world was in some ways more tiring than just going there, and certainly more time-consuming, but at least I knew the general area in which he could be found.

Robin Goodfellow, perhaps the only subject who remained truly loyal, had flown all the way to Taliesin's town and scouted the area for me, so when I did find Taliesin, Robin could open a portal for me. I could not use magic to reach a place I had never been, and I doubted I had the time to fly there as Robin had.

Robin had returned and was with me now, quieter than I had ever seen him, kept silent by the gravity of my situation and particularly by my need to find Taliesin as quickly as possible. Even Robin's breathing was a whisper of what it normally was; a tomb would have been only a little more silent than this tiny chamber in which my body sat while my mind reached out into the mortal world, searching for Taliesin.

I did not immediately find him, but in my visions of his world I did find a structure Robin told me was the Santa Brígida High School gym. The door was shut tightly, but I could still hear the music—or at least what passed for music with human teenagers—from inside. I could almost feel its vibration in the otherwise still night air, though certainly that must have been my imagination. Robin had heard there was to be a dance in commemoration of Saint Valentine's Day, and if this was that event, it was more than likely Taliesin was inside. If so, how was I to reach him without attracting unwanted attention from other mortals?

I noticed there were two teenage males standing outside the gym, looking around in a way that suggested they did not wish to be observed. One was tall, blond, and muscular. The other was shorter, had black curly hair and a leaner build. I had only seen Taliesin's warriors once, but I was almost positive these two teenagers were two of them, Daniel Stevens and Stanford Schoenbaum. Heartily sick of the feeling of being spied on everywhere, I had not intended to eavesdrop on them, but I needed to make sure I was right about them. If my memory had served me well, they would know where Taliesin was and could probably call him to me, saving precious time and reducing risk.

Daniel, if that was who he really was, gazed at the one I assumed to be Stanford as if Daniel were trying to stare him down. Stanford looked nervous but did not seem ready to back down.

"Stan, we have to tell Tal!" Daniel said in what I took to be an attempt at a commanding voice.

"Tell him what?" replied Stanford. "That he's under a spell?"

"He has to be!" Daniel insisted. "What other explanation is there?"

"We asked Nurse Florence to check," replied Stanford patiently. "She couldn't find any hint of a spell, remember? And Tal's mom is a seer. She can sense things happening on other planes of existence. You think she would miss what's happening under her own roof?"

"We've seen many things that didn't make any sense but were true anyway," replied Daniel stubbornly, "and you know that as well as I do."

"Has it occurred to you that Tal might actually have fallen in love with Carla on his own? Dan, you suggested that he give her a chance yourself, didn't you?"

Daniel laughed in a way that made me shudder rather than want to join in. "Yeah, and that's one of my reasons for thinking something's wrong. One or both of us has been Tal's best friend as long as any of us can remember. Has either of us ever been able to talk Tal into anything when his mind was already made up?"

Stanford didn't respond right away, and I thought about opening a portal at that very moment. I knew the Tal they referred to was Taliesin, so they must be who I thought they were. I hesitated, though, because of the possibility that Taliesin really was under a spell. Something like that could doom my effort from the very beginning. Rather than commit myself too hastily, I decided I needed to listen just a little while longer.

Daniel seized the opportunity created by Stanford's silence. "Nothing to say, Stan? You know I'm right. The guy's part mule for sure. And even if Tal were easier to convince, look at all the other things in this situation that just don't make sense. For four years now Tal has been pining for Eva, trying to recapture that childhood crush they had. Then, suddenly in a twenty-four-hour period, Tal decides he and Eva are just friends, after all—"

"We know a lot of guys who've changed their minds pretty quickly...where girls are concerned," interrupted Stanford.

"But not Tal, you must admit!" replied Daniel, again attempting an authoritative tone. "I don't know if it's because of being able to remember all of his previous lives or what, but Tal isn't anything like most guys our age as far as romance is concerned. Look at the number of girls on this campus who would have been happy to take his mind off Eva. No, don't even worry about them. How about the *women* who wanted him? Ceridwen, Morgan le Fay—"

"Both of whom were evil!" protested Stan. "Anyway, they were just toying with him."

"Yeah, right. I know a lot of teenage guys who would turn down sex with a beautiful woman because they weren't sure of the woman's motive. Sure! But forget about them, too. What about Aphrodite? The Greek goddess of love, in the flesh—quite literally, from what we could tell—and Tal turned her down because he didn't want to be disloyal to Eva...and he and Eva hadn't been a couple for four years!

"You remember when we first arrived on Olympus, and Aphrodite greeted us with a little of her charm? I would have done her right then and there. So would you, in front of everybody if need be."

Stanford blushed intensely but said nothing.

"We got only a small dose of what she could do, Stan, only a fraction of what Tal got later. Yeah, yeah, don't say it, I know his will is stronger than ours, I know he has magic, but still...do you really believe he could have resisted if not for his stubborn determination to cling to Eva no matter what?"

Stanford shifted awkwardly from one foot to the other. "I'll admit that Tal's resistance to temptation would be...hard to explain unless he had some very strong motive to resist."

"And then," said Daniel, pressing his advantage, "even if he were ready to move on, how could he pick Carla right then? You and I both heard that shouting match. Carla tried to trick him into thinking the only way to ever be with Eva would be in another life...after marrying Carla in this one."

Stanford nodded his head reluctantly. "Tal did feel betrayed."

"Well, buddy, I know more about what Tal does when he feels betrayed than anyone else. If not for that...situation in the Underworld, I don't think he would have forgiven me yet...or ever, maybe."

"The circumstances aren't even remotely the same," insisted Stanford. "You aren't a supernova-hot girl, for one thing."

"And yet," Dan interrupted quickly, "Tal himself pointed out to Carla that I was much younger when I...did what I did." Daniel paused, looking uncomfortable, perhaps haunted by the memory of that past betrayal. Stanford, looking just as uncomfortable, waited for Daniel to continue rather than taking the opportunity to jump in.

"What about the fact that Nurse Florence couldn't find any trace of unexpected magic on him?" asked Stan finally. "Wouldn't it be impossible to cast a spell on Tal that couldn't be detected by someone who knew what to look for?"

"You know what, Stan, I don't have a clue, but after all that we've been through, is there really anything that could truly be impossible? Tal and all of us have magic weapons, which we carry around with us invisibly, with no more thought than other people give to carrying cell phones.

"And why do we carry magic weapons everywhere?" asked Daniel more loudly.

"Keep your voice down!" cautioned Stanford.

Daniel rolled his eyes. "Yeah, like anyone could hear us over the music. I think it's starting to vibrate the fillings out of my teeth.

Anyway, you know what I mean: we carry them just in case some bad guy, who may or may not be human, but probably not, tries to get the drop on us. We carry them so they'll be handy in case we need to take a quick trip to Annwn, or maybe Olympus, and who knows where next? I spend every day half expecting to be told that Narnia is real and that we have to go there to save someone or retrieve some artifact."

"Be—"

"Tell me to be quiet one more time, and we'll do some impromptu combat training right here! I could be shouting so loud my lungs would pop, and nobody inside would hear us." Stanford looked a little annoyed, but also just a little uneasy. I could understand that feeling all too well, and I knew Taliesin had been told in no uncertain terms that there could be no more information leaks to mortals— under any circumstances. Daniel was right, though; that music would cover their conversation even if he screamed. I also noticed that they, accustomed to observing their surroundings in combat, were keeping a watchful eye, each looking over the other's shoulder. They had positioned themselves so they could see anyone coming to or from the gym.

"Stan, we've fought the undead, witches, rebel faeries, mortals hyped up on nectar and ambrosia, giants, demons, former Greek gods, and even a dragon once. A year ago, hell, six months ago, we would have said that none of those things existed.

"And look at our little group," Daniel continued without giving Stanford a chance to respond. "Tal is the reincarnation of King Arthur's bard, you're a reincarnation of…King David." Again Daniel seemed hesitant, and I remembered Robin had told me there were rumors that the David presence in Stanford was a separate consciousness, which would mean David could easily be listening in. Perhaps being overheard by someone like that intimidated even the generally self-confident Daniel.

"Oh, and we can't forget that Shar was once Alexander the Great…mostly because he never lets us! Carla is the sorceress Alcina returned, our school nurse is a modern-day Lady of the Lake, Shar's family has adopted someone his parents think is a fugitive but who is really a half djinn, and, oh yeah, until a few weeks ago my little brother was a dead nine-year-old haunting us, and now he's a very much alive sixteen-year-old, even though nobody knows how that happened. You know what? None of us can really say impossible anymore."

"Suppose you're right," replied Stanford a little defensively. "What can we do about it? We have no proof. If Tal is under a spell, what makes you think he's going to listen to us?"

"Honestly, Stan, grow a pair!" snapped Daniel. "It's a risk, but not any worse than any of the other risks we've run. And Tal is still Tal, spell or not. He may not believe us, but I doubt he's going to whip out his sword and hack off our heads for suggesting the idea.

"I get it," he continued, much more gently. "I know you don't want to do anything that would hurt Tal, and he seems so happy now. It's fake happiness, though. I'm sure of it. Maybe real happiness will come his way, maybe not. Whatever happens, he deserves the chance to find out, and he'll never get it if Carla is bewitching him somehow."

Stanford leaned against the wall, looking almost sick. I imagined that with all his heart, he hoped Daniel was wrong...and so did I. What I had to ask of Taliesin would be hard enough to accomplish when he was at his best. It might well prove impossible if he were compromised by a spell.

Nonetheless, Daniel could be wrong, and Taliesin remained my only real hope, even if hostile magic had impaired him somehow. I realized listening to the conversation had been a waste of time after all. Placing the weight of all my plans on this one teenage human was a risk either way...and either way I had to take it.

I opened my eyes and nodded to Robin, who quickly cast the spell that opened a portal, its swirling silver glow inviting me to step through.

By now Taliesin's men were so preoccupied that, vigilant as they had been, they did not see me coming.

Chapter 2: My Heart is Yours (Tal)

It had been some time since our band, the Bards, had played together, and Carla and I took a rare moment to just enjoy the companionship and the music. It was Valentine's Day, after all. Not only that, but it was 2013, a year I was once sure neither one of us would live to see. Both of us still had our share of worries, but tonight we had agreed to take a holiday from them.

Carla was soloing in Demi Lovato's "Give Your Heart a Break," and everyone on the dance floor so successfully moved in rhythm to the music that from where I was standing, the scene looked more like Hollywood choreography than real life. Carla's raven-black hair sparkled in the lights, her model-perfect face seemed to glow, and her voluptuous body called to me, making me ache to answer. She, too, looked like someone from a movie scene…or from Olympus. Yeah, I know—I'm not the only guy who ever compared his girl to a goddess. I am, however, the only mortal guy in quite a few centuries who could have made the comparison from firsthand experience.

I was playing the guitar right now, but my solo turn would come next, with Bruno Mars's "Locked out of Heaven." We would follow that with a duet: "Breaking Free," the romantic number from near the end of *High School Musical*. Corny, I admit, but what can I say? I'm a hopeless romantic, and given the occasion, I could get away with being one. I know life isn't really a Disney movie, but wouldn't everything be a lot easier if it were one?

Carla got enthusiastic applause, especially from the guys, and I started my solo performance. I was putting a little magic into the music—don't worry, not enough to set off a Dionysian orgy! Just enough to get everyone feeling so good they could escape their troubles as I was doing. The magic the original Taliesin had gifted me with, to say nothing of the musical ability, meant that even on a bad day, putting an audience in whatever mood I wanted was not much of a challenge.

Maintaining my own mood, however, abruptly became more challenging. I didn't know why I suddenly felt a twinge of uneasiness. Perhaps something reminded my subconscious of the

Halloween party that had turned out to be a trap set by Ceridwen...a trap that had nearly killed me and all of my friends.

Knock it off, I told myself, but uneasiness continued to gnaw at me. I kept most of my attention on the music, but I allowed myself to glance around the room, looking not just with eyes but with my magical senses as well.

Nurse Florence, who managed to chaperone every event I attended, seemed completely unconcerned. She was near the back of the gym, dancing with Coach Miller, the only other staff member who knew my secret. Frankly, they looked as if they could use a chaperone! I couldn't really blame Coach, though; aside from Carla, Nurse Florence was the most beautiful mortal woman I had met in this life. Coach and Nurse Florence looked mismatched, since he was older and pretty ordinary looking. Then again, he had risked his life on Halloween and was willing to put up with his girlfriend's quick exits whenever an emergency presented itself.

Carlos, Shar, and Gordy were all dancing with their girlfriends. Jimmie was sitting and talking to his date. I paused a little when I came to him. Even from a distance, I could feel his unhappiness. His date seemed totally into him—and oblivious to what was going on in his head. I couldn't do much for him right now, but figuring out what his problem was definitely on my to-do list.

Suddenly I realized what was out of place: Stan and Dan. Dan had come stag, probably still doing his penance for breaking Eva and me up four years ago so he could have her. I was more than willing to forgive and forget; our mutual desire to save Jimmie, Dan's actual brother and someone I loved like a brother, had helped me to realize the importance of forgiveness, and I wasn't shy about letting Dan know how I felt. Still, he made of point of coming by himself to this kind of function, ignoring all the girls who would have crawled across half a mile of scorpions to be his date. I knew he had been here earlier, but now he was nowhere to be seen. Of course, he could have stepped outside to get some air. So what?

Stan's absence, however, was more conspicuous. He had finally started dating Natalie Kim, a girl he had been crushing on for months before finally getting up the nerve to ask her out. It wasn't like him to just leave her standing around looking impatiently at the door he must have exited through a few minutes ago. Even if he hadn't been hot for her, he was too much of a gentleman to just abandon her. Could something be up?

It took me only a few seconds to find them, standing outside the gym in what appeared to be very serious conversation. They were clearly having an argument, and I could easily have tuned in to find out what was going on, but I didn't feel any fear from either one of them, so I decided not to poke my nose in where it didn't belong. Had there been some supernatural emergency, they would have shared it with me. Apparently, there wasn't one—for once.

I got applause as enthusiastic as what Carla had gotten when I finished my solo number, and then we started on "Breaking Free." Staring into her eyes as we sang, my earlier uneasiness faded away...

Well, that is until a psychic blow like a spike being pounded into my skull hit me with such force I nearly staggered. If this were indeed a magical attack, I had to do something about it without any of the hundreds of students and others in the gym ever knowing what had happened.

Carla was looking at me with concern. She was too close not to pick up on my sudden pain, though I think I was camouflaging my feelings well enough to keep anyone else from catching on. I could easily have alerted her and gotten her help. I could have done the same with the guys and Nurse Florence.

I didn't for one basic reason: at that moment I realized the attack was coming from inside me. There could only be one source for such an attack: my old "buddy," Dark Me. Only I could do much about him, so I signaled Carla not to worry and tuned in on his evil frequency, which I had tried so hard to jam in recent weeks.

"Sorry about the headache, dude, but I needed to get your attention," I heard him whisper from the depths of my mind. The tone was oddly friendly. Most of the time he screamed obscenities or insults at me. He was a sore loser for sure, not at all happy that I had kept control of my body away from him.

"You got it, but not for long. What do you want?" I mentally whispered back, hopefully keeping our mental conversation too low for Carla to pick up on.

"I've been trying to warn you for days, ever since we returned from Annwn. You just haven't been listening."

"I'm listening now," I thought impatiently. *"Spit it out."*

"Carla cast some kind of spell on you when you were recovering from that fall from the sky. I don't know what it was, and I must not have been conscious at the time, but given your sudden change of feelings, I can guess."

I wanted to laugh out loud but couldn't risk that, so I had to settle for laughing inside, laughing in my most derisive way. I didn't want Dark Me to have any doubt about my reaction.

"I don't know what your game is, but you aren't coming between me and Carla." Dark Me wasn't totally evil any more than I was totally good; however, he was a product of the unusual workings of my brain and my ill-advised use of dark magic. I couldn't trust a word he said...even if what he said made any sense, which it certainly didn't.

"Wake up!" he snarled. *"Wake up, you pathetic excuse for a hero. You and I always used to agree on one thing: we both loved Eva. I still do. Whatever spell Carla used only affected you, not me."*

I gave him another contemptuous laugh. *"Love? You don't even know what love is. You just want to distract me for some reason. Well, like all your plans, this one will fail."* I clamped down on him with all my strength, shoving his lies back into his throat. He screamed in protest, and I knew I would have a headache tomorrow, but I had heard the last of him for a while. I hadn't figured out how to completely reintegrate him with me yet, but I could damn well keep him quiet.

We finished the number, and scanning the audience, I sighed with relief; no one had caught even the smallest glimpse of my inner turmoil. Apparently, I had been able to keep the performance going and deal with Dark Me at the same time.

However, I hadn't been able to mask all of the ordeal from Carla. This was the time for one of the band's scheduled breaks, so she took me in her arms and whispered, "What's wrong?"

"Dark Me was getting a little temperamental," I whispered back. "Nothing to worry about, though. I suppressed him again."

"Aren't you having to do that more and more often?" Even in a whisper, I could hear the concern in her voice. "Perhaps Nurse Florence and I could help."

"You remember what Merlin said," I replied quickly. "I need to be able to handle Dark Me for myself if I am to ever be free of him. If people help me too much, he will win in the end."

Carla frowned—just barely, since she needed to maintain the illusion that we were just exchanging whispered I-love-yous. "Merlin doesn't know everything."

I matched her almost-frown with the ghost of a smile. "In my experience, he does. Anyway, Dark Me's safely tucked away again, so let's not let him spoil the evening."

Carla looked unconvinced, but I gave her my best I'm-too-cute-to-argue-with smile, and she reluctantly dropped the subject. If I had the power to create a girlfriend by magic, I could never fashion one better than her.

At that moment, I noticed Stan reenter the gym. As soon as he made eye contact with me, he pointed at the door; clearly, I was needed outside. However, I still didn't sense fear, so at least the campus wasn't under some kind of supernatural attack.

"Carla, I need to step outside for a minute," I told her quickly.

"Break's almost over," she noted, looking around nervously.

"Change the playlist a little and start with some of your solo numbers if you have to. The guys will follow your lead."

"If you need me—" she began.

"I promise I'll come get you," I replied. "I don't think it's that much of an emergency, though." She looked worried again—who could blame her, given recent history? Nonetheless, she didn't try to hold me any longer, and I raced over to the door.

Outside I found Stan, Dan, Nurse Florence...and Titania, queen of the English faeries. The hood of her brown cloak partially concealed her face, and she wore what was, for her, a subdued dark green gown, but even so, she stuck out like the proverbial sore thumb. Even without her faerie luminescence glistening in the dark, her sheer beauty would have been eye-catching enough to draw the attention of anyone but a blind man.

She must have noticed my worried expression, and with a wave of her hands, she shrouded all of us in invisibility.

"Pardon this intrusion, Taliesin, but there is no one else to whom I can turn."

There was a time when I wouldn't have had the first clue how to deal with royalty, let alone faerie royalty, but by now I was used to drawing on the experiences of the original Taliesin to get me through these situations, even ones like this one that could require diplomatic skill as well as manners.

I bowed to Titania, but she immediately signaled for me to stop almost before I could complete the motion.

"Your courtesy is much appreciated, but I fear we have no time for such niceties tonight." Normally, I could not read the mind of such a powerful being and would not have attempted to, except in urgent circumstances, but I could not help feeling the anxiety radiating from her. She had reason to be anxious, but I had no idea why she thought I could help.

"I am at your service, Majesty," I assured her.

"I am glad of it, for I much need your aid. Only you can save my husband…and me."

Just when I thought the universe had no more surprises in store, Titania came along and sent shock waves through my whole body. I could see the others had been caught off-guard just as much as I.

"Majesty," I began, uncertain what I wanted to say but knowing I couldn't just stand there with my mouth hanging open, "forgive me for hesitating, but I do not see what I can do for your husband…or, meaning no disrespect, why I would want to do anything for him. He has allied himself with Morgan le Fay against me. As if that were not enough, he sent me on a quest he hoped would kill me, and, when I actually completed it, instead of accepting the outcome, he tried to murder me outright, threatening my friends in the process."

Titania bowed her head in what looked like genuine shame, though I didn't know her well enough to be sure.

"Taliesin, I must agree with what you say. He has done all that you claim…and more. Yet I must ask you to come to his aid anyway."

"Queen Titania," interrupted Nurse Florence, "perhaps the Order of Ladies of the Lake could be of service—"

"The Order will do me no good," cut in Titania impatiently. "I mean no disparagement to your age-old organization, but they will judge me in the same way you do, and I do not wish to be seen merely as the doting wife too foolish to fully appreciate her husband's corruption."

"I beg your pardon, Majesty," I said, trying to be as diplomatic as possible, "but what makes you believe I won't think exactly the same thing?"

Titania pulled back her hood, allowing her luxuriant black hair to flow over her shoulders. I wondered for a second if she would actually sink as low as to try to seduce me. Surely not with three other people watching.

"When others wanted to condemn me for my role in Oberon's plot, you recognized I had been deceived and defended me. You also spoke for mercy to Alexandros, despite his alliance with Oberon and my Olympian cousin, Ares. Alexandros would be spending eternity in Tartarus if not for you. You were willing to look beyond your desire for revenge and seek justice instead."

"You *were* deceived," I said slowly, "and Alex was a bullied wreck tempted into an evil he would never have pursued on his own. By our standards, he would not be considered fully responsible for his actions. Oberon's case is not like yours or Alex's. What defense can you offer for Oberon? What possible extenuation can there be for a king who deceived his own people, his own queen?"

Titania smiled weakly. "There is wisdom in your words...but Taliesin, you knew Oberon long ago, at King Arthur's court. He was manipulative, truly. He was...a politician. But was he evil? Was he at all the man he seems to be now?"

"People change," replied Nurse Florence, "especially when they have centuries to live."

"Majesty, I knew of Oberon at King Arthur's court, but I would never have claimed to know him personally. Besides, Nurse Florence is right."

"Except that he did not change over the centuries," insisted Titania. "He changed only recently...as if by magic."

I was tempted to laugh at Titania's grasping at straws, but laughing at a formidable spell caster with an army of faeries at her command would have been stupid, and there was something in her glance that would have stopped me anyway. She might be talking nonsense, but she believed it. Of that I was certain.

"Surely Oberon is too powerful to be conquered by an ordinary enchantment," I protested, "and if someone powerful enough to enthrall him actually existed, surely magic that potent would be easy for someone like you to detect."

Titania shuddered. "I have known Oberon for centuries. Though I cannot sense any alien force working upon him, I know there must be one. Someone has developed the ability to cast a spell both powerful and subtle, undetectable by me because I do not know what to look for."

I could have sworn Stan flinched at those words. I made a mental note to ask why later.

Then I thought I saw something even stranger: Titania looking knowingly at Stan as if she understood why he was flinching. That really had to be my imagination. I needed to stop looking for nuances that weren't there.

"We all know Morgan le Fay convinced him she had been his mother in a previous life, but a spell such as you describe is far above anything Morgan could do," I argued. "Who did you have in mind for this enormously powerful sorcerer? Surely someone with that much might would have shown his hand in some other way."

Titania locked eyes with me as if she were trying to gaze right into my soul—or inviting me to gaze into hers. "Someone summoned a demon powerful enough to impersonate Merlin and nearly kill you."

Nurse Florence shook her head. "Hell magic *is* powerful, but I have never known it to be that subtle. Of course, a powerful enough caster might have crafted the spell and summoned the demon as two separate, magically unrelated acts. However, the fact that a demon was summoned doesn't mean a powerful and skillful caster had to be involved. Anyone with even a little magical ability, plus a willingness to sell his soul and to commit vile enough acts in the service of Hell can raise a demon"

Titania looked annoyed but tried not to show it any more than she could help. "What about the disappearance of my Olympian cousins? How many souls would it have taken, how many vile acts would have to have been performed for Hell to make Zeus, Hera, and Demeter vanish? And what about the sudden hostility of Ares and Poseidon? I suggest that the same force that corrupted Oberon attacked the Olympians, enchanting some of them in the same way Oberon was enchanted and somehow banishing the others. Do you have a better explanation…any of you?" she added, almost as if challenging Nurse Florence.

I had to admit it was an interesting theory. When we had found a way to reach Olympus, sent by Oberon on the supposedly impossible quest to bring back the lyre of Orpheus, Apollo had told us of the unexplained absence of the three elder Olympians. Ares, from what I recalled from my Greek lives, was a nasty customer who might have turned to evil on his own, but Poseidon, though temperamental, didn't seem a likely candidate to turn on his own family so completely.

"There is one more thing," continued Titania, perhaps sensing I was wavering. "When the Amadan Dubh stole the lyre, his act, though evil, made sense. He is a musician, after all, and the lyre makes him several times more powerful. But what did Oberon want with it?"

"It was just a pretext to get me killed, remember?" I replied. "He never expected me to return with it."

"Ah, yet when he intervened on Olympus to keep you from coming back, do you remember his final attempt? Having gained the upper hand, he offered to spare your friends in exchange for you…and the lyre. Why? He is no musician! I suppose he could have made some use of it, but it would not have done anywhere nearly as much good for him as it did for Dubh. Why then bother with it at all? Including it in the deal made it more likely the Olympians would balk.

"There can be but one explanation," she continued triumphantly. "The…being who has bewitched him wants it for something."

She might have been just a woman trying desperately to save the man she loved, but the theory was weirdly convincing.

"Oh Queen, if all this is true, why come to us?" asked Nurse Florence, still unconvinced. "You have all the faeries of England at your disposal…and Olympian cousins far more powerful than Tal. They would surely be interested in fighting the being who made Zeus disappear and corrupted Poseidon."

"Lady of the Lake, I would not be so contrary if you came to me for help," replied Titania, but her voice had more sorrow in it than reproach. "The truth is that my subjects, fooled by Oberon, would not help me now. If I tried their loyalty in such a way, there would be a revolt, and I would be overthrown. As for the Olympians, they distrust me after the plot in which Oberon involved me. They will not heed my call, and, as you know, I cannot travel to Olympus to plead my case without their consent."

Much to my surprise, Titania knelt before me and clasped my hand so hard I thought for a second my fingers might fracture. "Taliesin, please! You are my only hope!"

I sighed audibly. I always was a sucker for a damsel in distress.

Gently I pulled her to her feet. "Majesty, I can promise nothing…but I will investigate your theory."

"Tal—" began Nurse Florence.

"Investigate!" I reiterated. "Queen Titania, I am not convinced that what you say is true, but even if it is only partially true, it raises issues we cannot ignore. Oberon's odd behavior by itself could be disturbing, but, added to the disruptions on the Olympian plane, the fact that a high-level demon is lurking around somewhere, and the fact that a madman is running around loose with the lyre of Orpheus…well, the possibility of a connection is alarming.

"Nurse Florence," I said, trying to forestall an objection, "we already planned to figure out who had summoned the demon and how to eliminate it as a threat. Besides that, we have promised to help recover the lyre from Dubh as soon as Gwynn ap Nudd can figure out where he is. If the queen is right, we can aid her without deviating much from our plan; if she's wrong, we stand to lose very little."

Nurse Florence looked as if she might have objected further, but the sudden shimmer of a new portal right next to Titania drew her attention—and everyone else's. Titania herself backed away from it, and she seemed even more apprehensive when Robin Goodfellow shot through it, out of breath and totally unlike his normally mischievous self. I had only met him once before, and I hadn't imagined his playful face capable of such a display of abject terror. Even facing possible imprisonment by the Olympians, he had been far calmer than this.

"My queen, Nicneven comes!" he shrieked, hitting the ground with a thud. Picking himself up quickly, he added, "Run!" in an even higher shriek.

Having the relatively gentle Titania on campus was nerve-wracking enough. Having Robin Goodfellow around made me far more nervous; even when not quaking in fear, his unpredictability made him a problem. But having Nicneven, the bipolar queen of the Scottish faeries whose moods found expression in a physical form that varied from a beautiful young maiden to a hideous old crone? No, I couldn't take the chance.

Another portal erupted in the shadows nearby. Without a second thought, I turned my will against it, and it collapsed. Stan's and Dan's swords flashed in the dark, and I drew White Hilt, which flamed to life in my hand. Robin, however, did not follow our lead.

"Are you all crazy?" he asked, his voice still almost at a scream. "You can't block her like that without suffering her wrath! Our only hope lies in flight!"

That was easy for Robin to say. He and Titania could flee back to her castle in Annwn. Theoretically, I could take Stan, Dan, and Nurse Florence with me to Alcina's island.

What I couldn't do was take the whole gym full of students and teachers with me. Leaving the architecture aside, there would never be time to portal that many people out of harm's way. Besides, the various faerie rulers would be angry enough to make Nicneven look like a girl scout if I revealed my magic to that many mortals. No, I couldn't evacuate the area, and I couldn't chance running and having Nicneven land here and take her frustration out on a mass of innocent bystanders.

Another portal flickered into life, and I squashed that one, too. Robin stared at me, silenced by his inability to believe that anyone would risk Nicneven's terrible vengeance.

"Taliesin, I should leave you," said Titania quickly. "Nicneven is coming for me, not you."

"Can she sense your presence?" I asked. "Will she know you've gone and try to follow you, or will she appear here whether you leave or not?"

"Alas, I know not," admitted Titania. "I do not even know how she found me here in the first place."

"Treachery!" wailed Robin. "Someone has betrayed your whereabouts to Nicneven."

I blocked another portal, this one throbbing with the rage of its maker. At least it appeared that Nicneven was alone and could open portals only so fast. However, now that she knew someone here was blocking her, she might decide to come back later with reinforcements.

"What does she want, Majesty?" asked Nurse Florence.

"I have heard whispers that she wants to take my throne and unite the English and Scottish faeries under her rule. Oberon's situation has weakened my position, else she would never have dared such a thing."

As usual, I didn't have any really great options. Assuming Nicneven was alone, Nurse Florence, Titania, Robin, and I should be more than a match for her magic. She might have soldiers with her, though, if she aimed to capture Titania. In that case, I should try to summon Carla and the rest of the guys. How could I do that without someone noticing? My absence was probably already conspicuous enough. Carla was the band's only other vocalist, so she couldn't just leave without tipping off everybody in the room that something was wrong. The same held true for the other guys. Natalie, Stan's date, knew the truth about us as a result of being trapped with us when Ceridwen attacked, but the other guys' dates were completely in the dark and needed to stay that way.

"Majesty, can you tell where Nicneven is?" I asked tensely, stifling yet another portal.

"Not easily unless you allow a portal to open," replied Titania sadly. "I would not advise that at this point. However, I can guess she is in or near her castle."

"Which is…" I prompted. The original Taliesin had never met Nicneven, and his memory didn't provide me with any clue except her Scottish origin.

"In Elphame, of course, but there is a fixed portal that connects to this world at Caithness, and another is said to lead to a secret exit somewhere in the area of Ben Nevis."

"What difference does it make where she is?" asked Dan.

"Because," I replied with a grim smile, "the best defense is a good offense."

"Tal!" protested Nurse Florence, "you can't mean to attack her! That would pit you against every faerie in Scotland!"

"And the alternative is…what exactly?" I asked impatiently. "Wait until she breaks through here? I can feel her anger even though she's still in Elphame. I can block her for now, but what is to prevent her from coming through later and catching us by surprise? We have only two choices: appease her somehow, or fight her."

"I will not allow you to risk yourself," said Titania firmly. "This is my fight, not yours. Let her through, and I will go with her."

Suddenly the previously sniveling Robin grew a spine. "I will not permit this, Majesty! Once you are her prisoner, all hope is lost." He was still even paler than usual for a faerie, and his whole body was shaking, but suddenly there was a silver sword in his hand.

"She will still have to abide by faerie law," replied Titania with as much conviction as she could manage. "If she remains clearly the aggressor, she will not have the sympathy of the other faerie rulers. It would not surprise me if she were trying to provoke conflict that she can then somehow blame on me."

I had seen quite a bit of faerie politics in recent months, and I was not as confident in the system as she was pretending to be. I could imagine a lot of faeries being perfectly willing to sacrifice Titania if by so doing they could avoid war with Nicneven.

"Robin is right, Majesty," I said forcefully. I think even Robin was surprised to find me on his side. "Letting Nicneven take you gives her too much of an advantage. Besides, it's, it's…an affront to my authority. You are here as my guest, and you are under my protection!"

I was pretty much pulling rank I didn't have with that last line. It's not as if I was the mayor of Santa Brígida, much less its king—but my status was…unusual, and faeries sometimes had strange ideas about hierarchy.

I found myself getting a headache as I squeezed another portal out of existence. I had gotten much better at that kind of maneuver with practice, but even so it drained a lot of power. I could feel myself weakening and knew that we had to act quickly.

"Tal, even if fighting Nicneven is a good idea, which I doubt," began Nurse Florence, "trying to attack her in her castle is suicide. She's sure to have enough troops on hand to overwhelm us. If we take her on, let's do it here, where we have a chance of facing her alone."

"Not at school!" I responded in the most peremptory tone I could manage. "We'd be handing her hundreds of potential hostages."

"Or hundreds of reasons for restraint," suggested Titania. "Nicneven angers every other faerie ruler if she reveals her magic to mortals."

"I won't take the chance, Majesty," I replied, gently but firmly. "The presence of mortals did not stop Ceridwen or Morgan le Fay from working dangerous magic."

"One of them is dead and the other in prison," countered Titania.

"Which only demonstrates that the wrath of the faerie rulers is not that much of a deterrent to them."

Titania was not accustomed to being contradicted, particularly by a mortal, and she opened her mouth to speak again but then closed it. "What then would you have us do?" she asked finally.

This was a bad time to have no answer, but that was exactly my problem; though Titania finally considered following my lead, I realized I had no idea where I was going.

Much as I hated to admit it, Nurse Florence was right: it would be foolhardy to surprise Nicneven in Elphame or in Scotland. Yet I, too, was right: having a magic battle just yards away from my fellow students would be like exploding a small nuke right next to them.

"I have an idea," offered Robin, looking a little less shaky. I turned expectantly in his direction. "Any port in a storm," as the old expression has it.

"You don't want to fight here. There is no need to. We can divert Nicneven to any place of your choosing."

I tried hard to conceal my disappointment. "Robin, I know I could theoretically redirect her portal, but that takes enormous energy, and the results are as unpredictable as..." I trailed off, realizing I had been about to say, "as unpredictable as you."

"No, no!" said Robin, starting to shake more noticeably, but this time more with enthusiasm for his plan than with fear. "I don't mean that. Just open a portal directly in front of hers. She'll stride through, and, if you can be quick about it, before she realizes she isn't in the right place, you can jump through your portal and close it behind you."

"That…that just might work," I said, caught a little by surprise that his suggestion was actually good.

"I have learned a few things from playing tricks on people for centuries," he replied with a grin.

Then I had to slam shut an emphatic effort to open another portal, and my headache began to twitch into migraine territory.

"We need to do this fast!" I told everybody. Nurse Florence looked concerned but nodded her head in agreement.

"The others—" began Stan.

"No way to get them out without causing a scene."

"Leave that to me," said Robin with a wink, suddenly looking much more his usual, playful self now that he had something besides Nicneven to think about. He sheathed his sword, pulled out a faintly glowing wand, and then vanished so quickly I had no time to protest. I had the sinking feeling his attempt to extract the guys from the dance was going to be a train wreck, but I didn't have the time to go chasing after an invisible faerie who was one of the fastest moving of his kind. I did take the time to send a quick mental message to Carla, telling her to make some excuse for the band to take an early break and then try to work with Robin so that he made as small a mess as possible. She naturally wanted to join me right now, but she was the only one inside who had any magic—or any real possibility of guiding Robin.

I could feel the energy for another portal building. Instead of squelching it, I just slowed it a little.

"Nurse Florence, as soon as you can tell where Nicneven's portal is going to open, open one to Alcina's island right in front of it." She nodded and began building her own mystic energy. It suddenly occurred to me that it really should have been Robin matching the two portals, since he'd had centuries of practice with it. However, there was no use worrying about that now.

"Be ready!" I ordered. I should probably have addressed Titania separately and more diplomatically, but I had no time for courtesy right now. Fortunately, she didn't seem offended.

"We'll only get one chance at this," I added, though everyone knew that.

Nicneven's portal shimmered open, and a second later Nurse Florence's covered it completely. So far, so good, but if Nicneven wasn't in a hurry, we were sunk.

I had never met Nicneven, but I could feel someone passing from one portal to another...someone with a great deal of power.

"Now!" I barked, jamming Nicneven's portal closed, then plunging toward Nurse Florence's, boosting my speed up to faerie levels. Even so, if she wasn't surprised enough, she might conceivably jump back into Santa Brígida before I could reach the portal. The next few seconds would be crucial.

No one had emerged by the time I threw myself through the portal, a battle cry on my lips and White Hilt wreathed in flames, Titania at my heels and the others surprisingly close behind. This was going to work after all!

And it might have, too—except that we came tumbling through the portal and into the early morning sun on Alcina's island to confront...someone who couldn't be Nicneven. I had worked enough with faeries to recognize one even when the faerie was shape-shifted, at least if I concentrated hard enough. The gray-robed, gray-haired woman who stood before us did have power, but she was human, not fey. We had caught her by surprise, but since she wasn't the one we needed to surprise, we had to figure out what was happening quickly. From a different plane I could no longer block Nicneven's efforts to open a portal into Santa Brígida. On the other hand, I couldn't leave whoever this woman was roaming around on our island; I had to figure out what she was up to...and quickly!

"You there!" I said in my most authoritative voice, this time borrowing liberally from my life as Hephaistion, one of Alexander the Great's commanders. For good measure I pointed White Hilt at her. Nothing unnerves most people more than a flaming sword. "What is your business here?"

To my surprise, the woman didn't even flinch. If anything, she stood up taller and gave me what I imagined was her haughtiest expression.

"It is my mistress's business I do. Who are you to demand anything of me?" She looked oddly familiar, but I couldn't quite remember in what context I had seen her before. It had been some time in this life, though.

"Who do I have to be?" I countered. "I am now Taliesin Weaver. Once I was Gwion Bach, who drank from the cauldron of knowledge and was reborn from the womb of Ceridwen as Taliesin and became a member of the court of King Arthur. Before that I was Hephaistion, son of Hephaestus and commander of the army of Alexander. Before that I was Heman, son of Joel, son of Samuel, friend to King David of Israel. Before that I was Patroclus, who fought at Troy with Achilles. I can go on if you like." No, I'm not anywhere nearly that arrogant, but in the supernatural realm pedigree can be very important, and most people couldn't remember even one of their past lives, let alone all of them.

The woman remained unmoved. "I care not who you were. My mistress *is* a queen, and she will not hesitate to punish you for capturing her envoy."

"Well, I *am* a queen as well," said Titania, stepping forward. "If you will not answer to Taliesin, answer then to me, for it was I who ordered your capture." I raised an eyebrow but did not contradict Titania.

"Queen, yes...but for how long, I wonder," sneered the woman. If nothing else, she was gutsy. I wondered if she had any reason to justify such confidence.

"Long enough to make you regret your insolence," said Titania, quietly but somehow menacingly at the same time. I would have been interested to see how this battle of wills played out, but I couldn't spare the time. I tried to reach into the woman's mind, but she met me with what felt like formidable shields. Breaking through them would take time.

"We need to imprison her," I said to Titania and Nurse Florence, "and then we need to get back to Santa Brígida. Nicneven could be there by now."

"Imprison me? That you will not," said the woman harshly, after which she flew straight up in the air. Well, I knew she had power, so I really shouldn't have been surprised.

She might have expected Titania to fly after her, but she seemed genuinely shocked when I also took off and headed right for her. Unfortunately, she didn't freeze but continued to fly at high speed away from us.

Despite obviously being a follower of Nicneven, the woman didn't seem to realize how foolish it was to try to fly away from a faerie. As humans, the woman and I both had to expend magic to move through the air, and both high speed and long distances burned lots of magical energy. Titania, on the other hand, had the innate ability to fly—and she was much faster than a human. She caught up with Nicneven's fleeing minion and wrestled with her until I caught up. The woman might have been a physical match for Titania, as humans are normally stronger than faeries, but she was no match for me. Though I had an instinctive aversion to hitting women, dealing with the likes of Ceridwen and Morgan had more or less cured me of that, so I didn't have too much trouble stunning this stranger with a punch. Once she wasn't able to cause any more trouble, Titania and I easily carried her back to ground level.

"Now, ladies," I said to Nurse Florence and Titania, "if you would be so kind as to bind her with a powerful sleep spell, we can get back to Santa Brígida and see what's up." I hardly dared to voice my fear that Nicneven was already there committing mayhem, or if not, that Robin Goodfellow's plan to get the guys out of the dance unseen had gone hideously wrong.

"Might I suggest that you probe her mind first, Taliesin?" suggested Titania. "She is clearly in the service of Nicneven and might have valuable information."

I hated to spend the time, but I didn't want to refuse Titania's request, either; perhaps this woman knew something that could make the difference between life and death for the faerie queen.

I entered the stranger's mind with surprisingly little effort, aided by her unconscious condition. However, she still resisted instinctively once I was in, and it took a few precious minutes for me to extract anything useful.

I got her name almost immediately: Alisa MacDougall. Knowing who she was might be useful later if we needed to interrogate her, but right now it made little difference.

One of the first real tidbits I extracted from her was a memory of a meeting with Ceridwen during the time Ceridwen had been using the Carrie Winn identity. That explained why I had recognized Alisa; I had been at Awen as Carrie Winn's intern when Alisa met with her. Apparently, Ceridwen had been trying to form an alliance of some kind with Nicneven. So Ceridwen's agenda had been even more complex than we thought—not exactly useful intel now that Ceridwen was dead, though. Digging deeper, I pulled out the memory of Alisa standing next to Nicneven just minutes ago, and I breathed a sigh of relief.

"We don't have to worry about Nicneven right away," I told Titania and my friends. "She was using Alisa here to open the portal to Santa Brígida." I should have remembered that even someone as powerful as Nicneven couldn't open a portal to a place she had never been.

"As far as Alisa knows, she's the only one who has been anywhere near Santa Barbara, so at least Nicneven can't make any further attempts to reach our area for the time being."

"That's good news," said Nurse Florence, "but why haven't the guys and Robin joined us, then?"

"Robin must be having trouble finding a discreet way to extract everyone else from the dance," I said with a confidence I didn't entirely feel. "Let me see if Alisa knows anything else, and then we'd better head back."

I dug around for a while but found nothing we could not have guessed. I was about to withdraw when I brushed against something that made me shudder: a connection between Alisa's mind and someone else's. The someone else was trying to be subtle, but the tie between them throbbed with power. Nicneven!

"Titania, Nicneven is joined to Alisa right now." Titania motioned for us all to be quiet and cast a quick spell to render Alisa temporarily blind and deaf.

"It wouldn't do to have Nicneven hear the rest of our conversation," explained Titania. "I have no doubt she can hear through Alisa even if Alisa is unconscious. As it is, she knows we have people back in your world that we are worried about, even if she can't get at them this minute."

"You mean—" I began.

"Yes, I am afraid so," cut in Titania. "Alisa is a witch, and Titania is her power source."

"Pardon the interruption, Your Majesty," began Stan nervously, "but I don't understand the connection between a witch and her power source."

Despite the seriousness of our situation, I had to chuckle to myself. Stan always wanted to gather data in an effort to understand the principles that governed magic, much as he already understood the principles of physics. Well, if anyone could succeed in making science out of magic, it would be Stan.

Although Titania was obviously tense, she smiled at Stan. If I recalled correctly, she actually enjoyed interacting with mortals and probably hadn't had the opportunity in years, maybe even centuries.

"Power always comes from somewhere," began Titania. "Even in your world this is so, yes?" Stan nodded.

"So it is in Annwn, or Elphame, or any of the other magical realms. We faeries create within us the energy that fuels our spells. In much the same way, the Olympians draw the power for their special abilities from within.

"Most mortals have to approach magic differently, though. Humans, like all thinking creatures, can produce some magical energy, but only a small number of them create enough energy for significant spell casting. The rest must find another way if they would follow the path of magic. Druids, for instance, have mastered the ability to become one with nature and draw strength from it. Others find their power in the increasingly rare magic objects that still exist in your world.

"'Witch' means different things in different human societies, but faeries use the term for those humans who swear allegiance to some magical being in exchange for power."

"You mean…like Satan?" asked Stan. I could just imagine David squirming inside him.

"There are witches dedicated to Satan or a high-level demon, but it is wrong to think that Satan is the only source. Any entity with enough power could serve as the source. I have known witches whose power sources were good beings, though faeries tend to frown on witchcraft anyway. There aren't all that many humans who can resist the temptations of that much power."

"Faeries are not entirely immune to those temptations, either," I mentioned gently.

Titania laughed in a surprisingly light-hearted way. "Well spoken, Taliesin. It is the rare being, mortal or immortal, who can wield great power and remain unchanged by it."

"If Nicneven could listen in on us through Alisa, then the bond between witch and source must be strong enough to work even across worlds," said Stan.

"Very good, my young scholar!" replied Titania. "Yes, once the bond has had time to take root in the witch's very being, it can function across such boundaries. 'Tis too bad in a way; if infernal witches had to stay in Hell to have any power, there wouldn't be so many of them!"

"What about beings like the Olympians, who are more or less trapped on their own planes? Could Hecate, for example, still serve as a source the way she did in ancient Greece?" asked Stan. He had evidently read up on Hecate after our return from Olympus.

Titania suddenly became grim. "Why would you ask about her?"

"During our stay with the Olympians, we had to fight Hecate," I explained, wondering why the mere reference to her name would have cast such a shadow over Titania.

The faerie queen, who had been showing great courage at the thought of falling into Nicneven's clutches, actually started trembling a little. "I...I did not realize you had ever faced Hecate."

"Not to worry," said Dan. "We defeated her. She's probably in Tartarus by now for trying to overthrow Hades and seize the Underworld for herself."

"You do not understand. It is not Hecate herself I fear, confined as she is to the Olympian realm. But the young scholar is right: Hecate can be a power source, even from Tartarus. No new witch could pledge herself to the Triple One, but established bonds would continue to function. There have been rumors for years that Nicneven has combined her inborn faerie magic with powers of witchcraft...derived from Hecate."

Now Nurse Florence looked just as alarmed as Titania. "As a sworn servant of Hecate, she will want revenge then."

Titania nodded reluctantly. "In his eagerness to keep me safe, Robin completely misunderstood the situation."

"What do you mean?" I asked shakily, knowing perfectly well what she meant.

"Nicneven wasn't coming for me, at least not this time. She was coming for you."

As if to punctuate her words, a portal shimmered to life right next to the fallen Alisa.

Chapter 3: Faerie Fiasco (Carla)

I wished about ten times a day that Tal could get over the idea that I needed to be protected, and this was one of those times. After all, I had all the power of my past self, the sorceress Alcina. If some Scottish faerie queen was attacking, I could take care of myself just as well as he could—but here I was, ready to babysit Robin Goodfellow while Tal threw himself into deadly danger. No, I wasn't fooled by the excuse that I would need to make sure Robin didn't botch everything up. Tal wouldn't admit this, maybe even to himself, but he was being overprotective. Again.

Damn chivalry!

I spared a few seconds to wonder if I should have stayed on Olympus with Artemis. Then I got the band to take a break by pretending to feel faint.

And that's another thing: the band members had also been with us on Samhain when we fought Ceridwen. They knew perfectly well that I wasn't some frail flower who had to be protected, even though they had been unconscious during the most dramatic parts. I could have told them what was really going on, for that matter, but I didn't want to risk being overheard. I didn't blame them because I had to lie to them. I blamed them because they believed that particular lie so easily.

Not having to perform, I was able to devote my full attention to watching for Robin Goodfellow. He was invisible, but, like Tal, I could generally see invisible beings if I knew one was around and concentrated hard enough.

Sure enough, I could make out someone moving surreptitiously but very fast near the back of the gym. He was wearing a tunic of such bright green it was practically a neon light, and he looked almost completely frazzled.

"Robin! Over here!" I thought as loudly as I could. Tal was better at projecting his thoughts, but I did it well enough to get Robin sprinting to the stage.

"My lady," he whispered with a quick bow, "we must join Taliesin and my queen at once. Can you call Taliesin's men over here?"

I broadcast as well as I could to Shar, Gordy, Carlos, and Jimmie. It took a couple of minutes for them to extricate themselves from their dates, but they had caught the urgency in my call, and except for Jimmie, they were pretty used to this kind of emergency.

Once they had reached me, I motioned for them to be quiet and whispered to the still invisible Robin, "You need to cover our exit so no one will follow or miss us. Perhaps a sleep spell—"

"Where's the fun in that?" whispered Robin. He winked at me and said, "Tell Taliesin's men to stand right next to you." I got us together quickly, and Robin used his wand to draw a magic circle around us. I could see it glowing faintly, though of course the guys could not.

"What do you mean, 'where's the fun in that?'" I whispered worriedly.

"Shush!" replied Robin, putting a finger to his lips. "I must concentrate." At that moment I noticed he carried a willow flute as well as a wand. He stuck the wand in his belt, put the flute, pulsing with magic of its own, to his lips, and began playing for all he was worth.

I had seen Tal channel magic through his music before, but Robin, perhaps motivated by the urgency of the situation, played almost hysterically, energy pulsing wildly in every note. Everyone outside the circle seemed momentarily stunned, and I thought for a second that Robin had just been teasing me and was going to put them to sleep after all. The frenetic quality of the music should have told me differently. Robin clearly had other things one might do in bed on his mind.

I couldn't read people's thoughts the way Tal could, but the emotional feedback from hundreds of teenagers suddenly overwhelmed by sexual passion would have been hard to miss even if I had not had any magic at all. Suddenly, as if on cue, dozens of couples locked together in steamy embraces. I had to do something while all the clothes were still on. Oops, well, most of the clothes anyway.

"Stop it!" I hissed at Robin. He winked again and played on, even more energetically. I could feel the power of his music swelling to unbelievably high levels. I had only felt such power once before, from the lyre of Orpheus. How Robin had endowed his flute with that much mojo I had no idea—and no time to worry about his methods. I needed to find a way to stop him, though, and quickly.

I could hear Gordy chuckling behind me…until he saw his date in someone else's arms. Then he had to be restrained from jumping out of the magic circle. I could hear the guys tussling a little but had to focus on Robin. I tried knocking the flute out of his hands, but he dodged away from me. The band members, just as entranced as everyone else by the music, had climbed off the stage and were looking for single girls. I didn't have much time before someone did something that couldn't be undone—even by magic!

Unfortunately, in trying to restrain Gordy, the guys had scuffed the magic circle enough to break it. I knew because I was staring in Robin's direction, and suddenly he was looking fine. He was looking hot. No, more like volcanically hot.

Think about Tal, I told myself. If Tal had been able to resist Aphrodite herself, surely I could resist this little…adorable…sexy…

The guys, including Jimmie, had gone racing toward their dates. Thinking about Jimmie helped me reinforce my feeble grasp on sanity. I felt more protective of him than anyone else in the room. Physically, he was the same age as Tal. The problem was he'd been dead from age nine to age sixteen, and handling instant puberty was hard enough without being overstimulated by some…really, really gorgeous faerie.

Maybe if I closed my eyes and pretended he was Tal…

I threw myself at Robin. For a split second I think he imagined he was about to get lucky.

I had to depend on the fact that faerie anatomy and human anatomy were basically the same.

Yeah, apparently they were. At least similar enough for a kick in the crotch to put Robin out of action. He dropped his flute and fell to the floor, clutching himself. Again I congratulated myself on having taken those self-defense classes.

Fortunately, his spell was apparently not completely woven. People snapped out of their hormonal frenzy almost immediately. Also fortunately, at least as far as I could tell from where I stood, no frontiers had been crossed.

Unfortunately, we had lost any chance of making a quick, unseen exit. Oh, we could still get out, but I'd have to use some very hasty magic and take the chance it wouldn't be completely effective.

"Young man, put your shirt back on!" I heard Principal Simmons order someone across the room. I gave her some credit for gathering her wits so quickly, though it seemed to me she should have spent a minute or so being ashamed of the way she had been rubbing up against Coach Miller just a few seconds ago. At least he had managed to resist. Still, I didn't think that was a story I'd be sharing with Nurse Florence any time soon.

"Get the hell over here...now!" I barked at the guys, but they weren't all situated in such a way that they could come back right away. Gordy had paused in his search for sex long enough to punch the guy who was all over Gordy's girlfriend. Looking more closely, I could see the guy clutching his nose. There was blood, and the guy was mumbling something about his nose being broken.

None of Alcina's specialties—generating overwhelming love, commanding sea creatures, and changing people into other forms—would be much use now. I could make myself or any of the guys invisible, but most of them were in very public situations, and I couldn't just make them disappear right in front of everybody—particularly not Gordy, who was in the grip of two teachers, and poor Carlos, who was being yelled at by Principal Simmons and seemed unable to find his pants. Apparently he had moved faster than most other guys. Well, if it had to happen to one of them, at least Carlos was a swimmer and used to appearing publicly in his Speedos. All things considered, he probably looked better in boxers than most of the guys in the room would have anyway.

Robin had gotten up and was eying me as if deciding which faerie curse to cast on me.

"Sleep spell now!" I forgot to whisper. In fact, I came pretty close to shouting. Luckily, the room was in such chaos that no one seemed to notice. Any teacher looking my way would have seen a fully clad girl yelling nonsense at thin air and figured I was the least of the problems right now.

"Mortals anger faeries at their peril!" said Robin in what I imagined was his best effort to seem ominous. Needless to say, my patience with macho nonsense was pretty much exhausted by this point.

"Yeah, well, faeries anger me at their peril! Now, do what I tell you, or I'll cut off your manhood and throw it to the nearest dog!" I was drawing on things Alcina might have said in the same situation and had no intention of doing anything of the kind, but Robin didn't know much about me except that I was a formidable sorceress and clearly had a temper. He muttered something about the good old days when women knew their place, but he did pick up his flute and start to play, a soothing tune this time. In about two minutes almost everyone was asleep. I had warded myself enough to be unaffected, and Shar must have had the presence of mind to touch the hilt of Zom, his sword that protected its wielder against magic. He and I awakened Carlos, Gordy, and Jimmie while a sullen Robin Goodfellow eyed us with mischief—or murder—in his heart. We had to help Carlos find his pants, which slowed us down a little, and I made a mental note to speak to the crimson-cheeked Jimmie, who looked thoroughly mortified, later. No, actually, I should have one of the guys do it, but right now there was barely time to think, much less play mother to the poor boy who lived under the same roof with his parents but couldn't tell them who he was. Later I promised myself to take care of him, though.

"Should we bring Eva?" asked Gordy, rubbing his reddened knuckles. For a moment I froze.

Why did references to Tal's ex still bother me? I couldn't really say. Maybe it was that I had been in Eva's shadow for so long while Tal had eyes only for her. That time seemed like a half-forgotten dream now. Tal and I shared a bond more real than anything he had ever had with Eva. Still, the past sometimes refuses to stay in the past; as someone whose past-life persona had once controlled me and still remained a part of me, I knew that better than anyone.

"No more than we should bring the band members or Natalie," I said, hoping no one had noticed my momentary hesitation. "They know about us, but Tal still wants them treated as civilians and not involved any more than necessary." He had never actually said that in so many words, but I was sure he it was what he wanted. And if not, well, it was definitely what I wanted, and he would understand.

"I'm more concerned about the guy with the broken nose, Gordy. What were you thinking?" I asked as we returned to where Robin was standing.

"Like everybody else, I wasn't," said Gordy, his tone a cross between apologetic and defensive.

By now we had reached Robin, moping in the corner. "Well, we need to fix this mess before we can let any of them wake up, but Nurse Florence would be better at healing the nose, and Tal would be better at rearranging memories. I could try, but with this many people—"

"There is no time anyway!" burst in Robin angrily. "We need to rejoin Taliesin and my queen immediately."

"Which we could have done already, I'll point out, if you hadn't decided tonight would be a good night for a Roman orgy!" I said in a scolding tone. I would really have liked to hate Robin at this point, but despite his centuries of life, he managed to remind me of a child—a very obnoxious one, perhaps, but still a child.

"Roman? It would have been a perfectly Celtic party, in honor of Saint Valentine!" Robin snapped defensively.

"If Saint Valentine had actually ever met you, he would have denounced you as an imp of Satan and had you burned at the stake!" I snapped back. "No more arguments! Draw your swords, everyone, and be ready to attack at will. I'm just about to open a portal." Robin pulled out a small silver blade, clearly of faerie manufacture. Gordy's fear-evoking sword glistened as if eager for battle. Carlos's drowning sword sparkled with muted blueness. Jimmie's Black Hilt, the dark twin of Tal's sword, shimmered with cold. Shar's Zom blazed with emerald waves of antimagic. As soon as I conjured up the portal, I would draw Artemis's bow, and we would be ready. I would have liked to retrieve the dragon armor for the guys, but Tal had stored it in his attic behind wards only he could get past. I now realized that plan might not always be the best idea, but I couldn't do anything about it until Tal got back. I focused my thoughts, summoned a portal...and then cringed as someone on the other end crushed it. Could this night get any more frustrating?

"What's wrong?" asked Carlos as the last traces of the portal flickered out of existence.

"I think Tal is blocking me," I replied, rubbing my temples.

"Why would he do that?" asked Jimmie. "He wants us to meet him."

"Because he knows her," growled Robin.

"It's hard to tell who is on the other end of a portal until it actually opens, Jimmie," I replied, ignoring Robin, who, whatever else he might be, was clearly not a good fellow. "I have to assume Tal has been fending off someone else's efforts to reach Alcina's island."

"From a strategic standpoint, isn't it also possible that some-one else is on that beach by now?" asked Shar, frowning.

Gordy rolled his eyes. "Yes, oh great Alexander, what orders have you for us?"

"What's your problem?" replied Shar irritably.

"Gordy, he's right," I said quickly. The last thing we needed right now was a battle of male egos. "The beach we normally use as a rendezvous point may not be safe. There's really no easy or fast way to tell from a different world. I'll take us to Alcina's castle instead, and then we can figure out what we are up against."

I had another portal open as fast as I could, partly because Tal and the others could be in danger, but partly because it was the best way to forestall discussion. In moments we had left the gym and stepped into the great hall in the castle of my past self.

Chapter 4: Faerie Fracas (Tal)

"Tal, what's wrong?" asked Nurse Florence.

"I think I might have just blocked Carla's portal by accident," I said ruefully. "I can't be sure, but that last one felt different."

"How could Nicneven come here?" asked Stan, still trying to figure out how magic operated. "She's never been here, has she?"

"She could have been when Alcina was in charge, for all I know," I said. "But Nicneven might be able to use her connection with Alisa to open a portal here."

"I can put a stop to that," said Titania, who began weaving some kind of softly glowing containment spell around Alisa. I turned my attention to locating Carla, but I wasn't that used to trying to probe one world from another one, and at first I felt nothing. I was just making a mental note to research bonding myself to Carla in such a way that we, too, could have a connection that persisted across worlds, but then I felt her nearby.

"She's come through somewhere else on the island," I said happily, relieved that everyone would be together and safe—at least for a while. "She's moving," I continued after a short pause, "and the guys and Robin are with her. They'll reach us in five minutes or so."

Sure enough, Carla, moving as fast as she could in her party dress, showed up five minutes later, almost to the second. She must have scanned ahead, and, probably because she could sense Alisa, she had Artemis's bow drawn, and the guys had kept their swords out.

"Stand down, guys!" I shouted as they came into sight. They hesitated, perhaps fearing I was an illusion or a shape-shifter, until Carla nodded, at which point they sheathed their swords. I ran over to them, apologizing for having blocked them, and then I took a few minutes to brief Carla and the others.

By the time I was finished, everyone else had walked over. Titania did not look happy.

"Taliesin, I could not break the bond between the witch and Nicneven. It is already too old and too strong. The best I could do is make it…dormant, I think you would say. At least Nicneven can't use her as a way to open a portal here."

"Thank you, Majesty. Now, the question is, what are we going to do with her?"

"Vanora could keep her prisoner in Awen," suggested Nurse Florence.

"For how long?" I asked skeptically. "I know that dungeon underneath the building is designed for magical prisoners, but do we really want to get into the business of running a prison?" My life was already a three-ring circus as it was; I had no desire to open a fourth ring.

"Robin and I will take her back with us," said Titania firmly. "We have better ways to secure prisoners, and since we know Nicneven is really after you—"

"When did this happen?" said Carla, clearly alarmed. I told her what we had learned from Alisa's mind, and she looked even more alarmed.

"Nicneven has never been anywhere close to Santa Barbara, Carla, so she isn't an immediate threat. Without Alisa, she can't reach us by magical means. Somehow, I can't see her flying commercial to get here." I smiled, but Carla pointedly did not smile back.

"What is commercial?" asked Titania. "Remember, Taliesin, Nicneven *is* a faerie. It would take many hours, but she could fly from Scotland...you know, as the faeries do." Well, that demolished any chance I had of getting Carla not to worry herself sick.

"Majesty, I know faeries can fly; I've just never heard of one making a transatlantic crossing that way."

"Truly, it is not the most practical way," the faerie queen conceded. "Poor Robin exhausted himself completely when he flew to your town to give himself the ability to open a portal there, and Nicneven would be far more conspicuous than he were she to try the same thing. However, Caithness is visited by many...tourists, as you would call them. All Nicneven need do is find a tourist from California, link to that person and use his connections to places he has been to open a portal somewhere near you."

Well, Titania had now given everyone nightmare material for days.

"The portal method makes it easier for her to bring her troops through. The faeries could fly across the sea with her, but the witches would use too much power that way—"

"Witches?" interrupted Carla, obviously shocked by the plural. Perhaps because Titania was depending on me for help, she did not betray any annoyance at being interrupted yet again by a mortal.

"Nicneven has often denied her connection with witches, but she is every bit as much the queen of the Scottish witches as she is of the Scottish faeries," Titania explained patiently to Carla. "If she thinks she can get away with it, she will bring as many of both as she can manage."

The day just kept getting better and better.

"If the witches are drawing power from her, doesn't that mean they weaken her?" asked Shar.

Titania's answering laugh had not even the slightest touch of good humor. "I wish it were so simple. When such a bond is first made, yes, but the bond takes on a life of its own eventually, almost as if it creates power rather than just channeling it. Up to a point, one of Nicneven's witches can summon magical energy without immediately affecting Nicneven's own supply."

Ceridwen had been only one witch, though a very powerful one, and Morgan le Fay was only a half faerie, yet each one of them had come close to besting me in magical combat. True, I continually practiced to improve my skills—but now we were talking about armies of witches and faeries, not even counting Nicneven. I did not like these odds one little bit.

"Do not fear, Taliesin," said Titania, picking up on my mood. "You have agreed to help me; do not think that I will abandon you in your hour of need. Robin and I will take Alisa back to Annwn with us, as I have said. Once I have arrived there, I will communicate the nature of Nicneven's trespasses to my fellow rulers. I do not doubt they will realize the danger and forbid Nicneven to intrude into the mortal realm. They may not all be willing to fight her directly, but my army by itself should be sufficient to hold her at bay. Worry not," she continued, responding to my skeptical expression. "My troops would not support an attempt to rescue Oberon, but they will certainly obey me in a struggle with Nicneven. She will never reach your hemisphere, much less your town."

I bowed and offered my thanks, but in my heart I doubted much of what she said. Oh, her words were sincere, but I was not about to trust my life and the lives of my friends to faerie politics. We would need to have a plan B—and a damn good one, by the look of things.

"Before you depart, there is one other matter I beg leave to bring to your attention," said Carla. Like me, she tended to borrow words and style from her past self when dealing with supernatural dignitaries.

"You may speak," said Titania with a nod.

"Robin Goodfellow has caused…tremendous harm in our world."

"She lies!" the faerie screeched indignantly. "I did but do what I had promised. It was she who ruined everything…and assaulted me besides!"

"Majesty, a simple sleep spell would have enabled us to join you. Instead, Robin cast some kind of spell to…sexually arouse everyone present."

I could see that Titania was not really seeing the problem. We had already had some trouble with faeries not quite getting our different sense of sexual morality.

"Majesty, in our world most of the people involved are not…permitted to engage in…sexual conduct—and certainly not at a school function."

"That did not seem to keep them from enjoying it," muttered Robin grumpily.

Titania nodded. "Gwynn has told me something of this difference in our cultures."

"I knew nothing of these peculiar customs!" protested Robin. "And my spell would have permitted Taliesin's men to steal away unobserved."

"I told you!" replied Carla angrily. "You wouldn't stop." She turned quickly to me. "Tal, we have a big mess to clean up at school. Carlos and several other people are probably facing suspension, and Gordy may be in even a worse spot for breaking someone's nose."

"And Jimmie got very, very badly embarrassed," she thought to me. *"I don't know exactly what happened, though. Dan's going to need to do something to make Jimmie feel better about the situation."*

I nodded to Carla, then took a second to wonder how Gordy's sexual passion could have gotten someone's nose broken, but I quickly decided I really didn't want to know.

"Robin!" snapped Titania, now as angry as Carla. "What have I told you about playing tricks on mortals?" Robin hung his head and said nothing.

"I command you to apologize to all of them at once. I further command you in future to do no harm to any of them, or to anyone they know."

"Yes, Majesty," Robin mumbled, still not meeting her eyes.

"Robin is bound by the most solemn oath to obey me in all things, Taliesin. Will my commands to him suffice?" I had been about to insist on some kind of *tynged*, a binding agreement among the faeries, to keep Robin out of our hair in the future, but I didn't want to suggest his obedience to Titania was insufficient security. Nonetheless, I hesitated for a moment. I could tell from Carla's expression that she wanted to smear Robin with honey and tie him to an anthill—and after I saw the mess at school, I might perhaps agree with her.

Titania moved closer and whispered to me, "Robin is… impulsive, and I will personally guarantee that his pranks will never trouble you again. He is, however, almost literally the only subject I can trust completely at this point. If I have to place him under a *tynged*, it will be an affront to him, and it will make me look weak, for it is not the practice these days for faerie rulers to doubt the obedience of their own followers in such a way."

I nodded. "Your Majesty, I would not dream of creating any new problems for you at such a troubled time. Your guarantee is more than enough for me."

Truth be told, *tynghedau* had not served me that well anyway. I always missed some potential loophole that bit me in the butt eventually.

Titania nodded in acknowledgment of my courtesy, then motioned to the shamefaced Robin to help her with the still limp Alisa. Once they were ready, Titania bid us farewell and opened a portal. Robin continued in sullen silence and made a great show of not even looking in our direction. I could not help but breathe a sigh of relief once they were gone.

"We'd better get back ourselves," suggested Nurse Florence. "The dance should be ending just about now, and it won't take some parents long to start missing their sons and daughters."

Nurse Florence took charge of opening a portal, being careful to have it connect to the space right behind the gym, just in case someone who had not been at the dance, like one of the custodians, happened to be around. Fortunately, that part of the campus seemed completely empty, except for the sleeping multitude in the gym.

When we entered I winced a little despite myself. For an instant all the bodies strewn around gave me the feeling I had stumbled upon some massacre. However, I could feel the life all around me, catch snatches of dreams, and see the gentle breathing of the sleepers.

The gym clock told us that it was just past eleven, exactly when the dance was supposed to end. That gave us only minutes to figure out what to do.

Carefully, I probed a few students to see how much they remembered. The short answer: too much.

"I don't think we can just erase the memories of the...almost-orgy," I told the others grimly. "What happened created such an emotional charge that some residue will remain; people will have the feeling of something missing, and a few may keep picking at that particular mental scab until they unearth part of the original memory. It would be better to embed some rational explanation in their heads. The problem is I don't have a clue how to explain what happened."

At first my statement was greeted by eerie silence. Clearly, nobody else had a plausible mundane explanation, either. Fortunately, our group had a lot of collective brain power. Together we came up with a reasonable cover story.

In our revised reality, a stranger had gotten into the gym near the end of the dance. Principal Simmons had spotted him and asked him to leave, but apparently not before he had managed to spike the punch with some kind of mixture derived from prescription sleep aids—a bad mixture that greatly increased the probability of hallucinations and other side effects. Mostly, it just put everybody to sleep, but it caused some students and staff members to experience fairly vivid dreams.

"Some people might be inclined to share their 'dream' experiences," I said, "but probably not too many, given their...awkward nature. Anyway, it'll be easier to give them a dreamlike fuzziness than it would be to erase them. People will have a hard time holding on to the details, and that should be enough bury the whole thing eventually."

"Isn't the idea of some intruder coming in and drugging the whole student population going to start some kind of panic?" asked Carlos.

"At first, perhaps," admitted Nurse Florence, "but that can't be helped. Any story we create to explain this set of facts is likely to have a scary element of some kind, but nobody is going to have any long-term damage, and that should take the edge off the fear pretty quickly."

"That story will cause the police to waste a whole lot of manpower trying to find the nonexistent intruder," pointed out Dan.

"Give me a day or two, and I will be able to whip up enough evidence that the stranger isn't from around here and that he fled to parts unknown," replied Nurse Florence. "It will be tricky, but I think I can get that case to go cold quickly."

"I'm still not loving this idea," said Stan slowly. "It's going to make people uneasy for months. That's not fair to them."

"What you have to ask yourself," replied Shar, "is whether the truth would be any better, even if we could afford to tell it. Do you think anybody, aside maybe from a few RPG nerds, wants to think supernatural beings are hovering around waiting for a chance to mess with them? The lone intruder who is now gone is not anywhere nearly as scary as the reality."

It took a few minutes, but eventually we got to unanimous agreement on the plan. As the best mental manipulator of the group, I created the basic template for the memories we needed to implant: the average-looking teenager whose image we could use for the intruder, the scene with Principal Simmons, a Valentine's Day toast that got everybody to have a little punch. Once I had the details worked out, I downloaded them to Nurse Florence and Carla, who could then insert them into the evening's memories of each person in turn. We also cast a dreamlike mist over the chaotic sexual frenzy, and that was pretty much it. Then I used Nurse Florence's medical knowledge to create the appropriate kind of residue in the punch bowl. It was too risky to try to introduce similar residue into people's bloodstreams, but we picked a drug that didn't leave too much trace, so if anyone got a blood test, the absence of a drug in the system would not send up too many red flags.

While I was busy transmuting the punch, Nurse Florence healed the nose Gordy had broken. That incident would become just another blur in the hallucinatory haze in everyone's mind.

We finished only a few minutes before the police showed up. Some parents had called their kids' cell phones, the call had gone straight to voice mail, and the parents had understandably gotten nervous—especially when they compared notes with other parents. The Santa Brígida police force is small, but then, so is Santa Brígida, so it didn't take too long for a car to arrive after the first mildly panicked parent phone calls.

When the doors of the gym burst open, we, acting somewhat groggy, were shaking our fellow students awake, or so it appeared. We had just lifted the sleep spell, leaving just enough of it in force so that everyone else would look a little groggy as well.

The police did their job meticulously, and I felt a pang about having to deceive them. Shar was right, though: the truth would have been far more frightening than any story we could concoct.

The one drawback to the spiking-the-punchbowl story that none of us had thought of was that the police wouldn't allow anyone to drive home. That meant that after going through police questioning, we all had to sit and wait for our parents to pick us up. Of course, Stan and I lived in walking distance, so we could in theory have left earlier, but the delay gave me a good chance for a quick council of war with Nurse Florence and the guys. Standing in the corner and cloaked in a little don't-notice-me magic, we could talk in comparative safety.

"Nurse Florence, we need to protect the town against Nicneven, just in case," I suggested.

"Already on it. I've made Vanora aware of the situation. That magical network you and Stan helped her create is going to pay off again. Just as she did when we were trying to keep out Morgan, Vanora will spread her security men out across Santa Brígida, increasing her effective range tremendously. If Nicneven does find a way to get here, Vanora will spot her fast and use her guys as conduits to zap the faerie queen as quickly as possible. There is just one problem."

"Isn't there always?" I asked, rolling my eyes.

"It's going to take her about twenty-four hours for the defense plan to be fully operational. I know," she said in response to my impatient glance, "that's not ideal, but remember Vanora will be tied up pretty much twenty-four/seven in order to maintain proper surveillance. She needs time to prepare herself and her men—not to mention changing her schedule as Carrie Winn in such a way that she can be out of sight for a while without attracting too much attention."

After we had defeated the witch Ceridwen, Vanora, who was among other things an accomplished shape-shifter, had taken over Ceridwen's Carrie Winn identity, both because Carrie Winn's sudden disappearance would have led to investigations we didn't want and because being able to exploit Carrie Winn's financial empire and status in the community would be very handy. If any other private citizen deployed armed security men all over town, the city government would raise objections and ask uncomfortable questions—lots of them. However, if Carrie Winn did exactly the same thing, the city government would send a thank-you note. And if the guys and I needed to be out of school for some emergency in Annwn, Carrie Winn could announce we were attending some highly prestigious activity she had arranged, and the school board would send her a thank-you note.

All that convenience had a high price, however. Vanora had always struck me as being a little too willing to let the end justify the means...but the longer I knew her, the more I worried about her belief that *I* was the end. Having bought that absurd "Tale of Taliesin," which I was quite sure the original Taliesin had never written, Vanora became increasingly insistent that I pursue my destiny, a destiny she visualized in melodramatic messianic and apocalyptic terms. She was a little difficult to laugh off, as I would have loved to do, because she did not hesitate to throw around her Carrie Winn resources, her magic, even her high rank in the Order of the Ladies of the Lake, to get what she wanted. Fortunately, she hadn't decided exactly how to "help" me to achieve my destiny. When she figured that part out, I could only hope she really wasn't as obsessive as she seemed.

With friends like that, who needs enemies?

Trying to get Vanora out of my mind, I switched the conversation to a different aspect of our problems. "Of course, if Nicneven realizes she can't easily enter, she might try to capture people leaving Santa Brígida and use them as hostages," I said quietly. I didn't want to worry anybody—particularly Carla, whose arm around me gripped me progressively harder as the conversation continued. I tried to make my arm around her as reassuring as possible, but I could feel the tension radiating through her body.

"There's nothing we can do about that," said Nurse Florence, "except hope that the faerie rulers do what Titania wants."

Shar scoffed openly at that suggestion. "The faeries probably won't take on Nicneven directly. For all Titania's bluster, I don't see her being willing to do the job alone. We need to find a way to beat her ourselves, just in case."

"If Titania's assessment is accurate, Nicneven has forces even more powerful than those Ceridwen threw at us on Samhain," I pointed out. "I'm not sure we can do this alone. We know even friendly faeries aren't likely to venture into our world in large numbers to help out, and our Olympian allies can't." I could feel Carla start to tremble. I gave her a reassuring squeeze, but again it failed to calm her.

"There is only one way I can think of to have enough power at our disposal to be sure of winning: we have to recover the lyre of Orpheus."

"We need to do that anyway," said Nurse Florence, "but we're still waiting on Gwynn. So far, he hasn't been able to locate the Amadan Dubh or the lyre."

"Can't your mom help out, Tal?" asked Carlos.

I had been dreading that question, because answering it meant dumping yet another worry on everybody. "My mom...doesn't seem to have her abilities as a seer any longer."

"When did she lose them?" asked Nurse Florence sharply.

"When we came back from Annwn that last time, she told me she wasn't having feelings or dreams any longer. To be honest, I think she's kind of relieved."

Was I imagining things, or did both Stan and Dan look more shocked than everyone else? That didn't make any sense, though. Yeah, I guess fatigue was just getting the best of me.

"Tal, this isn't normal. A seer's powers don't just vanish overnight." Nurse Florence's tone was urgent. "I need to examine your mother tomorrow."

"I'm not sure she's going to be happy about that, but OK, I guess I can drag her in," I said reluctantly.

"Maybe if Nurse Florence can unblock her, we can find the lyre quickly," suggested Carla.

Damn! Why were Stan and Dan both staring so fixedly at Carla? There really was something weird going on here.

"We'd still have to rip it away from the Amadan Dubh, though," said Gordy. "That guy is even more unpredictable than Robin Goodfellow."

"Oh, that reminds me!" said Carla quickly. "Tal, did you notice anything unusual about Robin's flute?"

I glanced into her eyes and saw something—shock? Fear? Nothing good, that was for sure. "No, should I have?"

"When he started playing, I felt enormous power, not quite like the lyre of Orpheus, but close. Tal, it wasn't just that he drove everyone crazy; he did it in seconds. What does that sound like?"

I frowned. "Well, it sounds a lot like the lyre, doesn't it? How did Robin get hold of that much power? I guess I need to pay Titania a visit, but when am I going to find the time?"

"I thought things were going to get easier now," said Gordy glumly.

Yeah, fat chance as long as you're one of my warriors, chum!

"Shar, your parents are here," said Nurse Florence quickly. I turned, saw she was right, and gently eased us out of the spell so that people would notice us again.

Much to my surprise, as soon as we could be seen, Eva came running over.

"Tal...is something...wrong?" Eva, who had experienced some of our recent adventures, knew what fuzzy memories and a wild story to explain them meant.

"I'll tell you later, Eva. Your parents just got here, and it's late."

"OK," she said reluctantly, but she didn't move. I couldn't figure out why she would want to linger at this point.

"Tal, I…hallucinated…some guy I didn't even know…trying to have sex with me. It was very unsettling."

"Things didn't actually…go too far, did they?" I asked, suddenly profoundly uncomfortable.

"No, but Tal, I wanted them to…with someone I can't even remember having seen before. And he wanted them to. If I hadn't managed to say no, I…I don't want to think about what would have happened."

"You said no?" asked Carla—a question neither Eva nor I would have expected at that point.

"Sure," replied Eva a little too loudly, sounding offended. "Carla, the weird part was that I felt like doing anything in the first place, not that I said no to it."

"Oh, I didn't mean it like that," replied Carla, blushing a little. "It's just that most people didn't summon up that much willpower."

"I knew it!" said Eva emphatically but quietly. "It wasn't a hallucination. What I thought I dreamed…actually happened."

"Eva, not now," I replied nervously. "Your parents are coming over. I promise I'll explain everything tomorrow." Eva looked eager to continue the conversation, but her parents were right behind her by that time, and she knew enough not to continue that kind of conversation with them in earshot. They said hello to me more out of obligation than anything else—they hadn't really liked me in years—and then they got Eva out of there as fast as they could, pretty much as if they were fleeing from the plague. Actually, that's the way a lot of the parents were reacting. I had another pang about our cover story.

"Why was Eva able to resist?" asked Carlos in a low voice. "Is she developing some kind of magic?" Given how people who spent enough time around me tended to develop whatever latent magic they had, his question wasn't a bad one.

Before I could answer, though, Carla said softly, "She must be in love with someone. That's the only way anyone could resist that barrage of sexual energy."

"Good," I said quickly. "It's about time she got together with someone. I wonder who it is." Then I saw a forlorn look in Carla's eyes and knew immediately what she was thinking.

"You aren't jealous, are you? If Eva had been interested in me, she had four years to make a move."

Carla pulled away from me. "Of course I'm not jealous," she replied, but she didn't make eye contact with me. Instead, she stepped away, ostensibly to say something to one of her friends.

"Weird!" I muttered.

"Not as weird as you think," said Carlos, who had overheard me. "A guy is never as attractive to a girl as when he's with another girl."

"That's pretty cynical, Carlos!"

"It's pretty true," he replied with a wink. "Didn't Eva come alone tonight?"

Just then I was rescued from that awkward conversation by the arrival of Carlos's parents. With Carla evidently wanting to be alone, I found myself with Stan, Dan, and Jimmie. All three weren't great company at the moment. In fact, Jimmie was looking downright miserable, and I remembered Carla telling me he had been embarrassed somehow. I'd get Dan to talk to him if Dan didn't notice the problem on his own.

Speaking of problems, I couldn't help noticing that both Stan and Dan were unhappy, too. Well, this hadn't exactly been the greatest Valentine's Day for either of them, but we had certainly handled worse situations. Compared to fighting Cerberus or an army of dead knights, for instance, the evening had been tame. One witch, one trickster faerie, one messy situation to clean up—not exactly a hard day for us.

"OK, guys, what's up?" I asked. "This is a Valentine's Day dance, not a wake! Well, what's left of a Valentine's Day dance anyway."

"Nothing's up," said Stan, fidgeting. "It's just been a long day, and Natalie wasn't very understanding about my sudden absence."

One of the dilemmas of being able to read minds is the constant temptation to use the power. I could tell that Stan wanted to tell me something but was too nervous to do it. Dan opened his mouth, then closed it again. He wanted to say something too, but he apparently didn't want to reveal whatever was weighing on them unless Stan was willing to join him. Neither one of them had magic;

hence, neither one had natural shielding against a mind probe. Whatever they were worrying about was right on the surface of their minds. It would be so easy, so easy—but I had very definite ethical standards on this subject. I could freely read the mind of an enemy, particularly one who was attacking, but I would only read the mind of a neutral or a friend without permission only in a dire emergency. This situation did not seem quite that urgent...yet.

At that point Dan's parents arrived and offered to give Stan and me a lift. We could easily have walked, but it was around 2:00 a.m. by now, so we both gratefully accepted the ride.

Once home, I brought Mom up to speed; thankfully, Dad, who didn't know my secret, was out of town on business. Tired as I was, I should have gone to bed as fast as possible, but Nurse Florence had me worried about where my mother's abilities as a seer had gone. I had been assuming that a seer's link with higher powers might fade naturally, but apparently, I had been wrong. While we talked, I scanned her carefully for any sign of hostile magic. At first I found nothing, but just as I was about to relax and forget the whole thing, I noticed tiny threads of pulsing redness.

Hell magic!

Nurse Florence had said that she had never known hell magic to be subtle, but clearly there were exceptions, and this was one of them.

I said nothing to Mom. What would have been the point? I had been honest about Nicneven, so Mom clearly had enough to worry about without knowing that some demon had violated her mind.

Before I went to bed, I reinforced the wards on the house, adding a new one that specifically protected against hell magic, though at this point that was a little like locking the proverbial barn door after the horse was out. Still, beefing up the protection made me feel better, if nothing else.

People used to fall asleep by counting sheep. This night I had to resort to counting enemies instead. Nicneven was obviously number one on that list, but that demon, who had evidently been lurking around ever since I stopped him from killing me during trial by combat, had to be at least a close second. Then there was the Amadan Dubh, called the bringer of madness and oblivion, hidden away somewhere with the lyre of Orpheus; his theft of that supremely powerful instrument might end up costing me my life—or more than that. Then there were a multitude of faeries who feared me because of my unique nature. Oh, and Ares and Poseidon would cheerfully execute me as painfully as possible if they ever got their hands on me because I had thwarted their attack on Olympus. Wow, now that I thought about it, Hecate, rotting in Tartarus right now because of me, probably hated me even more and was whispering across worlds to Nicneven. Should I count Morgan le Fay and Oberon, both in prison because of me?

Thinking about Oberon brought me back to Titania's theory. What if there were a being out there powerful enough to control the faerie king, yet subtle enough to do so undetected?

If such a creature existed, one thing was certain.

It, too, hated my guts—and had a much better chance than any of the others of ripping them out.

Chapter 5: Ghost of a Chance (Jimmie)

I knew it was very late, and I had school tomorrow, but I sneaked downstairs anyway. I opened the front door as quietly as I could, made sure it was unlocked, closed it gently behind me, and sat on the front porch for a while. It must have been around three in the morning, but I didn't feel cold, even though I was in just pajamas and a robe.

I didn't know how long I stay there, just staring at the moon and stars. The moon was pretty skinny, right between new and first quarter, but at least it had some company up there…unlike me.

Even as I thought that, I knew how ungrateful it sounded. I couldn't have a better brother than Dan—that was for sure. The other guys were just as great; all of them would risk their lives for me…and they had. Everybody had my back. That was for sure, too.

So what was I whining about?

Long story short: I couldn't return the favor.

When I was a ghost, everything was different. Then I could contribute something to the group. I even saved Tal a time or two.

Then I…resurrected…or something; nobody really knew quite what. I got flesh and blood again, anyhow. At first I thought it would be great. I really did. I'd never seen Dan so happy. Nurse Florence was nervous about the balance, or something like that, but even she got on board pretty fast.

Then reality smacked me in the face hard enough to make my teeth rattle. Shar was a patient teacher, and he knew just about everything when it came to handling weapons and to unarmed combat. After a few weeks, he didn't say so in so many words, but I could tell he was frustrated with my lack of progress. I just didn't seem to have any physical coordination to speak of. None. Zip, zero, zilch.

My body looked good. Hanging around for seven years as a ghost, but only able to watch what was happening until near the very end of that time, I felt Dan and Tal, my best friends from when I was alive, slipping away from me, getting older while I stayed the same nine-year-old. What was it Nurse Florence called it? Oh, yeah, age progression. I age progressed my ghost self, so when I was finally able to appear to them, I looked sixteen, just like Tal, just like Dan had a year earlier. I looked like I thought I would have looked if I'd lived through those years. Ghosts can pretty much appear however they want, so I made myself look handsome, like Dan. Hey, I'm his bro, so I could have turned out that way. I threw in a little extra height because I liked basketball and figured I would have played it if I had lived.

So far, so good. When I became flesh, I looked just like the shape I had given my ghost self. There was a difference, though. As a ghost, I could imagine moving, and it happened. I imagined swinging my sword, Black Hilt, and it swung exactly the way I wanted. Too bad my flesh body wasn't as easy to maneuver. The muscles were as strong as they looked, but they were brand-new, not used to moving. Oh, I could walk and stuff like that, simple stuff. Elaborate combat moves? No way! I couldn't even hold a sword right, much less swing it effectively. Basketball? It took me all these weeks to be able to dribble…sort of. I couldn't even think of trying out for next year's team. I'd be an embarrassment to myself and, even worse, to Dan. Maybe I would improve with time, or so Shar kept assuring me. If I could read minds like Tal, though, I bet I'd find something else going on behind Shar's intense eyes. Trying to figure out how to tell Dan and Tal I was hopeless, probably.

And girls? Wow, disaster waiting to happen! Again, I had the look. I had no trouble getting dates, but I wasn't used to making conversation with girls. As a ghost I had the opportunity to study Dan's and Tal's techniques, but I wasn't expecting to ever have any use for them, so I didn't pay enough attention. I felt awkward whenever I went out. Girls put up with me anyway, but I could tell all they really liked about me was my looks. OK, so I'd rather have nice abs and biceps than not, but even I knew there should be more to a relationship than that. All the other guys seemed to have it easy. Dan was deliberately staying away from girls for some weird reason, but Tal had Carla—I ached just to look at her—and he had been with Eva, just as beautiful as Carla. All the other guys had beautiful girlfriends. Still, there were a number of beautiful girls at school who were unattached right now. I was at a total babe buffet and couldn't figure out how to place an order.

I could have asked Dan or Tal, or probably any of the guys, about how to talk to girls. Asking them about sex, though, would have been a whole other problem. Even though they all knew I was a nine-year-old in a sixteen-year-old body, they still looked at me and assumed somehow that I automatically knew what to do. I felt the same hormonal blast everybody else did at the dance, but even with most of my brain effectively shut down, I still realized a painful truth I had somehow missed before: when the moment came to make love, even though I was overwhelmingly in the mood and with a girl who was by that point more than willing, I had absolutely no idea what to do. Only Carla's putting an end to the spell had spared me an ultimate humiliation far greater than how much I could embarrass myself on a basketball court.

I knew I could ask Dan for help, but how could I admit the extent of my ignorance? I knew Dan wouldn't laugh at me or anything like that, but that was the scene I keep seeing somewhere in my head, and I just couldn't take the risk.

I could have gone to Dad, but that brought up a whole other range of problems.

You see, my dad didn't know who I was. Neither did my mom.

I wanted to tell them, every minute of every day, but that truth they might not be able to accept, and then what? Would they think I was playing a cruel trick? Would they think I was nuts? Hey, maybe they'd think both.

That's how I had become Rhys James Stevens, the distantly related orphan from Wales, in the first place. Everybody said that was the best way to get me into the house, and Dan assured me that, once I was there, they would eventually love me as a son.

"It hasn't been that long," everyone said. "Give them more time," everyone said. Nobody really knew what that was like, though. I was a guest in my own house. Oh, my parents had adopted me, but because that was what one should do for a poor relative alone in the world, not because of any affection for me. They were as kind and considerate as anyone could ask, and superficially they treated me as well as they treated Dan. They didn't love me, though. In their hearts I was a distant cousin, not a son.

Part of the plan was for me to say I was called Jimmie back in Wales on the assumption that my parents would start calling me Jimmie, even though they didn't know I was the same Jimmie. Well, that idea failed epically. Mom teared up a little at the suggestion and said she'd rather call me Rhys. In that moment I saw she still felt grief for the old me, and I longed to say, "But you should call me Jimmie because I am Jimmie, *your* Jimmie, and I'm back, and I'll always be with you." I knew I couldn't, but I wanted to so bad I was sure my heart would explode right out of my chest and splatter all over the walls.

Not only didn't they know I was their Jimmie, I got the pretty strong vibe that they didn't like me all that much, not that they would ever say anything like that. A guy can tell, though, after a while. They still missed Jimmie, the cute nine-year-old. Having an awkward, angsty teenager suddenly dumped on them wasn't exactly the answer to their prayers. Oh, they'd never say, but I could totally tell.

All those ghost years I thought that being near them but invisible and inaudible to them was hell.

Nah, that was just purgatory.

Now I knew what hell really was.

I knew it for sure…and every so often I caught myself wondering exactly how sharp those steak knives really were, or whether razor blades would be a better choice. I cut myself shaving so often anyway. Everybody would probably write it off as an accident.

What was I thinking?

After all, I had my own sword.

My increasingly morbid mood did not prevent me from seeing someone standing on the sidewalk and waving at me. Our front yard was huge, and the sidewalk was farther away than you might think, but even so I could see a woman—no, a teenage girl, about my age—and the wave was unmistakable. I was self-conscious about being in pajamas, but at least I *looked* like a hunk, so perhaps I could succeed in rocking pajamas, at least in the dark. I got up and walked in her direction.

Even from a distance, I could see that the girl was dressed in a light gray gown and that she had a faint glow, like that of a faerie. As I got closer, I could she was about the most beautiful girl I had ever seen, a faerie version of Eva, somewhat shorter, and with light blond hair that sparkled even in the faint moonlight. Her deep blue eyes shone like stars, no, more like star sapphires. Her luminous skin made her alluring figure even more evident—the gray fabric of her gown was a little more translucent with her glowing inside of it than perhaps she realized.

I froze for a moment. I had heard faerie girls tended to want sex all the time. Was this one here for that? Was I doomed to be humiliated tonight after all?

"Jimmie!" she called to me softly in a sweet, musical voice. "Don't fear me! I am here to help you."

All right, Jimmie, man up!

I pushed myself forward. She took a few steps away and beckoned for me to follow her. I left the grass and felt the cold concrete sidewalk beneath my bare feet. Only then did she stop backing away. Instead she moved toward me, took me in her arms, and gave me a gentle kiss on the cheek. Her arms were oddly cold, as were her lips—but she was hot, and that was enough.

I had been dead for seven years, but I was still a guy, and I found her presence overwhelming. Despite all my anxieties about sex, I found myself getting excited. This couldn't be good!

However, instead of trying to jump me right there in the street or become offended by my current state, the faerie girl just smiled.

"Jimmie, I am flattered more than I can tell you."

"I..." I began, then didn't know where to go with that sentence. Could I tell this stranger the truth?

"I told you there was nothing to fear," said the faerie calmly. "When the time comes, I can teach you." She continued, answering the question I would never in a million years have had the nerve to ask.

Well, OK then!

"I am Gyre-Carling, the giver of many gifts. I am she who walks in winter." She looked around at the green lawns deep in shadow and at the palm trees. "I must say though, that in this land winter takes a strange and unfamiliar shape."

Her connection to winter would explain why I felt like her arms were going to give me frostbite. Well, if I was going to end up as an ice cube, at least I'd be a happy one!

"I cannot stay long," she continued, "but I know of your pain, and I have a gift that will ease it." Perhaps it was my shivering that caused her to stop hugging me, but I noticed a silver medallion in her hand, a medallion I could swear hadn't been there a second ago.

"How do you know so much about me?" I had been told supernatural beings could be temperamental, so I probably should have kept my mouth shut, but my curiosity got the better of me.

Gyre-Carling laughed her sweet laugh yet again. "News travels fast in the faerie realms, and I dare say there is hardly a faerie anywhere who has not heard of Jimmie the Twice Born. No one in centuries has conquered death as you have. Somehow, you are more than mortal, yet your rising has not been complete. Your body does not obey you as you would wish, yes?"

I nodded, unhappiness clutching at me again.

"I would like to help you achieve your destiny." She handed me her gift, which I immediately recognized as a silver Saint Sebastian medal.

"That's more of a Catholic custom," I said without thinking.

"But not forbidden to Episcopalians," she said. "I checked. And you certainly honor the saints, do you not?"

"I guess so," I replied uncertainly. "To be honest, I'm not the most...regular churchgoer." I went to services with my family, but I hadn't really gone during the seven years of my death. I was afraid God would see and snatch me up to heaven before I was ready. In my defense, I was nine.

"Nor am I," admitted Gyre-Carling. "Like all faeries, nature is my church, yet no one had a problem with my taking this medal to give to you. It is no ordinary trinket. It was blessed by the saint himself and sent down from heaven especially for you. I am honored to be the bearer of this gift."

I suppose a resurrected ex-ghost who had seen Annwn and Olympus shouldn't question the idea of getting a gift from heaven, but it did seem a little...random. Why me? Why now? Still, there was that old saying about looking a gift horse in the mouth...

"Saint Sebastian is the patron saint of athletes and soldiers, among others. As long as you wear that medal, you will achieve your full potential on the athletic field and the battlefield."

Despite the fact that the medal had come from Gyre-Carling's cold hand, it felt warm, almost alive.

"I...I don't know what to say," I told her. "This is such a wonderful gift, and it comes at just the right time."

"I know," she replied. "That is no doubt why it was sent now. There is, however, a condition."

Fear gnawed on me a little. "What kind of condition?"

Gyre-Carling smiled. "It is a small thing. You must keep it a secret. No friend may you tell, nor any of your kin. If you breathe one word of this to anyone, it will at once lose its power."

Somehow, that didn't sound right. "I've never heard of a miracle that people couldn't share."

Gyre-Carling looked at me indulgently. "Have you not read the gospels? Did not Jesus sometimes tell people he had healed to tell no one? I know not why you are enjoined to secrecy in this case. I am but the humble messenger. Perhaps if anyone knows, God's purpose for you will not be fulfilled."

God's purpose? I know some people thought that Tal had a great destiny, but me? I'd never even considered the idea. Could it be true? A little voice inside me said, "Why the hell not?"

"I promise I won't tell anyone," I said solemnly. Gyre-Carling gave me a smile as bright as sunshine hitting ice.

"But," I continued reluctantly, "what am I going to say when people ask about it? If I'm wearing it around my neck, someone's bound to see it."

"The saint has provided for just such a situation, Jimmie. Try it on, and you will see." I put the silver chain around my neck. The medal came to rest on my chest. Both felt warm. Then I fastened the clasp.

Immediately both chain and medal burned as if I were wearing a necklace of flames. I had to grit my teeth to keep from screaming. Gyre-Carling took me in her chilling arms and told me the pain would only last a second, that it would be worth it.

Much to my surprise, she was right. I went from fiery agony one minute to feeling terrific the next. Every muscle tingled, but the feeling was invigorating. Suddenly, I felt as if I could run a marathon without tiring.

Gyre-Carling opened my pajama top a little and put her cold hand on my chest. I could her skin against mine, no medal between us.

"You see, Jimmie? The medal is part of you now. No one can ever see it, and no one can take it away from you."

My earlier anxiety forgotten, I kissed her wintry lips, a kiss she returned enthusiastically.

"Thank you, thank you!" I said, probably too loudly for early morning.

"I must go now," said Gyre-Carling sadly. "I have much to do, but I will return to you later,"

"When?" I asked eagerly.

"On the twenty-fifth of your month of February when the moon is full. The Celts called the February full moon the moon of ice, for it is a time sacred to me." She smiled even more broadly than before. "On that night will I teach you of the mysteries of love."

She gave me another arctic kiss and then vanished.

I could hardly believe my good luck. In one moment all of my problems had been solved. Well, OK, she hadn't solved the problems with my parents, but once I stopped being the awkward and angsty teenager and started being the charming star athlete, I felt sure they would welcome me into their hearts.

I would have whistled all the way back into the house, but I didn't want to wake everybody up.

There would be time enough to celebrate later. There would be tomorrow…and the rest of my life.

Chapter 6: Cold Hands, Warm Heart (Tal)

I tried to get up when my alarm went off, but the sheets struggled to hold on to me. As soon as I pulled free of them, I realized they were trying to protect me from the cold. The floor felt chillier against my feet than I could ever remember. After all, this was sunny California, but this morning it felt more like Washington State in the middle of a winter rainstorm. I threw myself into the shower as fast as I could and cranked up the hot water as far as possible, but the water took its time warming up. Could the weather really be that much colder than yesterday?

The Valentine's Day dance mess had kept most students from getting much sleep, and my guess was attendance at school was going to be pretty low today, particularly since it was Friday. Actually, going back to bed was looking more and more appealing, but I had been absent so often I really couldn't afford to stay out just because I felt like it. Anyway, I never knew when some emergency would keep me out. It was better to drag myself in if I possibly could.

I dressed as fast as I could…in a heavy sweater. Just yesterday I had worn a T-shirt, but this did not feel like a day that was going to reinforce my worries about global warming.

When I got downstairs, Mom had hot oatmeal and hot chocolate ready. As we ate, I had to bypass the usual small talk and get down to business quickly.

"Mom, when's Dad getting back from his business trip?"

"Next week if all goes well," she replied.

"I need you to see if you can get him home earlier than that," I said, trying hard not to sound alarming. Needless to say, Mom got alarmed anyway.

"What's wrong?" she asked quickly. I could see her hands shake just a little as she clenched her hot chocolate harder without even realizing it.

"Nothing specific," I answered reassuringly. "But I'd feel better if he were here. I can't efficiently protect him while he's out of the area."

"Can't you cast a protection spell over him?"

I almost laughed out loud, not because it was a silly suggestion—though it was impractical—but because even a few weeks ago,

I would never have imagined having this kind of conversation with my mother.

"Magic tends to weaken with distance, Mom. I'd need something where he is to use as a local focus and amplifier. Dad's blood-tie to me might work, but I've never tried that, and I'm not sure that kind of connection would be enough to make a long-distance casting work. Trying might just call attention to him. I can't pop up to San Francisco, either; I've never been there." I was beginning to realize I shouldn't have brought up the subject in the first place.

"Don't worry, though," I continued. "I doubt Nicneven has had time to research my family, and even if she has, she's not going to be able to affect him that easily in San Francisco, either. When he gets back, I'll cast a protection spell on something he always has on him, like his wedding ring, and then he'll be safe when he travels."

"This would be a lot easier," said my mom, staring at her oatmeal rather than making eye contact, "if you could just tell him—"

"Mom, we've been through this before. I'm already distrusted by many faeries...and for the ones who help me, like Gwynn, I think I'm becoming a bigger and bigger political liability. If I do something that makes me look like an even more serious threat to the peace of Annwn, Dad and all of us could end up in even more danger."

Mom sighed loudly. "I know, I know, but promise me one thing: tell him if there is ever a more immediate threat. You can't just let him walk into danger without having any idea what he's up against."

"You know I wouldn't do that," I reassured her. "If a situation like that arises, I'll tell him everything, and damn the consequences."

My mom gave me a reluctant smile. "Yes, dear, I know that. I just wish our lives didn't have these dangers in them."

You and me both.

"Oh, Mom, before I forget, I'd like you to go to school for a little while and talk to Nurse Florence."

Mom stiffened immediately. "Why?"

"Is there a problem?" I asked. "I thought you and Nurse Florence are friends."

"Viviane and I are friends," she conceded. "It's just…is this about the fact that I don't seem to be a seer anymore?"

"Yeah, she just wants to check you out and make sure everything is all right. You know her; she worries as much as you do."

After an uncomfortably long pause, Mom said, "I'll go in, but Tal, if she can restore my abilities, I'm not sure I want her to."

"Mom, I get that. That's your choice. Just make sure nothing's wrong; that's all I ask."

"OK," she replied, still clearly reluctant.

I got up and kissed her on the cheek. "That's more like it." She took hold of my shoulder as I started to stand up.

"The day will come when I will ask you to return the favor," she said solemnly.

"And so I will!" I replied. "I better get going now, though," I said, glancing nervously at my watch. "Stan is going to think I've forgotten him."

"Take a jacket," suggested Mom.

"I'm sure I don't need—" I started, then opened the door and got hit by a blast of wind that bit right through my sweater. I ran upstairs, grabbed a jacket, ran back down as I zipped it, waved goodbye to Mom, and went out into the coldest February morning I could ever remember in Santa Brígida.

The weather forecasts for this morning had predicted an early morning temperature close to sixty, but I could see my own breath as soon as I stepped out the door, which would make the temperature more like forty-five, despite the bright sun mockingly shining down on me. I reached out with my mind, looking for any sign of magical interference with the weather, but I didn't feel anything out of place…well, not in the immediate area anyway. That didn't mean something wasn't going on farther away. When I got the chance, I'd check, just to be on the safe side.

When I got to Stan's house, which was only three doors down from mine, he was standing on his front porch, shrouded in warm clothes: a jacket that looked almost like a parka over what appeared to be a very heavy sweater, at least judging by the extra bulk. His curly black hair was hidden beneath a cap he had pulled all the way over his ears.

"Are you expecting it to snow?" I teased as he walked over to meet me on the sidewalk.

"What I'm expecting is that my mother is still watching me through the blinds," he said grimly.

"Oh, so this is the overprotective mom outfit?" I tried to ask with a straight face, but I didn't quite succeed.

"Yeah, well, I'll make some adjustments once I'm sure we're too far away for her to see anymore." Stan sighed, then realized he could see his own breath.

"It really is cold this morning. Tal, is this normal?"

I chuckled. "You mean, is magic at work? Not as far as I can tell, but I'll check later."

"If this keeps up, maybe we should break out the dragon armor," Stan suggested. I couldn't quite tell whether he was serious or not.

"Stan, I don't think there's any immediate danger of Santa Brígida reaching arctic temperatures. Yeah, dragon armor would keep us warm, but concealing our swords is tricky enough. I'd hate to have to weave a full-body illusion around each of us."

"I meant underneath our clothes," replied Stan, slightly irritated. "And I wasn't thinking about cold protection. I was thinking about what happens if this is magic. I was doing some reading about Nicneven. Isn't she associated with the onset of winter in early Scottish belief?"

"She'd either have to expend enormous power to make our weather here change, or…"

I had been about to say, "She'd have to be nearby," but somehow I didn't want to speak those words. It was improbable at best that Nicneven was any nearer than Scotland. Still, if she had found a California tourist…"

"Well?" asked Stan. "Or what? Or she's here, right? You can just say it. I'm a big boy, despite the outfit. I can take it."

"I know," I said quickly. "I just didn't want to worry you."

"Friends sometimes have to worry each other," he pointed out. Which reminds me—"

"Wait a minute, Stan. Now that the idea is in both our minds, let me just check it out." Stan nodded, though he didn't look completely happy. I checked my watch. We didn't have much time, but surely there was enough to try to sense Nicneven. She could attempt to conceal herself, of course, but someone as powerful as she was would not be able to do that easily, and if she was announcing herself by changing the weather, perhaps she was being careless.

I took a quick look around, verifying that no one was watching us. Then I threw a don't-notice-us spell around Stan and me. It wouldn't do to have passersby see what I was doing; even if they didn't realize the truth, they would think I was crazy.

I sang quietly in Welsh. I didn't always have the time to build power that way in the middle of combat, but music strengthened my magic when I had the opportunity to use it.

Stan fidgeted as a jogger came near, but the runner didn't skip a beat as he passed us. I had practiced concealment so much I could hide now almost reflexively.

When I could feel the power rising within me, I let my mind wander—literally. I reached out gradually in all directions, looking carefully for any unusual power sources that might indicate the presence of a strong faerie witch. Even someone operating at Olympian levels wouldn't register much if he or she wasn't actually using magic, but I should be able to feel at least some small trickle of mystical energy from such a powerful caster in the immediate area if I was actively looking for it. It also seemed unlikely that Nicneven would come alone, and the more faeries in the area, the harder it would be to miss all of them.

My sword and Stan's registered first. As I stretched my mind out further, I could pick up other familiar magical signatures. I could sense Nurse Florence, already on campus. I got a ping from each of the guy's weapons and from Carla's bow, as well as Carla herself. I could discern Khalid's half djinn nature as he hurried off to middle school. I could also tell that Jimmie was somehow different, but unlike the reading I got from Khalid, I couldn't really tell *how* Jimmie differed from the human norm. I hadn't been able to since Jimmie's resurrection, though, so I was hardly alarmed I couldn't get a clear reading from him today.

Widening my mind's reach still further, I could feel the steady flow of communication through Vanora's network, and finally I picked up Vanora herself near the north edge of the town. I also felt the wards in various places, functioning exactly as they should be, at least as far as I could tell from a distance.

By now my consciousness had spread like a thin film across the town. When I thought about it, there was a frightening amount of magic in the air, but it was all coming from friendly sources. There wasn't even the slightest hint of anything I couldn't identify.

I let my focus return to my immediate surroundings and let the enchantment concealing Stan and me fade.

"All clear," I said simply.

"But—" Stan began.

"Yes, someone could be hiding from me," I finished for him. "But that isn't all that easy to do, so I'm not too worried."

Actually, I was worried, but it was clear Stan was going to stay vigilant regardless of whether there was an immediate threat or not, so why worry him?

As it was, he still looked unhappy, and I was about to say something else comforting when he cut me off.

"Tal, there's something else I need to get off my chest—"

"Could it wait, buddy?" I said, looking at my watch. "We've only got about five minutes to get to class, and we're still three blocks away from school."

"All right," said Stan tightly, his tone indicating it was profoundly not all right.

"Just a second," I told him. I reached out with my mind toward the school. It took longer than I wanted because of the distance, but I finally managed to connect with the school's automated clock system, setting it and the bell system connected to it back five minutes.

Yeah, being the only person I knew of who could use magic to directly influence technology had advantages.

I felt a little guilty doing something like that, but it wouldn't hurt anybody, and I was only doing it to give Stan a chance to unburden himself.

"OK, Stan, I just bought us five more minutes by adjusting the school's clocks. Any more than that, and too many people would notice it. I hope that's enough."

"I think that'll be enough," said Stan uncertainly. Then he stared at me for a minute and looked down at the pavement. I waited patiently, but still he said nothing.

"Stan, the clock's ticking," I pointed out gently. "I thought you said this couldn't wait—"

"I think you're under a spell!" he blurted out.

I hadn't seen that one coming.

"What are you talking about?" I asked quickly. "What kind of spell?"

Stan was studying the pavement again.

"Buddy," I continued, sounding a little less gentle, "you can't just drop that kind of bomb without an explanation."

"You're under a love spell," said Stan so quietly that I almost missed it. As soon as I realized what he was saying, I couldn't help laughing.

"Stan, I really love Carla."

"That's what you thought before, too," said Stan, now almost in a whisper.

"You got me there," I said, somewhat impatiently. "Carla cast a spell on me by accident before she knew what magic was. And later, when Alcina had control of Carla's body, she hit me with the ultimate nuclear love spell. If it makes you feel better, I'll have Nurse Florence check me out, just to be sure."

Stan made eye contact with me with visible reluctance. "Dan and I had her check you out two weeks ago. She didn't find anything."

"You did what?" I said, much louder than I intended. "You went behind my back? Why not just talk to me?"

"Because if you were really under a spell, you wouldn't have listened anyway…just like you aren't now," replied Stan, his volume also rising.

"You're the scientist among us," I reminded him, annoyed by the idea that my two best friends were somehow conspiring against me. "It isn't very scientific to propose a hypothesis there is no way to disprove. I also wouldn't listen to you if I really loved Carla, which I do. Where does that leave us? And why didn't you and Dan realize you were wrong when Nurse Florence couldn't find anything?"

"You have to admit it's strange…strange how fast you got over Carla's deception and then decided you had really loved her all along."

"The prospect of being without Carla made me realize my true feelings. Yeah, I was angry, but after I told her we couldn't be friends anymore, I started to think about the situation, and the more I thought about it, the more I realized I didn't want to cut myself off from her, no matter what she'd done. After that, I didn't take much more thinking to realize that the reason I didn't want that kind of separation was that I loved her. Is that really so unbelievable?"

Stan sighed. "I guess not, but…but—"

"Spit it out!" I said abruptly. "We've got to get to school pretty soon."

"Titania believes it's possible to cast a strong spell in a subtle way, so that it can't be detected," he replied, fidgeting in a way that suggested he wished he hadn't brought the subject up.

"Titania is grasping at straws to save Oberon, and she could be wrong," I pointed out. "Even if she is right, the existence of such a spell doesn't prove I'm under one."

"Don't you think it's an odd coincidence that your mom, whose seer visions have always alerted her when anything was wrong with you, suddenly loses that ability right before your sudden change of heart?"

"There is magic involved there," I agreed, "but it's not Carla's. It's very definitely hell magic, and Carla isn't a demon. Even Alcina, had she somehow managed to control Carla again, wouldn't cast spells in a way that would show up as demonic. Satisfied?" I knew I sounded curt, but Stan was being unreasonable, and with all the real problems we had, I didn't have to time to deal with invented ones.

"All right," Stan said, "that does make sense, but—"

"No buts!" I said impatiently. "I love Carla, period. Now stop worrying about nothing!"

Stan nodded, eyes focused once again on the pavement, and I knew I hadn't convinced him, a fact reinforced by his silence as we hurried the rest of the way to school, arriving in class just before the bell rang.

I tried to concentrate in school, but aside from Nicneven and Hecate haunting me, Stan's words kept replaying in my head. To make matters even worse, Dark Me whispered his agreement with Stan over and over again, his grating voice as always sounding like my own, his tone growing more and more strident by the minute.

I willed him away with difficulty. I should have Nurse Florence check me out and make sure that something wasn't wrong.

Nurse Florence, who had spied on me for my "friends."

I had a harder time willing away that idea than getting rid of Dark Me. Nurse Florence had come to Santa Brígida in the first place to watch over me when my past life memories had first awakened, though I didn't know that until a few months ago. She had risked her life for me. So had Stan and Dan. Intellectually, I knew they were just doing what they always did: looking out for me. Emotionally, though, it was hard for me to get rid of the feeling that I had somehow been betrayed.

At lunch I made excuses to skip my usual get-together with the guys and sought out Carla. Stan had looked guilty and Dan sullen, but neither had said anything. The others winked or otherwise implied I just wanted a little fun when I had the chance. Sadly, fun was not on today's agenda.

Without hesitation, I told Carla everything Stan had said to me. She reacted with more understanding than I had.

"They can't read minds, Tal," she said quietly. "I never thought about how odd your actions would have looked to everybody else."

"I guess so," I replied reluctantly, "but even after I explained, Stan remained unconvinced. I'm afraid his paranoia about this is going to come between us."

"Well, we can't have that," said Carla. "Why don't you probe my mind? Go as deep as you want. Then you can report to Stan and Dan that I couldn't possibly have cast a spell on you. They'll have to believe you then."

"Are you sure?" I asked. "I don't really like the idea myself."

"Tal," she said, taking my hands in hers, "I want to share everything with you anyway. There's nothing in my mind that you aren't welcome to know."

Carla had never looked more beautiful to me than she did at that moment.

"All right, if you're sure…"

She nodded. I could feel her mental barriers lowering, and I entered effortlessly.

However willing she was, I had no intention of doing a scavenger hunt in her head. I focused narrowly on the period between the Amadan Dubh's escape and our return to our own world, for it was during that time that I realized I was in love with Carla. I felt her pain from my angry rejection of her, and I almost cried for having caused it. I saw myself through her eyes, saw with her as she looked at my broken body after I had fallen from the sky, wondering if I would survive. I again heard our conversation from the time while I was healing, and I felt her joy when I confessed that I hadn't known what I was doing when I cast her away, that I wanted her with me always, and not just as a friend.

When I ended the probe, there was no shadow of doubt in my mind; when I had pledged my love to her, I had done it of my own free will. I had to have—she had no memory of developing the kind of spell Stan was theorizing, much less of actually casting it.

"Now I can assure Stan and Dan that my love for you is real. In this crazy life, I sometimes think it's the only thing that is."

I could see a tear shining on Carla's cheek. I wiped it away and kissed her, long but tenderly.

"Oh, Tal, Tal, I don't know what I would do without you," she whispered.

"Don't worry!" I whispered back. "I'm yours forever."

Somewhere inside of me, Dark Me was screaming his head off. In Carla's warm embrace, though, I hardly heard him.

Chapter 7: Saint Sebastian Does His Stuff (Jimmie)

When I woke up the next morning, the house was very cold, but I barely noticed the difference. I threw myself into a hot shower, not because I was trying to warm up, but because I was eager to get to school.

Dan heard me singing in the shower, and since I hadn't done that in days, naturally he popped into my room after I got out of the bathroom to ask me what was up. (I say "my room," but it really belonged to Rhys, the guy I was pretending to be. The room I thought of as mine was down the hall, set up like some damn shrine to the old me.)

"I have a feeling that today is going to be my lucky day."

"What's that on your chest?" he asked, squinting at something.

For a split second I thought he could see the Saint Sebastian medal, but that was silly, of course, since it had buried itself in my chest. I glanced down and noticed a tiny scar where it must have bored its way in. Given how painful the whole process had been, I actually wouldn't have been surprised to see a much bigger mark.

"Oh, that," I replied that. "I noticed that the other day. I don't know where it came from."

"Have Nurse Florence take a look at it," Dan said in a voice that sounded much more like a command than a suggestion. "Given your...unusual—"

"Yeah," I said quietly. "You want to make sure I'm not turning back into a ghost or something. I'll stop by and see her, but don't worry. I've never felt better."

Dan caught me by surprise by giving me a bear hug that made me feel like my ribs were going to collapse.

"OK, little bro, but see Nurse Florence anyway."

I saluted him mockingly, and he was still chuckling as he walked downstairs. In a couple of minutes I finished dressing and went down for breakfast.

Mom had made incredible omelets. I thought of her as "Mom" even though she had no idea that she really was my mom. I couldn't help remembering the way things were when I had been alive the first time. Anyway, she was my adoptive mom now, so I guessed I had the right to think of her that way. She even accepted my calling her that, but I could tell she wasn't used to it, as if it were some new name she'd gotten from witness protection or something.

I picked midway through breakfast to ask Dan about trying out for the baseball team.

Dan looked surprised…and not in a good way. "J—Rhys, the tryouts were a while ago now. The first game is in about two weeks."

"I heard one of the players moved away, though," I said innocently.

"One of the first-string varsity players, yeah," said Dan, now even more uncomfortable. "Rhys, I don't think that's a good idea." He didn't finish, but I knew he was thinking that I would never make varsity. No, scratch that: he was thinking I'd never make any team.

"If there is a space, and the boy wants to try out, why not let him?" said Dad, pouring himself another cup of coffee.

"The boy?" Really?

OK, he didn't know I was his Jimmie, either, the same one he used to play catch with. If he had tried to play catch with me recently, he would have known what Dan was fretting about, though. Dan's attempts to play catch with me had been complete disasters. Plus, Dan had no doubt talked to Shar and knew what a freaking disappointment I was athletically. Caught between a dad who didn't know me and a brother who loved me so much he didn't know how to tell me I would just embarrass myself if I tried out, I would have been discouraged, but I knew something they didn't know.

Saint Sebastian was on my side. Oh, and I didn't forget Gyre-Carling either. How could I forget someone that hot? Anyway, with that kind of backing, how could I miss?

"Dad, I don't think Coach is going to have another tryout anyway. There was a guy who just missed the cut in the first tryout, and he's already on the JV team, so it'd make sense to just move him up to varsity. Unfortunately," Dan continued, looking at me to make sure I was listening, "the JV team already had more players than it needed, so I doubt they'll be a space there, either."

"I'll bet Coach would look at me if you asked him," I said hopefully. I was immediately sorry I had said it. Dan looked like a condemned man who had just lost hope of a pardon. I didn't mean to put him on the spot like that.

"I don't have as much pull with the coaches these days, Rhys, not since the soccer team didn't make it past the first round in CIF playoffs." I knew that Dan and Tal, the two best players, had been worn down by the quest to find the lyre of Orpheus and all the stuff that went along with that, but of course the coaches didn't, and so both of my friends just looked like they didn't have their heads in the game.

"Dan, it might be good for Rhys to be on the team," said Mom, unexpectedly joining the conversations. She didn't know much about sports and had always confined herself to the occasional, "That's nice, dear," in response to one of Dan's athletic achievements.

"Did you play baseball in Wales, Rhys?" she asked, turning to me.

Unlike the person I was pretending to be, I hadn't grown up in Wales, but what can I say? Thank God for Tal's Welsh history lessons—and the Internet.

"Welsh baseball is a little different from American baseball, but I believe I've picked up enough of the US version to be able to make the switch," I replied as modestly as I could. It was hard to sound modest when I felt like I could play like a pro right now.

Dan kept a neutral facial expression, but I noticed he was clenching his fists under the table. "Tell you what, Rhys. Let's you and I talk about it on the way to school and see if we can figure something out." I knew perfectly well that he was lying for the benefit of Mom and Dad, but I wasn't about to call him on it. They both seemed satisfied, and I could talk to Dan more frankly when we were alone anyway.

In just a few minutes we were in Dan's silver Lexus and on our way to school. Yeah, I knew his ride seemed pretty showy for a high school guy, but Shar had told me he'd seen the same kind of thing in Beverly Hills.

At first Dan said nothing. Finally he looked at me when we were stopped at a signal and said tensely, "Jimmie, what are you thinking? You know you aren't ready for this."

"If by 'not ready' you mean I suck, yeah, I kinda got that that's what you think. Have a little faith, bro."

"I don't think you suck, Jimmie, but you have to admit you need work still. Your body just needs a little time to learn to work properly, that's all. It could happen any time."

"Maybe this is any time. Dan, I feel different this morning...way different. I know I can do it."

Dan shook his head sadly. "You couldn't have changed that much since yesterday. I'm sorry, Jimmie, but I won't ask Coach to give you a tryout."

His words hit me like a slap. I could hardly believe my ears. I was sure I could talk Dan into helping. I looked down at the floor of the car and muttered, "It was easier being dead."

The light turned green, but we didn't move. Instead, Dan reached over and grabbed me by the shirt front.

"Don't say that!" he almost shouted. "Don't ever say that."

I didn't know how to react. Except in play, Dan had never gotten physical with me before. I half expected him to smack me. He didn't, though. Instead he just kept on gripping my shirt like he was a drowning man and it was a life preserver.

"Jimmie," he said a little more calmly, "when you say that kind of thing, it gives me the creeps, like...like you're thinking about doing something to yourself." He started tearing up, and I froze. I had seen him cry plenty of times, especially in my early ghost years, but I had never actually said something stupid that caused it before.

His death grip on my shirt morphed into another bear hug. "I know...I know you're unhappy. Everything will get better, though. You'll see." My shoulder was wet with his tears. The moisture on my cheeks, though, was my own.

"Dan," I sputtered, "I didn't mean—"

"I know, but promise me, promise me you never will. Promise!"

"I promise," I whispered. People had begun to honk behind us. Dan slid back over to the driver's side and started up again as if nothing had happened—that is until he took a right instead of going straight and headed over to Winn Park. I tried to ask him what he was doing, but he just kept shushing me.

Since school was starting in just a few minutes, the park was deserted when we got there. Dan unlocked the trunk and pulled out some of his baseball gear.

"What are you doing?" I asked, though it should have been obvious.

"What I should have done in the first place, Jimmie. Letting you show me what you can do."

I took a deep breath, suddenly nervous. What if my feeling was wrong? Then again, how could it be? Put another way, how many times did faeries meet you in the middle of the night to drop off saint medals that didn't do anything? That would be kind of anticlimactic, if you asked me.

We only had a few minutes, but that's all I needed. It took me all of about two to convince Dan I could throw and catch decently. No, better than decently. I could tell I was surprising him, but in a good way this time. I really had him, though, after I hit his most devious pitch and knocked the ball halfway across the park.

"You really are good now!" he said approvingly, slapping me on the back.

"Oh, I see," I replied playfully. "My rising from the dead you take in stride. But my being good at something…that you can't believe!"

"Get in the car," he said, ignoring my joke but smiling as broadly as I had seen him smile in weeks. "We're going to be late as it is. Don't worry, though. Something tells me we can get an excuse from the school nurse."

Much to Dan's surprise, however, we didn't need one. As if Saint Sebastian decided to help me out again, something weird had happened to make the school's clocks run slow, and we got parked in plenty of time to make it to our classes.

"Jimmie, I'll see you at tryouts today," he said casually as he left me. Just like I thought, that whole "I don't have as much pull with the coaches these days" routine was only a way to discourage me. As I expected, he was absolutely confident he'd get me a tryout. Apparently every coach on campus still thought the sun shined out of his butt.

I waited impatiently for school to end. Yeah, even more so than usual. At times it almost seemed as if the clock had started to run backward. Finally, I was free to join Dan at the baseball diamond near the gym.

The whole team was standing around, apparently waiting for me, some of them with ill-concealed impatience. The ones who looked so out of sorts were probably friends with the JV guy who wanted to move up, and a new student, even Dan's adopted brother, was not exactly their idea of a good replacement. In fact, almost the only exception to the general annoyance with me was Gordy, who gave me his usual grin and seemed unaware that some of the other guys were looking at me like they had just found dog excrement on their shoes.

As I walked in their general direction, Coach Arnold eyed me appraisingly. Fortunately, I'd been taking weight training for PE, so the coaches had seen the strength of my body, but not its obvious lack of coordination.

"Rhys, Dan's told me a lot about you," said Coach, grabbing my hand and squeezing it hard. Yeah, he was one of those my-grip-is-stronger-than-yours guys—except that, in this case anyway, it wasn't stronger. Also, I was taller than he was, and he was actually pretty old, one of those fixtures of the school who would keep on coaching until he dropped, which might not be too much longer to judge by how paunchy he was. I'd never understood how someone in coaching could let himself go like that, but some of them did.

"Coach Arnold, Dan speaks very highly of you. I hope I will have the honor of playing for you."

"We'll see, son," he said in a somewhat skeptical way. Yeah, great! This stranger called me "son," but the best my actual father could manage was "boy."

"You should really have been in baseball conditioning if you wanted to play," said Arnold, looking me over in a way that suggested I couldn't possibly be good enough to be on the team without the proper preparation.

"I just moved here a few days ago, sir," I said respectfully. The coach was making sure I understood I was not getting on the team just because I was a distant relative of Dan's. Or maybe he was signaling Dan that only the moon shined out of Dan's butt. I wasn't entirely sure. All I was sure of was that I was ready to show what I could do.

"Dan tells me you played Welsh…baseball," he said with a half snicker. Apparently the idea that there could be a different form of baseball in the world struck him as too ridiculous to credit. He must also have thought rugby was just a practical joke someone was playing on him.

"Yes, sir, for several years. Last year, I was on the junior team that represented Wales against England." I probably shouldn't have said that, since the coach could look that kind of thing up online, but he would never have believed I just appeared out of nowhere—or climbed out the grave, for that matter—with no previous experience. Anyway, once he saw me in action, he wasn't going to bother checking my credentials.

"Well, I don't know how they did things in Wales, but we take baseball very seriously here, Mr. Stevens. *American* baseball. Are you sure you have what it takes?" I was trying really hard not to dislike the guy, but…well, what can I say? He just wasn't very likable.

"Yes, sir," was the best I could manage. I was afraid if I said too much, my tone would give me away.

Now I understood why Dan had originally been so opposed to my trying out. It wasn't just that he didn't want me to be embarrassed. He knew I would be facing a pretty hostile audience. Well, I was going to show them.

As I warmed up a little, I glanced over at the bleachers and froze for a second. Sitting right in the middle were Mom and Dad. He must have changed his work schedule so he could come and watch.

Now I was really nervous. I had another moment of doubt, but I brushed it aside.

After all, why worry when you have God on your side?

I also noticed Shar in the stands. He played football in the fall, but otherwise he spent so much time on martial arts and weapons training of various kinds that he played no other team sports. He wouldn't have come just to watch a practice. He must have come to see me try out, which meant Dan must have told him.

With Shar, of course, was Khalid. Like me, he had to disguise his true identity. Shar's parents would never have believed Khalid was an abandoned half djinn, though they no trouble believing he was a Middle Eastern refugee, happily took him in, and pretended he was a cousin, all in order to keep him safe from imaginary bad guys. Unlike me, though, Khalid enjoyed pretending to be someone else. Well, it wasn't as if he was the Sassanis' actual son and just couldn't tell them.

Shar gave me a thumbs-up, and Khalid waved when they saw I was looking in their direction. I wondered whether Shar was asking himself how I could possibly have gotten so good so fast, but like the rest of us, he was surrounded by magic all the time, so perhaps he just figured my sudden increase in athletic ability wasn't all that shocking.

Eva joined Shar and Khalid; I could see that strawberry-blond hair of hers even from this distance. Had she come to see me, too? Unless she had a new boyfriend on the baseball team, why else would she be there? She also waved at me, and my heart skipped a beat. After all, she was still single as far as I knew.

Of course, she was also my brother's ex—and Tal's. I guessed I would have to talk to them before making any kind of move. Being a teenager was way more complicated than being a little kid. Ah, just one more reason to envy Khalid.

Then, just seconds before I would have to prove myself, I had a vision. No, not a product of an overactive imagination! A real vision, the kind that if I told people about might result in a shrine being built right next to the baseball diamond.

I saw Saint Sebastian himself, his muscular body tied to one of the fence posts, the arrows of his executioners still sticking out of him, blood dripping from each wound.

I wouldn't have minded a quick thumbs-up; a replay of his whole martyrdom seemed like overkill, though. Worse, he seemed to be trying to tell me something. His piercing eyes (no pun intended) were staring right at me, and his lips were moving, but I was too far away to hear what he was saying. Why visions should obey rules about how far sound could travel I had no idea. I would have to move closer if I wanted to hear him, though.

"Stevens!" barked the coach. "We're ready for you."

This wasn't the kind of moment where I could say, "Sorry, Coach, but I have to go over and talk to Saint Sebastian, who's tied to the fence over there, even though you can't see him." Come to think of it, I guess there never really was a moment for that. I glanced at the saint again. He was still staring, and he looked even unhappier than before.

"Stevens!" repeated the coach.

Reverently, I sent Saint Sebastian a mental apology for not taking the time to hear what I was sure would have been an excellent pep talk. Then I proceeded to show the coach and everyone else just exactly how ready I was for American baseball, my medal pulsing warmly inside of me and sending coordination out to every muscle as I did so.

The coach used the best pitcher to try to strike me out, but I hit a home run instead, knocking the ball over the fence in the process. Figuring that was a fluke of some kind, the coach had the pitcher try to strike me out three times more, and each time I hit the ball right out of the field. Sure I couldn't be as good a fielder as I was a hitter, the coach had the best hitters try to pop flies over my head, and I caught them all. He tried every other conceivable scenario, and I owned all of them.

Despite himself, the coach was impressed. So were the team members. They may have liked the guy I just aced out of a space on varsity, but they also wanted to win. Mr. JV was going to have to wait until next year. As for me, I was not just varsity; I was starting varsity.

I looked up at the stands and saw my parents beaming with pride. Shar, Khalid, and Eva gave me a standing ovation. Dan and Gordy were applauding from the sidelines.

I looked over toward Saint Sebastian. I wasn't expecting applause from him; after all, he was tied to the fence. I would have settled for any sign of approval. Instead, all I got was empty air. At some point, the vision had ended, but I had been too preoccupied to notice. I couldn't really be too critical of his odd behavior, though, considering all he had done for me.

Coach got me a uniform, I suited up, and practice started. The rest of the afternoon was kind of a blur after that. I kept feeling the medal throbbing in my chest until the sensation seemed as natural as my own heartbeat. Something else that became natural was my interaction with the team. By the end of the two hour practice, it felt like I had always been part of the team—as perhaps I would have been, if only I hadn't died. However hostile or uncertain any of the players had been in the beginning, they were all my friends by the end. All it took was being able to play well.

When Dan and I emerged from the locker room, I was surprised to find Mom and Dad right outside waiting for us. I hadn't noticed, but they must have stayed through the whole practice, as had Shar and Khalid. I was a little disappointed that Eva wasn't still there, but I was too happy about everything else to let her absence drag me down. Anyway, just having her there in the beginning had been more than I was expecting.

"Rhys, I had no idea you were such a skillful athlete," said Dad, giving me a hug a little less rib-cracking than Dan's tended to be. "Why didn't you say something?"

"I don't like to brag," I said simply. He didn't need to know that until today I didn't have anything to brag about.

Then it was Mom's turn. She made a valiant attempt to enclose me and Dan in a kind of group hug, though her arms wouldn't go all the way around the two of us.

"My two sons! I'm so proud of you both!" I had to struggle not to tear up. She and Dad had adopted me, legally accepting me as their son, but this was the first time either one had actually called me that.

Then I saw that she was crying, and I knew she was thinking about the old me, about what I might have been like. At the same time, she was making room for the current me in her heart. I couldn't read minds, but I knew it. I could see it in her eyes.

"Your dad and I would like to take you out to dinner to celebrate making the team," said Mom, dabbing her eyes with a handkerchief. "Your friends can come too, if they like," she added, pointing at Shar and Khalid, who accepted immediately. Dan got the invitation extended to Gordy, and everything was almost perfect. I would have liked to have Tal there. And girls, too! Well, at least one girl in particular.

As we headed to our cars, I wondered if Gyre-Carling had any Saint Valentine medals.

Chapter 8: Justice? (Tal)

I sometimes wondered how I managed to do so well in school. Days like today, I was so distracted that whatever the teachers were saying rippled around me but somehow didn't penetrate either ear. My mind was absorbed almost entirely on my to-do list.

After school I stopped briefly at Nurse Florence's office.

"Did my mom stop by?" I asked her.

Nurse Florence nodded. "She did…and you were right. Hell magic is definitely involved, quite probably from the demon we faced before."

"Can you undo the damage?" I asked.

Nurse Florence smiled. "You mean, assuming she wants me to? She is pretty conflicted about that. The short answer, though, is yes. Her abilities as a seer have been blocked, not destroyed. I have a call in to the Order, and I'll consult with Vanora, too, once she doesn't have to worry about Nicneven every second.

"I'm more concerned about motive," she continued solemnly. "Assuming the same demon is involved, someone invoked it for a job in Annwn. We suspected that Merlin impersonation it pulled off was designed to get Morgan freed from custody by deliberately losing to her in trial by combat. When you refused to let the fake Merlin face her, it tried to kill you, though I don't think that was its original objective. Either way, it failed at that as it had failed to free Morgan.

"You know as well as I that demons don't just give up if they are thwarted. Presumably, someone sold his or her soul to bring that creature up from Hell in the first place, and it will not stop until it fulfills its part of the contract. I just checked with Gwynn less than three hours ago, and there have been no attempts to free Morgan, even though weeks have passed in Annwn."

"So what can we conclude from that?" I asked. "That we were wrong in the first place, that freeing Morgan isn't really the demon's objective?"

Nurse Florence frowned a little. "I can't rule that out, but I think it's more likely that the demon is developing some elaborate scheme to free Morgan. She is well guarded by faeries, and even such a powerful demon as this one is would have a hard time fighting its way in and rescuing her directly. There isn't any way we can know until the demon makes its next move. Unless, of course, the demon already has made its next move."

"OK," I said, "I can see where you're going. What I don't see is how blocking Mom as a seer advances any possible effort to free Morgan. There are seers all over Annwn that Gwynn can consult if he needs to. The only way depriving us of a seer would help would be if we were holding Morgan ourselves."

"That's my thought as well," said Nurse Florence, sighing, "yet I can't shake the feeling that I'm missing something. There is another problem, though. Your mother was never in Annwn, and typically demons summoned by pacts can only act in the realm in which they were summoned or, if the person can travel from one world to another, the realm in which their summoner resides."

"So the signer of the pact is on Earth now?" I said, my apprehension mounting.

"Or at least was on Earth at some point. But there is an even scarier possibility."

"I might have known," I said grimly. "And what might that be?"

"When a demon has risen from Hell to fulfill a pact, that demon has the power to interact in the world in which it is working. It could conceivably find another vulnerable soul and seduce that person into another pact.

"At first I tried to figure out how your mother could relate to Morgan's imprisonment, just as you did. Well, what if there is no connection? What if the demon is acting on an unrelated plan stemming from a completely different pact?"

I slouched down in the chair, feeling more overwhelmed than I had in days.

"A demon that powerful, with an unknown agenda, loose in Santa Brígida? This could be way worse than I thought."

"At least on Earth the demon will have a harder time using magic than it did in Annwn, and it will have to be more discreet, but yes, it would present a formidable danger. If I'm right, we need to figure out what it's after, and fast."

"This would be a great time to consult a seer," I said nervously. "Too bad we don't have one anymore."

"Exactly! Fortunately, as you point out, there are plenty in Annwn. I'll go there right now and ask Gwynn if he can arrange something."

"That's a good idea. While you're at it, see if he can also arrange an audience with Titania. I was going to ask if she can find out why Robin Goodfellow's flute is now so powerful."

Nurse Florence rose quickly. "I'll go right away. Why don't you get the guys together?"

"I'm not sure that's necessary...or wise," I replied. "We're just going to get some information, not fight, and we should be back quickly. I'd rather leave them here, just in case—"

"Got it!" said Nurse Florence. "I'll advise Vanora that we'll be in Annwn for a short time. You do the same with Carla, just to be on the safe side. The two of them can coordinate with the guys if necessary."

It took us only a few minutes to bring Vanora and Carla up to speed, and only a few minutes more for Nurse Florence to visit Gwynn and return.

"Gwynn is eager to see us," she said quickly, a little out of breath. "We are in luck. He is with Titania near the border between his kingdom and hers."

"Good," I replied. "We can pick both their brains at the same time."

Because of the ban of Arawn, the former king of Annwn, I still couldn't open a portal to it, but Nurse Florence as a Lady of the Lake had no problem getting us both there. She also had the further privilege of being able to take us right to Gwynn, wherever he might be. In this case he was in a clearing in the middle of a vibrantly green forest; like everything else in Annwn, it was more vivid than its counterparts in the human world, though its brightness was muted somewhat by the mist that invariably swirled in the Annwn air.

Gwynn ap Nudd, uncharacteristically large and dark skinned for a faerie, towered above everyone else in the clearing, his appearance made even more impressive by sparkling faerie plate mail I had never seen him wear before. Possibly it was the equivalent of his dress uniform, donned for his meeting with Titania. Next to him stood his war horse, and behind him lay his three hounds, one white, one black, and one red. Discreetly positioned around the western side of the clearing were a dozen of his knights, though they, too, looked more ornamental than necessary. I had to remind myself that looks could be deceiving, especially in Annwn's strained political climate, and one could never be too careful.

Standing next to him was Titania, wearing a shimmering gown of sky blue that made her raven hair look even darker. A dozen of her knights lined the east side of the clearing, with Robin Good-fellow in their midst. He did not seem the least bit glad to see me.

"Did you bring *her*?" he asked, taking a step back from me and looking around suspiciously as if he expected Carla to appear from nowhere and attack without warning.

"Robin!" snapped Titania. He immediately bowed and kept his mouth shut. She turned back in my direction, worry plain on her face.

"Well met, Taliesin! We much need your counsel in this try-ing time."

After Nurse Florence and I bowed appropriately to both Gwynn and Titania, I stepped forward.

"What troubles you, my queen?" I asked, though I could make a pretty good guess. "How can I help?"

"Omens of impending ruin multiply all around us," she re-plied grimly. "I know Nicneven is planning something, and I long to strike out at her, but I fear making me look like the aggressor is ex-actly what she desires." She paused and stared at me intensely. "And I fear for you, Taliesin. I have registered a complaint against her for her attempt to attack you, but so far the faerie authorities have not responded."

Shocker.

"Fear not for me," I said in my most reassuring tone. "I have two Ladies of the Lake, a sorceress, and several brave warriors at my side, and my town is well watched by magic. Nicneven will attack again at her peril."

Gwynn eyed me appraisingly. "Yet you come here without most of your allies, armed, it is true, but not wearing your dragon armor. I had thought you more cautious than this." I had been some-what willing to dismiss Titania's concerns, but if even the warlike Gwynn thought I was at risk just by being in Annwn, well, that was a completely different situation.

Before I could answer, a portal shimmered to life in the middle of the clearing. Gwynn and Titania made no attempt to block it, so neither did I, but I drew my weapon as everyone else did, and White Hilt flamed comfortingly to life in my hand.

Three faeries emerged, one man and two women, all royally attired—and all much angered to see so much steel pointed in their direction.

"What means this display?" asked the male faerie. "Gwynn ap Nudd, do you not recognize Finvarra, high king of the faeries of Ireland? Titania, I might ask you the same. Have your men sheath their weapons." He looked at me, clearly puzzled. "Why are there humans here? Ah," he continued, his eyes reflecting White Hilt's swirling fire and his tone softening noticeably, "this must be the young Taliesin. What brings you here?"

While he had been talking, both Gwynn and Titania had gestured for their men to put their weapons away, and the tension became much less marked.

"I come seeking the wisdom of the faeries," I said, sheathing White Hilt and bowing. "I had not thought to be honored by your presence."

Finvarra smiled approvingly at my courteous response. Rumor had it he was generally well disposed toward humankind, but it never hurt to be cautious.

The high king was not as physically imposing as Gwynn, but he had a quiet dignity about him that would inspire respect.

"Indeed, Taliesin, you can consider yourself thrice honored when I introduce my colleagues," he said, gesturing toward the two faerie ladies. "May I present the Korrigan, faerie queen of Brittany, and Princess Doirend, daughter of King Midir and granddaughter of the Dagda?"

Both ladies were as beautiful as faerie women almost invariably are, but in very different ways. The Korrigan's beauty was that of an ice sculpture or the depths of Broceliande in the middle of winter. The original Taliesin had met her while training as a druid—and it had not been a happy meeting. She wore a dark green gown, shadowy like the depths of the forest, and she eyed me with frosty disdain. Doirend's beauty was more like that of a spring field, but her gown shifted from one color to another with alarming frequency. Rumors suggested she was moody, but I would not have expected her clothing to follow her example. In contrast to the Korrigan's undisguised contempt, Doirend looked at me with curiosity. I bowed to the two women as custom required, but as soon as that necessary courtesy was dispensed with, I promised myself I would do my best to keep my eyes discreetly on the Korrigan as much as possible, not because she was beautiful but because she was legendary for setting traps for the unwary.

"Are you the tribunal selected by the lots to hear the case I have brought against Nicneven?" asked Titania quickly.

Finvarra seemed like a man not easily disconcerted, but it took him a moment to answer. "Alas, Titania, we are here to prepare for a charge filed just before yours and thus needing to be disposed of first. It is a charge leveled by Nicneven against Robin Goodfellow." Gwynn and Titania were both visibly shaken by that revelation, and Robin, normally faerie pale, turned white as chalk.

"What is the charge?" asked Titania with just the slightest quiver in her voice.

"That Robin Goodfellow used magic on mortals in a public setting, disrupting their lives and jeopardizing the security of the faerie realms," replied Finvarra solemnly.

The Valentine's Day dance! I thought to Nurse Florence. *How could Nicneven know of that?*

The gym wasn't warded against any kind of detection. She could have used a dozen different methods, thought back Nurse Florence.

"Majesty," I said, addressing Finvarra, "may I be heard?"

The high king of Irish faeries looked somewhat surprised. "You are not a faerie, nor a party to this action, Taliesin. What is your concern in this matter?"

"I have heard that Robin acted overzealously, but he did so to free my men to help defend his queen, who had come to seek my aid and thus fallen under my protection."

Finvarra was not easily bluffed. "Are you now a lord among men, Taliesin, that you have official protection to extend? I had not thought your status so changed."

"Taliesin does not proclaim his status among men publicly," said Gwynn, "lest by so doing he also compromises the security of the faerie realms himself. He has men who are loyal to him, and to the extent they can in his culture, they have pledged themselves to him."

For an off-the-cuff legal pronouncement, Gwynn's argument was pretty smooth. I hadn't thought of my position in quite those terms, but his explanation did fit.

"He also acted as proxy for me," said Nurse Florence, "and under faerie law, we would all agree that a Lady of the Lake has protection she may extend, would we not?"

That was an even neater theory, but if it took this much effort to even get Finvarra to agree that I had enough connection to the case to speak, it was going to be a long, long day.

Finvarra nodded. "Taliesin, you may speak, but briefly. Having found Robin Goodfellow, it is our duty to bring him to the place of judgment."

"Wait!" interrupted the Korrigan sharply. "I do not agree that Taliesin has the standing to speak. No mortal who has not agreed to be bound by faerie law should have such a privilege."

Finvarra nodded again, this time reluctantly. "Doirend, what say you? Shall we hear Taliesin or not?"

I glanced in Doirend's direction and became profoundly uncomfortable. She was eying me in a way more suitable for the bedroom than the courtroom.

It wasn't that I completely lacked self-confidence, but it seemed to me I was just an OK-looking guy. I had never been able to understand my allure for supernatural women. At least this one probably didn't have an agenda beyond wanting to bed me, but that by itself would conjure up a world of trouble.

Of course, I could never betray Carla, but even if I were single, having a little fling with a member of the tribunal before which I was giving testimony seemed wrong. Besides, I had no desire to get embroiled in faerie politics any more than necessary, and Doirend's ambiguous role in that political system ought to give any man she cast her eyes toward some pause.

Her grandfather, the Dagda, had been a high king among the Tuatha de Danaan, the ancient race the Irish had once worshiped as gods before the Tuatha had wisely retreated from that distinction and became the faeries of Ireland. Though he was thought to have died in battle, one could never be too sure he would not somehow return; after all, I had seen evidence that faeries did occasionally reincarnate, and then all someone would need to do would be to use on him the awakening spell once used on me, and presto: instant high king returned.

An even more likely outcome of any connection between Doirend and me would be sending those faeries who already feared me spiraling into blind panic. After all, might not the consort of a high king's granddaughter one day seek the crown for himself?

Any way I looked at the situation, Doirend was trouble.

I had dropped my eyes as if in virginal reluctance to meet her gaze, but when I chanced a glance up again, she winked at me. Not good, not good at all!

"There is no rule precluding us from hearing testimony from anyone, as far as I can remember. Let Taliesin speak," Doirend proclaimed, causing the Korrigan to glare at her.

I was uncomfortably reminded of the only other faerie tribunal with which I had dealt. Its majority had been unstable, and so was this one's. Finvarra could be counted on to be fair, but Doirend's voting habits might shift if she forced me into a situation in which I had to reject her, and the Korrigan appeared to have a very large axe to grind. If she was anything like the Korrigan I remembered, she could easily be in league with Nicneven, though I had no way of telling.

"Majesties," I said, trying to push the political calculations in my head aside, "Nicneven sent the witch Alisa MacDougall to attack me and would have come herself as well, but I managed to block her attempts to reach me."

"If she did not get through, as you say, you cannot be sure it was she," interrupted the Korrigan, "nor can you be sure that the witch was in her employ."

"I have learned the art of reading minds," I responded, keeping my voice neutral. "The witch was definitely under the sway of Nicneven. As to the other portals, I could feel Nicneven's anger through them." The Korrigan looked at me as skeptically as if I had just announced that the moon was made of green cheese.

"I hold the witch at my castle," added Titania. "It would not be hard for the tribunal to determine from whence her power comes."

"Even so, that doesn't prove she attacked Taliesin under Nicneven's orders, nor does it prove that Nicneven was about to come through another portal," objected the Korrigan. Yeah, this was going to be a very long day.

"Perhaps Taliesin should be given the opportunity to prove his ability to read minds," suggested Doirend. "He can read mine if he has the power."

Predictably, the Korrigan objected, but equally predictably, the vote went two to one against her. However, reading Doirend's mind opened up a whole new minefield of problems.

"Majesties, I do not like to invade the mind of another, except under the most dire circumstances."

The Korrigan snorted derisively at that. "Just as I thought: Taliesin is nothing more than a charlatan!"

"Clearly more than that!" Finvarra objected immediately. "It was he who defeated Ceridwen and Morgan. It was he who outwitted a dragon and held his own against a powerful demon. Surely there can be no question that he has magic."

"I do not question his magic," replied the Korrigan, sneering at me as she did so. "I question his ability to see what is written in the soul of another."

I sighed. "If the princess is willing, and if she agrees to forgive me my trespass in advance, I will read her mind." The Korrigan was clearly dissatisfied, but equally clearly she could not think of another objection now that I had agreed to the test she had been demanding only a moment before. Finvarra gestured for me to proceed.

"Princess," I said, trying to conceal my nervousness, "anyone with magic will reflexively resist a mind probe. You must try very hard to suppress this response."

"Taliesin," she said playfully, "I am ready for you to penetrate me at any time it pleases you." Finvarra raised an eyebrow, but I had found playing dumb worked best in that kind of situation, so I ignored the play on words and reached gently into her mind.

Evidently, she had conceived this as an opportunity for some intense yet secretive flirting. She was projecting an image of her own beautiful naked body, followed by an image of the two of us lying in the grass and making love so furiously that the earth was shaking. Well, at least I think it was the two of us. The guy she was with looked so handsome it took me a second to be sure it was me—or at least, me as she saw me.

I gave myself the mental equivalent of a cold shower and tried to push beyond the sexual slide show, but I found myself hitting a blank wall. I closed my eyes to block out visual distractions, but greater concentration didn't help.

"Princess," I said aloud. "You are fighting me. You need to open your mind to me. I don't want to hurt you."

"You want me to spread my...mind a little more widely, Taliesin? Why, certainly!" I was focused both visually and mentally on Doirend, but I did catch the Korrigan's disgusted muttering in the background.

The solid wall in front of me softened, then melted away, and I found myself plunging past her increasingly intense display of desire and into the depths of her mind.

Apparently, she had not really believed herself that I could do any more than sense general feelings, because her thoughts were now totally unguarded in a way that few people can achieve in the presence of someone they believe can read their every thought. That's probably why I picked up on a secret far greater than any she planned for me to have.

The Dagda was alive!

From what I could tell from the brief glimpse I got before she realized what I had stumbled upon and tried to push me out, he had used the second battle of Magh Tuiredh as a way to fake his own death. Weary of the kingship, he had let it pass to someone else while he hid himself away on an isolated island near Mag Mell, the Irish paradise.

The problem was that he was not so weary anymore and wanted back into the game. No one knew that, as far as I could tell, except his favorite granddaughter, with whom he had found some way to communicate.

Talk about minefields! The one in her head had a nuke in it that could explode the whole current political alignment of the faerie universe. Even if the Dagda meant to seek some position less exalted than high king, everyone would assume he was scheming to get that crown, and the counterschemes would grow so thick they would come close to suffocating faerie society.

"You cannot tell anyone!" she shouted in my head.

"I have no intention of saying anything, as long as you meet certain conditions," I thought back, trying to sound soothing but probably coming off as calculating. Well, whatever! As long as I got what I wanted, if I had to settle for her thinking I was a jerk, so be it.

"What conditions?" she asked quickly. I was still in her head enough to know she was hoping I was going to demand sex.

"First, I am in love with someone in my world. Beautiful as you are, I must ask that you stop tempting me to betray that love." I could tell that she was disappointed, but also relieved that I had not demanded something impossible, and my diplomatic wording worked well enough to avoid offending her.

"Agreed," she thought, with just a hint of regret.

"Second, you need to reveal some secret to me that I can share. Only in that way can I overcome the Korrigan's objection."

"Agreed," she thought quickly. I could again feel he relief that I was not demanding more.

"Third, in exchange for your agreement to the first two conditions, I am willing to give you a guarantee of my perpetual silence, but you must accept that my guarantee will only hold as long as the Dagda does not attempt the violent overthrow of any faerie ruler who governs virtuously. In particular, any threat to Gwynn ap Nudd will void my guarantee."

I could tell that last part did not please her, possibly because she was not sure exactly what the Dagda intended to do, but in the end she had no choice. She agreed because she knew how much trouble I could make for her and her grandfather if I said anything. I could hear the Korrigan making impatient noises in the background, but I ignored her long enough to set up the *tynged* that spread a golden net over us, binding us to our respective parts of the agreement. It was unusual to weave a *tynged* using just thought agreement rather than spoken agreement, but I could feel its magic holding satisfactorily.

I opened my eyes and told Finvarra and the Korrigan a secret I had seen in Doirend's mind, some recent love affair whose details she had just fed to me. Doirend feigned a blush to make us not look somehow complicit.

"Well, Korrigan, what say you?" asked Finvarra when I was done. "Would you agree that Taliesin can indeed read minds?"

"I will agree," said the Korrigan reluctantly, "but that the witch thought she was doing what Nicneven wanted does not make it so. Nor does it mean that the anger felt from the other side of the portal was coming from Nicneven."

"With all due respect, Majesty," I said, addressing the Korrigan directly, "I have enough experience in these matters to know what I am picking up from someone else's mind. In Alisa MacDougall's mind I saw her memory of Nicneven giving the order. On that point there can be no doubt."

"And if you are right," the Korrigan persisted, "What of it? How does that affect the charges against Robin Goodfellow?"

"That is a fair point," conceded Finvarra. "Regardless of what Nicneven may have to answer for later, her charges against Robin Goodfellow have not been proven false."

"But surely Nicneven's motive in filing the charges can now be questioned," insisted Gwynn. "She knows as well as we do that proceedings against her cannot begin until her earlier charges have been investigated. What is she doing, if not playing for time?"

"Regardless of her motives, Robin Goodfellow must answer for his crime," said the Korrigan in an annoyed tone.

"If it please the court, you have given me leave to speak, but almost immediately I was interrupted," I said quickly. "May I please finish my statement?" The Korrigan started to object yet again, but Finvarra cut her off with a wave of his hand.

"Yes, you have already been granted the right to speak," he said firmly. "Say what is in your heart."

"As I have mentioned, Robin may inadvertently have used magic in front of mortal eyes in the interest of defending his queen, but a Lady of the Lake and I undid the damage by giving our fellow humans a logical explanation of what they had experienced. The security of the faerie realms has not been put at risk."

Finvarra's eyes widened. "Viviane, can you confirm this testimony?"

"I can," Nurse Florence replied, stepping forward a little bit. "We planted appropriate false memories. No one who did not already know of the existence of faeries learned of it that night."

"This new evidence requires consideration," said Finvarra.

At almost exactly the same moment, an arrow whizzed past, missing him by an inch at most.

Chapter 9: Surprise Attack (Tal)

Before Finvarra had a chance to recover from his shock that anyone would dare to open fire on him, other arrows began raining down on us. Gwynn and the armed escorts that had accompanied him and Titania were at least somewhat armored, but the tribunal members, relying on their authority, had not come prepared for battle.

Nurse Florence had already begun to cast a deflection spell that would make it more difficult for the arrows to hit us, and the faerie soldiers had drawn bows to return fire. However, assessing the situation as best I could under such tense circumstances, I could tell we were in trouble. Between them Titania and Gwynn had brought twenty-four men as escort. The tribunal doubtless had a small group standing by somewhere ready to step through a portal and arrest Robin Goodfellow, but that group did not immediately appear. Perhaps whoever was attacking us had blocked them somehow. Gwynn, Titania, Robin, the tribunal members, and I did not have long-range weapons, and Nurse Florence had no weapon at all. Magic we certainly had—but it was likely our adversaries had as well, or they would never have launched on attack on such a powerful group of spell casters in the first place.

The faeries sweeping down from the clouds and bombarding us with arrows were far more numerous than we were; I couldn't get an exact count, but the number of minds I could feel suggested at least two hundred, maybe even more. Even from a distance, I could feel magic building somewhere above the first ranks, readying either to break our defenses or fortify their attack.

For some reason, Nurse Florence's efforts at deflection were less effective than usual. Possibly our attackers included a spell caster adept at interfering with that defense. I couldn't immediately be sure, but I knew we needed to adopt a different strategy. Accelerating myself to faerie speed, I drew White Hilt and directed its fire to form a flaming roof above our heads. It would prevent our archers from fighting back effectively, but given how grossly they were outnumbered, it was more important to prevent the attackers from aiming. I could feel arrows hitting the fire, and I did my best to make it hot enough to incinerate them. A few arrows penetrated my defense, and they were burning, but at least they were few enough to make it easier to dodge them.

"Taliesin, this is dangerous!" barked Gwynn, stating the obvious. I looked in his direction, and he added, "The fire may anger the forest." I was embarrassed to admit that was something I hadn't thought of, though I should have. I had seen an outraged forest in Annwn get the better of a dragon. Right now only a few flaming arrows had hit the ground and set the grass ablaze, but if the process continued, the forest might awaken, and clearly Gwynn was afraid it would blame me, even though I was carefully keeping the fire White Hilt was generating away from the greenery.

"Good point, your Majesty, but what else can I do?" I asked. "We are grossly outnumbered, and deflection spells alone may not be enough to protect us."

Gwynn paused for a moment as if listening, and then he replied, "The forest still seems calm, but take great care you do not let the flames get out of control."

"I'm always careful," I assured him. He nodded, and since he knew me well enough to trust me, he started giving orders to his own men.

I was painfully conscious that we could have only seconds before some of the faeries dropped to ground level and started shooting at us unimpeded. If they did, however, they would have a much narrower window than they would have had firing from above us, and the archers on our side could retaliate more successfully.

Finvarra magicked open a portal, not to flee himself, but to usher the ladies away. However, it collapsed before even the Korrigan, who seemed to have no qualms about leaving, could step through it. At least one of our adversaries had to be a powerful enough sorcerer to thwart Finvarra's efforts.

"Let us unite our strengths to open a portal," suggested Titania quickly. "We have little chance of prevailing here today."

By now I had molded the fire carefully around us, not quite touching the ground or any of the surrounding trees, but coming so close the attackers would have to practically be lying on the ground to get a shot. Unfortunately, I couldn't keep up this defense indefinitely, and the job was made more challenging by having to maintain such a high temperature on the outside. The faerie assailants were making the job even more difficult by shooting volley after volley of arrows in rapid succession, requiring me to keep reinforcing the integrity of our ceiling and getting enough flaming arrows through to interfere with the spell casting efforts of pretty much everyone.

"There are fixed portals nearby—" started Gwynn.

"Unless 'nearby' means inside my fire wall, Majesty, we aren't likely to reach them. However, now that I think of it, you might make it in faerie armor. Perhaps you should go and bring back aid." The moment I said it, I knew Gwynn would decline.

He shook his head and frowned. "I cannot leave now." At some point he had drawn his sword, which sparkled midnight blue in the air. "It will take several minutes for me to return, and by that time it could be too late. I will stand or fall with the rest of you."

Glancing around me, I had another idea. "Robin!" I said. He was lost in concentration, trying to conjure up some defense, but I called to him both verbally and psychically, and he reluctantly abandoned his effort to look quickly in my direction.

"Robin, I hear your flute is supercharged these days. Hit our attackers with something like fear or confusion." A similar tactic had worked for me on Olympus with the lyre of Orpheus. From what Carla had told me, Robin's instrument wasn't quite that powerful, but the force we were facing was smaller than the one I had bested.

Robin's face went blank, as if he had only thought of the flute's power in terms of pranks. However, once he registered on what I was suggesting, his reaction was swift. Pulling the flute from his belt, he began to play, and I felt an immediate surge of power from the music. Carla had been right.

Unfortunately, Robin had evidently not had enough practice with his new power to know how to aim it well. Too late I remembered Carla had said he had enclosed her and the guys in a magic circle before beginning his playing.

There was no magic circle protecting us here, and every one of us got a good strong dose of soul-numbing fear before it even touched our opponents. The faerie rulers and I had strong enough wills to be resistant to such an enchantment in the short term, but some of our troops dropped their bows, shrieked, and curled up into a fetal position. In a few minutes, that would be all of us. Already, I could feel my heartbeat speeding up, my muscles trembling, a scream building at the back of my throat, and, worst of all, a shuddering in my fire wall. I would lose concentration on it altogether if I wasn't careful.

Gwynn, Titania, and I were all yelling orders at Robin to aim better or stop, but he looked dumbfounded and continued playing. It occurred to me that Robin should be able to use the music like the fear effect on Gordy's sword, so that it only affected enemies, but I didn't know how to communicate that idea fast enough to the confused faerie.

Eventually, Robin might have gotten his magic sorted out, at least if he was still alive to think about it. I realized, however, that a faster solution would be the tactic I had used against the Amadan Dubh while he was stealing the lyre of Orpheus: deafening everyone nearby, placing them outside the lyre's power. A similar tactic would almost certainly have worked here. Unfortunately, while I was trying to summon the magic necessary for such a spell at the same time I was trying to fight the fear and keep us shielded, our foes, realizing that getting close enough to hear the music quickly sapped their courage, abruptly changed their tactics—or so I sensed, though I could not see them do it. Several of them soared into the clouds and then shot down like bullets, counting on momentum to carry them through the music—and right into my fire wall.

Someone must have decided that if they could break that barrier, they could take out whoever the musician was from a distance. The idea was sound in theory, except that it required a number of the hostile faeries to make human torches out of themselves. What commander would sanction such a move?

Well, whoever was giving the orders here, apparently. I felt five of the faeries hit the flaming ceiling and then come screaming right through it.

Luck was almost with us. Four of the five hit the ground head first, probably killing themselves in the process. The fifth one, though, came plunging through right above Doirend, who, already shaken by the fearful music, froze at the sight of a faerie fireball descending on her.

My first order of business should have been to complete the deafening spell, but the sight of Doirend about to get hit hard enough to shatter her bones and set her on fire as well got the better of any strategic calculation, and I threw myself at her with all the strength and speed I could muster. I knocked her clear and, as an added bonus, sent her sprawling into Robin, knocking the flute from his hands and sending him tumbling to the ground.

I moved just fast enough to be only grazed by the plummeting faerie, who hit the ground with a sickening crunch and lay as still as his fellows.

I worked to seal the gaps in our fiery ceiling as fast as I could, but a number of arrows sailed through before I could. Fortunately Gwynn, slowed by his plate mail but only slightly, flew back and forth, letting the arrows crash harmlessly against his armor or knocking them off course with his sword. His defensive moves, coupled with Nurse Florence's attempts at deflection, which now seemed more effective, got us through that part of the attack with only Finvarra and one of the archers getting grazed.

We didn't have to fight the runaway fear effect any more, but the smell of burning flesh had rapidly become overpowering. Instead of making us all deaf, I deadened our sense of smell. However, I couldn't speak for everyone else, but to me the sight of the burned faeries and their crushed skulls was almost as bad as the smell. I couldn't blind us, though, and masking out the bodies with illusion would take too long.

A more pressing problem was that, though we now had a pretty good idea of how many enemies we were facing, we still didn't have a good idea of just how much magic they could hit us with. Someone had been fighting Nurse Florence's deflection, as well as snuffing out any attempt to open a portal, but aside from that, I could feel distant power but not see any sign of its use. If anything, the crude effort to use faerie bodies as battering rams suggested sorcerers who were either very weak or very unimaginative. I could have figured out several ways to destroy or weaken my fire defense, including some that Morgan had used to good effect, like torrential rain storms and lightning. There were probably a dozen ways to get the job done, none of which involved using faerie archers as cannon fodder, yet whoever commanded our attackers didn't seem to have lifted a finger to even try any of them.

Just as I thought things couldn't get any weirder, the attack broke off. I could feel the faeries soaring away and at first feared that they were all going to plunge down and through the fire shield, breaking it beyond repair, setting all of us on fire or burying us beneath dead flesh in the process. Instead, they just kept going. By the time we realized they were retreating, it was too late. Gwynn would have given chase, but someone unleashed at least a little magic, setting up what amounted to mystic static that would make the fleeing attack force hard to track by supernatural means. Since they were already out of sight, Gwynn reluctantly dropped the idea of pursuing them, and I breathed a silent sigh of relief. Gwynn could perhaps outdistance our withdrawing assailants on his war horse, but the rest of us, confined to ordinary flight, could never catch up, and even Gwynn had little hope of beating nearly two hundred skilled faerie fighters all by himself.

"I will find out who is responsible for this outrage," he vowed through clenched teeth.

"You will not have to wait long for that knowledge," said the Korrigan. "Look at these bodies."

That was about the last thing I wanted to do, but if there was evidence of who attacked us, we all needed to see it.

It did not take anyone long to notice what the Korrigan wanted us to see. The bodies were badly charred, as was their leather clothing, but not so badly that we could not make out on two of them a small but distinctive patch: a dark sky crisscrossed by lightning, with a stylized *O* in the center.

It had been a symbol of obedience to Oberon but was still, pending his trial, the badge of the faerie armies of England.

"You cannot think that I—" Titania began.

"Indeed, how can we not?" asked the Korrigan, watching Titania suspiciously. "It was your men who attacked us."

"Anyone may sew a false patch on his leathers," Finvarra pointed out.

"Perhaps," agreed the Korrigan, "but her trusted man, Robin Goodfellow, already stands accused, and did you mark how he tried to sabotage us today?"

"I tried something beyond my skill," admitted Robin quietly, "but not from malice or treachery."

"Your incompetence was most conveniently timed—for our enemies," noted the Korrigan angrily.

"Even if these events furnish more evidence of Robin Good-fellow's possible crimes, that does not necessarily mean that he acted on Titania's orders," said Finvarra slowly, weighing his words before he spoke them. Perhaps he was beginning to wonder about Titania himself.

The Korrigan turned to Gwynn. "Are you not still the guide of souls to the lands of the dead, son of Nudd? If so, why not question these dead?" Gwynn nodded, faded to gray scale, and then vanished completely. Apparently he was sufficiently attuned to whatever plane the recently slain inhabited that he did not need to open a portal to get there.

After a few minutes of strained silence, Gwynn returned, first as a shadow, then as gray scale, and finally as himself in living color. "They will not say aye or nay to me. I think I could sense the truth or falsehood of their words, but they seem to know that, and for that reason they decline to answer. Even when I threatened to prevent them from moving on, they remained silent. I cannot know with whom their allegiance lies."

"Titania must at least be arrested on suspicion, then," demanded the Korrigan. "Her involvement in this attack may be innocent, but let a proper tribunal determine that, as ours should determine the fate of Robin Goodfellow."

"Majesties, if I may speak—" I began.

"What, again?" snapped the Korrigan. "Taliesin, you presume too much. You are not the equal of faerie kings or queens and should learn not to meddle so much in our affairs."

"Korrigan," began Finvarra, "Taliesin is not faerie royalty, nor does he claim to be, but surely his valiant efforts to protect us deserve to be acknowledged. I say he shall speak." Doirend nodded enthusiastically, and the Korrigan gestured dismissively, as if the matter was no longer important to her.

"Let me then begin with a question. How does this attack benefit Queen Titania in any way?" I asked.

"Perhaps her husband's lust for power has rubbed off on her," replied the Korrigan in a pseudopatient tone, as if she were explaining to an idiot. "Look around you. Here you have, all gathered in one place, the high king of Ireland, the king of Wales, the queen of Brittany, and...others," she said, with another dismissive wave, this time at Doirend. "With Nicneven and Titania herself, we are now the highest rulers in the faerie realms, at least in this part of the world. Gwynn came at Titania's behest. Finvarra, Doirend, and I came to apprehend Robin Goodfellow, whom Titania brought here for no apparent reason."

The Korrigan paused for dramatic effect and stared into my eyes. "Is it not obvious even to a mortal such as yourself, Taliesin, that Titania plots to rule all of the faerie realms herself? Nicneven she has already slandered. If she can kill the rest of us and convince the remaining influential faeries that Nicneven is responsible, then Nicneven ends up deposed, or worse, and Titania is...how do you say it in your world? 'The last man standing.'"

Someone was definitely being framed here—and it wasn't Nicneven. "Majesty," I answered her quickly, "there are several things wrong with that theory. Surely if Titania wanted to use her own men to attack you, she would have disguised them, probably in Nicneven's favorite gray, rather than having them conveniently crash down upon us with the badge of England prominently displayed."

Finvarra, Doirend, and Gwynn all nodded at that. I needed to push just a little more to keep Titania from getting railroaded.

"And if the plan were to kill all of you," I continued, "why was the attack broken off in the way it was? We were badly outnumbered, with no way to retreat, against an enemy clearly not afraid to take casualties. Why send just five against my fire defense, when fifty would have had a much greater chance of actually accomplishing what you say their objective was?"

"They would not have beaten us," said Gwynn firmly.

"Perhaps not, Majesty, but if we were so strong they knew we would win, why engage with us at all?"

"Because their plans were disrupted by your unexpected arrival," said the Korrigan mockingly. "They were not anticipating having to fight the great Taliesin. They had not counted on a wall of flame blocking their way to us.

"Yet there is merit in what you say," continued the Korrigan, her sudden change of direction catching everyone by surprise. "I cannot answer all the arguments you raise. However," she said, looking straight at Finvarra, "the question is not whether the case against Titania proves her guilt. Perhaps it does not. The question before us, though, is whether there is sufficient evidence to convene a tribunal to consider the matter. Finvarra, do you doubt any faerie authority would decide otherwise?"

Finvarra paused for a moment to consider. Then he looked at me apologetically and said, "Though Taliesin has offered a defense of Titania that is in some ways compelling, he has not dispelled all possibility that she is guilty." By now the guards who were to accompany the tribunal had finally made their appearance.

"We must," continued Finvarra, "take into custody both Robin Goodfellow, on the accusation of Nicneven, and Titania, on the accusation of the Korrigan." His men moved toward both. I noticed that Titania's own guards didn't move at all. Faerie law would have precluded them from interfering, but the fact that they did not even look in Titania's direction was telling.

They didn't trust her, either.

"I...I am...innocent," managed Titania, overwhelmed by the speed at which her life was crumbling.

"And you shall be given every opportunity to demonstrate as much to a tribunal's satisfaction," said Finvarra gently. "In the meantime, your daughter, Tanaquill, can rule, can she not?"

Titania nodded.

"That is well," said Finvarra, "for we cannot leave England leaderless at such a dangerous time."

"Majesty, I do not like this," I thought to Titania. *"I might doubt Oberon's innocence, but not yours. I will do what I can to investigate."* She nodded slightly and tried to muster a smile for me. She didn't quite manage one, though.

Actually, I didn't have any idea how I was going to do that. Finding the real source of the attack might take weeks, even months in Annwn, or perhaps other faerie realms as well. Even with the faster progression of time here, I couldn't vanish from Santa Brígida for that long.

There was also the problem of Nicneven. She could well be responsible for this attack herself. That would be reason enough to investigate. On the other hand, it was also reason to get back to Santa Brígida and help to protect my family and friends. For all I knew, she had noticed my presence in Annwn and tried this attack as a diversion to keep me here. The defensive strategy Vanora was using would only hold together for a few days at most because of the strain it placed on her. Sooner or later, holes would develop, and Nicneven could exploit them.

A grim Titania and miserable Robin were already chained and would be led away in moments. That sight might have drawn all my attention, but Doirend motioned for me to join her. I think she wanted to kiss me, but the *tynged* prevented her.

"Taliesin," she whispered, obviously not wanting to be overheard, but in a place filled with faeries, most of whom could, at will, amp up their hearing, that could be tricky. "Taliesin, enter my mind for a minute."

Ah, her thinking was the same as mine.

"Yes, princess, what do you want of me?" She could not read minds as I could, but I could project to her, or pretty much anyone. Someone with magic could respond loudly enough for me to hear.

"I want only to thank you," she thought back. *"I will not forget that you saved me today. Nor will my...family forget it."* Even in a communication no one else could overhear, Doirend was cautious.

Normally, I probably would have done my, "Ah, shucks, it was nothing," routine. I couldn't claim I had even thought my little rescue through; rather, I had reacted instinctively. However, in this case I hesitated. Months of exposure to the puzzling and often threatening world of faerie politics had made me realize one thing: I should never miss a chance to make an ally. The fact that the ally in question was probably on par with Zeus made the deal even more tempting, not to mention the fact that Zeus could no longer enter my world, while the Dagda theoretically could. He would have to lie low until he revealed he was still alive, but he clearly meant to do that very soon.

I had to remind myself that I had no idea what the Dagda's agenda was, and past history suggested that I might inherit a lot of enemies with this particular ally.

"Princess, I did not act with any thought of reward, nor do I expect one. I am happy to have done you service."

"Taliesin," she thought back immediately, *"I am no seer, yet I could have prophesied that answer. The fact that you did not expect a reward does not mean that you will not receive one."*

Before I could respond she firmly broke off contact, turned, and walked away.

Well, I had tried to stay out of the potential mess. There could be worse things than being owed a favor by one of the most powerful faeries who ever existed.

The tribunal and its guards left very rapidly with their prisoners. Finvarra clearly feared another attack, though he did not say as much. Titania's men departed as well, presumably to notify Tanaquill of what had happened. That left Nurse Florence and me alone with Gwynn and his men. I had hoped for an opportunity to speak with him, but that was not to be.

"Taliesin, I must go and pay my respects to Tanaquill. She will need my support in this difficult time."

"Of course, Majesty," I replied. "We can only hope this bitter time will be short-lived, and that her mother will rapidly be exonerated."

My words seemed to surprise Gwynn. "Why do you think I wore this armor, Taliesin?" The question seemed like a non sequitur.

"I'm afraid I have no idea," I replied.

He looked at me grimly. "I wore it for the same reason I brought my hounds along: because I do not trust Titania. Nor should you. She may be innocent, but it would be unwise to take chances."

"I trust Nicneven far less," I said quietly.

"I do not trust her, either," admitted Gwynn, "but there is no reason I may not distrust both if I please. You would do well to do the same."

I nodded and did not try to pursue the conversation any further. He was clearly impatient to be away, and now did not seem a good time to tell him I intended to try to prove Titania's innocence. He would probably have advised me to stay out of the matter, I would have had to refuse, and our relationship might become strained. Gwynn was really the only faerie ruler I trusted without hesitation, and he had been more than generous to me in the past, so I didn't want to risk his friendship by arguing.

"For what it's worth, Tal," said Nurse Florence after Gwynn had mounted his war horse and flew away, followed by his hounds and guards, "I think you're on the right track. Nicneven must be behind this attack, not Titania."

"It's too bad we don't have anything remotely resembling proof," I said irritably. "We have some ghosts who won't answer Gwynn, but not a single live hostage from whose mind I could extract the truth. Whoever was providing the magic stayed far enough back that none of us could get the flavor of it and trace it back to a particular caster."

"I'll say one thing, though," said Nurse Florence. "Your dad would be proud of you. You have the makings of a natural lawyer."

"Following in Dad's footsteps has actually never occurred to me," I replied.

"I'm not trying to pressure you to do that," said Nurse Florence reassuringly. "I just can't help but be impressed by the speed with which you can weigh evidence and produce logical arguments. I've noticed it before, but today you really outdid yourself."

"Not enough to do any good," I said with a touch of bitterness.

"Don't be too hard on yourself," Nurse Florence replied, patting me on the arm. "I think Finvarra would have agreed with you under normal circumstances, but after Oberon's inexplicable lunge toward the dark, he seems more risk averse than normal. In his position, would you want to cast the deciding vote to free Titania, only to have her turn out to be evil later on?"

I sighed loudly and then said, "I guess not. Still, this makes our situation even more difficult. If Titania is right about Oberon, there is some far greater evil out there that isn't on anyone's radar yet except ours." I noticed something lying in the grass, almost hidden by the blades as they regrew with amazing speed, erasing the fire damage. I reached down and picked up Robin's willow flute.

"Well, at least I can answer our question about this," I said, holding it up for Nurse Florence to see. Then I let my mind reach out to it, searching for the secrets of its magic. It took me only a few minutes, as the magic was familiar.

"What's the verdict?" asked Nurse Florence. She, too, was studying the instrument closely but could not perceive its essence as well as I could.

"Robin's flute must have been blessed by Apollo and Hermes right before Robin left Olympus. I can feel the presence of both of them in its wood. I don't get it, though. They had only just cleared him of being involved in Oberon's plot, and as far as I can remember, they were still not exactly on friendly terms. He seems a strange choice for a gift of such high-level magic."

"Apollo can sometimes act as a powerful seer," Nurse Florence reminded me. "I'm guessing he saw a possible future in which giving Robin a magical boost would produce a good result."

I frowned a little. "Well, let's see. So far Robin has nearly converted the Valentine's Day dance into an orgy and caused the arrest of Titania. I'd say Apollo is zero for two right now."

"Circumstances may have changed," Nurse Florence suggested. "The possible future Apollo saw might have been rendered impossible by some other development. Speaking of which, we didn't make arrangements for a seer, and with Gwynn preoccupied, we won't get any help finding one right away. I would recommend we return to Santa Brígida for a while."

"Yeah, we should check and make sure Nicneven hasn't been up to any mischief in our absence," I agreed.

It took Nurse Florence only a short time to open a portal, but getting through it was another matter. It did not open on my back yard, as she had intended. Instead, we saw something that looked like a wall of magically charged ice, sparkling blue but filled with moving shadows. I had never seen anything like it in any of my lives, and Nurse Florence could not recall anything in the records of the Order that even remotely resembled it.

"Is Nicneven borrowing from Robin's playbook?" I asked. "Are we seeing through someone else's portal at the end?" We experimented and quickly disproved that theory. No matter how rapidly Nurse Florence opened portals to different locations in Santa Brígida, we always got the same cold welcome. It wasn't plausible that someone else could travel fast enough to be in every location and open a portal right in front of ours. Nor could we believe that there were casters all over Santa Brígida, each one thwarting us at a different location.

However, when we tried other destinations, we were able to connect and step through the portal every time. We tried Cardiff, London, and Los Angeles, all without incident.

"Now you try," suggested Nurse Florence. I couldn't open a portal into Annwn as a result of Arawn's ban, and I had just assumed that I couldn't open one from Annwn, either. I was very pleased to discover I could, and I was successful in connecting to every location I tried. Well, every location except Santa Brígida.

"So it isn't just me!" said Nurse Florence. "It looks as if traveling by magic to Santa Brígida has been blocked."

We tried opening a portal together, with the same result. This time, though, I reached out with my mind to probe at the magic, though I knew what I would find.

The barrier was an amalgam of two magics: the ice was Nicneven's. The shadows? Well, they were special. Hecate's magic, channeled through the bond with Nicneven, had crafted them. Apparently the stories about Nicneven pledging herself to Hecate were true.

Ice, even magic ice, I might have melted through with White Hilt. The shadows, though, would not burn, and I knew instinctively that trying to push our bodies through them could have dire results.

"If Nicneven wants to keep us out of Santa Brígida that badly, we need to get back right now," I said.

Nurse Florence nodded. "The obvious way would be to use a portal to some nearby spot and then walk back in. Tal…"

"Yes?" I prompted.

"It's possible that whatever is surrounding the town might block us physically as well as magically. Nicneven must surely know we could reach any point near town. She'd hardly waste all the magic that went into crafting that barrier if it could be so easily circumvented."

Nothing was ever simple!

Chapter 10: Runaway Djinni

As I drove Khalid home from Jimmie's celebration dinner, I could tell that my little...well, brother (in every way that mattered) had a question.

"Shar?" he said finally, after what, for him, was an uncharacteristically long silence.

"What?" I asked, keeping my eyes on the road. I might end up dying in battle at some point, but I wasn't going to die in a stupid auto accident.

"Will I be able to play sports like all of you when I get into high school?"

The answer should have been a simple yes, but Khalid's special abilities made the situation more complicated.

"We can work something out, I'm sure," I told him, "but you probably shouldn't play anything that requires speed. You'd have an unfair advantage."

There was a pause so long I realized I could hear Khalid breathing. Finally, he said, "But doesn't every sport require speed?" I hadn't thought about it, but certainly most did.

"What did you have in mind?" I asked.

"Football like you and Dan and Gordy in the fall, soccer like you and Tal in the winter; Gianni and I could be on the soccer team together. Oh, and baseball like you, Gordy, and Jimmie in the spring."

I chuckled. "Well, I'm glad you're ambitious, but all of those require running, and you know you could outrun a car."

"I'll...I'll hold back," he said, sounding desperate. His tone made me sad. If he had asked me for the moon, I would have tried to pull it out of the sky for him.

"Under the pressure of competition, I don't think you could, Khalid. Your adrenaline would take over." He sighed in a way that almost sounded like a moan.

"But," I continued, "you've got three friends with magic. We know there are already spells that can change someone's speed or strength, and there's even one that can get people to perform at their best. Somehow the spell knows what their best is. I'll bet Tal, Carla, or Nurse Florence could whip up a spell that would work the other way around and keep you from exceeding the best you could do if you were an ordinary human." Yeah, I shouldn't have made that statement without checking. Despite being surrounded by magic all the time, what I knew about it could fit in an eye dropper. Still, I knew Tal in particular could explore new magic faster than anyone else. I also knew he would do whatever he could for Khalid. I wasn't a gambler, but I would have taken a pretty big bet that Tal could figure something out.

Apparently Khalid felt the same way, because my answer satisfied him, and he went back to smiling as broadly as he had been during dinner. As we got closer to home, he also started humming. Khalid might be magical in more ways than one, but carrying a tune was not one of his abilities. However, I didn't care how grating his humming was. If he was happy, I was happy.

As soon as we stepped into the house, my mother made a fuss over both of us. She had always been loving, but during my teenage years I had gotten her to dial it down a notch, at least in public. Something about Khalid, though, sent her maternal instincts into overdrive. In a few years he was going to try to get her to back off a little, but for now he loved the attention, and why shouldn't he? Where his mother was, only God (or I should Allah?) knew, and his father had abused him and abandoned him on the street.

My parents thought Khalid was a Middle Eastern refugee they were more than willing to pretend was a distant cousin of theirs because they believed he needed protection. I thought my mother at least was already wishing she could adopt him, and that was just fine with me. It would be easy to pretend our "cousin's" parents had died and adopt him. Then he would be my brother under law as well as in my heart.

Oddly enough, the only obstacle to that outcome was Khalid himself. As much as he loved us—and he did, I had absolutely no doubt—he still expected that somehow he could find his father and get him to take Khalid back. Since his father had rejected Khalid after discovering that the little guy's mother was a djinni, I couldn't imagine that man treating Khalid like anything other than some kind of abomination. I couldn't tell Khalid this, but, like Tal, I had no intention of letting Khalid ever get within a thousand miles of his father. Somehow, someway, I would get him to forget that false dream.

Finally I managed to pry Khalid loose from my mother and take him upstairs to his room. He gave me a big hug and promised to get ready for bed, though he was so excited, I doubted he would sleep as much as he needed to. Well, tomorrow was Saturday, so at least he didn't have to get up for school. He would have to go to temple and pretend to be Jewish again for the sake of his cover, though. I knew that was a strain on him, but he always did it without complaint, insisting when I asked him that Allah would forgive him.

I went to my room for a little while and went through my teenage rituals, like checking e-mail, Facebook, Twitter, Instagram, and pretty much any other social media I could think of. I sometimes laughed to myself about what would happen if I started to post things about my real life. Imagine how fast a selfie taken on the peak of Mount Olympus—the home of the old gods, not the physical one—would go viral.

After a short time I went down to check on Khalid, who wasn't there. He had his own bathroom—my house is pretty big, if I haven't mentioned—but the door was open, and there was no sign of him. I covered the whole second floor, but there was no sign of him anywhere. I went back to his room—still empty. I would have heard my mother talking to him if he had gone back downstairs, and I was pretty sure he wouldn't have done that anyway.

I began to get nervous. Tal had warded our house some time ago against supernatural attacks, but I tried to remember when those wards had last been renewed. Had Tal checked them since Nicneven had emerged as a menace? I called him, but his phone went straight to voice mail. Then I remembered he was going to Annwn for something and probably wasn't back yet.

I was being silly. Vanora was monitoring the whole town like crazy, and there was one of her security vans parked discreetly at the end of the street. She could psychically monitor through her men, even cast spells through them if needed, and they could also respond if a physical menace threatened. I was almost better protected than if I had been hanging out with the president in the White House.

Still, where the heck had Khalid gotten to?

His laptop was open on his bed. I didn't want to be the kind of Big Brother who was snooping all the time, but I couldn't just stand around and do nothing. Finally, I looked at the screen—and then my heart almost stopped.

Khalid had been doing what I was doing: checking the latest developments on his computer. I noticed he'd clicked through to some news story about Beverly Hills. I'd told him that I used to live in Beverly Hills, and from that moment, he always wanted to know what was going on there.

Apparently, there was an evening career program of some kind going on at Beverly Hills High School, and one of the speakers was an Egyptian businessman. Even a casual glance at the images with the story would have led anyone who knew Khalid to remark on how much that businessman looked like him.

Khalid had found his father.

Surely he wouldn't just take off without saying anything?

Yeah, surely, but where was he then?

His window was open. I now realized how odd that was, given how cold the weather outside had gotten.

I looked out into darkness that wouldn't have been menacing if Khalid hadn't been out in it. He could jump higher than a normal person his age—or mine, for that matter. Still, it was hard to imagine him jumping down from the second story. Unless…

I quickly checked his closet. Sure enough, his dragon armor was missing.

Tal had our dragon armor stored in his attic and heavily warded, but a few days ago he had let Khalid borrow his to practice flying. Khalid was supernaturally fast, but he couldn't normally fly. However, his set of dragon armor gave him that ability.

I glanced at my watch. It was already after 8:00 p.m., and the meeting at which Khalid's father was speaking ended at 9:00 p.m. Even running his fastest, which he couldn't possibly have done clear down to Beverly Hills, Khalid would have taken several hours, and by then his father would have vanished into some nearby hotel, probably to leave the next day. Flying, though, Khalid might be able to cover the distance in an hour, so if he had started a few minutes ago, he might just be in time to confront his father.

Quite aside from the fact that his father was an abusive bastard, once Khalid left Santa Brígida and Vanora's security network, he became far more vulnerable. Khalid was probably flying invisibly, but if someone supernatural had been watching Santa Brígida, as Nicneven and her allies probably were, they could have noticed him easily enough. Even I knew enough from experience to realize ordinary invisibility didn't hold up well against people with magical abilities, and using his dragon armor to fly would put out enough of a magic signature to be detectable from some distance.

Basically, anyone who wanted to kidnap Khalid and use him for leverage or worse would have an easy shot at him tonight.

Wishing I had Tal's ability to send out a psychic call to all of us, I did the next best thing and phoned Vanora. Any one of us had the privilege of getting through to her immediately.

"Shahriyar, is something wrong?" Vanora asked, knowing something was, or I wouldn't be calling. I could hear the fatigue in her voice. Our current security high alert was preventing her from sleeping very much.

"I think Khalid has run away and is flying to Beverly Hills. Can you tell me where he is?" I asked.

Vanora paused long enough for her consciousness to spread through her security men across the entire city. Finally, she said, "I'm not feeling him anywhere nearby, but…flying, you say? Yes, I can see what might be the residue of something like that heading south. I…Shahriyar, there's some kind of interference outside town. I can't tell where he went after he crossed the border."

"Interference," I said, my panic mounting. "Does that mean—"

"It could be Nicneven, yes, but that doesn't mean she has Khalid. It just means I'll need time to figure out where he is. Aside from making sure Nicneven or her minions don't sneak in, locating Khalid will be my top priority."

"I should go look for him," I said quickly. "I'll be back as soon as I can."

There was a long pause, but finally Vanora spoke again. "Shahriyar, I know you're worried about him, but what good can you do driving around aimlessly?"

"I think I know where he's gone," I assured her. "He's headed for Beverly Hills High School to find his no-good father."

Another pause greeted that revelation. Then, just when I thought Vanora might have succumb to fatigue, she picked up the conversation again.

"Did he take anything like a GPS device with him?"

I looked around quickly. "His phone still seems to be here," I replied. Clearly, Khalid had been in a real hurry to get out, or he would have taken it.

"Has he ever been to Beverly Hills?" she asked.

"No, he's been in this area the whole time I've known him…well, except for when we've gone to other worlds."

"Then how on earth do you expect he's going to find his way there? He can't do magic. He can't reach out with his mind and figure out where he is. Just flying south, particularly along the coast, might get him to Santa Monica, but Beverly Hills is farther inland than we are. For that matter, how is he going to know Santa Monica, or any nearby point? What's to keep him from flying right past and ending up in San Diego?"

Great! Now on top of worrying about someone finding Khalid, I had to worry about him getting lost.

"OK, I get that I can't just start driving and find him. But how are you going to find him from here with all the static?" This time the pause was even longer.

"I don't know yet, but you haven't given me a chance to find out. Shar, I understand why this upsets you so much, especially with Nicneven probably spying on us." Vanora had never called me Shar before. I didn't know whether the fact that she was doing so now should make me feel reassured or even more worried.

"Trust me, though," she continued, "Khalid is not in as much danger as you think. Even if Nicneven is watching us, and we don't know for sure that she is, she can't possibly be watching everything in Santa Brígida at the same time. She might have missed Khalid's departure, but suppose she didn't. You know how fast he can move in that dragon armor. She probably couldn't even tell who he was, and she would have had a hard time keeping up with him. To track him, she would have had to stop watching us. Draw a little on the tactical knowledge of Alexander the Great for me. What's the likelihood that Nicneven would do that? Wouldn't she suspect we had figured out she was watching and were creating a diversion to draw her attention away. I know that's how I would see it if I were in her place."

I had to admit Vanora had a good point, but the thought of Khalid out there alone had dug its claws in hard, and now it was all I could think about.

"Look, you're stuck here," I said slowly, "and you have a lot of other things to worry about. Why don't Carla and I get a little way out of town, and then she can try to locate Khalid? If we can get a fix on him, I've been all over southern California, so Carla can use my memories to portal us close to where he is, and we can bring him back fast."

"Shar, if Nicneven is keeping an eye on us, she could take advantage of even a short trip by you and Carla. Tal and Viviane are taking longer than expected coming back from Annwn, so our defenses are already low. At the moment, Carla is the only one in town besides me who has any magic to speak of, and you and that sword that makes you immune to magic have the best chance of anyone of warding off an attack physically."

"On the other hand, if one of our enemies captures Khalid, you know Carla, Tal, Nurse Florence, all the guys, and I would do anything to get him back. He'd be the ultimate hostage. Even if we get lucky and no hostiles notice his magic, he's only eleven, remember? We can't count on him to be discreet. If he does find his way to his father, there could be a big scene with no one around to magick away all the memories of it. Khalid has the idea that if his father can see what he can do, he will be proud of him and take him back. How would you like the little guy shifting from visible to invisible in public, or maybe doing a human air show over the high school, or even throwing himself into fire and emerging without the tiniest burn?"

Vanora sighed loudly. "And of course everything that happens in Beverly Hills tends to get picked up by the wire services. Khalid could make national news—"

"Or go viral on YouTube," I suggested.

"Yes, true," she agreed, "and then the faerie rulers would be very, very angry with all of us." She paused again. "Oh, all right, take Carla and see what you can find out, but promise me something."

"What?" I asked suspiciously.

"If Carla can't figure out his location pretty quickly, promise that you and she will return to town right away. If you can't rescue Khalid anyway, there isn't any point in risking yourselves or the security of the town."

"You got it, Vanora. I'll keep you up to date on what's happening, too."

Though clearly still not happy with the idea, Vanora was satisfied with my promise. We said quick good-byes; she was no doubt eager to get back to surveilling the town, and I wanted to try to grab Khalid before he could confront his father if at all possible.

Carla only lived a block and a half away. She arrived at my front door about two minutes after I called her. I hadn't been exaggerating when I told Vanora we would do pretty much anything to protect Khalid.

"Khalid's had time to get to Beverly Hills or some equally distant point, right?" she asked.

"I'm afraid so," I said.

"Well, then," she replied, looking around his room, "we need an object, something personal, that will help me reach for him. If I have to cast my mind out in all directions and scan for him, it could take me hours, and the farther away he is, the less likely my search is to find him."

Together we searched and picked out a photo of Khalid and me taken right after he had first come to live with us. Khalid also had a digital version, but he kept the physical print on his desk, and it was well fingered, suggesting that he held it every chance he could get.

Carla closed her eyes for a minute. "This is good; I can feel him on it...and you. Since you're with me, your connection, both to the photo and to him, will help. It wouldn't hurt if we had some hair or something like that."

We found a couple of hairs in his comb. Carla pronounced them satisfactory.

"Can we look from here?" I asked, just to be sure.

"No, Vanora was right. I can still see what's going on in town, but there is some kind of interference beyond that. I don't know how far we'd have to drive to get out from under it, but if Nicneven's doing it, I doubt she can mess with an area much larger than the town." She patted me on the arm. "Don't worry, Shar. We could have him back in half an hour."

We took my Lexus and went north on San Ysidro, then turned left into the parking lot for Manning Park once we got into Montecito. We cleared the interference some time before that, but Carla wanted an isolated area, and the park closed at sunset, so it seemed as good a spot as any. We parked. She made both the car and ourselves unnoticeable, conjured up a little light, and then went to work. Not for the first time, I wished I had magic so I could help out, but at least if there was trouble, my sword arm was more than good enough to protect both Carla and Khalid if need be.

In a very short period of time, Carla looked up from contemplating Khalid's picture and his hair. "He's in Beverly Hills, after all."

"I should have known Vanora was being too pessimistic," I said. "He's really enthusiastic to learn about the place. He's probably been taking virtual trips on Google Earth for days. Can you tell where in Beverly Hills?"

She nodded quickly. "I even managed a brief glimpse through his eyes. Older-looking building, French Norman architecture."

"That's the front of the school. If you can get a more precise location, we can zap in right next to him," I said. "He's not going to want to leave without making contact with his father. We need to physically grab him before he flies away."

"Probably wise," Carla agreed. "I could fly after him, but in the dragon armor he's faster than I am, and if he moves fast enough, I'll have a hard time seeing through his invisibility."

She closed her eyes, and after a minute she began talking again. "He's invisible, so at least he's being cautious. He's on the move. He's gone up some steps, taken a right, and now he's trying some doors, but they're locked. Here, let me show you." She took my hand, and since her magic was not hostile, Zom didn't block it.

I found myself at the front of the high school, looking out through Khalid's eyes. He was in the process of picking the lock on one of the doors leading to the auditorium.

"Something's wrong!" I said, dropping her hand. "The program should be over about now, but the building is already locked. That doesn't make sense."

Carla had the portal shimmering next to us without my having to ask. Since Khalid could see the portal opening on the other side, we jumped through before he had a chance to run away.

Though it had only taken us seconds to reach Khalid's former position, he had already gotten the door open. I charged into the lobby of the auditorium. The area was dark, and Khalid must still be invisible, so even though there was a little light coming in through the door, I had no clue where he was. I prayed Carla could get in fast enough to spot him. I didn't want to have to chase him all over the city…or beyond.

I could hear Carla's footsteps behind me, but I could also hear Khalid in front of me, picking the lock on one of the doors that went into the auditorium itself. Unfortunately, he had developed pretty good lock-picking skills during the time he lived on the street. Right now he was surrounded by locked doors, but if he got into the auditorium and then out one of the side doors near the stage area, he could take off again, and, as Carla had pointed out, we wouldn't be able to follow.

It occurred to me that I had no idea how the alarms worked or where security cameras were located. Neither would have been a problem if I had Tal with me, but Carla's magic, like most people's, didn't work on modern technology.

Damn! Beverly Hills Police had a really fast response time. We'd have to make this quick and worry about any evidence of our visit later.

I heard a click, and I could see movement in front of me as one of the doors swung open. Carla was right behind me, but in the darkness she clearly hadn't been able to spot Khalid yet. As fast as he could move, he'd be away before we could stop him.

Khalid had obviously seen us, so I had nothing to lose by yelling, "Khalid, your father isn't here!"

"He must be!" I heard his high-pitched voice, shaky with desperation, somewhere in front of me; I stumbled forward and into the auditorium, with Carla following. I knew I needed to keep Khalid there until she could pin down where he was.

"Khalid, I think it's a trick of some kind. You remember what I told you about Nicneven?"

Khalid didn't answer.

"Look," I continued, wondering if I was talking to myself, "even if you just missed the meeting, there's no way everyone would have left this fast. There's no way the auditorium would have gotten locked up so fast, either. There was no meeting here tonight. You're a smart guy, Khalid. You know what that means as well as I do. This is some kind of trap."

"I've magically locked every exit except the one Khalid used to come in," Carla thought to me. *"I still can't tell exactly where he is, but if he tries to run, his attempts to pick a lock will give him away."*

"Anyone here besides us?" I thought, hoping she was listening, because, unlike her, I couldn't project my thoughts.

And that was exactly the moment the lights came on. Momentarily blinded, I spun in the direction from which we had come, a safe guess since I hadn't heard any other doors or seen the glow of a portal, and drew Zom.

"Shar?" asked a familiar voice from my past.

Even before my eyes fully adjusted to the light, I realized I had just drawn a weapon on my freshman English teacher. He would see it as a fencing foil and not as a sword, but still, my drawing it must have looked odd, to say the least.

"Mr. H., I didn't expect to run into you,"

"Clearly," he observed dryly. He looked just as I remembered him: midfifties; gray, thinning hair; kind of pot-bellied. However, his normally friendly expression had been replaced with a suspicious one.

"So," he continued, "what are you and the young lady doing here?"

"We..." was all I managed to get out. I had faced dragons without getting jittery, but right now my stomach was doing flip-flops. It wasn't that I had bad memories of Mr. H's class or anything. Actually, he was one of the people I really missed after leaving Beverly. Maybe that was the problem: I didn't want him to think I was some kind of juvenile delinquent. Stupid, especially considering Carla would undoubtedly end up wiping his memory, but that's how I felt.

"They were just looking for me, sir," said Khalid. I almost jumped at his voice right next to me. "He wanted to show me the school where he used to go, and I decided to play a trick on him and Carla, so I ran and hid. The door was open, sir, so I came in here." Khalid was doing his best I'm-much-too-cute-to-do-anything-wrong act, and I could see that it was working, but not completely. I could still see the skepticism in Mr. H's eyes.

"Shar, I don't remember you fencing. You played football, right?"

"Good memory," I said, praying that my voice wouldn't give me away. "I took up fencing after I moved north."

"Oh, yes, you moved to…Santa Barbara, right?" he asked. He seemed to be relaxing, and I breathed a sigh of relief and relaxed just a little myself.

"Actually, a little place called Santa Brígida, just east of Santa Barbara," I replied.

"You like it there?" he asked.

Interestingly, I had to think about my answer for a second. Leaving all the supernatural hijinks aside, and the fact that I would never have met my closest friends, to say nothing of Khalid, if I hadn't gone there, what did I actually think of the school?

"It's different," I said slowly, looking around the dark burgundy decor of the auditorium, refurbished from its original 1930s design. "SB's a very new school. Everything is pretty shiny and new, but I kind of like Beverly for its traditions. I look around here and see history everywhere."

Mr. H. nodded and smiled. "I feel the same way."

"Also," I added, "I was happier being part of a Persian community. In SB my family and I are the only Persians for miles. It's a good thing I've made some really good friends there." Suddenly remembering my manners, I introduced Carla and Khalid.

"So Shar, now that we've all been introduced, you think you could put the fencing equipment away?" I was so nervous I had forgotten I was clutching Zom. I chuckled and sheathed it.

"Sorry, but I had just come from fencing practice with an old friend, and when you turned the lights on, I just reflexively grabbed it."

Mr. H. laughed heartily at that, and I relaxed completely. "I guess it's a good thing, then, that I wasn't closer—you might have run me through!" Then we all laughed, and I knew everything was going to be all right.

We chatted as we walked back out into the auditorium foyer. It was lit now, too, and I got distracted by showing Khalid the WPA mural that portrayed the Norman contributions throughout history. I should have thought about the fact that I was holding up Mr. H. As it turned out, I should have been thinking about a lot of things I wasn't.

"I'm so glad you're still interested in history," said Mr. H., "since very soon you're going to be history." Khalid was prattling on so much about the mural that at first Mr. H's words didn't register on me. Actually, I didn't know what was up until I heard a crunch and spun around to see Carla crumple to the floor, clutching a bleeding nose that from the sound of things was broken. "Mr. H," who was clearly an impostor, lunged at me far too fast for the middle-aged man he was.

I drew Zom again, this time for real, and I could see the emerald-green reflection in his eyes. He could see through the illusion, as I knew he would.

The fake Mr. H. began to mutter a spell, which told me two things: he was a spell caster as well as being a shape-shifter, and his intel was remarkably poor. Zom made me immune to any kind of hostile magic…unless of course I wasn't the target. Carla was relatively defenseless. Khalid had gone invisible at the first sign of trouble, but I knew the stranger could probably see through that if he had the time.

The smart play from a military standpoint would have been to take off his head with one stroke just to be safe, and I could easily have done that, but, aside from the fact that I couldn't bring myself to kill that casually, I also started second-guessing myself. What if he really was Mr. H.? He had been such a perfect counterfeit in the beginning. Maybe someone…or something…was possessing him. Rather than use deadly force, I rushed forward and smacked him across the chest with the flat of the blade. He staggered, both his nearly finished spell and his disguise destroyed by Zom's touch.

He was still middle aged, but much leaner and meaner than the man he had been impersonating so well, and his eyes were cold and heartless. Before his magic could come back online, I knocked him out with one blow, yelled to Khalid to keep an eye on him, and ran to Carla's assistance. She was already recovering, but I helped her stop the bleeding, and, drawing a little strength from me, she bounced back quickly.

"I'm not as good a healer as Nurse Florence," she said, looking at her swelling and vaguely crooked nose in the mirror. "I'll need to see her or Vanora before I go home; this is one thing I can't explain to my parents."

"Who is that?" asked Khalid, looking suspiciously at our unconscious adversary.

"The gray robe tells us he is one of Nicneven's," Carla explained to him. "Shar was right in thinking this was a trap."

"It was a pretty sucky trap, then," Khalid observed cockily.

Out of the mouths of babes! It was indeed a pretty sucky trap. One of Nicneven's minions, trying to capture a sorceress, a half djinn, and an experienced fighter with magic immunity? Even on his best day, he could never have pulled that off. Nicneven herself probably couldn't have. His only chance, had I not been immune, would have been to zap all three of us at once before we realized who he was, and he didn't even try to do that.

"I hadn't been paying attention at first," admitted Carla. "That's how he got the drop on me. Seconds before that, though, I realized his mind was shielded, and that he seemed to be operating on a pretty high-power level. From the way he acted, I guess he already had some protection against physical attack in place; he just didn't know about Zom."

"He sure knew a lot about me when I was a freshman, and about Mr. H. Carla, I have to know. The real Mr. H. isn't lying somewhere dead, is he?" I hoped I was being silly, but I couldn't quite shake the image of his dead body lying in a blood-spattered classroom. Given the way we lived, who could blame me?

Carla closed her eyes for a minute, clearly sending her mind out to look. Then she opened her eyes, and smiled. "He's sleeping peacefully in what I imagine is his classroom. I took off the magical constraint keeping him asleep. He should wake up in a few minutes and just think he dozed off."

"Our mystery attacker must have probed him before we got here so he could lull us into a false sense of security," I said, wondering what I would have done to the guy if Mr. H. had been dead. As it was, Nicneven's minion was just a logistical problem rather than an object of swift vengeance. "Does that mean this guy can read minds like Tal?"

"Could be, but that gift is pretty uncommon," said Carla. "It's more likely he used some sort of compulsion to get your teacher to talk about you before putting him to sleep. Either way, what are we going to do with our prisoner? I don't have a direct line to Gwynn the way the Ladies of the Lake do, or I would suggest getting Gwynn to lock him up. As it is, it would take a lot of time to locate a faerie ruler, and I don't want to stay here longer than necessary."

"Yeah, I promised Vanora I'd get us back just as soon as we snagged Khalid. Oh, and by the way, young man, we are both so happy to see you...and so ready to wring your neck for putting yourself in danger."

Khalid shifted effortlessly into poor-little-me. "I'm sorry," he said, hanging his head after I had seen a strategic tear drift down his cheek. "I didn't mean to worry you, but...but I knew you would try to stop me from coming if I told you." He hugged me hard and started sobbing. Either he was destined to get an Academy Award, or I had been wrong, and he was crying for real.

I could feel my heart breaking as I clutched him to my chest. "I wouldn't have wanted you leaving Santa Brígida right now. That's true."

His red eyes looked up at me. "You and Tal don't believe my father will ever be proud of me and love me, but I know I can convince him if I can just see him."

I couldn't deny the truth of what he said about Tal and me, but at the same time, I didn't want him to start thinking I wasn't on his side. "Khalid, I admit I have my doubts, but that's because I don't think your father can see who you really are. I can see, little guy, and I love you, and so do my parents."

"And so do we all," said Carla softly. I glanced in her direction and saw she was tearing up, too.

"Could that be enough, Khalid? I know we aren't your real family, but—"

"Shar, you're like the best brother ever, and your family has been so good to me. Everyone has been. It's just…well…I can't get my father out of my mind, see? I think about him all the time."

I did see, and I wished I could make his father love him. Probably Tal or Carla actually could, and I had brought up the subject once. Tal made me understand that compelling someone's emotions in that way was never a good idea, especially not if the compulsion had to continue long-term. Intellectually I got it, but emotionally I ached to find a way to give Khalid his wish.

"Shar," said Carla gently, "we should get going."

I did the best I could to dry Khalid's tears, though most of them had already been wiped on my shirt front. He nodded when I asked him if he felt like going back home now. I could see in his eyes that he knew his father was nowhere near here, so staying would be pointless.

"We still don't know what to do with our friend over there," said Carla sadly. "We probably shouldn't just leave him here."

"We could just phone in an anonymous tip to BHPD about a break-in at the high school, but I'm hesitant to do that without knowing more about this guy's power. He could hurt someone in the process of escaping custody," I said.

"We can't portal directly into Awen," replied Carla, "but we can come out right in front. Let's turn him over to Vanora's security. She may want to question him, and she certainly has the facilities to keep him out of trouble until we figure out how to deal with him."

"That's sound like a plan," I agreed. Together Carla and I got our unconscious assailant up and dragged him through a portal to Annwn. That was the easy part. Coming back out in Santa Brígida proved to be more complicated.

"Something's blocking the portal," said Carla worriedly. "Look at that!" Khalid's eyes got very big, but I couldn't see a thing. She took my hand, linked her mind to mine, and suddenly I knew what she was talking about: a wall of ice with weird shadows floating through it.

Carla tried several spots in Santa Brígida, but always with the same result. "I don't know how Nicneven is doing this," said Carla slowly, "but she has found a way to block portal travel into Santa Brígida."

"Why don't we just take a portal back to the car?" I suggested. "We're only a few minutes away from town. We can easily drive back."

"Something tells it may not be that easy, but we should obviously try that," she agreed.

"I'd better give Vanora a progress report," I said, pulling out my cell.

As soon as I got her, I tried to explain the problem, but she cut me off. "Shahriyar, I already know," she said tiredly. "Taliesin and Viviane are having the same problem. I should have spotted this issue sooner, but the spell doesn't block outbound traffic, just inbound, so I couldn't immediately sense it, and my attention was mostly focused on making sure there was no hostile magic in town. I couldn't do that and watch the immediate surroundings at the same time." Her tone sounded almost apologetic. It was the closest I had ever heard her come to admitting an error.

"Can't we…break the spell somehow?" I asked.

Vanora laughed bitterly. "It seems to be an amalgam between the winter power Nicneven has always had and the dark magic she gained as a witch pledged to Hecate. It's going to take some research to break it."

"Our parents—" I began.

"Have already been taken care of," she finished. "As soon as I got the call from Viviane, I figured the three of you might not be coming back tonight. Your parents think you are helping me with a project of some kind and are spending the night here. Yours were a harder sell than Carla's; they couldn't figure out why you and Khalid would have just left without saying goodbye. I had to use a little magic—just a little, don't worry—to keep them from being too suspicious."

"They'll expect us for temple," I reminded her.

"Let's cross that bridge when we come to it," she replied, sounding weaker than I had ever heard her. Right now we have bigger problems."

"Don't we always?" I asked facetiously.

"Don't be flip, Shahriyar; this is serious. Be Alexander for me again. Aside from the obvious supernatural problem, does anything strike you as odd about this situation?"

I thought for a minute, not sure why she didn't just tell me what she was thinking instead of making me guess all the time. "It all seems weird to me...wait, the meeting in which Khalid's father was supposed to participate was fake. There wasn't any function here tonight."

"I suspected as much," Vanora said, "but what does that tell you?"

I thought again. I wasn't a half-bad strategist myself; years of martial arts training had helped my planning abilities as well as my combat capabilities, but somewhere deep inside of me, the memories of Alexander did have something to offer as well.

"I thought at first that someone was trying to kidnap Khalid and use him as a hostage. Then I thought perhaps the whole thing was a trap for us, but Nicneven only sent one male witch, and he didn't seem to realize what we could do. Not much of a trap. Even Khalid noticed the preparations weren't exactly great. That's because it wasn't really a trap, was it? Nicneven wasn't trying to capture us. She just wanted us to leave town!"

"Exactly!" replied Vanora. "I have no doubt she will try to lure others out if she can."

"That means we can't just drive back in, right?" I asked, pretty much knowing the answer.

"Viviane and Taliesin already tried opening a portal near town and walking back in. Neither one of them could get through, though they saw a couple of pedestrians and at least one car cross the town boundary without incident. The spell may be specific to the members of our little group."

"Tal and Nurse Florence didn't have Zom," I pointed out. "Now that I think about it, I could probably just cut right through."

"No!" said Vanora in a tone that sounded oddly panicked. "We can't risk that without knowing more about the spell involved. Taliesin has studied the spell a little bit and believes breaking the barrier might release dark energy against the town. You'd be safe, and Carla could probably protect herself and Khalid, but there's no way to shield everyone in town from it."

"Are you sure about that?" I asked. "Could the barrier be that powerful?"

"It's hard for me to tell from inside it. I can only barely perceive it, because at the moment all its energy is still directed outward. Taliesin examined it from outside, though, and he believes it is...what would you Americans say? Oh yes, booby trapped. He thinks it's booby trapped."

I started having a light bulb moment. "That means Nicneven knows about Zom," I said. "But she knows more, doesn't she? I've used Zom in Annwn. A lot of faeries know about it. And except for you, all of us have been seen together in Annwn, so I can understand her designing a spell that keeps us specifically out. But who knows about Khalid's father? Nicneven would have to know how Khalid would react to seeing his father was nearby. How could she possibly know that?"

"There are only two ways I can think of," replied Vanora. "Perhaps Nicneven has found a method for using magic surveillance on us, directly or by proxy. I must be slipping if she could get away with that under my nose." She had gotten away with putting a magic force field around the town, but I decided it would be unkind to mention that.

"The second possibility you aren't going to like, but it has to be considered," she said quickly, as if trying to get the theory out before I could stop her. "Someone in the group is helping Nicneven."

"Impossible!" I blurted out. "I would trust any of them with my life."

"It seems unlikely to me as well," Vanora admitted, "but how else could someone have information that only one of us would know?"

By now I was channeling Alexander big time. "This is one of those times in which the best defense is a good offense. Vanora, can you use your pull as Carrie Winn to get the town evacuated?"

For a moment my question was greeted with silence. Finally, she said, "That might be beyond even Carrie Winn's considerable influence. But suppose I could? What does that gain us?"

"Assuming the 'booby trap' blows dark magic inward, we can make it safe to break the spell with Zom if we can get everyone out."

"I suppose," she reluctantly agreed, "but without knowing the exact nature of the magic involved, we could end up poisoning the whole area, rather like setting off a small nuclear blast. I don't know yet whether the spell only affects people."

"How about creating a magic shield of some kind just inside Nicneven's barrier?" I asked. "Could you shield the town from whatever might spray out if the barrier is disrupted?"

"That's an idea Taliesin already suggested," Vanora replied. "The problem is I'm the only one left in the town who can do magic, and I'm getting closer to collapse every minute. We'd need to bring in more spell casters for that plan to work, which we may or may not be able to do. We're assuming the barrier blocks just members of our group, but for all I know it could block other spell casters as well."

I groaned a little at that.

"Don't lose hope yet," said Vanora. "Taliesin and Viviane are on a mission to recruit other casters to help us. We'll put the theory to the test, and if everyone is blocked, at least we'll have more eyes on the problem."

"We could help speed up the recruitment," I suggested.

"I appreciate that," said Vanora, "but there's no way to add more people now. I've asked Taliesin and Viviane to stay out of Annwn and work through the Order exclusively."

"Why?" I asked impatiently. "Surely it would be faster to contact the faerie rulers directly rather than working through intermediaries."

"It would indeed," she agreed, "but now that we've established that Nicneven is a master strategist, how can we be sure part of her goal isn't to get some of you into Annwn? If she doesn't want every other ruler united against her, she has to be at least a little careful in our world. In Annwn, she can be much more forceful, and her magic will be even more powerful."

"I'm not afraid of magic," I said, reflexively touching Zom's hilt.

"Are you afraid of a faerie arrow through the heart?" she asked irritably. "Because without your dragon armor, that'll be how Nicneven tries to take you out."

"I guess you're right," I conceded. "I hate to just sit around and do nothing, though."

"Then don't," she replied. "Stick to our world and start scouting locations. If we do have to evacuate the town for one reason or another, we could do with a decent temporary headquarters. Find some place suitable and have Carla start warding it. Perhaps we can catch Nicneven by surprise for a change. I'll call you as other ideas occur to me."

I had the feeling she was just assigning me busy work to keep me out of trouble, but I decided not to call her out on it. Instead, I thanked her and said we'd keep in touch. Actually, finding a safe place for Carla, Khalid, and me wasn't a bad idea. As things stood now, Nicneven could make a move against us any time.

Then I realized I was an idiot. We already had exactly the right place.

"Carla, if you take us to Alcina's island, can you still monitor developments here?"

"It's a lot more work, and it will take time to set up, but yes, there are ways to see from one plane what is happening in another," she replied.

"Vanora wants us to set up a base in case Santa Brígida has to be evacuated." She raised an eyebrow at that.

"I'll fill you in later," I assured her. "For now, Annwn may not be safe, but the island should be." I didn't have any intention of hanging out there for days, but it would be a good place to park Khalid if we needed to come back without him. He would profoundly hate that idea, but he couldn't open a portal himself, so if we timed things right, we could keep him from tagging along and putting himself in danger.

Naturally, we couldn't evacuate the whole population of Santa Brígida to the island without revealing too much and getting ourselves in trouble with the faerie rulers. I would have to talk to Vanora again and work out a plan for what to do with the other evacuees.

Of course, getting to the island, getting it set up properly, and figuring out where to put everyone else was the easy part. Defeating Nicneven was going to be tougher…much tougher!

Chapter 11: Calling the Order to Order (Tal)

Much as I valued security, especially at a time like this, the precautions taken by Order of the Ladies of the Lake struck me as too much of a good thing.

Vanora and Nurse Florence had both sent the Order an SOS already, requesting immediate assistance to stop Nicneven. The Order reminded us of the number of members who had been lost in a plane crash when they had been dispatched to help us deal with Ceridwen. The Order didn't refuse to assist us, but its leadership wanted Nurse Florence and me to come to headquarters to talk strategy first. Wasting that amount of time seemed reckless at best, but the leaders were adamant. Nurse Florence told me I was the victim of my own reputation. Having beaten Ceridwen, Morgan le Fay, Oberon, Hecate, Hades, and Ares, among others, I'd have to get used to people wanting to pick my brains for strategy tips—or just rub my head for luck.

"None of those were exactly one-man efforts," I pointed out.

"No, but none of those victories would have been possible without you," Nurse Florence said, then smiled. "Be patient with them, Tal. In recent years the Order's work has become more and more research oriented."

"Really?" I asked. "That's not how it used to be, at least not if the original Taliesin's memories are accurate."

Nurse Florence nodded. "Things have changed quite a bit over the centuries, though Coventina, you know, the original Lady of Lake, still plays the role she always did: maintaining the connection with Lynn Mawr, the underground lake to which all members of the Order are tied, and protecting that lake from anyone who would attack it or try to learn its secrets."

"Didn't you tell me once that she never leaves headquarters anymore? Wouldn't that mean some of the other Ladies would have to be pretty active in the world, just as you and Vanora are?" I asked.

"You'd think, but that's not the way things work out in practice," she replied. "Most members of the Order now play much less active roles than they would have even a hundred years ago. Oh, occasionally someone from the Order gets dispatched to deal with a ghost, a small-scale faerie incursion, maybe even a minor demon.

That would be a quiet day for us in Santa Brígida. Vanora and I have probably had more actual experience with supernatural threats than all the other living human members put together.

"I also have another theory," she continued. "The Order always likes to appear to be in control of everything. I think their request to see us is rooted partly in the fact that no one available at headquarters right now has ever been to California. They need to use our memories to travel there by portal, but none of them want to admit that's why they want us."

We both had a good chuckle over that. Unfortunately, the Order's stubbornness on another issue was not so funny.

The leaders absolutely, positively refused to open a direct path for us. Nurse Florence had asked them to relax security long enough for us to enter by portal, but they summarily dismissed that idea.

The Order's headquarters had the unique security arrangement of occupying some cubbyhole between different planes of existence, not fully in Annwn, but not fully on Earth, either. There was theoretically an entrance on the campus of the University of Cardiff in Wales, but anyone trying to approach that way from the outside could search every inch of the university, both scientifically and magically, and never find the entry. Only someone who had recently been in the headquarters could perceive it, let alone enter it. In much the same way, there was a fixed portal in Annwn that led to headquarters, but we couldn't just use another portal to reach it; we had to travel at least two days across Annwn, or the fixed portal would not function for us. Having tried that trek when we had sought the Order's help to free Carla from a coma, I was not enthusiastic to do it again. Even with an escort provided by Gwynn ap Nudd, clear evidence that we were under his protection, we had faced an undead army, the Chapel Perilous, and a dragon, and we had to turn back without reaching headquarters—and that was when only Morgan le Fay was trying to stop us. Nicneven apparently had far more resources. I shuddered to think how big a faerie-witch combination force she could deploy if given half a chance. No, the Annwn route was out of the question. Nor could Nurse Florence use the Lady of the Lake specialty and travel from some outside body of water to the lake in the center of the complex. That trick, too, only worked for those Ladies of the Lake who had recently been at headquarters.

Fortunately, there was another route, designed to be almost as cumbersome as the two-day trek across Annwn, but not as dangerous under the present circumstances. In the not too distant past, some strategist in the Order, recognizing that the Annwn route might not always be safe, had created a series of fixed portals in every American town named Cardiff. Theoretically, any spell caster who stumbled across them could use them, but they had to be visited in sequence: each one led, not to headquarters, but to the next portal in the series, which could only be used by someone relatively fresh from the preceding portal. Not only that, but each portal deposited the would-be user a few miles from the next one, so it took some time to navigate them. The setup was designed to be time-consuming, because using the portals set off some kind of alarm at headquarters, and the way the portals were spaced out gave the Order plenty of time to prepare if an enemy found out about those secret gateways and tried to use them.

We went by regular portal to the approximate location of the first one, Cardiff-by-the-Sea, a little place near Encinitas, somewhat north of San Diego. Luckily, my parents and I used to vacation there; driving down from Santa Brígida would have added another three hours or more to our trip. Cutting those hours off was more than worth taking the small risk of setting foot in Annwn for a minute.

We had dinner at my favorite Pancake House before proceeding, mostly because neither one of us expected to be able to eat again until we reached the Order's headquarters, but I couldn't really enjoy my ham and cheese omelet. I was too worried. We ate quickly, and then to avoid using any more magic than necessary, we took a cab over to San Elijo State Beach, the location of the first portal.

Actually, the portal was adjacent to the beach, hidden on the granite pedestal that displayed *The Magic Carpet*, a bronze sculpture locally known as the Cardiff Kook and representing a boy novice surfer riding a nonexistent wave. By now it was close to 9:00 p.m. and relatively dark, but there was still a fair amount of traffic on the Pacific Coast Highway, so I cast a don't-notice-us spell around us and then levitated us to statue level so we wouldn't have to try to climb in the dark.

"The location suggests that someone had a sense of humor," I said, "but shouldn't the portal have been placed in a less public location? The statue is a major tourist spot during the day."

"I think that particular Lady of the Lake was using a hiding-in-plain-sight approach. Precisely because the location is so visible, it isn't exactly the first place someone would look for a portal, even if he or she knew this route to headquarters existed. You'll notice too that even standing right on top of it, you can perceive only the slightest trace of magic."

"True," I conceded. "Would you do the honors?"

"Certainly," she said, and with a wave of her arm, she stirred the portal to life, and a glowing doorway appeared, uncomfortably close to the statue, though there was enough room to squirm past the statue and reach the portal.

Or at least there would have been, if the portal hadn't had magical protection. When I unavoidably brushed against the statue, I was suddenly not on the granite pedestal at night. I was on a surfboard at midday, preparing to catch a promising wave.

I knew this must be an illusion of some kind, but I was shaken by how fast it had engulfed me. I could smell the salt spray; I could feel the sun against my skin and even the dampness of my board shorts. Normally, conjuring up an illusion that detailed took time.

I suddenly realized I didn't want to go back to that dreary night. I wanted to be out here in the sun, I wanted to catch the wave, I wanted to forget the winter queen and revel in the summer sun, now and forever.

Fortunately, I had enough willpower to pull myself back to reality before it was too late. Another few seconds, and I might not have been able to break away, at least until someone spotted me, and the police came out to arrest the nut surfing next to the Kook.

"What the hell?" I said to Nurse Florence. "I thought we were dealing with the Order of the Ladies of the Lake, not Robin Goodfellow." Much to my surprise, she just shrugged.

"I'm beginning to think someone doesn't really want us to visit the Order," she said. "At the very least, I should have been told about the security precautions. They must be pretty new."

"Nicneven?" I asked, feeling the chill of the night.

"No, that felt like Lady of the Lake magic to me. Just in case the illusion is not the only defense the portal has, let's get through it before anything else happens." How could I argue with such a good idea? Doing our best to avoid the statue this time, we both stepped through the portal.

Our next stop was Cardiff, Illinois—or rather, we emerged about five miles from where Cardiff used to be. The town had rapidly vanished after a mine explosion and the eventual closure of the second attempt at mining, but the place still existed legally, and someone had the bright idea to use something that hardly qualified as a ghost town for the location of the next portal.

It was after 11:00 p.m. local time, and we had to trek miles through farmland and wooded area to reach the spot. I could have flown us there, but carrying Nurse Florence, who had never quite mastered flying, would require an enormous amount of energy and make us too conspicuous if someone was looking for us, so I settled for enabling us to see in the dark and speeding us up. Even so, the trek was frustratingly slow, and the night was overcast and very dark, even with magical night vision. I was glad when we reached the cement slab that held the miners' memorial—and the portal.

There was a large planter almost right behind the monument, as well as an impressive plaque, and of course the portal was sandwiched in between the two. This time there was no avoiding touching the back of the monument, which predictably threw us into an illusion that we were trapped in a mine collapse and running out of air. We had had the presence of mind to hold hands, and, fighting the illusion together, each of us pulled the other through the portal. The illusion dissipated once we were on the other side, and none too soon. My lungs were convulsively pulling in oxygen as if I really been trapped underground.

"On the whole, I think I preferred the Encinitas surf," I wheezed. Nurse Florence nodded, too angry now with her colleagues to even try to make conversation for a few minutes. Finally she managed to stifle a stream of profanity and content herself with the observation that someone should have told her how to disable the defenses—or at least mentioned them.

We appeared about five miles from Cardiff, Alabama, now a very small town, having been partially destroyed by flood in 2003. It was already past midnight, and both Nurse Florence and I needed rest, but it wasn't exactly as if there was a local Howard Johnson's to check into, and I was having waking nightmares owing something to the imagery in the movie *Deliverance*, so it seemed best to press on.

In this case the Lady of the Lake who created the portals had cheated: the portal was not actually in the town of Cardiff, but in Cardiff cemetery, which was technically in Graysville. Either way, we made a long hike in record time, and the place seemed deceptively pleasant. In daylight it would have been parklike, its green grass dotted with little clusters of pink and purple flowers, its old white tombstones mostly on a hill surrounded by a wide variety of leaf-covered trees. I thought to myself that this would be a nice place to be buried. I almost got my wish.

This time the portal was situated right in front of a tombstone, so that anyone using it would actually have to step on the grave. I found the placement offensive, more worthy of a necromancer than a Lady of the Lake. I whispered an apology to whoever was buried there and to God.

I was prepared for the illusion of a ghost springing out of the grave and trying to grab me. Nonetheless, the hallucination was so vivid I could feel the ghost's clammy touch upon my arm, and his howling sent shivers down my spine. Ignoring this imaginary specter, I tried to step through the portal and found that I couldn't move. Could I be paralyzed by fear? No, I had been prepared for the attempt to frighten me. What I had not been prepared for was the vines gripping my ankles and sinuously sliding up my legs.

Whoever designed this obstacle course wanted us to think that only illusions would try to keep us away from the portal, lull us into a false sense of security, and then pull off a surprise that might just end us. Looking down I saw that I was in the grip of magically enhanced kudzu. The normal variety had engulfed the abandoned parts of Cardiff long ago, but there had been none in the graveyard. Our approach had evidently triggered some kind of explosive growth, kudzu on steroids. Within a minute it would cover both of us completely, probably with the intent of suffocating us, though if it were strong enough, it might also try to crush us with its grasping vines.

It would have been hard to cast a decent spell fast enough, especially with the distraction of the plant wrapping itself around every part of us. Fortunately, the one who crafted this trap had not anticipated a weapon like White Hilt. I managed to draw it before my sword arm got pinned; the sword flamed to life, and in no time the regular kudzu had been turned to extra crispy and cut into thousands of tiny pieces. More kept growing from the ground, but I managed to sear the roots as well, being careful not to disturb the graves themselves.

"Someone will answer for this!" growled Nurse Florence.

"Pity Vanora isn't here to enjoy this with us," I observed, and we both practically fell over laughing. Nurse Florence would give the leaders of the Order a piece of her mind; Vanora would be plotting their deaths right about now, plotting them with a positively Machiavellian glee. I usually didn't appreciate her more fanatical side, but I would have made an exception this time.

We found ourselves in Cardiff, Tennessee, five miles from the next portal, again a cheat, since it was again in a Cardiff Cemetery, this time in Rockwood, right off Highway 27. Here the graves were on a gradually sloping hillside and interspersed with trees, some of them evergreens, perhaps symbolic of resurrection. This time I didn't make the mistake of thinking it would be a nice place to be buried, but we still had to go through another trap: bolts of lightning from the nearby power lines. My hair realistically stood up, and a near miss burned me, but this time it was just an illusion. Again I had to apologize as we had to step on someone's grave to enter the portal.

Our next stop, the village of Cardiff, Pennsylvania, again had a cemetery nearby, though not actually in it: Saint Mary's Roman Catholic Cemetery, between Cardiff and Blacklick Township—a rather unimaginative choice, considering it was the third cemetery on the route. This time our anonymous Lady of the Lake, whom I could not help but loathe, had set up an uncomfortably vivid illusion of the Virgin Mary warning us to go back. Mary seemed uncharacteristically wrathful, as if ready to call down fire from heaven on us, perhaps for stepping on two graves. I bowed apologetically to Jesus's mother and looked appropriately contrite as I had to step on a grave once again to get to the portal.

"When we finally get to Cardiff, you know, the one that's actually in Wales, I'm going to complain about all this sacrilege," I said angrily. "It seems unnecessary."

"And oddly counterproductive," added Nurse Florence. "It's hard to see Nicneven's minions or someone like that being upset by the vision of Mary, but a more moral person would be."

"How many more steps are there?" I asked, fatigue nibbling away at my energy and my peace of mind.

"This should be Cardiff, Maryland. The next stop is Cardiff, New York, unless the Order decided to extend the route through the two Canadian Cardiffs. Oh, and did I mention there's one in New Zealand and one in Australia?"

"You'd better be kidding," I said grimly.

The Maryland portal was behind what was now an apartment building but used to be headquarters for the Cardiff Marble Company, which had once prospered because of the presence of an unusual green marble in the area. Here the illusion, which I had to admit was creative, if incredibly annoying, was suddenly being marble. Yup, I actually found myself part of the facade of the Empire State Building, not feeling the icy winds because, well, I was now stone. A little less willpower, and someone would have found me lying on the ground tomorrow, babbling about hanging from a skyscraper, and carted me off to the nearest lunatic asylum.

I knew Cardiff, New York, was the last stop, and our Lady of the Lake outdid herself. Not only did we get the illusion of being buried in the Bear Mountain avalanche of 1993, but we also had to fight something like the "Cardiff giant," a famous hoax, supposedly a petrified giant dug from the earth. The difference was that this one was animated, like a golem, and standing between us and the last portal, fittingly right in front of the sign commemorating the original Cardiff giant.

The creature would have been strong enough to crush bones with a single blow, but fortunately it was also slow moving, doubtless to give interlopers a chance to run away if they were so inclined. I wasn't. I had never tried White Hilt on stone, but it did its job adequately, slicing through the creature as it normally sliced through regular armor. In no time the thing was a pile of rubble by the highway. Then it vanished as the burned kudzu had, leaving no trace behind.

Though nearing exhaustion, Nurse Florence and I ran through the portal, just to be sure nothing else tried to get us. On the other side we found ourselves in a very anticlimactic hallway with plain white walls and light blue carpeting.

"Is this it?" I asked Nurse Florence.

"Doesn't look like much, does it?" she said, smiling. "I think this hallway was designed in the unlikely event someone somehow found the entrance and managed to walk in through it." She pointed to a plain white door whose upper third was glass. Having been on the Cardiff University campus in one of my nonmagical lives, I couldn't resist peeking out to see where the headquarters of the Order intersected with the physical world.

It was about 5:00 a.m. local time, and I could see the beginning of dawn's touch, but much of the view right in front of me still lay shadowed in a way that suggested I was looking from the southeast, with the sun rising not quite behind me, to the northwest. Across a street that must have been King Edward VII Avenue, I could make out Alexandra Gardens, beautiful even in shadow, and much farther, across Museum Avenue, rose the impressive facade of the campus's Main Building—its actual name, not just a description. The large structure, ghostlike in the early morning light, was slightly obscured by just a touch of mist but still looked as impressive as I remembered.

"We're between Bute Building and Glamorgan Building, aren't we?" I asked. Nurse Florence nodded.

"I was a student here in an earlier life. How often I walked right past this spot and never realized! How often I probably walked right through this area!"

"I don't want to risk it right now, just in case there's some other new wrinkle in the security, but if we have time later, I'll show you how this building looks from the outside—or rather, how it doesn't. If you're connected to my mind, you will be able to see the door, but that's all. It's just close enough to the mundane world for a Lady of the Lake who has recently been inside to perceive it. The rest of the building isn't on this plane at all."

"I'm beginning to think we need an arrangement like this back home. Like a panic room, only it would be a panic building we could flee into if we needed to hide out—"

We both jumped at the sound of someone clearing her throat behind us. Turning, we saw a woman slightly older than I was, maybe twentysomething, pretty, but not Carla's equal. The girl had long blond hair tied up in a ponytail and wore the long white robe favored by the order.

"Viviane, Coventina is expecting you," said the girl, beckoning us toward the interior door at the end of the hall. The door had been closed when we arrived but now stood ajar. Inviting as it was, a bed might have been more inviting. I hadn't expected to walk right into a meeting with the Order's leadership. At least the leaders were finally doing something, so I knew I shouldn't complain, and in truth we might not have much time.

We followed the woman through the door, and our surroundings became much less commonplace. The hallway through which we now walked was lit not by electricity but by the luminous walls themselves. I was reminded of Gwynn's palace and wondered if the building was of faerie construction. Probably, given how closely the faeries and the Order were allied with each other, not to mention the fact that Coventina was a faerie herself.

The hall was descending, making me wonder if we would end up underground, yet another security measure in case the magic defenses were somehow breached. Could even the Ladies of the Lake be that paranoid? Perhaps.

Both walls were covered with elaborate murals portraying the history of the Order from its early Celtic beginnings to modern times. I would have loved to study these murals, both for their artistry and for any light they might shed on the Order's structure. Even the original Taliesin had not learned much about the background of the Ladies of the Lake, though they played a tremendously important role at Camelot.

As we walked, I realized that we were not only descending but circling; the hallway spiraled down into the earth...or into something anyway. I didn't know whether we were really beneath anything remotely resembling soil, since we weren't on Earth anymore. Again, I would have liked the time to examine our surroundings magically, but it didn't seem likely that I would get that even after our business was concluded. Something told me that almost everything about the Order was kept on a need-to-know basis.

Finally we reached the heart of the spiral: a vast chamber reminiscent of a cavern, but not a natural one, for every surface was polished to glowing smoothness and covered with the best ancient Celtic art I had ever seen. I was not surprised to see Celtic spirals in almost hypnotic patterns all around, glowing in a subtly different way than the walls did.

To my surprise, the chamber's center was a lake—Lyn Mawr itself! Its surface reflected the surrounding glows in such a way that it, too, seemed hypnotic. I tried to avoid looking at the slowly shifting patterns on either walls or water, but avoiding them completely would have required me to shut my eyes, which I could hardly do at this point.

Aside from the way in which we had entered the chamber, I counted three other entries spaced more or less evenly along the walls, so that the passageways corresponded to the four cardinal directions. From what little I knew of headquarters, I guessed one led to the dormitories, since the trainees and some of the experienced members lived here. Another probably led to the training facilities, and a third to the vault in which the Order stored goodies like Excalibur. I felt just a little queasy remembering that the Order also had the pieces of the black altar on which I had nearly become a human sacrifice. Who knew what else they might have?

White-robed Ladies of the Lake lined the walls, some trying to look impassive, some willing to let their curiosity show, all more than capable of catching my eye under ordinary circumstances. The scene made me wonder if physical beauty was an entrance requirement.

Our escort pointed us to two chairs, the only visible pieces of furniture in the room. No sooner were we seated than the lake in front of us began to bubble and churn. Then from its depths rose a woman even better looking than Nurse Florence. Almost too perfect to be flesh, the woman had the most intensely blond hair and penetrating blue eyes I had ever seen. This could only be Coventina, the original Lady of the Lake, and I could see why the ancient Celts had worshiped her as a goddess of the waters, even well into Roman times. Could any ancient man who had seen her doubt that he stood in the presence of the divine? Only the memory of Carla kept me from getting completely enthralled by Coventina's beauty.

The original Taliesin had never met her...but the original Taliesin had never faced a crisis of the magnitude that now confronted us. As annoying as this seemingly unnecessary trip to Wales had been, I couldn't help but feel honored that Coventina wanted to see me in person.

Nurse Florence and I both rose and bowed. Coventina nodded in acknowledgment, then gestured for us to sit back down. I wondered for a second why our escort had seated us to begin with, but perhaps she hadn't known how quickly Coventina would appear. I wondered for a little longer why there was no sign of any of the other leaders. I had never been to headquarters before, but I knew the Order was governed by a council, not by Coventina alone.

"Well met, my friends," began Coventina warmly. "Taliesin, I have long wished to meet you, and Viviane, it is a pleasure to see you here once again. I had not thought you would have to remain so long in America, but we have had our share of surprises of late."

"Forgive me if I am too bold, my lady," I said, drawing again on the original Taliesin's manner, "but I was not expecting quite so many surprises on my way to see you."

Coventina smiled indulgently. "We had reason to believe you might be followed, Taliesin. We knew you would overcome our little traps, and you did."

I should have just taken the compliment, but my nerves were raw, my diplomacy a bit ragged. "The kudzu trap in particular could have killed us." Nurse Florence poked me in the ribs, but I kept going anyway. "I have never been treated in such a fashion by an ally."

The archetypal Lady of the Lake looked confused for a moment. "Kudzu trap? Please explain. I recall no such snare."

It only took a couple more minutes of conversation to reveal the unsettling truth that only the illusions were part of the Order's security system. Both the kudzu and Cardiff giant attacks had been added by someone else.

"The situation is worse than I imagined," said Coventina gravely. "If enemies could create these menaces along the route, they must have known what the route was even before you took it."

"Your security has been compromised, then?" asked Nurse Florence.

"So it would appear," admitted Coventina. "Niniane! Arrange at once for the American pathway to be blocked." One of the ladies lining the wall hurried off down one of the passages. The others stood very still, shocked by the idea that someone knew the way to reach them.

"My friends," Coventina continued quietly, "from time to time a Lady of the Lake has been captured. It may be that the portal locations were tortured out of one of them. Only a member of the Order would know of that path's existence, let alone all the exact spots involved. Like this place itself, all the possible entrances are protected by the magic equivalent of Celtic knots so intricate that they would confuse even the vision of a seer."

"It also suggests that Taliesin was the target of this sabotaging of the path," added Nurse Florence. "We have reason to believe Nicneven is seeking revenge against him on behalf of Hecate."

Coventina's eyes widened. "I feared as much. In such a case, there is only one answer. Taliesin, you must stay here now."

I might have been inclined to wonder out loud how safe I was going to be if Nicneven had learned some of the Order's secrets, but I was too stunned by Coventina's plan to raise that objection.

"My lady, if Nicneven can't get to me, surely she will turn on my family and friends. I cannot place everyone I know at risk."

"Do not trouble yourself, Taliesin. The powerful spell surrounding Santa Brígida only prevents the magically endowed from entering, not from leaving. Is this not so?"

"It is," I began, "but—"

"The Order can arrange for the evacuation of certain people to join you here. You have parents, or so I have heard. We can make room for them, and for your men."

"What about my men's families? What about everyone I know at school? Even if I could somehow convince all of them to come, would you take them?"

Coventina moved closer, clearly not wanting to be overheard. "I see you do not fully appreciate the danger. Nicneven's combination of faerie magic with the magic of Hecate makes her one of the most dangerous casters alive. Were that all she had, your peril would be great. But that is not all. She has an army of faeries and an army of witches, perhaps the strongest force under the control of any faerie ruler at this time. Yet even that may not be all the might she can bring against you. She seems to have access to other powers, perhaps even darker ones. Taliesin, she may have become the first faerie to sell herself to Satan."

"Why would such a powerful faerie sacrifice herself in that way?" asked Nurse Florence, her skepticism obvious from her tone.

Coventina glared at her. "I cannot be sure, but a strange darkness is definitely falling on Elphame. If she has not herself made a bargain with the Evil One, perhaps she has induced some of her witches to do so. Either way, we are not in a position to fight someone who has marshaled unpredictable powers from Hell itself. Protection here I can and will offer you freely. More I cannot do without putting the whole Order at risk."

"Surely you can at least help me break the enchantment around Santa Brígida," I suggested. "Additional Ladies of the Lake could make the attempt. If they cannot quickly prevail, they can always return here."

Coventina shook her head sadly. "I wish I had enough proficient casters to put at risk such a group as you might need, Taliesin, but I simply do not. I lost a dozen of the Order's best in that plane crash and have lost others since. It becomes harder and harder to find humans with enough magical proficiency to become decent replacements for those who have been lost.

"If you were here for a while, perhaps four years, perhaps more," she continued, "that strange quality of yours that brings out latent magic in others could perhaps increase the number and power of our recruits enough to make it possible for us to stand up to Nicneven."

So there it was. Coventina had a hidden agenda. She would not give me the help I wanted unless I stayed with her and helped her restore the Order to its former glory. Maybe I would have been willing to throw away my whole life like that if I had been able to safeguard everyone else, but she wasn't offering me any way to do that.

"I'm sorry, my lady, but I cannot possibly stay here unless you can guarantee the safety of everyone Nicneven might try to slaughter because of me. You have already made it plain that you cannot—or will not—do that."

"Cannot," agreed Coventina. "I can save some of them, however. If you refuse my request, you may lose them all."

It was rare for me to get through a day without having to ward off some kind of emotional blackmail. Apparently, this was not going to be one of those days.

"Tal," thought Nurse Florence, *"Tread carefully. Try to turn her down without offending her. Vanora and I will see if we can change her mind later."*

In theory, Coventina could not read minds, but there was always some risk she might pick up mental communication that close to her. For Nurse Florence to take that risk, she must have been very concerned I would say the wrong thing.

She would have been right. I was having a hard time not shouting at Coventina by this point. I was that disappointed, that horrified by her willingness to write people off as collateral damage. However, Nurse Florence's suggestion reminded me that she and Vanora were both Coventina's subordinates. In theory the ultimate Lady of the Lake could demand that they both return to Wales, and if they refused, remove them from the Order. They would still have magic, but they would no longer have the unique ability to teleport through water, immediate access to Gwynn ap Nudd, information and support from the Order's vast nonmagical arm, and every other perk. Particularly in such a grave situation, I couldn't afford to lose either of my Ladies of the Lake.

"I will take council with my men," I said slowly, "but I doubt they will want to save themselves at the expense of their families."

"Make no mistake," said Coventina, her volume increasing as if she no longer cared who heard, "if it is indeed Nicneven who seeks to harm you, someone will die. I must ensure that it is not you. Your destiny is too important to be left to the whims of your men— or even your own, for that matter." I was disturbed by her use of "destiny," which made her sound uncomfortably like Vanora in one of her more fanatical moods.

"My destiny is my own concern, not yours," I insisted, suc-ceeding only with great difficulty in keeping my anger from boiling over. "And, my lady," I added, noticing that her staff, which I had barely seen before, now glowed much more brightly, "if you think to keep me here by force, think again."

Coventina looked at me sadly. "I will not try to hold you against your will, though in my heart I wish I could. I will, however, share my visions with you. Observe the lake!" she commanded, waving the glowing staff over it. The waters shifted, no longer reflecting the walls but now lit by the visions of Coventina, who must have been a seer as well as a sorceress.

First I saw a psychic view of Scotland, with darkness flowing over it, lit only by an occasional burst of what had to be hellfire. If this was a true vision and not a trick by Coventina, then yes, Nicneven had definitely tapped into infernal power somehow, and I could feel its unholy strength even through the vision. There was enough power there to dwarf Ceridwen and Morgan put together—and I had only barely survived encounters with each of them.

Then I saw Santa Brígida within the mass of ice and shadow I now understood how Nicneven could sustain so easily. I could see snow falling on the town; that would give the local weather girl fits for sure, but it would also attract press attention of a kind faeries usually avoided. If Nicneven was willing to risk something like that, or if she soon would be, then she could be an even bigger threat than I had imagined.

Next I saw a vision of war in Annwn, with Gwynn's Welsh forces pitted against those of Scotland and England, suggested that Nicneven had somehow formed an alliance with Tanaquill. Not surprisingly, Gwynn's army was losing...badly. Overwhelmed both by numbers and by magic, hundreds of Welsh faeries would be slaughtered, and Gwynn would end up besieged in his castle. If I had thought to get his aid in this crisis, I now realized he would have his hands full keeping the darkness from overcoming Wales.

The next vision looked as if it were coming from Olympus—not the physical one, but its spiritual double on the Olympian plane. I saw continued war and felt guilty that I had not yet checked back with the Olympians to see how they were faring. Apparently they had not defeated Poseidon as easily as they had imagined. I saw the seas in constant upheaval and filled with monsters. I saw Ares leading a new army from Thrace, massacring everything in his path. I saw Pan leading a frenzied mass of centaurs and satyrs from Arcadia. What I did not see was any effort by the remaining Olympians to stop these disruptions, nor any sign that Zeus and the others who had disappeared had been found.

Then I got a tiny, jolting glimpse of the Underworld. Even in a realm of shadow, a greater darkness was welling up. At its center was an indistinct figure, not someone I had encountered in my visit to the Underworld, but someone both more powerful and more evil.

Hecate had a backup plan!

With sickening speed, the vision changed focus, and I saw my friends in dire peril, fighting for their lives in a blurry battle. Its details were indistinct, as I had been told such visions sometimes were. Even the clearest often showed only a possible future, not an inevitable one. When they were this blurry, future events were being constantly impacted by a flow of new developments. Coventina might have intended to convince me through this vision that my only hope lay in accepting her offer, that I was the wild card keeping the future in flux.

If that had been her intent, she failed. The details might have been hard to make out, but the battle part was the same no matter how much the specifics shifted around, and so was the seriousness of the situation. If I was the wild card, then no choice I made was going to keep my friends out of harm's way.

I realized then that I was not visible in any of these foggy combat scenes. Perhaps my returning to my friends, rather than my staying here, could be the change that would prevent this future from ever taking place.

Abruptly a couple of elements became crystal clear. I saw Jimmie, alone and lying in a pool of his own blood on the floor of an unfamiliar castle. If only I could tell where he was! I had seen many castles in many lives, but I did not recognize anything about this one. He seemed to still be alive, but only barely, and when I tried to focus on his surroundings, they became too blurry for me to tell whether anyone was coming to his rescue or not.

I almost cried out when the scene shifted again, shifted too fast for me to find the clues I so desperately wanted to see. Instead, I was greeted by something I would have given anything not to see: Carla in the clutches of some demon, its claws digging into her flesh, its darkness blotting out her light. If the vision of Jimmie had nearly thrown me into a panic, the vision of Carla definitely put me over the edge.

I'm ashamed to say it, but my first reaction was to turn my fear into anger and use it like a weapon against Coventina.

"You lie!" I shouted, my whole body trembling. "You are trying to trick me!" I felt Nurse Florence's restraining touch on my arm, but I shook her off. "You don't care who dies, as long as you get what you want!"

The light from Coventina's staff disappeared abruptly, taking the visions with it. She stared at me as if she wanted to use that staff to strike me.

"Shut the hell up!" shouted Nurse Florence in my head. She never talked like that, to me or anyone. Her words hit me like rocks. I realized I needed to get a grip on myself, but my realization might have come too late.

"Arrogant, arrogant boy!" Coventina said angrily. "My visions are true, but you will not heed them! It is you who do not care who dies, for you would have me throw every one of my ladies into a battle they cannot win to save the people you care for. Mark my words: if the Order ever perishes from the earth, then chaos will come again. You would save dozens by killing thousands, perhaps even millions, in the future."

Before I could respond, Nurse Florence threw herself to the ground, a shockingly uncharacteristic gesture for her. "Oh Coventina, I beg your forgiveness on behalf of Taliesin. He spoke out of fear bred by your visions, not out of careful thought. He would never willingly sacrifice anyone, certainly not a Lady of the Lake. More than once he has offered his own life to save another's."

"He questions my honesty," said Coventina in a way that suggested she really wanted to summon a sea serpent into her lake and feed me to it. "His rashness will be the undoing of us all."

"Or perhaps it will be our salvation," replied Nurse Florence quietly. "I have seen it be so more than once. Even Vanora, at first his harshest critic, has doubtless reported as much to you. He lacks your wisdom, but his heart often guides him where even wisdom would fail."

By this point I was profoundly embarrassed, both by my own outburst and by the fact that Nurse Florence had to grovel on my behalf. Well, when in the lake, do what the ladies do. I threw myself on the ground right next to Nurse Florence.

"My lady, I offer my most humble apologies, inadequate as they may be. I know you would never deceive me." Really, I wasn't at all sure that was the case, but I couldn't afford to completely alienate her. "I spoke disrespectfully and unfairly. I was shocked by your visions, but that is not an excuse for what I have done."

After an uncomfortably long silence, Coventina said, "Rise, Viviane. Rise, Taliesin. I will accept your apology…this one time. But, as some human thinkers have said, 'Actions speak louder than words.' Are you prepared to lend strength to your words by acting upon my suggestions?"

I bowed low and tried to keep my voice as quiet and controlled as possible. "My lady, though I do not doubt the truth of your visions, even the clearest image of the future can yet be changed by our actions. Is this not so?"

Coventina, too, seemed to be struggling to maintain control of herself. "Yes, I have seen such things happen. Do you intend to use that as an excuse for ignoring my advice?"

"No. Rather I wish to amend my original request. The Order is safe for the moment, is it not?"

Coventina nodded. "The compromised pathway from America has been cut off, so we will have no uninvited guests, and no one has succeeded in divining our location in all these centuries. We should be safe enough for the moment."

I knew the next few minutes might make the difference between losing Nurse Florence and Vanora and keeping them with me, and I chose my words carefully.

"If you are secure now, then give me leave to return to America and help my friends. I will withdraw my request for the Order's aid. Instead, I will find a way to thwart Nicneven on my own. Meanwhile I will find a way to awaken the magical potential in any humans who may have much faster than the four years or so it takes for my mere presence to do it."

Judging by their facial expressions, I had succeeded in surprising both Coventina and Nurse Florence.

"Is this but a hollow promise, or can you really do what you suggest?" asked Coventina suspiciously.

"I cannot promise to succeed, my lady, but, as you may have been informed, I can develop and learn new magic at a very fast rate."

"I'm sure you have seen that in our reports, my lady," added Nurse Florence. "In a matter of days, he learned how to use magic to affect modern technology. Others have worked on that problem for centuries and still failed. He has learned powerful spells just by seeing them done once, when others would have taken months to learn them. If anyone can develop a spell to awaken magic potential, it is Taliesin."

I could see Coventina was wavering, so I did what I could to pull her toward agreement. "We believe my presence rouses magic in others because of the way in which I was transformed in an earlier life. As Gwion Bach I accidentally drank the potion of knowledge from the cauldron of Ceridwen. That gave me, an ordinary boy up till then, potent magic, and though it did not literally put every piece of information in the world into my head, it did give me the ability to swiftly learn whatever I needed. Apparently it gave me other things as well, some of which I have discovered only in this life."

"All this I knew before," said Coventina impatiently, "but the draught you had from Ceridwen can only be given to one person at a time. So long as you live, it is unique to you."

"I wasn't suggesting I could brew the same potion, my lady," I said as humbly as possible. "I cannot change the restriction on that formula. However, if I study the force that radiates from me, I believe I can replicate it and cast it as a spell in a much more intense form. Having a candidate for the Order have to wait four years to gain magic seems like an unwieldy method anyway, better than nothing, yet painfully slow. Why wait four years to see if someone's magical ability to blossom, when I could bring forth that bloom in an hour?"

"You are indeed clever, Taliesin," admitted Coventina, "but I see grave risk in this plan. Nicneven might well kill you before you can perfect such a spell."

"That is true, my lady," I conceded, "but it is equally possible, if Nicneven is truly as powerful as your visions suggest, that my presence here might draw her unwanted attention to you. Already one of her allies has forced you to abandon the pathway from America to here. If she focuses all of her resources on finding this place, is it not possible she might succeed?"

"She has a reputation for being single minded in the pursuit of what she wants," said Coventina reluctantly.

"Then perhaps the sooner I leave, the better," I said gently. "Give her something to think about besides trying to find me here, for the sabotage of the American pathway suggests she knew what my travel plans were. Surely in such a case she would have had eyes on the pathway. She must know I'm here now."

Coventina sighed. "There is wisdom in what you say, Taliesin. Now I have a dilemma, however. I cannot keep you here for fear Nicneven will find us, and yet I cannot let you go, for certainly Nicneven will find you if you return to help your friends."

"I do have a knack for survival, my lady," I said, trying not to sound cocky about it.

"And so you do," she replied, "but perhaps there is something I could do to give you at least a little more protection. I need only a little of your blood."

I looked reflexively at Nurse Florence, who nodded. I held out my hand, and one of the Ladies of the Lake stepped forward with a silver knife. One quick touch was all it took to prick my finger.

"Hold your hand over the edge of the lake, and allow a few drops to fall into the water," Coventina instructed. As my blood dripped down, her staff flared to life, bathing the blood in incandescence, then shining light into the depths of the lake as the blood dispersed into it. As the light continued to shine, Coventina began to chant in Celtic. The rhythmic sound of her words vibrated through the chamber, on and on, capturing me in its flow. I felt myself becoming one with the lake as my blood had become one with it, felt the waters rippling around me, engulfing me, taking me into their depths, though I could still breathe perfectly normally; the sensation was comforting, not aquaphobic.

Gradually I rose from those friendly depths and found myself back on shore again, perfectly dry. The feeling of being underwater must have been an illusion.

I felt something cool in my hand and looked down. I was holding an amulet of some kind; I could tell from the way it was subtly radiating magic. Its chain and setting were silver. The gem it was set with seemed like alexandrite or something like that, since it changed color as I looked at it, sometimes appearing blue like the lake, sometimes red like my blood. Into the gem some better-than-human craftsman had carved the image of Coventina herself, reclining on a leaf, holding a water lily in one hand and pouring water from an urn with the other. The image was superficially like that on some objects excavated from the area of Hadrian's Wall, though the artist had been far superior to the ancient Romans who created those earlier images.

I looked up and into the eyes of Coventina, who appeared exhausted. Whatever she had done had evidently required substantial mystic energy to accomplish.

"My lady, I thank you, but…pardon my ignorance. I don't really know what you have done."

"I have created…what would your people call it? A pass, let us say. A security pass. No matter how strictly we are guarded here, you will be able to travel here, just like a Lady of the Lake could, through water. The lake will always recognize you and allow you to pass. If you are in danger of capture or death, you can gain sanctuary here."

I had never heard of such an arrangement, and I could tell from the whispered conversations around me that the Ladies of the Lake had never heard of it, either. Even Nurse Florence had to abide by whatever security measures were in place. Hell, even Vanora did.

As if she could read my mind, Coventina said, "Only two beings can automatically travel here without restriction…you and I." With a sudden jolt I realized that Coventina *could* read my mind.

"My lady?"

"No, Taliesin, I cannot read minds in general," she said before I could ask. *"I can read yours through our common bond with the lake. I will not do so except in case of need, and I expect you to do the same."*

"That is my general practice with mind reading," I assured her.

"What other help I can give is limited, as you know," she said without acknowledging my agreement, which she probably took for granted. *"Nonetheless, you can call out to me in time of need, and I will answer if I can."* I tried hard not to think about how much her attitude had changed once she realized the value I could have for the Order. Fortunately, true to her word, she seemed to be only broadcasting her part of the conversation and listening for my responses, not trying to read my thoughts in general.

"Before you go," she said aloud now, adopting a kind of don't-let-the-door-hit-you-on-the-way-out tone, "I have some advice." Given how much she had just given me, her demeanor seemed remarkably detached. I wondered if she was feigning aloofness to reduce the possibility that some members of the Order might feel jealous.

"Yes, my lady," I said expectantly.

"Your best chance of keeping Nicneven from harming you or your friends is to boost your own power as much as possible. One chance of that would be to recover the lyre of Orpheus from the Amadan Dubh."

"Indeed, I would like nothing better, my lady…if only I knew where he was," I replied.

Despite her weariness, Coventina actually smiled a little. "Vast as Annwn is, Dubh must have realized that he could not hide in Annwn if he wanted to experiment with an artifact that powerful. Rumor has it that he found the way to Hy-Brasil, which would be west of Ireland, if in fact it really existed…on Earth. It is actually in another realm, though its occasional intersections with your plane caused it be included on maps for a good long time."

"That sounds vaguely familiar," I said. "I think the original Taliesin looked for it at Arthur's request and did not find it. Never having been there, I can't just open a portal to it."

"Indeed not, and neither could I, even though I have visited there once, for the place has some…unique security features," said Coventina in a matter-of-fact tone. "You will need to approach it more physically. Nonetheless, my memories of the place may aid you in your quest, though they are several centuries old. Now that we are linked through the lake, you can take that knowledge from my mind, can you not?" I was surprised the Lady of the Lake knew so much about my abilities…until I remembered that Vanora and Nurse Florence filed regular reports with the Order. With Coventina's permission, I copied every piece of information she had on Hy-Brasil into my own memory. Somewhere in that mass of detail might lie a clue to reaching the island before Dubh left it.

As it turned out, Coventina had one more surprise for me. "Even better than the lyre, though, would be the Holy Grail."

There must have been an audible thud as my jaw hit the ground.

"My lady, the original Taliesin was still alive during the Grail quest, but he did not participate himself. I wouldn't even know where to start."

Coventina turned to Nurse Florence. "Viviane, I'll have one of our researchers fax the Grail files to you." I imagined a fax machine rising out of the lake and almost giggled. Coventina realized my amusement and said, "You may not have time for a tour this visit, Taliesin, but we have offices in the human world that handle the mundane tasks, like setting up a fake identities for your friends, Jimmie and Khalid. We need several…fronts, I think you would call them, for dealing with the authorities and various others in the mortal world. We can't very well take meetings with regular humans down here…and I suspect getting phone service down here would be problematic." She made that last statement with a totally straight face, and I tried not to laugh, because supernatural beings in my experience don't like you to laugh when they aren't trying to be funny.

"One of those fronts," continued Coventina, despite my snicker, "is a publishing company, Gates of Annwn Press, which from time to time publishes works about Welsh history, culture, and mythology. That is where we hide physical copies of our research, disguised as raw material for future books. That is also where the fax machine is."

I was trying to wrap my head around a Grail quest, not exactly a casual undertaking. Yeah, the Grail was probably the ultimate artifact we could lay our hands on, but it had taken the knights of Camelot several years, and most of those who set out never returned. We didn't have several years. Nicneven was already on the move and would probably have made California fall into the ocean long before we could complete such a quest. Nor did I want to see my friends die or at least be lost forever in the search.

I was still weighing the pros and cons of even attempting such a drastic step as a Grail quest when I heard shouting echoing in one of the corridors.

Chapter 12: Strategizing for Armageddon (Vanora)

I was having one of those days in which my eyes seemed about to fall out of my head. At the very least, they were having a contest with my head to see if they could fall out before it exploded.

Usually my Lady of the Lake techniques for going without sleep worked for a few days when I had to be on constant surveillance, but here it was less than two, and I already felt as if I'd been up for a month.

Maintaining a security network across the whole town was more draining than anyone realized. I had to keeping switching my consciousness around, seeing through the eyes of one security guard after another—and not just physically. I had to scan psychically as well.

It would be a great deal easier if I could just ward the whole town and renew the wards every day, and indeed since last time I had been called upon to protect against a powerful enemy, I had managed to create a generalized "detect and protect" system that covered more or less all of Santa Brígida. Unfortunately, any shield spread across such a large area ended up being very thin, even if well maintained. It might slow down a determined intruder, who would rather look for a hole than tear through and alert me immediately, but sooner or later such an intruder would find a gap and slip through. A few individual points in town were protected separately, including all of our homes, but that still left all of us vulnerable during at least part of the day. My security men alerted me to anything odd that they observed, but they couldn't observe magic or similar goings on without my being in their heads. There was also the problem of people—or other beings—opening a portal into town. A perimeter defense wouldn't block that kind of nonphysical entry. I have wards that should, but again, they cover too wide an area to really be effective on their own. That's how I ended up being the last line of defense, the person whose job was to catch incursions the other layers of protection miss—with precious little help from anyone else, I might add.

And that was another thing. This was a group of teenagers with major entitlement issues. Well, Taliesin had at least proved a pleasant surprise in that his plans, no matter how ill advised, seemed to work anyway. That said, he would never listen to my advice, never.

Since his friends looked at him as a leader, they tended to ignore my instructions as well. Even the young ones, like that annoying half djinn, generally gave me little respect. Oh, they had no hesitancy about asking me to use my Carrie Winn persona to create fake alibis for their unexplained absences, some of which could have been avoided if they had just listened to me. Nor did they have any qualms about expecting me to protect the rest of the town while they were gadding about.

Take Shahriyar, for instance. OK, I understand why he wanted to go after the half djinn, whose inability to follow rules had gotten him into trouble yet again, and who sneaked right out of his own house because the Sassanis clearly didn't know how to look after someone his age. Nicneven was on the prowl, and the whole town was in danger, but Shahriyar had to go chasing after him right then and damn the consequences. Why didn't I just say no to him? Because he would have ignored me and gone anyway, and with that damn sword protecting him, I couldn't have stopped him with magic. I suppose I could have had security apprehend him, but that would have created a huge mess. Now he and Carla, who could have helped me maintain surveillance, were both trapped outside the town. That was all right with them, because they got to do just as they pleased, as usual, and what did I get to do? Clean up their mess, particularly covering for them, yet again. Even worse, the Sassanis didn't really trust me, and I had to use magic at a point when I am already spread too thin.

If you asked me, I'd tell you this all came down to parental discipline being too lax in the States. One of these days the willfulness of these kids was going to get one of them killed…and then they'd probably ask me to bring him back to life, or go off on some quest or other to bring him back themselves, leaving me alone here again to defend the whole town from whoever the menace of the week happened to be.

Why did I stay? I could certainly have requested another assignment. The Order wanted to keep control of Carrie Winn's assets, but that could have been handled without my having to stay here all the time. If the Order had wanted a constant presence, any other shifter could easily have done the job with a little training.

I stayed because of Taliesin, ungrateful though he was. I stayed because he was destined for greatness…if he didn't get himself killed first. I was determined to make sure he fulfilled his destiny, whether he wanted to or not. Right now he was in denial about it, but I knew I could wear him down eventually.

If I could play a role, however small, in keeping destiny on track, I would consider all the irritation, all the ingratitude, well worth it.

I took a moment off from my constant body-switching to sip a little tea and wonder how Taliesin and Viviane were doing at headquarters. Assuming they were still there, they couldn't exactly call me from another realm, but I found myself growing impatient anyway. I had hoped for some reinforcements outside, someone who could at least start to work on the barrier Nicneven had thrown around us. Given how much area it covered, I would have thought it would have obvious weak spots, just like my own, much less ambitious protection, but apparently Nicneven had found a way to overcome that particular limitation. Either that or she was operating at an unbelievably high-power level. No wonder I had a headache.

It was getting close to three in afternoon by the time Taliesin's little band—or what was left of it anyway—finally assembled for a meeting. I had wanted a meeting that morning, but Stanford had to go to temple, and two or three others made excuses as well. If my life ever depended on teenagers changing their schedules, I would start planning my funeral.

I greeted them in one of the conference rooms on the upper floors. I don't think any of them really wanted to be there, though they loosened up a little once they got inside my perfectly temperature controlled space, and I had the hot chocolate brought in. The temperature today was below fifty—Nicneven's doing, no doubt— and as much as I was not their first choice of company, they couldn't deny the appeal of being warm enough. One thing about Awen, Ceridwen's monstrous pseudocastle: it was shockingly weatherproof.

"I'll make this meeting brief," I assured them, "but as Taliesin and Viviane are not here, I knew you would want an update, and I may need your help."

"Help with what?" asked Stanford. His tone was not quite suspicious, but close.

"If we can't get Nicneven's barrier down, my ability to keep constant surveillance going without help is going to get spotty at best after a few days. I know none of you have magic—unless that's changed." With this group, one had to ask. Their collective situation hardly ever stayed the same for two days in a row.

All of them shook their heads…all except one. Jimmie, or Rhys, or whoever he was this week, didn't respond. It took me a second to realize he wasn't listening. Unlike the others, he had a goofy-looking smile on his face and was clearly daydreaming.

"Jimmie," I snapped. "Pay attention!" He looked at me guiltily, but the smile faded only a little. What did he have to be that happy about in the middle of a crisis?

"Sorry," he mumbled. I had a good mind to tell him to speak up, but I would need to get my mind back on patrol soon, so I ignored his lack of manners.

"I was just asking you and the others if you had acquired any magic I didn't know about." To my surprise, he looked guiltier.

"Magic? No, not magic," he said cryptically. I had no time for riddles.

"If not magic, then what?" I asked. He didn't meet my eyes, never a good sign.

"Sorry, Vanora," said Dan, clearly trying to intercede for him. "His new body's been giving him some trouble, but yesterday he finally got control of it."

"I'm sure coming back from the dead must have some unique problems," I said. I was trying to sound supportive, I really was, but somehow they all seemed to take what I was saying as subtle sarcasm. I was less concerned by that than I was by the fact that Jimmie still looked guilty. There would be no call for that if his brother's description of the situation had been accurate, but rather than try to get the truth out of him directly, I scanned him quickly with my mind.

There was something odd about him; that was certain. What it was, however, was another matter entirely. I cursed myself for not having looked him over when he first came back from Olympus. There was definitely magic in his body, but I couldn't be sure whether it was a by-product of his resurrection or was completely unrelated. It did seem oddly similar in some ways to the magic of his sword. Morgan had once wielded that sword, but she had been in prison long before Jimmie had risen. Anyway, the fact that she had used the sword didn't mean she had created it. I cursed myself again, this time for not having investigated the provenance of the sword earlier. Tal had been drawn to White Hilt, and it to him; in any case, its origin was well known. All the other unusual weapons the group had came either from Gwynn ap Nudd or from the Olympians—all except Jimmie's sword.

"May I see your sword?" I asked Jimmie. Like all of them, he wore it most of the time, sheathed in invisibility, but of course I could see it. He looked puzzled but handed it over willingly enough. Even the hilt was cold to the touch, and the blade dribbled ice crystals all over the table. As far as I could tell it was of faerie manufacture, though Govannon's mark was not on it. There had been other black-smiths in the faerie realms, though, probably several over the centu-ries.

The sword was iron, though darker than normal iron. The hilt had a pattern like fronds of some kind, or perhaps feathers, but so elaborately done that they might even have been parts of snow-flakes, which would certainly better fit what the sword could do. I could see within it the magic that caused it to radiate cold. It was a complicated magic, however, so I couldn't be sure that was all it did. Could it have somehow been responsible for Jimmie's return to life?

While pretending to still be looking at the sword, I scanned Jimmie's body again. The magic was still there, though I noticed as I looked more closely that it seemed mostly dormant. Possibly it was the explanation of his sudden acquisition of physical coordination rather than of his resurrection. That would explain why it was inac-tive while he was just sitting. In any case, the magic energy bore some resemblance to that of the sword, so it would not be unreasonable to assume it came from the sword. I had sensed the magic while making my rounds, but I had written it off as just the sword. Was some of that enchantment rubbing off on Jimmie? If that were the case, why wasn't he gaining the power to radiate cold instead of better physical prowess?

I gave his body an even more intense scan. I should have asked Jimmie to do something physical so that I could see what dif-ference exertion made, but I didn't want to draw more attention to what I was doing. The magic remained largely inactive, but with enough concentration I could perceive it flickering up and down his muscles and nerves, clear evidence it had something to do with his new coordination. However, there was one detail that didn't fit that theory well: the magic seemed to center on a point in his chest. Why would it do that? There weren't any voluntary muscles there.

A sudden burst of pain distracted me. I looked down at my hand and saw that I had cut myself on the blade accidentally. I must have been more tired than I realized. Unfortunately, I had to pause and heal myself. Taliesin's men dithered around a bit. At least they didn't ignore my injury, but they clearly had no idea how to deal with it. I might have lost a lot of blood if I had not had the magic to stop its flow.

"You must all learn basic first aid," I said, trying to be as businesslike as possible and frankly trying to cover my embarrassment at being so clumsy. "With the kind of lives you lead now, you may need it. Viviane and I won't always be there to heal you on the spot."

I glanced at my watch and realized I would have to investigate Jimmie's newfound prowess later. I only had a few minutes before I absolutely, positively had to be back on patrol.

"As I was starting to say before, none of you can help me with the magic end of security, but you can help my men with the patrols. Young as you are, you have all had more experience than they have with the supernatural and even with combat."

"We'll help whenever we can," said Stanford quickly. The others nodded. I'm sure some of them thought "whenever we can" meant "whenever we have nothing better to do," but a little help would be better than none at all.

"I also need you to be prepared to evacuate quickly if need be," I added.

"Is the situation that bad?" asked Carlos.

"I know you can't see it, but Nicneven has encircled the whole town with magic. Shahriyar, Carla, Khalid, Taliesin, and Viviane can't return as long as the spell is in place. Likely none of us could, but we can still leave if necessary. Shahriyar, cloaked in an illusion that makes him look thirtysomething, has been negotiating for me to rent several properties in the Santa Barbara area. Carla is setting up various protective spells on those properties. We can relocate almost at a moment's notice. Once outside, we have a better chance of resisting Nicneven."

"Unless of course she casts the same spell in our new location," said Dan.

"We have to hope that she can't do that very fast, as the spell is very powerful," I pointed out.

"What about our families?" asked Gordy. "I'm not leaving my folks in here."

"We'll evacuate the whole town if the time comes," I replied. "I'll invent some good cover story, and we'll take everyone with us. After all, we don't know that all Nicneven's spell can do is keep people out. The temperature drops can be connected."

"That sounds like a pretty tall order, even for you," observed Dan, obviously in his most skeptical mood.

"There are advantages to being Carrie Winn," I said, wishing I could be off in the Welsh countryside somewhere, far away from this whole mess. "I've already secured suitable office space for my operations, a new office building right next door that could in a pinch house the high school, two apartment buildings nearby into which we will place your families, and a large warehouse that can serve as an evacuation center for the people we can't fit in the apartments initially. They will probably only need to be there are a few hours. Shahriyar is putting together a list of every vacant space from Santa Maria to Carpinteria. Some people may be pretty far away, but everyone will have a place to stay.

"Best of all," I continued, "you and your families will be in a much more confined, much more easily defended space, something we can manage to protect better than we possibly can now."

"Is it really going to come to that?" asked Gordy glumly.

"Maybe not," I said, not quite managing to sound optimistic. "If Nicneven keeps intruding into our world, I think the other faerie rulers will unite against her." Actually, that group had a hard time agreeing on what day of the week it was most of the time, but even they could not ignore the kind of stunts Nicneven was pulling at this point—or so I prayed.

"I'm making preparations just in case," I added. "We'll have an easier time getting people to safety if we have some place to put them, don't you think?"

They all sat and stared at me like idiots for a little while. I didn't think my strategy was that difficult to fathom. I figured perhaps this was what came of watching too much television.

"Is something wrong?" I asked finally.

"We...I...didn't think you'd give so much thought to our families," said Gordy awkwardly.

I could see the truth in their eyes, all of their eyes. They thought of me as cold, heartless. Would I never live that Carla episode down?

The very day I arrived from Wales, I had to help Taliesin and the others fight Ceridwen, a battle we very nearly lost. At one point Ceridwen was using the awakening spell as a weapon, and Carla had been right in the line of fire. Taliesin, ever the martyr, had tried to intercept the blast, but we already suspected that a second dose of that spell might kill him, so I blocked him, and Carla took the blast instead. As it was, Carla took a second blast later that only sent her into a coma, but even had Taliesin been rendered comatose, we would all have died. His contributions later in the battle proved decisive.

Should I have let him be incapacitated, or worse? Should I have let him save her at the expense of all of our lives? Should I be distrusted forever because I could make the tough decisions nobody else wanted to make?

I longed to say all of this to them, but I feared they wouldn't believe me anyway, and I wasn't about to spill my guts for nothing. I settled for saying, "There is no need to put them at risk." I realized as soon as the words were out of my mouth that that statement could easily be interpreted as callous, that I wouldn't hesitate to let their parents die if I perceived a need. I suppose that was partly true, but only if there were no other way to avoid an even bigger disaster.

I suddenly became more eager for them to leave, and they were not exactly anxious to linger, so I dispensed with them in short order and made ready to start patrolling again.

Only after they left did the puddle on the table remind me of Jimmie. He had recovered his sword so quickly after I cut myself with it that I hadn't really noticed.

What I did notice was that there was no trace of my blood in the water, and there should have been. I realized I hadn't remembered seeing any on the blade, either. It was almost as if the sword had some vampiric property and had drunk the blood, though surely someone would have noticed that characteristic in combat. Perhaps the cold had prevented much blood from flowing. In my surprise and then haste to stop the flow, I hadn't really noticed.

Yes, the cold. Surely that must have been it. Surely.

Chapter 13: Speak of the Devil (Tal)

Coventina looked in alarm at the general direction from which the shouting had come. As it turned out, she had reason to.

Into the central chamber ran one of the Ladies of the Lake, hair disheveled, white robe torn. She had two others in hot pursuit, and at first I didn't see why.

"My lady!" yelled one of the pursuers. "Bronwen is a spy!" The runner, whom I took to be Bronwen, realizing she was cornered, spun around and sprayed ice at the other Ladies of the Lake. It did not take a genius to figure out that Nicneven had somehow planted one of her own within the Order itself.

I drew White Hilt and sent a blast of fire Bronwen's way, aiming it carefully to make sure I didn't catch the pursuers, who had already fallen, frostbitten. To my surprise, she spun quickly enough to intercept the blast, shielding herself with a wall of ice. That defense would not save her for long if I really turned up the intensity of the attack, but I hesitated to do that with so many innocents around.

You would have thought that, with the number of Ladies of the Lake in the room, Bronwen would have been quickly taken down, but most of them just stood there, paralyzed by surprise. I had taken them to be guards at first, but clearly their function had been more ceremonial. They were obviously not prepared for combat, though a couple did try to reach their fallen sisters.

Coventina, however, was another matter. She hit the ice wall with a concentrated blast of water that shattered it, then shot a continuous, high-pressure stream at Bronwen, intended to knock her down and keep her from casting.

Unfortunately, Bronwen was not just a witch whose allegiance to Nicneven would give her powers like Nicneven's. Her eyes burned bright red and countered Coventina's stream with a concentrated blast of flame that sent the Lady's attack up in steam. The smell of sulfur filled the chamber.

At first I thought demon, but the woman seemed human enough. Maybe she was possessed, or maybe she was proof of the theory that some of Nicneven's witches had also pledged themselves to Satan. Either way, she was several times more dangerous than I had thought at first.

I doubted if even Coventina could take too many direct hits from hellfire, and it was possible Bronwen was not so much spy as assassin. Otherwise, it was difficult to imagine why she would have run into this chamber to face the most powerful opponent in the whole complex.

I threw up a wall of flame in front of Nurse Florence and me. I had no illusion it would stop hellfire, but I knew from experience it could slow it down, and I hoped it would hold long enough to distract Bronwen and give Coventina time to make her next move.

"Set deflection around Coventina if she hasn't done it already," I thought to Nurse Florence. *"Give her time to mount a solid attack."* I sensed Nurse Florence's concern and knew she had started to ward me. *"I can take care of myself,"* I assured her. Then I sensed her doubt, but she did as I asked. Probably in this situation her first concern was supposed to be Coventina anyway.

I sang with all my might, sending a sleep spell Bronwen's way. I doubted I could overcome someone backed by both Nicneven and Satan using that approach, but I figured it would at least be a good distraction, and apparently it was. I felt a wave of hellfire hit my fire shield and start to eat through it, but by the time the shield really crumpled, I had risen into the air, and the blast missed.

I fought fire with fire. By now Bronwen had some protection up, but not enough to resist a continuous fire stream indefinitely. I threw everything I had at her, putting her on the defensive. At the same time, Coventina tried another high pressure water attack, being careful to target the water in such a way that it would not interfere with my fire. Bronwen was hard-pressed to defend against both at the same time, but she did not go down. Among her various power sources, which I recalled included not only Nicneven and Satan, but also Hecate through Nicneven's proxy, to say nothing of whatever she had gained from the Ladies of the Lake, it was possible she could still win if she could keep her defenses up long enough to launch more attacks.

Some of the Ladies of the Lake were still frozen in fear. Others were making feeble magic attempts that helped, but not much. Coventina had not exaggerated when she claimed the Order was too weak for her to risk any more manpower—or woman power, I guessed I should say. The only first-rate casters in the room were

Coventina, Nurse Florence, and me. Yeah, Bronwen could conceivably beat all three of us.

I didn't know why at first, but as the fire poured over Bronwen, so intensely now that it seemed as if it ought to melt the stone under her feet, I thought about Stan. Actually, I thought about Stan when David was in control. In combat David's presence made Stan's sword glow white and frighten evil creatures. David himself could not see this effect, but I had witnessed it many times. David didn't do anything consciously; it just happened. That glow had to come from some kind of divine blessing.

It wasn't that I didn't believe in God, and I had certainly done my share of praying, especially when Carla was in her coma. Somehow, though, my go-to persona in combat was always the original Taliesin, who had relied on his music and magic, not on the Judeo-Christian God. Like most of the people at Arthur's court, Taliesin was a nominal believer at best, still attached in some ways to the old gods. I had taken his basic music-magic formula and added reliance on White Hilt.

However, Taliesin was not the only person I had ever been. I had actually been hundreds of others. When with the Olympians, I had relied on Hephaistion and Patroclus, but neither of them could help me now. I knew all too well that the Olympians could not intervene much in our world any more. However, I had also been Heman, holy musician, friend of King David, writer of Psalm 88.

I knew God wasn't like a source of magic that could be invoked based on a set of rules. He had His own rule set that we didn't always know. There was no guarantee that a prayer would be answered in any obvious way. Still, I could feel Bronwen's resistance growing, not fading away as I had hoped. What I needed was a way to cut off Satan as a possible power source.

I kept up the fire attack, even raised its intensity a little, but I started to sing psalms in Hebrew, praying all the while that God would banish Satan from the room. No, I didn't think I was a saint to whom God would respond. What I was, was desperate, but at least I wasn't some atheist jumping on the bandwagon out of blind survival instinct—or so at least I hoped God would see the matter.

Nothing happened: no white glow on my sword, no army of angels descending, no sudden panic on Bronwen's part, no reassuring vision or divine instruction. Nothing. I knew I couldn't become discouraged, though. I had seen David's light flicker when Charon had made him doubt himself. Only if I had faith was this going to work.

By now Bronwen had made herself immune to fire, which she demonstrated by laughing as she let my river of flame wash over her. Someone pledged to Satan would naturally have been able to block a fire attack pretty quickly. Soon Bronwen would be sufficiently protected against Coventina's attack to go on the offensive. I had to do something before that happened.

Bronwen had been busy warding herself against magical attacks, but as far as I could tell, she was still vulnerable to physical attacks. At first that weakness didn't seem to make much difference. Trying to move in for close combat would make it more difficult for me to dodge her hellfire; actually, the idea was probably suicidal at this point. However, now that White Hilt's fire was useless anyway, I no longer need to keep the sword in my hand.

I gave myself a little strength boost and threw White Hilt at her with all my might. She dodged fast enough to keep the blade from piercing her heart, but it did catch her in the shoulder, wrenching a scream from her and causing her to drop to her knees. She did not completely lose concentration, but the injury had definitely slowed her down. What hellfire she could conjure up now was feeble, and Coventina started up her water attack again. I could tell she was tiring, but right now she had more to bring to the table than Bronwen. However, the witch was still not down completely. She pulled White Hilt loose and began to use her Lady of the Lake talents to heal herself, doing just enough to ward off Coventina to keep the battle going.

I thought about trying to invoke God's aid again, but Bronwen was getting stronger by the second. I didn't know how much power she could draw before she, too, became exhausted, but if I struck before she was fully recovered, I might have a better chance than relying on my less than perfect faith.

With a whispered apology to God for not being able to get my act together, I flew at Bronwen. Trying to fend off Coventina and heal herself at the same time gave her too much to think about to blast me with hellfire right away. I grabbed White Hilt, not for the fire, but again for the blade, and wounded her in the other arm. Her white robe, already red with her blood, became an even deeper hue as she bled freely. I made a couple more cuts, not to be a sadist but to be sure she could no longer fight back. I had no doubt Coventina would put her to death, but I still wasn't that comfortable killing people myself, and in any case I wanted whatever information she had.

Bronwen, unable to stop so many wounds from bleeding at the same time, finally succumbed, lapsing into unconsciousness on the burned and bloody ground. Suddenly Coventina was at my side.

"Why did you not just kill her?" the Lady of the Lake asked tiredly.

"We need to know what she knows, my lady," I said apologetically. "I can read her mind, remember? Would you not like to know exactly how much headquarters has been compromised?"

Coventina nodded. "There is much wisdom in that, Taliesin. Please proceed."

Anticipating just such a situation, Nicneven had built up Bronwen's mental defenses, but I sang myself into a psychic frenzy and ripped away those defenses one by one. I didn't especially want to do that any more than I wanted to kill her, but she had given her obedience to evil. I could only feel so much sympathy for someone who would have killed us all if she could have managed it.

Finally I was into the woman's numb and unresisting mind. Nicneven had apparently been thinking about casual slips near members of the Order, not the kind of psychic interrogation I could conduct. In any case, I didn't learn anything about how to counter Nicneven's magic in Santa Brígida, but I did learn what Coventina needed to know: Bronwen had brought another witch into headquarters, and that witch was soon to be in Nicneven's presence, which meant Nicneven could open a portal into any part of headquarters.

When I conveyed this information to Coventina, she immediately closed the Cardiff University entrance and assured me that she could quickly protect headquarters from Nicneven.

"Its..." she began, struggling for the right word, "its coordinates, I believe you would say, can be changed. Its location in this plane is...flexible. I must act quickly, though, and I am nearly drained. Everyone, gather round and lend me your strength." Nurse Florence and I, as well as all the Ladies who remained standing, joined Coventina, and I also lent my music to the effort. I couldn't tell exactly how Coventina was using her magic, but I could feel the stone floor vibrating under us.

The work nearly drained us all, but after an hour, Coventina announced that headquarters had been relocated in such a way that the information Nicneven had obtained would no longer do her any good.

"Taliesin, I have misjudged you," said Coventina apologetically. "The aid you have given the Order today was invaluable. I will never forget it."

I bowed to her. "My Lady, what I did was gladly done. I could never have done otherwise. You have given me the great gift of the lake. You gave it to me even before I had proved my worth."

"So I did," she said, "and now that you have seen the Order in operation, you understand why I have no great force to lend to you. Still, if I can see any way to free your town, I will gladly share that knowledge with you."

"I appreciate that offer more than I can say. If we all survive, I will find a way to fill your Order's ranks again." I probably shouldn't have repeated that idea without being sure I could do it, but I got caught up in the spirit of the moment.

"I have another proposal for you, Taliesin. I have long been without a consort. I would be honored if you would return to me not just to teach me a spell, but to make me your wife."

Crap!

My cheeks turned bright red. "My lady, I am honored more than I can say. Alas, I have pledged my heart to another. As a man of honor, I cannot wed you, though it grieves me to refuse you."

Coventina sighed. "I feared as much. Worry not—declining my offer in no way reduces my respect for you or my desire to remain your ally. May I at least offer you and Viviane a place to rest before you journey back?"

That offer we accepted, and as we walked to the chambers we had been lent, Nurse Florence said, "You had a chance to make history back there, you know. There has never been a Lord of the Lake."

I blushed again. "That's not funny! I'm glad Gordy wasn't here; he would have had a field day with this. What I don't get is why this keeps happening. Am I giving off some supernatural pheromones of which I'm not aware?"

Nurse Florence laughed. "In this case it's not at all sexual. Well, maybe a little," she added in response to my suddenly unhappy expression, "but really what happened is that Coventina realized how heroic you truly are. You could have fled when Bronwen started her rampage—some would have thought that the wise course of action, particularly since if the battle had taken just a few minutes longer, we might have had to face Nicneven's army, maybe even Nicneven herself. Instead of fleeing, you stayed and fought."

"Of course, if I'd thought to throw the sword at her earlier, the battle might have been over faster," I said ruefully.

"Don't worry about that too much," replied Nurse Florence, "in the heat of battle, there's no way to be sure what someone is warded against, and as long as Bronwen was vulnerable to fire, using White Hilt to blast away at her was by far the best play you had.

"I just wish the upcoming battles were going to be so easy," she added.

Well, that wasn't the best thought to go to sleep by...especially since she was undoubtedly right.

Chapter 14: Finding a Way to Hy-Brasil (Tal)

Despite our general exhaustion, Nurse Florence and I were both up by eight o'clock in the morning. It was Sunday, February 17, and the clock was ticking.

I could not attach an exact time frame or sequence to the visions Coventina had shown me, but she clearly believed her prophecies would be fulfilled very soon. Nurse Florence took a quick side trip to Annwn to warn Gwynn ap Nudd that he might soon be facing a joint attack by Scotland and England. She returned quickly with the welcome news that all was quiet, but that Gwynn would make what preparations he could. Whatever else happened, at least he would not be caught off guard.

"You know this means we probably can't get any aid from him to free Santa Brígida, at least not right away," said Nurse Florence. "He said without my even asking that he would send help when he could, but you and I both know he will put the welfare of his subjects first."

"He has to," I agreed, "but we couldn't very well not warn him. We'll just have to find another way."

"Fast, though," Nurse Florence pointed out. "I just checked with Vanora. Tal, she sounds terrible. She shouldn't be wearing down quite that fast. I suspect being surrounded by that hybrid force field of Nicneven's has something to do with it. But regardless of what is causing her strength to fade, she won't be able to maintain the defenses much longer. Oh, and the temperature continues to drop. It's near freezing now, though it gets a little higher at midday."

"Twenty or so degrees in…what is it now, three days?" I asked worriedly.

"Not even quite that long," replied Nurse Florence. "Vanora is getting ready to organize an evacuation. Shar's acting as her agent to arrange temporary housing and the like, while Carla is warding those properties. Vanora and I would both rather it didn't come to that, though. We have the sneaking suspicion that's exactly what Nicneven wants us to do. Once Vanora and the guys leave, they won't be able to return. Supernaturally speaking, that could leave Nicneven with the run of the place."

"I thought she was after me, not the town," I objected.

"There is no reason she couldn't be after both," replied Nurse Florence. "I've run across some evidence that the place was a kind of psychic hot spot even before Ceridwen built there. Besides, there's no denying it would make an excellent base if Nicneven wanted to make all-out war on us. We might be able to get people to evacuate the town, but we could never move them far enough away to be safe from Nicneven if she were operating in Santa Brígida."

"Are you serious?" I asked, knowing she was.

"The more I think about it, the more certain I am," said Nurse Florence. "Nicneven has no way of catching you if you get enough of a head start. With all the places you've been in your various lives, you could stay one or even a dozen jumps ahead of her as long as you could open portals. She needs to have some way of pinning you down. Hostages would be the best way to do that."

"Then we need to stop her before she starts taking prisoners!" I thought about the situation for a minute or so. "The Order and the Welsh faeries can't be of much help. The Olympians might give me another useful object or two, but they're still trapped on their own plane. Wait! Could they find some way to cut off Nicneven from Hecate?"

Nurse Florence pondered a minute. "Short of killing her, no...but now that I think of it, we should contact the Olympians right away. Remember Coventina had a vision of warning for them as well. If those prophecies have not yet come true, they, like Gwynn, might be able to prepare."

I owed the Olympians a heads-up at the very least. I lay down on the bed in the chamber Coventina and focused all my energy on making contact. Though I had been to Olympus, I couldn't just open a portal to it. One of the Olympians could open the way for someone, however...if that someone was connected closely enough to them.

The first time I had tried to make contact, I had failed. My previous lives as Hephaistion, son of Hephaestus, and as Patroclus, great grandson of Zeus, had not been enough. It took Shar, reincarnation of Alexander and Achilles, with a present life body descended from Perseus, son of Zeus, to do the trick, and even then I had to boost his signal to get through. Apollo had assured us that all of us, having tasted of Olympian hospitality, would be able to call on the

Olympians in the future, but evidently he had been overly optimistic, for I failed again. Nurse Florence lent me her strength, but even that was not enough.

"Maybe I still need Shar for this," I admitted as I got off the bed.

"Perhaps," said Nurse Florence doubtfully. She had always believed that my ties should have been strong enough without Shar if only we had known how to use them properly. "Why don't you give him a call?"

Coventina was busy somewhere, but after receiving our message, she reconnected the Cardiff University door to our plane so that we could walk out and use our cell phones.

We exited discreetly; it wouldn't have been very smart to appear suddenly in front of someone. Fortunately, there wouldn't be too many people on campus on a Sunday, so we didn't have to wait.

However, being outside in the early morning light reminded me of the time difference. Eight thirty in the morning in Cardiff would be one thirty in the morning in Santa Barbara. Readying an apology, I called Shar but got voice mail. Then I tried Carla with the same result.

"They've both got their phones off," I told Nurse Florence. "It could be hours before they get up. I'd hate to just stand around and do nothing."

"You're right," she said, "but we have to eat at some point anyway. Let's have breakfast and talk strategy."

The Ladies of the Lake would undoubtedly have fed us, but I wanted to stretch my legs, so we hiked over to Coburn Street and then went northwest, past a long stretch of brick buildings with very old-school chimneys. We kept going until we hit a cluster of restaurants near where Salisbury Road cut into Coburn. Looking at the brightly colored facades of a bewildering array of Italian, Chinese, Indian, and Sri Lankan eateries, I realized how hungry I was, a side effect of all those magic exertions. Nurse Florence steered me to a place fittingly called the Lady of the Lake, which she told me was a favorite hangout for the employees of the Order's various bureaucracies, including the ones that had faked papers for Khalid and Jimmie. Not coincidentally, it had a certain amount of subtle magical protection.

The exterior was a relatively demure pale blue, but the inside was surprisingly ornate, with wooden tables and chairs that looked as if they had been bought from a yard sale at Camelot. It had been quite a while since I had seen this much handmade furniture outside an antique store. The lighting was electric, but the fixtures managed to be a pretty good imitation of torches, complete with a flickering effect I thought must be off-putting to some people. The walls were covered with murals depicting Arthurian scenes such as the original Viviane giving Excalibur to King Arthur. Looking closely once we were seated, I could see they were hand-painted. I wasn't an art critic, but they seemed well done and somehow less overwhelming than the decor Ceridwen had picked for her pseudocastle.

"This place looks as if it should cost a fortune, but it doesn't," I said, looking at the menu in hungry fascination.

"The Order treats its employees well," replied Nurse Florence. "You should see their dental plan," she added with a smile.

The waitress, dressed in an outfit that looked vaguely medieval without being completely dysfunctional, came to take our orders. Against my better judgment, I ordered a pretty full English breakfast: bacon, sausages, poached eggs, grilled tomatoes, fried mushrooms, baked beans, toast, and tea. In some of my earlier lives, I had found this kind of fare to be pretty greasy and sometimes unevenly cooked in a lot of places, but I could highly recommend the Lady of the Lake for it. In fact, meals in Annwn and on Olympus aside, I ate one of the best prepared breakfasts of my life in that place.

As the pace of my eating finally slowed, Nurse Florence cast a little spell to prevent anyone from overhearing us, since there were a couple of civilians in the restaurant at that point.

"We do need to touch base with the Olympians," she said, "but maybe we should focus on catching up with the Amadan Dubh first. The lyre of Orpheus would up your power level quite a bit, and letting Dubh keep something that powerful is dangerous anyway. Now that we know where it could be, perhaps we need to grab it just in case Dubh moves."

"We've never been to Hy-Brasil," I said between bites. "And from what Coventina told us, even if we had, we might not have been able to open a portal directly there. I expected to find something useful in her memories of the place, but frankly so far I'm not seeing anything helpful in those experiences."

"Unfortunately, she's the only source we're likely to find," Nurse Florence answered quickly. "It hasn't been inhabited for centuries. Long, long ago it was the base for Braseal, a very early faerie high king, but he vanished hundreds of years ago. All I know is that it's an extra-planar island like Alcina's. There is some possibility it still has a connection to our world somewhere to the southwest of Ireland."

"Yeah, actually, if nothing has changed, Coventina remembers an entrance somewhere around there, but so far I'm not seeing any landmarks we could use to pinpoint the exact spot. If we got close enough, though, I'm pretty sure I could identify that entrance from her memories."

"Let's be optimistic and assume that's true," suggested Nurse Florence. "If so, we could in theory find the entrance by sailing or flying to it. I don't think you want to carry me that far by air, so sailing would be the best choice. Unfortunately, we can't exactly charter a boat to it. We could enchant someone to take us there, but I'd rather not involve civilians if we don't have to."

I could see the wisdom in that, since Dubh would probably fight us, but we couldn't exactly swim there. "Does the Order have any ties to any of the faerie rulers in the area?" I asked.

"In the days of Arthur, the Order had close ties to Avalon, another one of the western isles, but not so much anymore. Actually, there are several islands in the west, but their rulers keep pretty much to themselves. Some in the Order believe they are more miffed than our local faeries about having to give up their claims to godhood. If Coventina were less preoccupied, I might ask her to try to make contact, but as things stand that may be pressing our luck…especially," she added with a smirk, "after you declined her hand in marriage."

Despite myself, I blushed a little. "She said that wouldn't affect our alliance."

"I'm just teasing you," Nurse Florence assured me. "However, she's already told you where to find the Amadan Dubh and given you a connection to the lake that no man has ever enjoyed. It wouldn't be diplomatic to ask for more right away. Anyway, I'm not at all sure that any of the rulers of the western isles would respond to her, either."

"So where does that leave us?" I asked. "We know exactly where Dubh may be but have no practical way of getting there."

We spent a few minutes considering all the possibilities. It actually began to look as if a magically empowered swim might be the best choice—except that it would be like painting a target on our backs. Until we reached Hy-Brasil, or at least some other western isle, we would be radiating magic in a part of the sea otherwise relatively devoid of it. If, as seemed likely, Nicneven was watching developments in the general area, she or one of her agents might spot us, and we wouldn't be situated well for a fight. We also risked offending one of the western rulers; their reluctance to talk might not prevent them from being offended if someone passed near their domain without their leave.

"There may be one way," said Nurse Florence finally, "but you aren't going to like it."

"I'm not liking much about this situation anyway," I admitted, "but almost anything would be better than passing up a chance to recover the lyre. Try me."

Despite our protection against eavesdropping, Nurse Florence leaned forward, I suspected from reflex more than for any practical reason. "There are stories about faerie women coming occasionally from Tir Tairngire, one of the islands of Manann Mac Lir."

"The...lord of the sea?" I asked. Among other things, Manann had been an Irish sea god. "Oh, I get it. One of the women will carry a message to Manann, and he will help."

Nurse Florence looked uncomfortable. "It's not that simple. The faerie women won't be interested in carrying a message, and I have no idea whether he would respond to one even if they did. They are said to come with one particular goal: to find mortal men with whom to fall in love."

"What...oh," I said, slumping in my chair.

"I told you that you wouldn't like it," Nurse Florence reminded me.

"But surely they can't be doing that anymore!" I objected. "The faeries of the western isles must be as averse to letting mortals find out about their existence as the Annwn faeries are."

"Indeed," replied Nurse Florence, "but it is said that the faerie women look longingly at men on shore and then sail away weeping, for they can no longer approach them."

"How does that help us?" I asked. "What good is a faerie woman looking at me from a distance?"

"Don't you see?" asked Nurse Florence. "If you put out a little magical energy, they will know that you are safe to approach."

My whole body tensed up. "So you want me to...what exactly? Stand on the beach, exude some magic, and look attractive? Then what? Have sex with the first faerie who comes along, just to get her boat? Carla would never forgive me!"

In some of my earlier lives I would unhesitatingly have slept with a woman to advance the greater good...or at least, that's what I would have told myself was happening. Recovering the lyre could arguably be a justification. Still, Carla really wouldn't understand. I was sure of it.

"Tal," Nurse Florence said reprovingly. "I'm not asking you to have sex with anyone. These faeries are reputed to be relatively weak: servants in the western isles rather than rulers. If we can manage to get only one of them, between the two of us I believe we can weave a convincing illusion so that she will *think* she's having sex with you. While that is going on, you and I will steal her magic boat, and we can reach Hy-Brasil in short order."

"Gee, that isn't even remotely creepy," I said. "Isn't she going to be angry when she discovers the truth?"

"Undoubtedly, but with any luck she won't. Hy-Brasil isn't that far away if we travel by faerie ship, and it isn't that big. If Dubh is there, and we beat him, we can get back before the illusion runs its course. If we don't beat him, well, we'll have bigger problems than one vengeful low-level faerie."

"Manann won't be offended?" I asked, fishing for excuses to reject the whole idea.

"Unless his temperament is much changed, by all accounts he will find it amusing...if he learns of it at all."

I looked Nurse Florence in the eye and said, "There must be at least a dozen ways for this plan to go sideways."

"Well, if you'd rather, we could go after the Holy Grail," she suggested facetiously.

Despite its tone, that was more or less the winning argument. We needed more power somehow if we wanted to have any chance of defeating Nicneven. Since the Grail was surely unattainable, the lyre of Orpheus remained the most accessible source we had. Failing to grab it when we had the chance could cost us the lives of everyone I knew.

Nurse Florence put the charges on her account, and we left the restaurant quickly. We found a quiet spot on the street and took a portal to Valentia Island, one of the westernmost points in the Republic of Ireland, important to us because it was one of the places the western faeries were reputed to still visit. Fortunately, Nurse Florence had visited the island during her early training, so we could get there as fast as possible.

We couldn't make our attempt until after sunset, though, and it was only ten in the morning local time, so we made a little pilgrimage to Saint Brendan's well. Maybe I was trying to renew my faith. Maybe I was superstitiously looking for luck. Saint Brendan was believed by the Order to be a mortal who had somehow breached the barrier between worlds and reached some of the western isles back around the time of King Arthur. We wanted to follow in Brendan's footsteps...sort of. I'm pretty sure he didn't have to launch his attempt by making a faerie maiden think he was having sex with her.

*Of course, God, if you don't like the idea, perhaps you can offer us another way...*I thought as loudly as I could. God chose not to respond. Given the way my luck had been running lately, perhaps that was just as well.

We had to go squishing through a sizable bog to reach the well, and the large patches of grass sometimes concealed part of the mire underneath, which would have made staying on our feet difficult in places if we had not magically enhanced our senses.

The actual well wasn't very spectacular visually, though a rough semicircular stone wall made the spot more visible from a distance. So did the weathered seventh century stone crosses, one barely recognizable as a cross, and all eroded and partly covered by pale green moss. Entering the opening in the semicircle, we could see a stone altar rising from about the midpoint in the wall. The side facing the well had a stone cross covering its center and a smaller white cross hanging to the left of the stone one. Below the crosses was a shelf on which sat small statues, presumably of the saint, and a collection of small offerings.

Since this was Sunday morning in Ireland, we had the place to ourselves; everyone else likely to visit the well was at Mass. I stretched out my mind and tried to feel something, anything.

I could sense magic pretty easily. Divine power was a little different. I could see the light from David's sword, and since he couldn't himself, I had to assume I was perceiving it the same way I perceived magic rather than seeing it with my physical eyes. That said, I couldn't *feel* it in the way I could feel magic.

When Jimmie had still been a ghost and had sometimes been inside me to reinforce me in my struggles against Dark Me, Jimmie had claimed to see the white light he used when he chose to appear as an angel.

That seemed like a hundred years ago now. I wished I could see that white light inside me, feel it, something.

After a while I could feel something, not from within, but from the well, whose waters were too far down to see. My skin tingled, but just a little, and I thought I could see a faint glow from the deepest point I could see...or was that just an optical illusion?

I tried praying, but I felt as if I was talking to myself. Sometimes, when I had been trying to pray Carla out of her coma, I had sensed a connection. Had I just been fooling myself?

It wasn't that I was turning atheist. There were days, though, when I felt a little like a Deist, believing that God had created the world and then left us to run it.

If that were truly the way God operated, though, why was Satan so much more active? I saw evidence of his power practically every day. Less than twenty-four hours ago, I had been fighting a witch who could throw hellfire.

I wasn't expecting a fireworks display in the heavens every time I prayed. This was one of those days when I needed at least a firecracker, though.

Nurse Florence and I talked for a little while about a lot of things: my spiritual blockage, Dark Me's increasing activity, all of my other worries.

"The Dark Me part concerns me," Nurse Florence admitted. "You haven't been using dark magic, after all, or doing anything else that could feed his power, for that matter. If anything, he should be getting weaker."

"Tell me about it!" I replied in a light tone I didn't feel.

"As for the rest," she said, "you know what I think. Magical beings may not have any more answers than nonmagical. I have to think that if there is a God, he must be patient with our struggles to understand him."

I was reminded that I had no idea what Nurse Florence's religious background was. Somehow, now didn't seem to be the right time to ask.

"If we could visit a seer or cast a spell to get all the answers," she continued, "that wouldn't leave much room for faith, would it?"

"I guess not," I grumbled, "but with so much at stake, I might be willing to give faith a little less room, just this once."

We were still alone, so I decided to try asking for God's guidance one more time. I knelt and sang a prayer, first in Irish Gaelic, then in Hebrew. I wasn't trying to use the singing to draw magical power, just to make myself feel better. Not being stupid, I was well aware that magic could be used to manipulate the world, but it could not manipulate God.

"And yet you switch languages," said a voice behind me, "as if a prayer in Hebrew or Gaelic would be better than one in English." Whoever had somehow sneaked up on us had read my thoughts. I jumped up and spun to face the stranger, ready to draw White Hilt.

Nurse Florence was already staring in amazement at the newcomer, a middle-aged man, deeply tanned, wearing a simple brown monk's robe, his hair done in a Celtic tonsure (the front shaved). He carried a tiny model of a ship whose sail had a Celtic cross upon it.

Even without the subtle radiance that artists would have portrayed as a halo, I could tell our visitor was Saint Brendan.

Is this an illusion of some sort? I thought to Nurse Florence.

"I'm as real as you are," said Brendan, still reading my thoughts.

"Having had a number of encounters with shape-shifters and that kind of thing, I hope you will not consider it disrespectful if we…verify who you are," I said apologetically. The whole situation was profoundly awkward. If he was real, Brendan was obviously an answer to my prayers, and I had just been lamenting the fact that I hadn't received any sign. However, I knew he could be someone else in disguise, perhaps even an agent of Nicneven.

Brendan looked surprised. "I am not usually asked to…how would you say it? Present my credentials. You prayed, and God sent me to you. What more do you want?"

Well, when you put it like that…

"Forgive us, your…" Nurse Florence began, but then she faltered. How did one address a saint? I couldn't be any help there. The original Taliesin had been related by marriage to Saint David of Wales, but David obviously wasn't a saint in his own lifetime.

"Brendan will do," replied the saint.

"Brendan, then," said Nurse Florence. "As Taliesin said, we mean you no disrespect, but we have enemies who could easily pretend to be you. One of our poets wrote, 'The Devil hath the power to assume a pleasing shape,' and sadly, we have reason to know how truth that statement is."

Brendan paused for just a moment, his eyes closed, his expression reverent. Then his eyes opened again. "The Lord has advised me your fears are reasonable. Examine me as you wish."

Nurse Florence and I sensed what we could. As in other cases, I could see his aura, but I couldn't feel anything. I probed enough to know that he had no physical body, and shape-shifters have to maintain some physical form, so he couldn't be a shifter. Also, neither his aura nor his visible body had even a trace of magic. No spell could stand up that well to our insistent observation. That the figure before us had the power of God behind him I couldn't doubt.

I started to bow, but he gestured for me not to. "Brendan, you are indeed who you say. We are sorry to have doubted you."

He gave me a little smile. "After what you have lived through, your response is understandable. Now, can we get to the business for which I have been sent?"

"Yes, please," I said, still feeling awkward.

"Taliesin, God wants to do more than just run a puppet show," the saint told me earnestly. I frowned at the seeming non sequitur. Apparently saints, like other supernatural beings, liked riddles.

Brendan stared at me. "Was that not clear?" I shook my head. "You were wondering why God doesn't just destroy Nicneven, or at least imprison her in her own world, as he has with the Olympians."

I wasn't really aware I had been wondering that, but as soon as he had spoken, I realized that had actually puzzled me.

"Our minds are too small to comprehend the ways of God," continued Brendan. "We have to have faith that He always has His reasons."

"I know that's true, Brendan," I replied, "but what does that have to do with puppet shows?"

"I did not take you for such a literal thinker, Taliesin," said Brendan a little reprovingly. "God could destroy all evil in the world instantly. He does not because of free will. Ultimately, I have faith that evil will be vanquished, but when it is, that victory will come from God's creatures being able to follow His will, not from God acting entirely on His own.

"Suppose God made the world perfect on His own; He could wipe out all evil in less than a heartbeat. Then humans and other thinking creatures would have nothing to strive for, and so they would never reach their full potential."

"He could leave evil in our own hearts," I suggested.

"Indeed He could," agreed Brendan, "but what then? Would you have Him eliminate Nicneven but leave the likes of Hitler to wreak havoc? I have seen enough of recent eras to know that many criticized God for allowing Hitler to gain and continue in a position of power. Yet many thousands of people had to make sinful choices in order to bring about the unspeakable horrors of that time.

"If God eliminates evil from the human heart, then He is just performing a puppet show. If He allows evil thoughts but blocks them from being acted upon, he is still performing a puppet show. Would even the most sinful man try to do evil if he knew failure was inevitable? People doing right because they have no other real choice is not the same as choosing to do right. Had God wanted such an outcome, He could have just put Adam and Eve in the garden without a certain tree...or a certain serpent."

Needless to say, this wasn't the right time for a long theological discussion, and I knew I had more pressing questions to ask, but how often does one have an emissary of God to question? Before my life had been a constant string of battles, I had always been curious, and that curiosity got the better of me...or maybe it was just my desire to feel as if the fate of the whole world didn't rest on my every move.

"What about God's plan?" I asked.

At first, Brendan seemed not to know how to respond, more because he hadn't expected any question than because he couldn't answer the one I posed.

"God's plan," he began at last, "has an infinite number of layers. If a human stumbles off the right path, God shifts to a slightly different plan. He has no trouble producing as many paths to His ultimate goal as there are feet to walk them...and those paths shift if we make sinful choices, but the basic reality that there is a path never changes, nor does the final destination."

Before I could ask another question, Brendan continued, "Taliesin, you have often thought that God is not helping you. Ponder the course of your life for a moment. Your path has not always been easy, but He has been with you every step of the way, and if you had not endured the awakening of your past lives, many evils would already have come to pass that you have averted. Think, too, about your choices, and how they have helped you take advantage of what God has given you. Suppose you, as a popular boy, had paid no attention to the much less popular Stanford. Without that friendship, you would not have had Stan, or King David, at your side."

I must have looked puzzled, because Brendan looked mildly irritated again. "Think, Taliesin, think, for time is short! Did you believe that David reincarnated ended up living in your town by coincidence? Indeed, our Lord sent him to help you, but you would have lost that help if you had made the wrong choice. Similarly, if you had turned to anger against Shahriyar after your first hostile encounter, you would have lost another valuable ally. God has given you the tools, and you have had the moral sense to pick them up."

Brendan was sounding eerily like one of Vanora's rants. She had become convinced I was some kind of Celtic messiah, but evidently she had been right...up to a point.

"Then Nicneven—" I began.

"Can be defeated, despite all her power," replied Brendan, "if you keep making the right choices. If not...that will be a profound tragedy."

I had a momentary flash of the Arnold Schwarzenegger character, Jericho Cane, in *End of Days*. At one point Jericho said something like, "Enough of this religious nonsense! Just tell me which way to shoot!" That was kind of how I was feeling. I supposed that was ungrateful. I had asked for a sign and gotten one. Not only that, but I had been the one to turn the conversation in a very religious direction. Now I was tempted to whine because the sign hadn't come attached to a miracle that would make me immune to Nicneven's magic or give me some other unbeatable advantage.

Something about his demeanor told me he was getting ready to return to heaven or continue to his next assignment. I had to think quickly. I knew there were other questions I needed to ask, and if I didn't ask them now, I might never have another chance, at least in this life.

"Brendan, you know of our plan to reach Hy-Brasil?"

Brendan nodded but volunteered nothing more.

"What do you think of our strategy for getting transportation?" I asked.

"A better question might be, what do you think of it?" countered Brendan. "If what you are doing doesn't feel right, think about other ways to reach your goal." Nurse Florence tensed at that, but said nothing. Clearly, she couldn't see any other way—and neither could I.

I thought about asking Brendan if he could lend us his boat, but I already knew what answer I was likely to get. Instead, I surprised even myself by asking, "Can we succeed in a Grail quest?"

Brendan's expression changed from strict to sad. "The Grail can be won, but not by you alone. One of your band has the ability to set in motion events that will lead to that ultimate prize and save the day, but only at a great cost to you. Be sure, my son, that the Grail is truly what you need, because the harm the quest will inflict on you the Grail itself will not heal."

I sensed I had a shot at asking one more question, so I took it. "Brendan, why will I fail? Is it because I use magic?" Well, I had to ask. More than once David had expressed uneasiness about the source of my power, and the Bible had all those great quotes about not suffering a witch to live.

Brendan looked even sadder, giving me the sinking feeling I had asked the wrong question. "My son, what the Holy Scriptures condemn is the kind of power drawn from the Devil or some other evil source. The sorcerers and witches one finds in the biblical text all draw their power from evil and use their power to do evil, either against the Israelites or against the early Christians. Your power is part of your nature, much as the faeries' power is part of theirs. Such an ability is no more evil than the ability to swing a sword or write a song. It becomes evil only if you use it for the wrong purposes. No, what will keep you from the Grail is the other one within you, the one you call Dark Me."

Yeah, I should have figured. I had tried to use dark magic, and even though my purpose had been good, my disregard of the dangers had been arrogant. That episode had left me stuck with Dark Me, perhaps forever. In sickening clarity I saw how Brendan's revelations about God's plan related to me. Maybe I could have attained the Grail before, but now I was barred; worse, it sounded like a successful Grail quest would make me suffer in ways I couldn't even imagine. I might have gotten the Grail and avoided destroying myself in the process. Not now, though.

To my surprise, Brendan actually had a tear on his cheek. I knew the Grail could give us the power to stop Nicneven. He knew what was in store for me if I went down that fork in the road. I wanted to ask, but he continued before I could figure out how to frame the question.

"I must take my leave, but before I go, I give you one gift and one last piece of advice." He held up a vial of clear liquid that sparkled in the sunlight. "This is water from my well. God has empowered it so that it is now the holiest of water. As long as you have faith in it, it can vanquish any evil opponent, but be wary how you use it, for there is only enough here for one victory."

He handed me the vial and then vanished. His disappearance was more or less instantaneous, making travel by portal look slow and inefficient.

"Tal, are you all right?" Nurse Florence asked me.

"Be careful of what you wish for, because you might get it," I said bitterly. "Brendan restored my faith and took away my hope. The only way to win is to destroy myself."

"He didn't quite say that," replied Nurse Florence gently. "We don't know what the price is. We don't even know that we need the Grail to defeat Nicneven. Sure, we could probably win more easily that way, but Brendan also handed you water that can vanquish any evil."

"Yeah, once," I replied. "Toss it at the wrong foe in the heat of battle, and we're all done."

Then, realizing what an ungrateful bastard I sounded like, I prayed again, expressing my thanks to God for the exceptional help He had given me. After all, not everybody got a personal appearance by a saint, let alone holy water squared and some insight into how the universe worked.

Unfortunately, all I could think about was the probability I was going to have to organize a Grail quest that would be my undoing. The morning sunlight suddenly looked cold and gray to me.

As we squished back across the bog, Nurse Florence did what she could to cheer me up. "You know, Tal, what Brendan said confirms what I thought about the mutability of fate. A better solution than we can think of right now may yet present itself."

"He didn't seem to think so," I said gloomily.

"He's one saint, not God himself," Nurse Florence reminded me. "God can't have endowed him with the ability to see every possible future. Maybe we can work out a way to repress Dark Me for good and change the outcome of a Grail quest."

"Or maybe we'll lose our chance of success completely." I was determined to make myself as miserable as possible.

"I don't know, Tal," she said. "We've beaten pretty long odds before."

I suddenly realized I didn't want to talk about my grim fate any more. "Well, at least this puts to rest our discussion about the subjective nature of religion."

"Not in the slightest," said Nurse Florence with such firmness that I was caught completely off guard.

"The Order has centuries of records of supernatural visitations, and the only pattern seems to be that the one requesting divine assistance gets what he or she expects," she insisted.

"You mean—" I started.

"Yes. You got Saint Brendan because you belong to a religious tradition that still respects saints…though it's true Episcopalians don't typically expect them to be so active. A more radical Protestant might have gotten an angel or the voice of God, depending. Khalid might have gotten an angel sent from Allah. Your Hindu classmate might have gotten Vishnu. A Wiccan might have gotten the great mother goddess."

"It can't really be like that," I protested.

Nurse Florence sighed. "It may be that the higher power addresses us in ways that we can understand and appreciate, or it may be that some of us are in denial and see what we want to see, not what is truly there. I think it's safe to say that something is there, and that something cares about us. For me, that's enough for now. The next time a saint drops by, we can always ask for clarification."

I was tempted to think the last part was too flip for the occasion. I knew Nurse Florence meant well, but instead of cheering me up, she had done exactly the opposite.

Like most people I had met, I wanted to know the truth. At this point I doubted the truth would set me free, but damn it, I wanted to know it anyway!

The sky was still clear and brilliant blue, but as far as I was concerned, it might as well have been dull gray.

We still had quite a bit of time before we had to be in position to lure an unsuspecting faerie, so we moved by portal over to Knightstown and visited the Church of Saint John the Baptist—and no, I wasn't expecting him to put in a personal appearance. I don't really know what I was expecting. Maybe I was just a glutton for punishment.

The church was about 150 years old, and its weathered roofing and brick walls certainly gave it a venerable appearance. Shadowed by some of the surrounding trees but still partly lit by the afternoon sun, the house of worship suggested a peace I couldn't share anymore.

Though this was Sunday, the church was open only during the summer and at Christmas, so no one else was around. I sat down cross-legged in the grass on the shaded side of the building and tried to pray again, but I felt like Claudius in *Hamlet*: "My words rise up, my thoughts remain below. Words without thoughts never to heaven go." No matter what I did, I felt blocked.

By the time I got up, I had the beginnings of a migraine—not the best news, especially since I had never been prone to them before. Nurse Florence banished it without too much difficulty, but I could see the concern in her eyes.

"Tal, what's happening?" she asked. "You're...you're..."

"Not quite myself," I finished for her. "Aside from the fact that I feel as if disaster is creeping around somewhere nearby, waiting to strike, it's taking me more and more energy to keep Dark Me quiet."

She frowned at that. "That just shouldn't be the case. Perhaps we need to go back to headquarters—"

"We don't have the time for that," I said firmly. "I'll be all right. Maybe you could lend me a little energy, and I'll get him under control again." Merlin had told me I needed to be able to control Dark Me on my own or I would never be able to defeat him permanently, but right now I needed to take things one step at a time. We had to get the lyre back from Dubh, and we should do it now, before he moved from his current hiding place, and we lost him, perhaps forever. Nurse Florence lent me some energy without hesitation, and once I felt its warmth, the clouds within me parted a little.

Another jaunt through a portal, and we were standing on a relatively high place on the western coast of the island, Bray Tower behind us and the calm seas stretching out in front of us. I could see a couple of rocks jutting out of the ocean, but Hy-Brasil would be much farther out and not so easy to see, even for someone like me.

It was about four o'clock in the afternoon, local time, which made it about nine thirty in the morning back in Santa Brígida. Amazingly enough given the relative remoteness of the location, there was cell service, and I managed to reach Shar this time. Vanora was keeping him busy organizing the possible evacuation, but he understood immediately the importance of contacting the Olympians and promised to do so right away. I had to show him how the first time, but he was confident he could manage the trick on his own and assured me that he would call back if he ran into any trouble. Much as I would have enjoyed seeing him, Khalid, and Carla, I knew I really should be conserving my energy for the night ahead, as should Nurse

Florence, who had already done quite a few portal jumps recently. Given the situation, I was more than willing to take his word that he could get the job done. I did, however, also spend a few minutes on the phone with Carla.

"I've missed you so much!" I said lamely. She deserved better, but my poetic side seemed to be almost as beaten up as my spiritual one right now.

"And I you," she replied, her voice fuzzy with static. "Maybe Shar and I should join you. Isn't Dubh going to be hard to beat?"

"Remember, I've got his number; as long as I deafen us, he can't use the lyre's music to get inside our heads, and I can keep him at bay with White Hilt if he tries to get up close and personal."

"What if he has help?" Carla persisted.

"Dubh has always been a loner," I said reassuringly, "and he's going to be paranoid about other people being after the lyre—which they probably are. He also has to worry about being arrested by the faerie authorities, so he's got to keep a low profile. I'd be willing to bet he's alone, but if he somehow has an army with him, don't worry. We'll get out fast and bring in reinforcements."

"All right," said Carla, in a tone that even through the static suggested it was profoundly not all right. However, she knew I was going to do what I thought necessary. Besides, she'd never been anywhere near this part of Ireland, so she couldn't get here by portal on her own. And yes, I did figure that out before I called. I was afraid she'd insist on joining us, and with Vanora fading, I really wanted both her and Shar near Santa Brígida in case Nicneven decided to attack. After all, Carla was the only one nearby besides Vanora who had any magic at all.

Nurse Florence stepped discreetly away while I was telling Carla how much I loved her, coming back only after I had ended the call.

"You didn't tell her about...what we need to do to get to Hy-Brasil?" she asked.

"No, that's embarrassing enough without sharing," I said ruefully. "Speaking of which, I suppose we should work out our illusion." We spent most of the rest of the time until dark crafting a spell good enough to make even a discerning faerie truly believe she had spent the whole night making love to me. Then we watched the sunset from Bray Head and tried to ready ourselves for what could be a long wait.

"I'm going to move away a little, go invisible to make me harder for any faerie friends to spot, and summon up a little mist to hide you from any humans who might wander past. There shouldn't be too many visitors here at night, but we can't be too careful at this point. If a likely faerie visits, initiate the spell, and I'll join in."

"You want me to do anything special?" I asked.

"Sing, and put a little magic behind the words. What we need ideally is something inviting, something that will attract their attention. Make the magic low level, but make it carry beyond the sound, like a gentle ripple, as far west as you can. If there is a western faerie anywhere close, hopefully she'll sense the magic, come closer, hear the song, and we'll have her...oh, and take your shirt off," she added in a matter-of-fact tone.

"What?" I said. "Maybe if you wanted beefcake, we should have gotten Shar here."

"You'll do, I'm sure," said Nurse Florence, trying to sound professional but only barely managing to smother a giggle.

"Great!" I said, unbuttoning my shirt. "Maybe this would work better if I stripped completely."

"It probably would, but I didn't think you'd go for that," replied Nurse Florence, totally deadpan, though I was sure she was joking—at least, I hoped so.

I sat for what felt like hours—and probably was—singing and letting magic trickle toward the west. Although it was February, the climate on Valentia was mild enough to have a subtropical garden, so the salty night air on my chest felt cool but not freezing.

Finally, as the clock crept toward midnight, I saw a distant glow approaching from the west. As it moved closer, I could see it was a faerie boat with a solitary faerie woman on board. This was exactly the scenario Nurse Florence was hoping for. I wondered how disappointed she would be when I made a few revisions in the plan.

I upped both the volume and the magic, and the faerie boat picked up speed, surging impatiently toward the shore. I could now see the faerie maiden who piloted the boat almost clearly enough to make eye contact. Those eyes were green as emeralds. Her skin, pale and glowing, complemented reddish hair that cascaded clear down to her waist. Her sea-blue gown was practically translucent, her figure enough to draw any male eye in a hundred miles. I loved Carla and never wished that relationship to end. If, however, I had been free, there would have been worse things than making love to this faerie.

I floated gently down from Bray Head to the point far below where the sea caressed the land. The faerie covered the rest of the distance in under a minute, brought her boat to a stop and gazed admiringly at me.

"It has been centuries since I have found a mortal touched by magic as you are, and you...you knew a faerie would come to you here, did you not?" I nodded. "And have you come so that one of us would whisk you away to the western isles? Will you love me? Will you be my husband?"

I bowed to her. "I wish, fair maiden, that I could have such an honor, but my heart has already been given to another."

"What are you doing?" Nurse Florence, who had been monitoring my every move, yelled in my head. I ignored her.

The faerie looked at me in disbelief. "You...you do not want me? You have lured me here for some other purpose?" She tensed, ready to sail away as fast as the quickest mortal vessels.

"I mean you no harm," I insisted gently. "And I am most humbly sorry for giving you false hopes. I come to you, however, on a most grave matter. Many lives depend upon the help you can give me."

The faerie hesitated. Her disappointment was plain, but she was evidently not as prone to fits of temper as some faeries. I figured if she were still here, she might listen to me.

She'd better. I didn't have a plan B, except to try to capture her in the spell Nurse Florence and I had originally planned, and I really didn't want to do that.

"Evil is abroad in the land," I continued. "If allowed to continue growing, it will eventually become too powerful to stop. I seek passage to Hy-Brasil, where I expect to find an object of great power that may enable me to contain the evil while I still can."

"And in return for passage to Hy-Brasil, you will marry me?" asked the faerie hopefully.

"I cannot, for I have given my heart to another," I replied. The faerie looked ineffably sad, and her eyes glistened with tears.

"Then let your lady love take you where you want to go!" she whimpered. I knew she would sail back out into the sea as soon as she got control of herself.

I sank to one knee even though small waves quickly soaked me from the waist down.

"My lady, please! You could help save thousands of lives, human and faerie. You will become a heroine, remembered forever in story and song."

"Song?" she said, sniffling. "You will write me a song?" I hadn't quite meant that, but why not? The original Taliesin had given me the necessary skill, not only as a performer, but as a composer.

"Aye, if that is your wish," I agreed.

"I would much like a song," she said wistfully, "but my bed is empty. If you cannot fill it, you must find me someone who will."

"You know I cannot bring you another mortal man."

"Then again, you could provide a faerie lover," said a familiar voice behind me. I turned quickly and saw that Robin Goodfellow in stealth mode had quietly descended next to me.

"Robin, has the tribunal already acquitted you?" I asked, rising to my feet.

"Sadly, no," he said with a shrug, "but Finvarra has paroled me to help you. He and Doirend outvoted the Korrigan again, though I am bound by a *tynged* to return for trial and not to use my magic on or reveal myself to mortals. I'm more than willing, though, to reveal myself—all of myself—to this lovely maiden here."

The faerie looked him over somewhat skeptically. "The human looks as if he would be a better lover," she announced. Despite the seriousness of the situation, I had to struggle not to laugh out loud.

"His muscles are certainly bigger," agreed Robin with surprising affability, "but that is easily remedied." His body shifted like melting wax, and in moments he had transformed himself into a passable imitation of me.

"See?" he said, winking at her. "Now there's no difference."

"You do look the part," she admitted, "but human men love more vigorously than faeries. Why else would I sail so far from home in the usually vain hope of finding one?"

I expected that statement to stump Robin, but he smiled broadly at her and replied, "Sweet one, that too can be easily remedied. Taliesin, will you spare me a drop of your blood?" I must have looked surprised, because he added quickly, "I need it only to replicate you even more closely. The blood will be consumed by the spell I use, putting it beyond the reach of any who might mean you harm."

I had never heard of such a spell, and I didn't know Robin well enough to trust him, but did I really have a choice? I could travel to Cnoc Meadha to appeal to Finvarra, who would probably be happy to help, but he and the tribunal could easily be on the move, and finding them could take hours. Meanwhile, the Amadan Dubh could move on any time, leaving me no clue where he might have gone. With a faerie boat right in front of me, I needed to seize the opportunity it represented.

Despite the need for haste, I asked Robin to revert to his normal form and let me scan him physically and mentally to verify his identity. As he himself had reminded me, blood could be very useful to one of my numerous enemies, and shape-shifters were plentiful. I hadn't yet gotten to the point of burning my nail clippings or anything like that, but this particular situation did make me nervous. A brief inspection could not completely rule out a truly proficient shape-shifter, but physically he did look like the Robin I had met before, and his thoughts seemed sincere, though a bit disjointed. Such a pattern was consistent with his restless energy. Nurse Florence, observing discreetly from the top of Bray Head, confirmed my observations: as far as either of us could tell, the faerie before us was truly Robin.

Quickly I offered Robin my hand, and he pricked one of my fingers to get his drop of blood, which he then floated in the air and chanted over far longer than I would have liked. After about an hour, the blood drop, still liquid thanks to the magic, expanded into a reddish mist that surrounded Robin and then contracted until it was a thin film on every exposed piece of skin. At that point Robin shifted back into my shape, and his skin somehow absorbed the bloody film.

Yeah, gross, but the faerie maiden looked at him with new apprecia-
tion, for now he was a double for me in more than just appearance.

I should mention that shape-shifting had various degrees.
Any sorcerer skilled in illusion could assume the appearance of another, but in such a case the change was only superficial and easily
detected by anyone else who had magic. A true shifter could actually
transform the substance of his or her own body, taking on not just
the look but also the general physical structure of the creature being
imitated. In such a case the shifter acquired most physical abilities of
the new form, though not the mental ones. However, the transformed body would still differ from the creature being copied. Traces
of the original shifter body would linger at the cellular level.

Robin Goodfellow was a true shifter, but what he had used
my blood to accomplish took him far beyond the shifter norm, at
least from what I could tell. Nurse Florence, linked to me psychically,
confirmed what I thought I was seeing: so little was now left of Robin
Goodfellow that he could pass for human at the cellular level. Nurse
Florence guided me into an even closer probe, showing me that the
change now extended to the genetic level. Surely there must still have
been differences somewhere, but from what we could see, Robin was
now my physical clone. I didn't see how the faerie maiden could read
his DNA, but she was definitely seeing something different about
him—and liking it. She stepped past me to him and embraced him
passionately, her earlier objections forgotten.

"How did you do that?" I asked Robin, unable to contain
my amazement. I knew he was a good caster, but hardly good enough
to pull off something this spectacular on his own in so short a time.

"Clever, aren't I?" asked Robin, winking at me again. His
manner was somewhat different from mine, but otherwise looking at
him was disconcertingly like looking at myself in a mirror.

"Robin, spill. I know a thing or two about developing new
magic, and you haven't had time to do something this ambitious, at
least not unless you have secretly been working on it for a long time."

"Enough chatter!" said the faerie maiden, clutching Robin
more tightly. She seemed ready to lie down in the waves and let him
make love to her right there.

"My lady, you are welcome to have him if he is willing, but
first honor your deal and take us to Hy-Brasil," I insisted.

Robin pulled free from her grasp. "Yes, my lady, for though I greatly desire you, I cannot be yours until you give my friend what he needs."

"You will marry me?" she asked expectantly.

"I cannot promise that," said Robin hesitantly. "Only a short while ago you were ready to accept someone to warm your bed while Taliesin searched Hy-Brasil, and that I can do."

The faerie considered long enough to worry me that she would refuse. At last she nodded a grudging agreement, though getting her to that point required a declaration on Robin's part that his heart did not belong to another. The faerie, whose name I finally learned was Breena, seemed determined to start a permanent relationship, even if that relationship was based on my shape rather than any characteristic of Robin's. Robin did not seem the least bit put off by the situation. Evidently, he didn't have an overly large male ego. Either that, or the possibility of getting lucky was all he cared about. It seemed impossible that a faerie several hundred years old could be quite that adolescent, but stranger things had happened.

I brought Nurse Florence down from Bray Head. Breena seemed annoyed someone had been watching all along, but Robin was just amused, and she decided to follow his lead.

While she expanded the boat to comfortably fit four, I put my shirt back on, but Robin didn't bother with his.

"We are ready," said Breena, clearly eager to drop Nurse Florence and me off. We all moved into the boat, and Breena steered us away from Valentia and out toward the open sea.

"Tal," thought Nurse Florence, "You need to learn what you can about the spell he used. Being able to duplicate someone that exactly could be invaluable, especially if the knowledge that such a spell exists is not widespread."

I had never been particularly enthusiastic about shape-shifting, though I could do it if I had to. Nonetheless, I knew she was right. The day might come when someone's life might depend on my ability to successfully counterfeit someone so flawlessly.

Breena was busy steering the boat across the moonlit ocean, so striking up a conversation with Robin wasn't difficult.

"So, where did that spell come from?" I asked.

Robin smirked and brushed his hand through brown hair uncannily like mine. "Are you that sure I didn't create it myself, Taliesin? Why, I'm offended!" He had worked himself into an appropriate tone of righteous indignation, but then he giggled and ruined the effect.

"Robin, I thought you were trying to help your mistress. The more I know about everything, the better." I wasn't sure myself whether knowing the spell would help me do something for Titania, but Robin seemed to buy the reasoning.

"Oberon it was who first obtained the spell."

I immediately switched to high-alert mode. "Given what Oberon was involved in, is the spell safe?"

"I'm trying to save my mistress and myself, not curse all of us," Robin reminded me. "Of course it is safe! I have tried it before with no obvious ill effects."

"All right," I said, not entirely reassured. A quick scan, however, turned up nothing sinister about Robin except that he was still creepily like me. "Do you have any idea where he got it?"

Robin stroked his chin as he thought. I made a note not to adopt that gesture, which made me—him, whoever—look vaguely ridiculous.

"Part of it came from Olympus," he replied finally. "Titania brought it back for him. She told me she got it from Proteus."

That part certainly made sense, since Proteus was the best shape-shifter among the Olympians. As an added bonus, Proteus was genuinely not evil.

"Oberon took the original spell," continued Robin, "and collaborated with some medieval alchemist. A couple of them actually found the Philosopher's Stone, made themselves immortal, and then found that staying in the mortal world, never aging, but needing to keep their immortal a secret was…inconvenient. I think they visit your world from time to time, but long ago they found ways to reach one or more of the faerie realms.

"Be that as it may, Oberon consulted one. I was not there. I wish I had been, but by that time Oberon may already have felt the first effects of being dominated by whatever evil force had infected him and did not want anyone to know what he was up to."

Then Robin paused for an annoyingly long time. "And…" I prompted.

"Oh, I am sorry," said Robin. "I was trying to remember what little I have been able to figure out. The alchemists searched not only for ways to extend their own life spans but for ways to create new life, even human life. There are comments in their writings about hom…what's the word?"

"Homunculus?" suggested Nurse Florence.

"That is it!" answered Robin happily. "A homunculus is supposed to be a tiny human created by alchemy. I think a small number of alchemists may have actually succeeded. I do not know what it was that suggested to Oberon that some combination of shape-shifting and alchemy might enable a shifter to become an exact double of someone else, undetectable except under intense scrutiny no one would think to apply if they didn't know such a thing was possible."

I doubted Oberon could have learned about human genetics, but the alchemists who experimented with blood and semen hadn't known about DNA, either. An intuitive spell caster wouldn't necessarily have to know the underlying science to craft such a spell, though I suspected a lot of trial and error might be necessary to get the right result.

"How long does the change last?" I asked

"A few hours, though the transformation can be longer if I use more blood," replied Robin.

"It sounds as if you've been working on this for a while," I said. "How did you anticipate it would be useful?"

"Much as I would like to claim credit, one of Titania's seers suggested it might come in handy one day…though she did also warn me that if I were not careful, the darkness would swallow me."

"What?" I asked, instantly alarmed again. "That's a big warning not to have told us about before."

Robin laughed at me. "Taliesin, seers always include a dire warning with whatever advice they give. That way, if things do not work out as they predict, they can use the warning as an explanation."

"We thank you for risking so much for us," said Nurse Florence with a little bow.

"I am doing it for my mistress," Robin insisted. "She has faith you will prove her innocence."

"Well, the spell certainly came in handy in this case, but it occurs to me it may not be as useful in other situations as I at first thought," said Nurse Florence. Robin looked offended, but she pushed ahead anyway. "Most casters don't try to identify a shifter through DNA; most wouldn't even know how to do it, and the ones outside the human realm generally don't even know what DNA is. They'd be more likely to use mental rather than physical examinations. Few people can read minds in the way Tal can, but often a good caster could pick up enough to tell the shifter was an impostor. I can tell you aren't Tal by the general…Tal's friend would say 'vibe,' the vibe you put out."

"Ah, yes, but I haven't shown you the best part!" replied Robin joyfully. "I don't know how Oberon and his collaborators got this to work, but I can make my mind look like that of the person whose blood I have used."

"That can't be!" I protested. "It's not as if our blood stores a copy of our memories and thoughts."

"No, but I believe the spell creates a link between the caster and the person whose blood is being used, at least if the blood is given freely."

"I would have noticed that close a connection forming," I insisted. "I felt nothing."

Robin shrugged. "Maybe my theory is wrong. But I can prove what I say about the spell's effect. Taliesin, scan my mind." He lowered his defenses again, and I entered a mind that at first seemed just like his from my earlier examination. Then my impression suddenly became indistinct. When focus returned, I was looking…straight into my own, or at least what appeared to be mine. If I tried really hard, I could still perceive Robin's own thoughts, but they were buried deeply, probably deeply enough to fool practically anyone, even a mind reader like myself.

Nurse Florence, who had joined me inside Robin's skull, gasped audibly. In another second, I gasped as well.

Robin now had access to every piece of information I had. If he ever turned hostile, or if a hostile force ever captured him, he would be a treasure trove of information that could become an unbeatable weapon against me.

Perhaps because I was still a little inside Robin's mind, he picked up on what I was thinking. "Do not fear, Taliesin; the memories fade when the spell wears off. I have tried everything I can think of, but in every test I have been unable to remember a single bit from the person whose blood I used. Your secrets will remain yours."

"Unless someone captures you and tortures them out of you while the spell is still in force," I pointed out.

"Killjoy!" he responded with a snicker. "If you desire, I will never do this again with you."

The boat stopped with a sudden lurch. "What about what I desire?" asked Breena. Her implicit threat was obvious.

"I agreed to make love to you once, not to marry you, and you agreed in exchange to take my friends to Hy-Brasil," said Robin in the gentle tone I would have used in such a situation. In our haste we had forgotten to bind Breena with a *tynged*, but supernatural beings who weren't evil tended to honor their agreements. Breena nodded slowly, and the boat surged forward again, so apparently she followed the general pattern.

I hadn't been conscious of passing through a portal, but I could tell from the feeling of subtle sorcery in the air that we were no longer in my world. Probably the boat could pass seamlessly into the western faerie realms and from one realm to another. If so, we would be even more inconspicuous than I had hoped. I doubted that Nicneven could monitor comings and goings in all the western realms, but a portal opening near Ireland might have attracted her attention.

I noticed the boat slowing and looked out across the waves toward a mass of glimmering mist right in front of us.

"Hy-Brasil lies beyond the mist," announced Breena.

"My thanks for bringing us here. Please allow a few minutes for Nurse Florence and me to prepare for our journey," I replied. Breena, clearly anxious to start the lovemaking with Faux Me, looked irritated.

"Allow perhaps a few more, my sweet, for I wish to help Taliesin retrieve the artifact he has come for."

"You will not leave me!" insisted Breena, her irritation escalating quickly to anger. "I have settled for little enough as it is. You will not slip away and cheat me of what we agreed."

Using a combination of his own cleverness and whatever about my manner and appearance Breena liked, Robin worked out a *tynged* that bound him to return to her and fulfill his part of the bargain. She still looked unsatisfied, but at least now she wasn't angry.

"Robin, we didn't ask you to risk yourself," I said.

"You did not ask, but I offered," he replied. "Surely the Amadan Dubh with the lyre is a formidable opponent. You could always use another caster, and I'm not bad with the blade, either, if it comes to that. Besides," he continued with a grin, "seeing two of you and not being able to distinguish which one is the original may slow Dubh down a little, don't you think?"

From what little I had seen of Robin, I had been tempted to write him off as a lightweight, but his ability to master new magic so quickly was impressive, and he had a point about confusing Dubh, so I agreed to let him help us.

I linked the three of us together mentally so we could communicate smoothly during combat. Then I deafened us so that we would be immune to the magic of the lyre. Dubh had learned how to project his paralyzing touch through the lyre almost the moment he had stolen it, and I was pretty sure he must know how to do the same with the touch that brought madness and oblivion, as well as generally being able to tamper with our emotions. Deafened, however, we could not be affected physically or mentally by the lyre's music.

Catching Dubh off guard was critical, though, because there was no telling what other uses he might have found for the lyre in the several weeks of Otherworld time he had possessed it. Since Hy-Brasil was in a little world of its own, he probably wouldn't be expecting company, but we would go in with all the magical concealment we could manage woven around us. Dubh might still be able to perceive us to some extent if he was keeping careful watch, but if we moved fast enough, we could greatly reduce the chance of being detected. We would fly in at faerie speed and hit him hard with magic before he had a chance to take countermeasures. Nurse Florence was prepared to try levitating the lyre out of Dubh's hands. I would blast him with fire from White Hilt. Now that we had Robin as well, he would use the Apollo- and Hermes-blessed flute to counter anything Dubh managed to do with the lyre. The lyre was far more powerful, but Dubh, who had to fend off two simultaneous attacks, would be at a disadvantage when trying to play his music.

Our plans in place, we bid good-bye to Breena, who insisted on kissing both Robin and me goodbye. I'm not sure what she did with Robin, but let's just say I learned from her kiss that faeries know how to use their tongues, and leave it at that. I was caught by surprise, so I didn't think Carla could really hold me responsible.

After casting and checking the proper spells, I raised Nurse Florence and me up into the air and started to fly toward the mist. Robin followed us, and together we three slid through the cold, faintly glowing curtain, readying ourselves for combat.

All we had to do was defeat a mad-as-a-hatter ancient faerie with a super weapon. What could possibly go wrong?

Chapter 15: Always Expect the Unexpected (Shar)

I knew I shouldn't be enjoying myself, but walking around wrapped in an illusion that made me look thirtysomething and gave me the credibility to negotiate deals on behalf of Vanora's Carrie Winn persona—that was a real rush. I had experienced a lot in my seventeen years, but being a businessman, even if only the agent for someone else, was new. Even better, I was good at it. I wouldn't have thought my previous life as Alexander the Great would have had much to contribute in this situation, but I seemed to be able to draw on his charisma, and people instinctively responded to the aura of leadership I could project.

I worked hard, jumping from meeting to meeting with little respite. There were, however, perks. To reinforce my cover, Vanora put us up in rooms at the Four Seasons Resort Biltmore in Santa Barbara, easily one of best hotels I'd ever seen. You would think that someone surrounded by Santa Brígida's Spanish colonial revival architecture wouldn't like the Biltmore, but somehow it seemed more real than my hometown (which had, after all, been created by the witch Ceridwen as a way to lure Tal's parents into the area). The hotel managed to suggest luxury everywhere you looked, but without being obnoxious about it.

Neither Carla nor I had exactly grown up in poverty, and actually my parents probably had more money than anyone in Santa Brígida, aside from Carrie Winn. Despite our house's Spanish facade, the interior was more like a really upscale place in Teheran's highest-class neighborhood during the last years of the Shah. Even we didn't have a fountain in the garden like the Biltmore did, though. We weren't sitting practically on the beach, either, and we lacked a pool with tropical landscaping, which was easily Khalid's favorite part of the hotel experience. I made him keep his dragon armor on (made invisible by an illusion Carla wove around him), but he didn't seem to mind. He really didn't mind anything I told him to do—at least, most of the time.

My favorite part of the experience was the food. My mother was an excellent cook, but my parents liked Persian cuisine most of the time, while I liked to experiment more.

I was weighing my brunch options, trying to decide between rack of lamb and wild salmon. Either way, I'd have some of the salad with five-spice duck breast in it, with eggs Benedict on the side—hey, it was breakfast! Their pancakes were really good, too. I would eat it all while staring across Butterfly Beach and watching the waves break on the shore. Khalid would eat almost as much as I did—djinn must have had very fast metabolisms—and Carla would tease me about the amount of food I was consuming. Khalid she wouldn't bother. Hell, the kid had to eat out of garbage cans for months before destiny brought us together. Who would begrudge him his omelet, loaded with every conceivable ingredient?

Carla's joke over yesterday's dinner—I had ordered two entrees, Pacific rock fish and lamb chops, followed by a chocolate sundae—was something like, "Be careful, Shar, or your body fat will get above one percent!" which told me she had taken favorable notice of my physique. At the risk of sounding arrogant, even through one of the finely tailored suits I wore to the business meetings, what woman was not going to notice my sculpted body?

Don't get me wrong: I know Carla is Tal's girl, literally the most inaccessible unmarried female in the county, perhaps in the state. I would never make a move on her. That didn't mean I suddenly went blind when she was around. That didn't mean I didn't occasionally wake up and discover I've been having…dreams about her. You'd think I would have a girlfriend of my own by now. I didn't have any lack of girls to date, but somehow I never felt as attracted to them as I was to Carla. That told me I wasn't really in love with any of the others, so I kept looking.

My reverie was interrupted by Tal's phone call, which pulled me back to unpleasant reality. Well, not exactly unpleasant. I had experienced Olympus, after all, and I would never have met Khalid in a more mundane life, but now I had to postpone brunch and figure out how to warn the Olympians. Since Coventina's prophecy, like so many others, had no time stamp on it, the threat might be months away…or seconds.

I was pretty sure I could connect to someone on Olympus, having done it before, but just in case, Carla offered to help me by lending her energy to the attempt.

The next question was where to make the connection. I was pretty sure I needed a quiet place. I had helped negotiate rental agreements for a large number of properties on Carrie Winn's behalf, but I didn't have any of the keys yet, and it was Sunday. I didn't want to attract unnecessary attention, though I could have gotten keys if I had made enough of a fuss.

We did have our opulent hotel rooms, but I thought it was better not to risk being interrupted. A lot of people had been sleeping in on Sunday, but it was nearly ten, and even the real sluggards were starting to stir, lured back from dreamland by the promise of Santa Barbara sun, gentle waves, mimosas on the terrace, whatever.

We discussed various spots that might not be frequented on Sunday mornings, finally setting on Godric Grove in Elings Park. Carla had been there once for a wedding, so she could take us there by portal. A quick check on the Internet revealed that area wasn't booked today, and the earlier morning crowd preferred the hiking trails and baseball and soccer fields. Until later, probably afternoon, sightseers wouldn't be in the area. Godric Grove it was, then.

Khalid always wanted to go everywhere with us, but Carla convinced him to get a swim in before breakfast. She thought, probably correctly, that his presence would make it harder to concentrate. I had to agree, though the truth was I didn't like being separated from him any more than he wanted to be separated from me. If all went well, though, we'd be back in minutes.

We stepped out of the portal right on the raised, stone-lined area used for weddings. It would have been a great day for one, actually: the weather was sunny but cool, the sky was bright blue, broken by a few white, fleecy clouds. The platform was shaded by large, older trees with dark green leaves. Behind us was a great view of the surrounding area: lighter, sun-washed trees as far as I could see. As possible sites for meditation went, I could hardly have done better.

Carla linked me to her energy, and I reached out to the Olympians as Tal had taught me. At first I felt nothing, but in a few minutes, I could sense someone answering my call. Before I had heard a voice and gotten the invitation to come to Olympus. This time a full vision of Aphrodite filled my mind. Had I wanted to see any Olympian, she would have been my pick, though her beauty threw me off a little bit, and she started speaking rapidly before I could even start my warning. She was speaking in ancient Greek, but thanks to Alexander and Achilles, I had no difficulty understanding her.

"Shahriyar, thank…God…that you have reached us. It is so hard for us to communicate with a human who is not actively trying to communicate with us. We were in battle, unable to answer when Taliesin called, and by the time we were able to respond, he was pre-occupied with something else. We haven't been able to reach him since."

"He was trying to warn you—" I began.

"Yet it is we who need to warn him. Shahriyar, we can observe much more easily than we can intervene, and we have seen much Taliesin desperately needs to know. There is a traitor in your midst."

"I can't—" I started to object.

"Silence!" commanded Aphrodite with surprising sternness. "I do not know how long we may have, and it is urgent I reveal the truth. I must caution you not to reveal what I say to Carla."

"You mean—" I started again.

"It is she who is the traitor."

I tried to object, but Aphrodite's cold glare cut me off.

"She has trafficked with demons. She has sold her very soul to be with Taliesin."

"I don't—"

"Silence!" This time Aphrodite roared. "I can read love better than any. Part of her bargain is a spell so subtle that no one can detect it unless they know exactly what to look for. He will not believe you if you tell him this. You must go to Viviane and tell her.

"But that is not the extent of her pact," continued the Olympian. "She also bought herself relief from the memory of what she has done. She believes that Taliesin truly loves her, forgetful of the free will she has stolen from him.

"For so much magic, the price was more than just her own soul, though. She had to agree to give the demon use of her body when the creature needs it. She still had conscience enough to try to bargain a guarantee that the demon cannot harm any of you, but mortals can never outbargain a minion of hell. The wording of the pact does prohibit the demon from physically harming any of you, but much ill can come from nonphysical attacks, as you well know."

"When did all of this happen?" I asked, relieved to finally manage to get a word in.

"If you ponder but a moment, you will know," she replied. "Do you remember Taliesin's argument with her on Olympus when she tried to trick him into giving up on Eva by impersonating me?"

"I have heard about it," I admitted.

"Did it not seem strange to you that he so readily embraced her less than a day later?"

"It did, but my life has been pretty strange in general," I pointed out.

"You are not to blame," Aphrodite answered. "I, who know well to what extremes love can drive people, should have realized how desperate Carla had become. Alas, I failed to do so, and when Carla and the rest of you were in Annwn, the very demon who had impersonated Merlin, having still failed to complete his last assignment, whatever it may have been, tempted her, and she succumbed. When Taliesin was recovering from his fall out of the sky, you yourself let her into his tent, and that is when she struck."

"I can't believe—" I started. This time Aphrodite did not interrupt. Instead, the connection between Olympus and me was abruptly cut off. Simultaneously, I felt a hand, swift as lightning, grab Zom out of its sheath, while another grabbed my cell phone. My reflexes were about the best anyone could have...any human, that is. Still, Carla, obviously magically accelerated, had levitated out of my reach before I realized what was happening.

I sprung to my feet and stared at her hovering above me. She was some distance away, but I could still make out her inhuman expression...and the reddish glow of hellfire in her eyes was unmistakable.

Possessed! Aphrodite had been right.

"Carla, you don't want to do this," I said gently. Unless she got closer, there wasn't much I could do except talk.

"Carla may not, but I do," said the soulless voice of the demon, deep and grating. The creature used Carla's hand to crush my cell phone and contemptuously sprinkled the tiny fragments on me. Much as I liked Zom, I had to admit that some kind of ranged weapon would be nice right now.

"Here is what is going to happen," it continued, staring at me as if it wanted to grow claws and tear me to shreds with them.

"I know you can't hurt me, so don't even think about bluffing," I yelled. Maybe if I could shake its confidence, it would make a mistake I could exploit.

"Physically, no," conceded the demon dismissively, "but there are worse things than physical pain, even than death. If you defy me, you will find out. If you defy me, I will take Khalid away, and you will never see him again."

That threat stopped me cold. Carla had access to Alcina's island, which we had all seen, but she also had the ability to visit other places she had never bothered with, Alcina's little secret hideaways in other realms. Assuming the demon could take advantage of her memories and open a portal to one such place, it could shove Khalid through, close the portal, and none of us would have had any way of finding the kid again. Its threat was no idle one.

The demon had chosen to strike when the logistics of the situation left me little chance of beating it. It could fly and open portals. I could do neither. The closest person with a cell phone could be a couple of miles away, and even if I could get to one, who could I call? Vanora couldn't leave Santa Brígida without letting its defenses collapse, and even if she could, I doubted she was a match for the possessed Carla at this point. Tal and Nurse Florence were probably both somewhere in the western faerie isles by now, out of reach of any communication I might send. I knew no one else who could get to the Biltmore before the demon could. Wearing Carla's face, it could easily get Khalid to follow it through a portal.

"What do you want me to do?" I asked, trying to keep my tone neutral.

"Listen carefully," cautioned the demon. "I would exile you to one of Alcina's little hiding places right now, and I will have to before Taliesin returns, for fear he sees the truth in your mind. For at least a few hours, though, you could be very useful. You will lure Taliesin's remaining warriors out of town. You will bring them to a place that I specify. Then I will exile you all. However, I will exile you together, so you will be with Khalid, and I will exile you to a place in which you will not be harmed. If you refuse to help me, the outcome will be…quite different."

My strategic mind had gone into overdrive. The demon had presumably realized through Carla's link to me that I knew the truth. However, as far as I could tell, that link broke when the demon cut off my contact with Aphrodite. Trying to look attentive to what the demon was spouting, I reached out with all the willpower I had to reestablish that communication. I was taking a big risk. If the demon still retained some tie to my mind, it might know what I was doing, and then Khalid would be a goner. On the other hand, it was probably setting up all of us to be killed, Khalid included. It couldn't do that particular dirty work on its own, but I was betting whoever had summoned it in the first place probably could.

"If you fail at any point to follow my instructions exactly, I will exile Khalid all by himself, and you will never see him again," the demon continued. "Fail me a second time, and I will find mortals not protected by Carla's no-physical-harm guarantee, and I will rip them to bits with her hands. I will not stop until you obey."

I could hear Aphrodite's voice in my head, but just barely.

"Get me out of here now!" I half begged, half commanded.

The Olympians could not normally intervene on Earth, but one exception was their ability to bring willing mortals who were related to them into their realm. If Aphrodite could hear me, she might be able to pull me to her before the demon could react. Then she could maybe return me to the Biltmore before the demon reached it. Desperate hope, but all I had.

The demon screamed when it realized what I was doing. It tried to exile me to one of Alcina's hideaways, but Aphrodite was a hair faster, and I found myself in the misty, luminous throne room of Olympus.

I was pretty sure the demon wouldn't carry out its threat to start shredding innocent bystanders, which would pretty much end Carla's usefulness to it, perhaps even void the pact, as she would certainly lose Tal's love one way or another after that. The threat to Khalid, however, I was sure it would execute, probably in seconds.

"Send me back!" I shouted to the startled mistress of love.

Chapter 16: The Song of Creation (Tal)

I expected Hy-Brasil to be something like a typical faerie realm: mistily luminous, covered with greenery, and somehow brighter and more vivid than the everyday world. I did not expect to see a twisted landscape with colors that hurt my eyes and unsettled me, colors from the brush of a lunatic painter. There was some kind of life stretched out like ground cover below, but it was squirming more than vegetation should. It seemed best not to look too closely. I did scan enough to determine that whatever it was, it wasn't a security measure. It did seem vegetable in nature, though it was every color except green.

The Amadan Dubh had been redecorating.

We flew as fast as we could toward the center of the island, our cloaking spells gripping us tightly, hoping to preserve the element of surprise.

Unfortunately, our plan went to hell as fast as the landscape had.

The Amadan Dubh sat on a platform near the center of the island, perched on what must have originally been Braseal's throne, though its first owner would no longer recognize it. I could still tell it was gold, but the carvings on it seemed much more like something out of a Hieronymus Bosch painting than anything a faerie monarch would normally prefer. They also seemed to be moving, though, as with other aspects of the island, I tried not to look too closely.

Dubh was playing furiously, though mercifully we couldn't hear him. He stopped, however, when we were some distance away and looked right at us. So much for stealth. It took me only seconds to realize that his music had created a magic field around him that dispelled our concealment. He might still not be able to see us with complete clarity, but the closer we got, the weaker our invisibility would become.

I could read lips well enough to tell he was saying, "It took you long enough." Then he strummed a couple of chords on the lyre, my ears popped, and my hearing suddenly snapped back on.

"I have managed to figure out how to cure a few afflictions like deafness with the lyre," he said with a crooked smile. I tried to reverse the effect, but apparently the same field that was wreaking havoc with our camouflage prevented me from returning us to deafness. I should have known! One of his first projects would have been to neutralize that defense.

We might only have seconds until he paralyzed us or drove us insane. I had already had White Hilt flaming, and I shot the strongest bolt I could manage in Dubh's direction. He had obviously prepared for that move as well. He played furiously, and my fire fell far short of him. Robin starting playing the flute for all he was worth, but if what he was doing made it more difficult for Dubh to fend us off, the effect was not immediately apparent. The air around Dubh pulsed with magical energy, power that I had no doubt protected him from any attack we were likely to make. All he needed to do was make that defense temporarily self-sustaining as he had his antimagic measures, and he would be free to launch a devastating attack we could not hope to resist.

"Are you ready to talk now?" asked Dubh, raising an eyebrow.

He had us cornered, and I think he knew it. As long as we remained relatively close to him and positioned to attack, he had to keep up his defensive casting, at least until it had achieved a certain level of momentum, but if we turned and ran, he could probably fry our brains with the lyre before we could get out of earshot.

"You made me wait longer than you should have," said Dubh, his serious tone spoiled momentarily by an almost maniacal giggle.

"You knew we were coming?" I asked. Normally, I wouldn't expect a useful answer to a question like that, but Dubh was unpredictable enough to actually reveal something valuable.

"Who do you think it was who spread rumors about my location?" he asked, and winked conspiratorially in my direction. "If I had not wanted to be found, I could have hidden myself here, and no one would ever have found me."

Yeah, I should have known finding him was too easy, but I had the cold comfort of knowing that Coventina had been taken in by his ruse as well, or she would never have passed the information on to me.

"Well, we're here," I said, not bothering to cover my impatience. "What do you want?"

"Nurse Florence," I thought, *"whatever protection he has in place may not block levitation. Try to rip the lyre out of his hands if you get the chance."*

"On it!" she replied.

"No need to be rude!" chided Dubh. "I am about to offer you a better deal than you would get from anyone else."

He paused annoyingly at this point. I didn't want to give him the satisfaction of asking, so I just waited too. Eventually, the game lost its appeal for him, and he continued.

"I am ready to make a trade for the lyre."

The words fell on me like bricks. I knew there had to be a catch...but what if there wasn't? Dubh was so devious. How would I ever be able to tell one way or the other whether his offer would be sincere or just another trap?

"What would you like in exchange?" I asked. I kept watching his hands, but his strumming never faltered. If he became distracted enough that it did, I would start spraying fire again.

"Your heart, ripped freshly from your chest and still beating, delivered to me on a silver platter." Dubh performed that line with an appropriate solemn manner, but then he giggled again. I had visions of him smeared with honey and tied to an anthill.

"No, Taliesin, I wish you no ill as long as you stay out of my way. I intend to stay out of yours, but in order to do that I need something that only you can give me."

"And what would that be?" I asked with affected boredom. I knew that tone would get me a faster answer.

"The song of creation," he said as if he were a neighbor asking to borrow some milk.

"What?" I responded, my disbelief fully on display. He giggled again, and I wanted to risk diving at him. If I were fast enough, I might get my hands on his throat before he could use his paralyzing touch on me.

"You know perfectly well what. You were with God at the beginning, were you not?" It took me a few seconds to decide he was serious. He actually believed that claptrap in the *Book of Taliesin*. He and Vanora should form a club.

"Dubh, I don't know the song of creation."

His eyes narrowed. "You don't remember, more like. Stay with me a few days, and I will get that memory out of you. You just have to be willing."

"What do you want the song of creation for?" asked Nurse Florence.

"Are you a dimwit?" asked Dubh, exasperated. "What do you think I want it for? I want to create my own world."

It was a measure of how stressed I was that his plan actually made some sense to me.

"Even with the lyre of Orpheus, Dubh, you aren't going to have the power of God, or even of the angelic choir."

Dubh frowned. "I don't need a big world. A little one I think would be sufficient. Once it has come into being, I will hand the lyre over to you, and I will stay in my world from then on.

"I have experimented here a little," he said. He couldn't point, but reflexively I looked around anyway. He certainly had been!

He must have read my expression, because his tone became much more defensive. "I have never tried to create from nothing before. I had to use what was at hand, and…the magic did not work out as I expected."

I had a feeling giving him the song of creation would just give him more power to screw things up, but I decided against saying that. I contented myself with responding, "Don't believe everything you hear. I was not with God at the beginning. If someone knows what He sang as He brought the universe into being, it's not me."

"Of course, if you want to make this difficult, I am more than happy to oblige." Dubh's smirk made it hard to take him seriously, but anyone with that much power could destroy us all. As far as I could tell, Robin's playing had prevented Dubh from switching from defense to offense, but that was about all. I could feel Nurse Florence straining, but her attempts at levitation could not get through Dubh's defenses. At best, we had a standoff, but Dubh had the better long-term power supply, and he would inevitably beat us if the standoff continued long enough.

"Taliesin, as much fun as killing you would be, I still need you. The rest of your party, however…" At first I thought Dubh was trying to use the pause to make his words sound more sinister. Then I realized he had gotten a good look at Robin for the first time.

"There are two of you?" he asked rhetorically...or maybe he actually expected me to answer. Either way, Robin's disguise had exactly the effect Robin suggested it would have. Dubh could tell the other me was no mere illusion; presumably he had enchanted the area to inhibit illusions in the same way it inhibited concealments. However, he clearly didn't know about the spell Robin had used. Dubh was so surprised that his fingers faltered for just a moment. I felt his protective aura shudder, and I hit it with every ounce of fire I had. This time my attack was not deflected, but Dubh recovered in time to keep his injuries down to minor burns, though the pain almost caused him to lose control again.

Robin took the opportunity to dive straight at him, leaving Dubh with a dilemma. Judging by his confused expression, he had no idea which one of us was the real me. If he had been sure Robin was the impostor, Dubh probably could have hit him with deadly force when Robin got close enough. Not knowing who was who, Dubh couldn't take that chance, but he couldn't let Robin reach him, either.

At the last minute Dubh must have decided that risking my death was preferable to being captured by me, and he changed the music just enough to make his protective aura physical. He didn't have time to do much, but the air around him hardened enough that Robin made a very disturbing thud when he ran headlong into it. He made another thud when he hit the ground. The sound wasn't exactly like breaking bones—yeah, I was all too familiar with that sound—but I couldn't rule out serious injury to his head. My psychic link with him went offline as soon as he hit the barrier, but he could be stunned...or he could be bleeding on the brain.

Renewing my fire barrage, I sought to keep Dubh busy long enough for Nurse Florence to get to Robin. Keeping White Hilt's blast aimed at the Faerie Fool, I dropped Nurse Florence low enough for her to jump down safely. Once on the ground, she ran toward Robin's crumpled form. The ground cover from hell writhed but did not try to stop her, confirming my theory that it wasn't another defensive measure.

At least we caught one break: Robin had apparently realized what Dubh was doing and had slowed down enough to avoid injuries as bad as I feared. He was already conscious when Nurse Florence reached him, and he even managed to play a little on his flute to strengthen and speed her healing magic.

Unfortunately, they were both too near the base of the throne on which the Amadan Dubh still sat, and he knew where they were. With only me attacking, Dubh had no difficulty restoring his defenses to full power, after which he made my fire bounce back at me, not because he wanted to burn me out of the sky but because he knew I would have to evade the flames, giving him a respite from constant defense.

Once Dubh was sure I was out of position for an immediate attack, he switched to a melody whose discordant tones would haunt my nightmares for years, perhaps even clear into my next life. I did not have to guess what he was doing; from the sound, I knew he was projecting madness upon us.

From past experience I had learned that his projecting one of his touch attacks through the lyre was not as powerful as actually being touched by him would be, though this way he could attack all of us at once. Still, it would be seconds before my mind started to melt into madness. What would be the best use of those seconds?

I could have flown right at him or blasted him with fire, but I could sense he was maintaining enough defense to give either tactic a good chance of failing. Instead, I decided to take a more defensive strategy. Faster than an arrow I flew to where Nurse Florence was crouching over Robin. Grabbing his flute, I cast protection against madness around us, using the magic in the blessed instrument to amplify its effectiveness. That approach would not work indefinitely, but it might give us minutes instead of seconds. In that time Nurse Florence might be able to heal Robin enough to get him back into action. Close as we were to Dubh, the three of us might yet be able to beat him...if only my protective measures held.

A hastily cast spell, though, never worked as well as one I had time to perfect. I could still feel the music affecting my mind, though not as severely as would have been the case without any protection. Indeed, the rending rhythm would not be having much immediate effect at all, except for one thing.

Yeah, that's right: Dark Me.

It had taken me inordinate effort to keep him under control in the last few days. Now I was tired, distracted, and under attack by mind-affecting music. I could tell he was going to take advantage of this situation. Sparing what little energy I could, I grappled with him internally. If he got control, there was no telling what he would do, but I was willing to bet he would try to make a deal with Dubh.

I doubted the song of creation was really buried somewhere inside of me, but if it was, giving it to the unpredictable Dubh could lead to horrendous consequences. Letting Dark Me have the lyre of Orpheus would be almost as bad. I'd give him about a week to have the faerie rulers united against him. He'd fight back with the lyre, and the apocalyptic vision of the future I had once had would become reality.

Nurse Florence was too preoccupied with Robin to lend me any aid, and the more I had to struggle with Dark Me, the less energy I had to defend against that infernal music, which came closer to shredding my mind with each passing second. If I had not had Dubh to contend with, I might have managed to get Dark Me back under control, but I doubted I could now.

I started getting a weird kind of feedback through my once more active link with Robin. It took me a few seconds to realize just how much more unmanageable the situation had just become.

I glanced down at him and realized I was not imagining what I was getting through the link. I could see it in his eyes.

Dark Me was looking back at me from the ground.

In my wildest nightmares, I had never imagined that in duplicating my mind, Robin's spell would also duplicate Dark Me, hidden away in some subterranean recess. The cloned Dark Me had been lying low, but after the blow to Robin's head and the insanity-provoking music, this new Dark Me had made his move.

I had had many weeks of practice in fighting Dark Me. Robin, on the other hand, had never faced that kind of split personality made literal, and Dark Me had wrenched control from him in seconds, probably even before Nurse Florence reached him.

Intent on healing his body, Nurse Florence failed to notice what was going on in his mind until it was too late. He smashed her in the face with a hard punch that probably broke her nose and certainly knocked her out. I had always felt inhibited in fighting women. Dark Me apparently had no such inhibitions.

I already had to fight Dubh and the original Dark Me at the same time. I had no magic to spare to stop the now possessed Robin. I might have managed a physical attack. He was still moving slowly, and I was probably good enough with the sword to have taken his head off before he could do much about it—but then I would have killed the innocent Robin, who, despite his prankish disposition, certainly deserved better than to die for something that wasn't his fault.

"We're on the same side right now, Tal," whispered the being I decided at that moment to call New Dark Me. He might or might not have realized I was weighing the merits of beheading him, but if he knew, he ignored the whole thing. "Neither one of us wants Dubh to have the lyre. Just stay out of my way."

With that, New Dark Me shot into the air with far more speed than I thought he was currently capable of. Looking up, I saw the sickening red flash as he cast the awakening spell. It was my use of dark magic that had spawned Dark Me in the first place, and I would never use it again. Unfortunately, he had no such qualms, and since I had learned the awakening spell, though I had never used it, New Dark Me knew how to cast it.

I could sense Dubh still had some defenses up, but he was pouring much of his energy into making all of us insane, and he had never seen anything like the awakening spell, which squirmed through his protections and hit him with its full malignant force.

Generally, faeries didn't reincarnate, which meant they didn't have previous lives whose memories could be awakened, but from what I could tell, the spell kept digging around in Dubh's brain, looking for what it expected to find. Consequently, he screamed, lost all focus on his music, and dropped the lyre, his brain now more scrambled than ours.

Free of the music's insidious erosion of my mind, I did everything I could to beat back Old Dark Me, still fighting with every ounce of energy he had to take over my body. New Dark Me tried to attack me through the link between me and Robin, which I promptly severed, but that was just the beginning of my problems.

New Dark Me had the lyre, which made him automatically far more powerful than I was.

The good news was that he knew as well as I did he might just vanish when Robin's spell ran its course. Having seen the spell done, he could probably cast it, just as I could, but he couldn't do it without my blood, which meant killing me was out of the question, at least until he had found some magical way to replicate my blood without me around. Anyway, neither one of us had Dubh's innate power to paralyze or madden, so New Dark Me couldn't project either effect at me. It would take him a short time to figure out how to use the lyre to best advantage. Those seconds might be my only chance to contain him until the spell ended.

I could probably have fried him with White Hilt before he figured out how to defend himself with the lyre, but I still didn't want to kill Robin.

I figured my best bet was to fight him. He should be my exact equal in combat, but his body had taken more punishment than mine had, and Nurse Florence hadn't finished healing him. I could practically feel him bleed from renewed exertion. He was even a little dizzy from his rapid movements. If I hit now, I could get the lyre away from him and probably beat him in a fair fight.

I shot up to where the throne was, stepped over the sprawling form of the Amadan Dubh, and reached for the lyre. New Dark Me was moving slower than I was, and his hands were shaky on the instrument.

I had a moment to feel optimistic again before Dubh, apparently dazed but now conscious, reached up and grabbed my ankle. Every muscle in my body seized up simultaneously, and I fell. The only blessing was that I struck my head, knocking me out. I know, that doesn't sound like a blessing, but with me under Dubh's spell, it would have been easy for New Dark Me to recover and help his older alter ego take me over. If I was unconscious, though, Old Dark Me would be as well.

I guess New Dark Me could have hung around and waited for me to recover, but he didn't. Nor did he try to manipulate my unconscious mind to allow Old Dark Me to assume control, or so I thought anyway. When I became conscious again, after what must have been several hours, I felt no evidence of any such interference, and Old Dark Me was quiet. My sluggish brain wondered for a couple minutes why New Dark Me hadn't at least tried to unleash his elder, who would have been a formidable ally.

I rubbed the considerable bump on my head and looked around. New Dark Me was gone, as was Dubh. Unfortunately, so was the lyre of Orpheus, Robin's flute, and White Hilt.

I tried to rise and made it to my feet, but then something cold was on my ankle, and I heard a click. I looked down and realized to my horror that a manacle I had not noticed had risen magically to enchain me. Its end was buried somewhere in the stone of the platform.

I could sense the magic in the chain, but I could not fight it. Somehow it chained not only my physical body but my magic as well. I strained my hardest, but I could not cast even a weak spell. I might have broken the chain with White Hilt, but I no longer had it. I could try to call out to the Olympians, but chained in this way, I was pretty sure my signal couldn't reach them.

I didn't know how to create this kind of magic trap. New Dark Me had perhaps gotten it from Robin's memories, tortured it out of Dubh, or taken some time to figure out how to do it himself. Like me, he was unnaturally fast at figuring out new magic, and we had seen something like this once in Ceridwen's dungeon.

New Dark Me realized, just as I would have, that he couldn't very well take over my life if I could pop up at any moment. He still needed my blood, but he could come back here periodically to feed me and bleed me. If what Coventina had told us was true, he couldn't just travel here by portal, but now that he knew where the place was, he could probably pop in close by and fly here.

"Tal!" I heard Nurse Florence call. She sounded shaky and had probably just returned to consciousness herself. At least New Dark Me had not killed her or taken her hostage. However...

"Tal, I can't move!" she yelled hoarsely. "Some kind of magic chain has me!"

Well, that answered the question forming in my mind: why had New Dark Me left Nurse Florence free? Clearly, he hadn't. The only consolation was that he hadn't just killed her, which would have been easier. I knew he wasn't totally evil, but how much good was really in him remained an open question.

Assuming Nurse Florence was trapped in the same way I was, how would we ever get off this island? New Dark Me had left with Breena and would probably be more than happy to make love to her, fulfilling the conditions of the *tynged* and leaving her little reason to care what had happened to the rest of us. Given the fact that Braseal had disappeared so suspiciously and so completely, faeries stayed away from this place for the most part, kept back by a kind of superstitious dread. It might literally be centuries before anyone came exploring.

The worst part was that my friends wouldn't even know I was gone at first. At whatever point New Dark Me betrayed himself and acted like too much of a rat bastard to possibly be me, they would still think they were dealing with my body, and they would waste time trying to free me, not realizing I wasn't really there in the first place. I had confidence they would figure out what was happening eventually—well, unless New Dark Me struck first and enchanted or killed them all. The problem was that eventually might not be soon enough. Nicneven could attack any day, and if she did while New Dark Me was still successfully pretending, no one else might realize they had a potential traitor in their midst until it was too late. New Dark Me wasn't an automatic ally for Nicneven, but he might align himself with her if there were any advantage to be gained. Even if he chose to fight against her, the guys would be expecting me to have their backs. New Dark Me would only have his own back. I bet he would probably sacrifice them all to save himself if he had to.

I thrashed around futilely for a few minutes in sheer frustration, ignoring even Nurse Florence's cries.

One way or another, my friends were in dire peril, and there was absolutely nothing I could do about it.

Chapter 17: Love Hurts (Shar)

I had baffled Aphrodite completely. "You want to go back? But—" she began.

"I don't mean back where I came from," I said, wishing I could communicate telepathically. "I mean back to our hotel. Carla's demon knows I know, and Khalid's in danger. You know where our hotel is?" I realized that explanation was pretty abbreviated, but fortunately Aphrodite had been watching closely enough to know what I was talking about and where to send me.

Well, almost. I think my panic flustered her enough to throw off her aim a little. I popped back into the regular world right over the pool where Khalid was swimming. In a second I hit the water with an embarrassingly loud splash. Incredibly, Khalid was the only one nearby. The lure of brunch must have been greater than the lure of the pool to most of the hotel guests today.

When I surfaced, Khalid was right next to me. "Shar, what happened?" he asked quickly. He could tell from my unusual entrance and from my facial expression that something was wrong.

"Carla's...been possessed," I said. The rest of the explanation could wait. "Khalid, she's dangerous now. We have to get you to Olympus. You'll be safe there."

Khalid looked frightened, but he controlled himself pretty well for an eleven-year-old. Of course, he had gone toe to toe with Hades in the Underworld, so I shouldn't really have been surprised.

"Just a second," I continued. "I need to connect with Aphrodite again. Then we'll get out right away." I would have preferred to go back to the room and dry out, but the demon would never have given us that kind of time. Indeed, I could see something flying toward us, closing fast.

The demon must have been driven wild by my escape. It should have taken a portal back to the hotel. Instead it was flying in broad daylight, apparently not bothering with invisibility. Unless...something was weird. The demon's edges seemed indistinct, flickery. I wondered if my Olympian blood was kicking in and letting me see through its invisibility. Well, I could worry about that later.

"Shahriyar!" Aphrodite thought to me.

I grabbed Khalid in my arms. *"Ready to go!"* I thought back.

Carla's body was close enough to recognize, but the snarl distorting her face told me the demon was still in charge. It was already close enough to cast a spell, but it just kept coming, hellfire pulsing in its eyes. It was leaving nothing to chance.

I saw the gateway to Olympus open in front of us. Unfortunately, Aphrodite, presumably still frazzled, had miscalculated again, and though we were still in the pool, the gateway was somewhat above water level, leaving us no easy way to get to it. Without a second thought I lifted Khalid and tossed him through it. Too bad there was no one who could do the same for me.

"Shar!" The demon called to me in a voice that might have sounded like Carla if not for the unnaturally angry tone. "You will regret this defiance!"

Since I no longer had Zom's protection against magic, I knew I was in trouble, but I would never regret refusing to help that thing. Nor could I regret saving Khalid. The demon could kill me if it wanted.

The original gateway had vanished, but I could feel Aphrodite opening another one nearby that I could just swim through. It seemed unlikely, however, that I would have the extra seconds.

Sure enough, the demon raised hellfire right in front of my escape route, sending a geyser of steam shooting up from the surface of the pool. If I didn't get boiled by the water, I'd get every inch of skin burned off me by the hellfire. I suddenly remembered that if the demon hurt me, it would automatically void its contract with Carla, though in this case it could argue that I would be making the choice myself if I deliberately braved the flames. Either way, burning to death would not be my first choice—or my hundred and first. My only option was to turn and fight.

Being in the pool left me at a disadvantage, though. I couldn't close the gap between me and the demon, for example. It was keeping its distance, knowing from Carla how effective I would be in a fight. I also couldn't really run. By the time I reached one of the sides of the pool, the demon could have blocked my way…if it didn't lose patience and just fry me first. I hadn't expected such aggressive action in such an exposed location, and the demon might catch "hell" for that back home, but it was apparently determined to beat me no matter what.

Luckily or unluckily, depending upon how one looked at the situation, the demon wasn't about to harm me physically if it could help it. When I looked back to see what it was up to, I saw its eyes flash and remembered too late what that meant. My last thought as myself was that robbing me of free will through a spell should be regarded as harm and free Carla. Then I felt my whole mind melting as my flesh would have in the hellfire. Maybe that would have been a better way to go...

Suddenly, I couldn't quite remember what I had been doing. In fact, I couldn't remember much of anything, except for the most important thing: I loved Carla more than life. And there she was, waiting for me by the side of the pool! I pushed toward her like an Olympic swimmer only seconds away from gold. She smiled at me, and I tingled all over.

"Silly, did you fall in the pool?" Carla said in a mildly reproving tone.

"Want to join me?" I asked slyly, making a grab for her slender arm.

"Don't you dare!" she said, backing away. "Listen, I need you to do something for me. Go to the room and get dried off first, though."

"I need to get all this chlorine off me," I replied playfully. "Want to join me in a shower?"

"Later," she said with another smile. "Meet me on the beach in a few minutes. Oh, and remember, you still look like you're thirtysomething, so act the part."

She left the pool area before I had a chance to ask any questions. I had no idea why I looked thirty, but if she said so, I must. I remembered she had magic, so my change in appearance must have something to do with that.

I have to say maneuvering through the hotel soaking wet made it more difficult to act thirty. I got a couple of very dirty looks from the staff, but I brushed my soggy bangs out of my eyes, they recognized me, and instead of scolding me for dripping all over the interior carpeting, they asked if I needed help. I said no, made my way to the room, stripped off my clothes, took a quick shower—alone, damn it—passed over the suits in the closet in favor of something casual, and went out to meet Carla.

The stretch of beach closest to the hotel was crowded, but she gestured me toward a little less populated area. Even there, she spoke to me in tones so quiet I could barely hear her over the waves.

"Shar, we're in trouble…bad trouble. I'm going to unlock memories for you, but you will recognize them as false memories."

I staggered a little as my mind flooded with unfamiliar images. Suddenly, a whole new life was jammed into my skull—one in which Carla and I were not together!

I started to protest, but she shushed me. "We may only have a few minutes before someone is watching again, Shar. I need to explain while we are still free of any surveillance."

I nodded to show I understood, and she continued. "I've been working on restoring you to normal, but I need you to remember what I have just revealed to you, yet know it isn't real."

"Why—" I started.

"Because," she interrupted, "if our enemies know that you have found out the truth, they will immediately try to kill both of us. I need you to pretend you are still fooled, and to do that, you have to recall those false memories. Otherwise, you're going to make a mistake sooner or later."

"Who did this to me? Who messed with my mind?" Whoever it was, they were going to regret it.

"The Olympians, Shar. They're real, I'm afraid, but they aren't the benign beings in those fake memories. They are trying to break into our world. They will stop at nothing to do so, in fact.

"Only Nicneven can block them," she continued, "but she needs our help. We need to eliminate the fake friends in those memories. Right now that's Dan, Jimmie, Gordy, Stan, and Carlos in particular. Pretend you are still imprisoned in that false reality, and lure them to Godric Grove in Elings Park. I'll be waiting there to trap them on another plane of existence."

My mind seemed to be working sluggishly, as if my thoughts were swimming in molasses. "What about…Tal? He's…he's pretending to be your lover!"

Carla looked alarmed. "Stay away from him, at least for right now. Oh, and Nurse Florence and Vanora, for that matter. Remember, they all have magic, and somehow they've gotten Zom away from you." I must have looked confused, because then she added,

"Zom, your sword! It's real, too, but you don't have it right now, so it's imperative you stay away from anyone besides me who has magic. Understand?"

I nodded again, feeling stupid. I should be able to keep up with her better than this. What was wrong with me?

Carla patted me on the cheek. "Don't look so sad, Shar. Just do what I tell you, and we will get through this…together."

She kissed me, and I wished the kiss would never end. I wrapped my arms around her, taking comfort from her warmth. All too soon, she pulled away.

"Go back to the hotel now. You can call the guys from the room. Oh, and Shar…"

"Yes?" I said, feeling a little sad that we were no longer kissing.

"From now on, assume we are being spied on by magic every second, unless I tell you otherwise. Even when you are alone with me, you must pretend that we are here doing business for Vanora…and that we are just friends. You can't even whisper to me without one of our enemies finding out we have broken free. And you can't make any romantic gestures. Our lives may depend on it."

"You can count on me," I replied, but now I was really sad. I didn't know how long I could hide my feelings for Carla. I hoped I wouldn't have to do that for too long.

We said good-bye, and then, knowing I shouldn't kiss her again, I just turned and walked back toward the hotel.

I would complete my mission no matter what. Saving myself would be good, but saving Carla was what really counted. I would give my life to save hers.

As I neared the hotel, I tried to think back to our first kiss and realized I couldn't. I had a vague sense of having been together for a long time, but why couldn't I remember the details? The false memories must have been interfering. I could hardly wait to defeat the Olympians so that things would go back to the way they were.

I wondered, too, where my cell phone was. Carla must have known I didn't have it, or she wouldn't have sent me back to the hotel to call my pseudofriends. Well, that was a small problem considering what we were up against.

Everything would be OK, though. As long as Carla and I were together, that was all that mattered.

Chapter 18: You Have To Be Taller To Take This Ride (Khalid)

I knew I should have acted like a big boy now; Shar would have wanted me to. But when I realized he wasn't coming to Olympus with me, I cried and begged Aphrodite to send me back to help him.

"Shahriyar wants you to be safe, little one," she told me sadly, patting me on the shoulder.

"But he isn't safe now, is he?" I almost shouted at her. "Please let me help him! Please!"

She wouldn't budge, though, no matter how big a tantrum I threw. Eventually I stopped screaming, sat down on the floor, and just sobbed. After a while, she took me in her arms, and I felt a little better, but not much.

Finally I got Aphrodite to show me Shar. I could tell she didn't want to do even that, but she couldn't argue there was any danger in just taking a look.

At first I couldn't believe what I was seeing. Shar seemed all right, and he was talking to Carla, who didn't look possessed to me. Could he have been wrong?

Then they started kissing, and I really couldn't believe that. Carla was Tal's girl, and Shar knew that!

"How can he be doing that?" I asked Aphrodite. She was the Olympian in charge of love. She must know something about it.

Aphrodite squinted a little at the image. "Khalid, Shar is under a very powerful spell. He doesn't really know what he's doing."

"Spell? Whose spell? Carla's?" I guessed she was dangerous after all. But why did she want to betray Tal?

"That's not really Carla," replied Aphrodite slowly, clearly not wanting to tell me very much. "She has…a bad creature inside of her."

"Possessed!" I said, happy at least to have an idea what was happening. "Shar told me that."

"Yes, little one, possessed," agreed Aphrodite sadly.

"You can help them, though," I prompted.

"You know the rules," she said even more sadly. "I cannot do much of anything in your world. If Shar invokes me, I can bring him here. I can send you back. That's really about all I can accomplish right now."

We listened to their conversation, but that just made me more unhappy. Somehow, Carla's demon convinced Shar that he had to trick the guys into leaving Santa Brígida. Then she was going to send them somewhere else, somewhere they couldn't come back from!

"We have to do something!" I pleaded again. I did my best cute-little-kid-in-distress expression; at least that's what Shar called it. But you know what? It didn't work. Now I was really stuck.

"Wait, child!" said Aphrodite. "Shahriyar is leaving, and I sense the demon inside Carla is going to communicate with someone else. We might learn something from this."

I knew when to get quiet, and this was one of those times. Aphrodite somehow adjusted the vision so that I could see and hear all that she could. Now I could see darkness all around Carla. She closed her eyes, and I could hear voices.

"Why did you cast that spell?" demanded an angry woman's voice. "It's so easy to detect."

"Nicneven, I'd have much rather just burned that oaf to a cinder, but if I do that, Carla goes free, and my master wouldn't like that. This way Shar won't reveal what he knows about Carla, and he will lure Taliesin's other warriors right into my grasp, just as I wanted."

So the demon was working with Nicneven! Wow, I needed to tell Tal or someone. That sounded important.

"Asmodeus!" snapped Nicneven. "I've already arranged for your master to have the souls of dozens of my witches. By comparison, Carla's one soul cannot be the priority."

Now it was Asmodeus's turn to be angry. "Do not presume to give me orders, faerie queen! Your witches got what they bargained for, and more: they can add the powers of hell to their already formidable abilities. What more advantage do you demand? I think that perhaps you are not a worthy ally if you cannot win with all that power at your disposal!"

"You know perfectly well some of them bargained their souls to rid me of Taliesin and his band," hissed Nicneven.

"And be rid of them you shall," snarled Asmodeus in response. "The methods you must leave to me. Sell your own soul if you want to determine the battle plan yourself."

Nicneven laughed bitterly in his head. "Why should I, when I can find legions of mortals to sacrifice themselves for me? It is not the number of souls at issue here, but your ineptitude. You gave the boy back his memories. You know that isn't the way that spell is supposed to work."

I could tell Asmodeus would have howled out loud if there hadn't been people nearby. "I know more about the human heart than you ever will. The spell holds, and it will continue to hold. So will the subtle one I placed on Taliesin. By the time you attack, they will already have defeated themselves. That is, of course, unless you invite my master's wrath any further, in which case you will find you don't need to sell your own soul to taste hellfire."

Nicneven did the magic equivalent of hanging up on the demon, who opened Carla's eyes long enough to let me see a flash of that hellfire. Then the demon seemed to fade away. I was looking into Carla's eyes, and she was looking confused.

I turned to Aphrodite. "She doesn't know?"

The beautiful Olympian nodded. "As far as I can tell, when the demon leaves her, she remembers nothing."

"I have to tell someone!" I insisted. "I have to go back."

At this point an armored woman carrying a spear emerged from the mist. Her gray eyes regarded me with surprise.

"Little warrior! I had not thought to see you so soon," Athena said to me. "What brings you among us?"

If I couldn't crack Aphrodite with a tantrum, I doubted Athena would be any easier. Still, she would appreciate the need to fight.

"My lady, Tal and my other friends need help, but Aphrodite won't return me to my world."

Athena raised an eyebrow and stared at her fellow Olympian.

"Shahriyar entrusted Khalid's protection to me, and I couldn't see a safe way to send him back," explained Aphrodite. "He is even more impulsive than the others."

Athena nodded, but her stern face suggested she was not going to let the subject drop. "You did well, my sister, yet we must do something to help brave Taliesin and his warriors. To plan a good strategy, though, I need to know all that can be known. Tell me what is happening in Khalid's world."

I let Aphrodite do most of the talking. When she was done, Athena's grave expression told me even she didn't see an easy way to help us.

"I have done much reading in the holy texts of the humans," she said, "enough to know we face forces far beyond Khalid's ability to overcome. Asmodeus is a prince among demons, a deadly enemy, though at least he is bound not to harm Taliesin and the others physically. Still, nothing seems to prevent him from subverting their minds with magic to prepare for Nicneven's coming. The threat looks at least as serious as the one from which Taliesin saved us some months ago. Remember, Khalid," she said in response to my surprised look, "time passes differently here. I know it has been a much shorter time for you. However, that difference will work to our advantage now. We can prepare a strategy carefully and still be able to send you back with only a few minutes having passed in your own world."

"Send him back?" said Aphrodite in disbelief.

"Do we have a choice?" asked Athena. "How else can we send help? Fear not, however. We will send Khalid back with…what is the mortal expression? Ah, yes, firepower! We will send Khalid back with enough firepower to protect himself and hopefully make a difference for the others."

"Thank you, thank you!" I said, running over to hug first Athena and then Aphrodite.

"Now there is much to do," said Athena as she recovered from being hugged by a little kid. "Since some of it will involve magic, we will need Hermes to help us." She hurried away, returning minutes later with the Olympian messenger, who patted me on the head and then asked for all the information we had.

"Hmmm…" he said after a little reflection. "This love spell is formidable, but if what you heard Nicneven say is right, Asmodeus may have compromised it by giving Shahriyar back his memories. The spell ensures the love of its victim by wiping out most of his memories. I believe Taliesin told us as much when he was here, and I was questioning him about what he knew of magic.

"There is also another possible weakness," continued Hermes. "The spell has made Shahriyar fall in love with Carla, but she is technically not the one who cast it. It was the demon, correct?" Aphrodite and I both nodded, and Hermes smiled. "In that case I think the spell may be much weaker than normal. It was designed to make the target fall in love with the caster, not with a third party. Skillful as Asmodeus is in the ways of magic, this kind of improvising may be his undoing."

"Then we can help Shar?" I asked, barely able to contain myself.

Hermes patted me on the head again and then ruffled my hair. "Yes, young warrior, I believe we can."

"Taliesin is under a love spell as well," added Aphrodite. "We need to free him too." Hermes asked for details and then expressed confidence that that spell would be even more easily eliminated.

"The problem, though, is how can Khalid safely deliver our cure? From what you have told me, Shahriyar may pretend to care about him, but he will regard him as an enemy, and Asmodeus will know he is a threat."

"Asmodeus wants to put Khalid in some other world in which he cannot be found," agreed Aphrodite. "We cannot allow that to happen."

"Make me big!" I said abruptly, surprising even myself a little.

"You wish to be a giant?" asked Hermes. "That kind of disruption in your world would bring the wrath of God on us, I think, as well as alerting Asmodeus immediately."

"I wish to be grown up, like the rest of Tal's men," I answered. "Then I can defend myself better. You can do that, can't you?"

Hermes continued to look startled. "Truly, I do not know. I have never tried anything like that, and I would never want to experiment on a child."

"Don't you see? I'm tired of being a child, at least in times like this. The other guys don't trust me to do things because of how young I am."

"Do you really want to leave Gianni behind?" asked Aphrodite gently. "And what about Shahriyar's parents? Suppose we could make you older, as you wish. How could that be explained to them? You would have to pretend to be someone else, with a new family."

I hadn't thought of any of that, and I didn't want to leave Gianni or Shar's family.

"I'll do it," I said slowly, tearing up despite my best effort to act grown-up. "I'll do it if it's the only way."

Hermes smiled at me. "I never cease to marvel at the group Taliesin has managed to assemble. Khalid, I know you would do whatever you could to help, but you don't need to make such a sacrifice. Why not become invisible and approach Shar without being seen?"

"Asmodeus can see through invisibility," Athena reminded him. "That by itself will not be sufficient protection."

Hermes glanced at Aphrodite. "Can your husband create a weapon that would be effective against demons? A bow, perhaps. We need something with which Khalid can strike from a distance."

"With a magic aim," added Athena. "We have little time to teach him bowmanship."

"I will check at once," said Aphrodite. She came back in a few minutes not with an answer, but with soot-smudged Hephaestus himself.

Bad as the situation was, I felt good that the Olympians were all willing to help. It made me feel a little less like we were all doomed.

Those good feelings took a beating for the next few minutes, though. Hephaestus had no idea exactly how to hurt Asmodeus.

"Would not a Jewish, Christian, or Muslim relic work better?" he asked. "He appears in all three traditions, if I recall."

"We do not have any," Athena pointed out. "And since God still sees fit not to answer our prayers, I cannot imagine He is going to deliver one into our hands now."

"Then I would suggest a variation on the arrows of Eros," said Hephaestus. "Taliesin has told us the power of love seems to work against evil in general. However, if we wish them to be as effective as possible, we should send Khalid somewhere to have them blessed. I don't recall. Does Asmodeus have a special antagonist?"

"In the Book of Tobit, it is Raphael," replied Athena.

"Israfel," I corrected her with the form in the Quran. "Oh, I'm sorry," I added, not wanting to offend her.

"Israfel it is, then!" said Athena. "Where can he be found? Well, anywhere, I suppose, just as the monotheistic faiths say of God. Still, I can't escape the feeling that a specific place couldn't hurt. A number of stories speak of miracles, and many seem to be connected with certain holy places. Ah, Saint Raphael's cathedral in a place called...Dubuque. Have you ever been there, Khalid?"

I shook my head.

"Well, it matters not," she continued. "We can figure out where it is."

Now I was in a bind. "My lady, it's bad enough that I have to fake being Jewish all the time so Shar's family can pretend I'm a cousin. Half the time I forget to do my prayers when I'm supposed to, and I'm not even sure where Mecca is anymore! I'm such a bad Muslim. Now I have to pray in a Christian church? Who is going to answer me?"

Aphrodite hugged me. "You are not a bad anything, little one. Surely Allah understands and forgives."

"A minute ago you were willing to let me practice on you magic I have never before performed," added Hermes. "Surely this cannot be any more terrifying than that."

"Perhaps no one will answer," said Athena, "but you will not have lost anything by trying, will you?"

I shook my head.

"Then let us try at least." I wished I shared her confidence.

"Even with a good weapon, Khalid still needs a chance to use it," said Aphrodite. "How can we protect him long enough for him to take his shot?"

"I'd like to help," said an uncertain but familiar voice behind me.

Despite myself, I jumped at the sound. I did not have to turn around to know that Alex had entered the chamber.

Alex, short for Alexandros, used to be a student at Santa Brígida High School. That was before he accidentally invoked Ares, who was his....great-great (and several more) grandfather or something. I remembered Alex had been bullied pretty badly, and Ares manipulated him to be against us. First Ares used him to try to kill Tal. Later, Alex fought against us on Olympus and pretty much broke every bone in my body. If not for Nurse Florence, I would never have walked again. Maybe I would even have died. He hit Carla and broke most of Stan's ribs too. Ares had fed him the food of the gods mixed with Ares's blood to make him so strong even Shar couldn't beat him. After the Olympians finally won, they would have thrown Alex into Tartarus. What Ares had done to Alex kept him from going home with us, but Tal begged the Olympians to try to clear up the mess in his head instead of imprisoning him. Tal also asked if they could maybe even cure him of what Ares did so he could come home. Eventually they agreed, so I guessed Hermes and Asclepius must have been working on him.

I spoke in favor of Tal's request because Alex hadn't had any friends to support him. If I'd been left on the street, I might have grown up like him. You know what, though? That didn't mean I wanted to hang out with him. I didn't even want to turn around and look at him.

"Hi, Khalid," he said unsteadily. I still didn't turn.

"This boy cannot be trusted yet!" said Athena emphatically.

"The risk is too great," agreed Aphrodite.

"Sisters," interrupted Hermes, "I must disagree. Alexandros was willing to change. The task was difficult, but Asclepius and I have some progress healing his mind."

"Progress?" rumbled Hephaestus. "You aren't sure, then, are you?"

Hermes hesitated a moment. "I would have preferred a few more months of time, but Khalid needs help now. Let this mission be a test of Alexandros's determination to continue his change. If he fails Khalid, then let our efforts to help him be at an end, and let him be cast into Tartarus. I am sure even Taliesin would not argue for him again."

"He can go to Earth, then?" asked Aphrodite.

"We have been performing what the mortals call transfusions on him," explained Hermes, "replacing the ichor that now flows in his veins with human blood. Unfortunately, his body still creates ichor, not blood, so the effect of the treatment wears off over time. When his veins fill with ichor, he is forced back here, tied to this realm just as we are. Gradually, though, the effect of the treatments has lasted longer. He could have a few hours in the human world to help Khalid before he must return here."

Aphrodite clutched me to herself. "How can we trust Khalid with him?"

"I will swear an oath on the River Styx," suggested Alex. I still couldn't look at him.

Athena looked puzzled. "Will that work, brother?"

Hermes looked uncomfortable. "Before we started trying to cure him of being Olympian, I am sure an oath on the Styx would have bound him as it binds us. Now may be another matter. Perhaps while the human blood is in his veins, the oath will not bind him."

"I'm nearly back to all ichor again right now," said Alex. "I can feel it. When the last of the blood is gone, I will swear the oath. Even if it does not bind me after the next transfusion, I will know it will bind me again when I again revert…and I will know the consequences will fall upon me then. No Olympian has ever broken the oath and lived. Even at my most twisted, I wouldn't have been willing to die just to hurt Khalid."

"What says Apollo to this plan?" asked Athena suspiciously.

"Apollo says it is, as the mortal would say, a 'crap shoot,'" replied the radiant Olympian, who had just arrived. "Alexandros has made progress. Whether the temptations he will face when he is away from our close supervision will overcome him I cannot certainly say. The future is jumbled and hard to interpret at present. He means well now—that much I will attest."

Aphrodite continued to clutch me as if I would blow away if she did not, and Athena and Hephaestus both looked skeptical.

"Khalid?" asked Alex. "Khalid, what do you say? Can I make up for what I did to you?" His voice shook, but I was still frightened of him, even with all the Olympians around us.

"Khalid, please!" he begged. Finally I looked at him.

He wasn't the best-looking guy, even with the much more muscular body Ares had given him. Somehow his face looked mean and nerdy at the same time. I was surprised, though, to see tears rolling down his cheeks.

Alex touched my shoulder, and I pulled away. I hadn't really meant to, but I kept feeling my bones breaking as he threw me on the ground with enough force to practically crack Olympus.

"Khalid fears him," pointed out Athena, waving her spear in our general direction. "How then can he possibly support Khalid? His presence will only make Khalid weaker."

"I'm not afraid," I said, but my voice sounded small, very small, and Aphrodite tightened her grip.

"Khalid, please! I can't finish my healing without your help."

"Why should I care?" I said as loudly as I could manage. "You tried to kill me."

Alex bowed his head in shame. "I...I know I did. But Khalid, I have changed. Maybe not enough, but some. I swear if you let me go with you, I will have your back."

I saw a tear hit the ground.

"Khalid," he continued, voice squeaking, "the Olympians will never be sure I'm really better unless I can do some good in the world. They'll never trust me, and I'll be stuck here. I'll never get to see my parents again."

I thought about my father, who had beaten me and thrown me out on the street when he found out I was half djinn, and about how much I wanted to see my mother, a djinni whose face I couldn't even remember. What would I give to actually have parents? What would it be like to have parents who actually wanted me and not be able to see them?

I looked at Alex again. "How can I trust you?"

"I hear the first thing you did to Shar was steal his sword, but he forgave you." That wasn't as bad as what Alex had done, but he did have a point.

I looked at Hermes. "I will take Alex...if he is willing to swear that oath thing."

Alex fell to his knees to thank me. I still could hardly look at him, but maybe he could be of some help.

"Remember, Alexandros," said Apollo pointedly. We all looked in his direction. "Remember that the very blood that enables you to walk the earth will weaken you. In that condition you can be killed."

"My lord, I would rather be dead than leave things the way they are now," replied Alex.

I figured it was easy to say death was better, and much harder to actually die. Still, Alex did seem honest about his feelings. Not for the first time, I wished I could read minds like Tal.

Apollo actually smiled, and his smile was like a sunrise. "Alexandros, I am beginning to believe in you. I can see a future in which Khalid and the others may forgive you. Beware, though," he continued, his smile replaced by grimness, "because the day Khalid smiles at you may be the day you die."

I remembered Tal joking about Apollo being "Lord Buzzkill." As usual, Tal knew what he was talking about.

My willingness to accept Alex's help seemed to help the Olympians make the decision…all except Aphrodite, who continued to hug me protectively.

"Time is short, then," said Hephaestus. "Hermes, let us hasten to my workshop. We need both weapons and methods to break spells. We have hours of preparation ahead. How long in the mortal world before Asmodeus springs his trap?"

"As time is flowing now, about one of their hours, or about eight of ours," replied Apollo. "Shahriyar has already made the call that will lure the others to where Asmodeus waits to exile them from this world. The demon seems to have exhausted the amount of time he can spend possessing Carla for this day, so Khalid and Alexandros will have clean shot at him…if we give them good enough weapons."

"My weapons are always good enough," said Hephaestus cockily. "But to finish in time, I will need everyone's help."

Hermes turned to me. "Since Taliesin showed us how to combine our wills as one, we have discovered that we can speed magical labors, such as Hephaestus's crafting of new weapons, tremendously. However, that means we all must leave you." He tilted his head in Alex's direction. "Shall I send someone in to…keep you company?"

I didn't want to look like I was afraid of Alex, even though he made my skin crawl, and I especially didn't want to look like I needed a babysitter. "No, I'll be fine," I lied. Apollo, who had once been god of truth, obviously knew, but he said nothing. The Olympians left us quickly after that, though Aphrodite made a visible show of her reluctance to let go of me.

I immediately realized how little I wanted to be alone with Alex. My heartbeat sped up, and I wanted to just fly away for a while and come back later, after the Olympians were back. Still, if I wanted them to have faith in me and let me go help Shar, I had to act like I could handle myself. Anyway, Alex was strong, but I was fast. As long as I kept my eye on him, he couldn't really do anything to me this time.

Alex started to walk in my direction. "That's close enough!" I insisted, tense and ready to fly if I needed to.

Alex looked hurt, but he kept his distance. "Khalid, I meant what I said about being sorry and about wanting to help."

"I guess," I replied. "Trust has to be earned, though, you know."

"I hear you," he said quietly. I'd always thought that was a stupid expression, but I decided I didn't need to call him stupid. I kind of wanted to, though.

"Look," he said after a while, "I know you don't like me."

"When you became an Olympian, did you want to be the god of stating the obvious?" I answered. I knew I was being mean. I just couldn't help myself.

"I deserve whatever you feel," he said after another awkward pause. "I know I do. But it's hard sometimes. Ever since I can remember, most people treated me like my face had 'kick me' tattooed into it."

"Poor you!" I said, floating myself a little above ground, just in case he tried to charge me.

"How are my…parents?" he asked.

"Fine, I guess. Tal's the one who sees them."

He looked relieved.

"Did you think Tal wouldn't keep his promise?" I asked coldly. "He always does what he says. Not like some people."

"Doesn't he ever say anything about the conversations he has with them?"

"Sort of," I said, trying to sound bored. "Tal creates an illusion so that they think they visit you once a week in the institution. He plays you and tells them you're getting better."

"He's not lying," said Alex. "I am." I knew he wanted me to believe him. I knew I couldn't yet, but I didn't make a big issue out of it.

Can you imagine trying to make small-talk with someone you basically can't stand for about eight hours? I didn't need to imagine it, because that's exactly what I had to do. The best I could say about those hours was Alex didn't do anything threatening. By the time the Olympians came back with our gear, I felt a little less afraid of him.

Hermes was holding two vials, one of clear glass and one green. "The green is for Shahriyar, Khalid. Throw the liquid on him, and it should break the spell. The clear one is for Taliesin. Do the same for him. Aphrodite helped me brew them, so they should work."

"A key ingredient is my tears," Aphrodite explained, "one of the most powerful weapons we have ever been able to find against a love spell."

"Khalid, here is your bow, your quiver and your arrows," said Hephaestus, handing them to me. The arrows sparkled like sunlight on water. I could feel their power just from touching them. "We did what we could to make them harmful to as many evil creatures as we could, just in case. They are imbued with equal parts love from Eros, for true love can free the heart from evil; the sacred hearth fire from Hestia, for evil creatures are warded off by the power of the hearth fire; and the rays of the sun, from Helios, for creatures of darkness cannot endure the sun. The quiver can produce more arrows, but since they are so powerful, creating new ones will take time. Therefore, use them wisely. Fire only when necessary."

"Thank you," I said enthusiastically, stunned by the responsibility he was letting me have. I guess the Olympians really did trust me.

Hephaestus turned almost apologetically to Alex. "Alexandros, we had to spend so much time on the arrows that I am afraid you will have to do with what weapons we had on hand." He passed him a weird-looking sword, shiny but with a curved blade, more like a sickle. "This is Harpe, the very blade Perseus used to behead Medusa. Like the faerie swords of Taliesin's men, it will cut through pretty much anything."

"Thank you, my lord," said Alex, with a bow.

I had a weird "daymare" of Alex taking the weapon and slicing off Hephaestus's head with it. It must have just been my own fear and not a prophecy of some kind, because Alex did no such thing. Weird, though, still weird.

"That is not all," said Hephaestus, gesturing for two of the cyclopes to come forward, carrying armor and a shield. I knew these one-eyed giants were gentle craftsmen, not monsters, but I still shuddered a little at the sight of them.

"Khalid is protected from all but the strongest weapons by his dragon armor. If you are to guard him, you must be at least as well protected. Take then, this armor, forged long ago by me for Achilles. Take also this shield, also forged by me, which once belonged to Ares." Alex froze at the name of the Olympian who had used him so shamelessly. "Take it," insisted Hephaestus. "It is not infected with his current evil. In fact, it is the Ancile, the symbol that guaranteed Rome supremacy as long as Rome possessed it. Though I cannot say for certain, it might even briefly withstand hellfire." Alex took the shield, his reluctance gone...or at least hidden.

"Take also these sandals," said Hermes, handing him...could it be? Yes! Winged sandals. "Khalid can fly by virtue of his dragon armor. To guard him, you must be able to fly as well."

"Finally," continued Hermes, passing Alex a ring, gold with a pulsing ruby in its setting, "we have been working on this token for you for a while, and we did have time to complete it."

"What does it do?" asked Alex, looking big-eyed at its rhythmic glow.

"We have had no time to test it," admitted Hermes, "but in theory it should keep regenerating your human blood. It will enable you to stay in the mortal world longer, possibly several days if all goes well. Be warned, however," said Hermes sternly, "that the steady pulsing you see in the gem is the very beating of Khalid's heart. The ring will at once cease to function if Khalid should die, turning your blood to ichor and returning you to us, possibly for judgment if you were negligent in any way. We will be watching.

"Heed even more this warning," continued Hermes. "If you yourself cause Khalid's death, your human blood will turn to the most violent poison we know of, and you will die within seconds."

Alex made a point of putting the ring on immediately. "Khalid has nothing to fear from me," he said solemnly, for the first time without the slightest tremble in his voice.

"Yet all the news is not good," said Athena in the closest to a sad tone I had ever heard her use, "for neither one of you has ever been to Dubuque, and it appears we cannot send you someplace you have never been. Our limits seem to be the same as the portal spell."

"Where else might they find Raphael?" asked Aphrodite.

Athena looked at us. "Madison, Wisconsin?" We both shook our heads. "Mission San Rafael Arcángel? Saint Raphael's Church in Devon? The naval museum in Lisbon?" One by one she went through every place named after Raphael, any church he patronized, even any place there was a major piece of art portraying him. We shook our heads each time.

"I do not know where we can send you, then," Athena finally said, sounding very sad.

"There is no need to send them anywhere," said a gentle voice that still made me jump. "I am here."

We all turned toward the voice, and sure enough, there he was, white robed and glowing like heaven itself: the archangel Raphael, uh, I meant Israfel.

Chapter 19: Unexpected Rescue (Tal)

There was no question that Nurse Florence and I were royally screwed.

I had hoped that the chain shackling me to the ground might have some flaw. After all, New Dark Me had to have produced it very rapidly. Surely it could not really be 100 percent effective. There had to be a weakness, right?

Wrong! I had seen such chains in Ceridwen's dungeon, which meant that Dark Me had seen them, too. If I could see something as unusual as the awakening spell cast once and then be able to cast it myself, I shouldn't have been surprised by Dark Me's ability to recreate magic chains he had only seen once. He was as good as me because, well, he was me.

That didn't prevent me from trying everything I could think of, including, despite my aversion to shape-shifting, changing my form enough to shift the chain off my ankle. Nothing worked. I continued to be able to sense the magic in the links, but that was the only magical operation I could perform. The chain blocked everything else.

I couldn't see Nurse Florence, trapped on the ground as I was trapped on the throne platform, but we were close enough to hear each other, so I was able to verify that she was just as stuck as I was.

A terrible thought occurred to me. Since time flowed faster here than in the "real" world, what if New Dark Me forgot about that discrepancy, and Nurse Florence and I were dead of thirst by the time he came back?

"Are you serious?" thought Old Dark Me from somewhere deep inside my mind. *"You wouldn't forget that, so why would he? And if he'd wanted to kill you, you'd both be dead."* Apparently the chain did not interfere with my attempt to talk to "myself," though I figured it would inhibit any move by Old Dark Me to take over.

"Look!" Old Dark Me tried to get my attention, probably because I hadn't responded. *"If we are going to get through this, there's one thing you need to know: I'm on your side...for the moment."*

I snorted derisively. *"Since when?"*

"Since that faerie idiot cloned you—and me," he replied bitterly.

"I would have thought you would be rooting for him," I thought back. I didn't really want to talk to him, but it occurred to me I might get some insight about New Dark Me, and it wasn't as if he was taking me away from something else.

Old Dark Me sighed. *"I don't see why so many people strive to be good when apparently all it does is make them stupid. Think, Tal! What have I always wanted?"*

I didn't have to think long about that. *"Control, power!"*

"Exactly!" he replied. *"And what do you suppose he wants?"*

I had a light bulb moment. *"The same thing!"*

"You'd get a gold star for that…if it hadn't taken you so long to get there," thought Old Dark Me sarcastically. *"We both want total control, but neither one of us can have it while the other exists. You're actually less of a threat to him than I would be. You hesitated when you could have just fried him because you would have killed Robin Goodfellow in the process. I wouldn't have hesitated for a second, and then we wouldn't be in this mess."*

I decided not to argue the point, since I had 0 percent chance of getting through to him. Instead, I figured I'd try to use our differences in perspective to my advantage. Perhaps he could find a way to overcome the chain.

Unfortunately, he had no more clue about that than I did, so eventually we talked about what New Dark Me would do next.

"Dense much?" thought Old Dark Me in answer to my question about New Dark Me's intentions. *"We can assume he took the Amadan Dubh captive. Dubh was only half conscious at best, and NDM had the lyre, so there would have been no chance of Dubh just escaping."*

"Why would he care whether Dubh escaped or not?" I asked.

"Because, moron," he replied harshly, *"Dubh knows too much. In particular, he knows about the spell that can duplicate you exactly. NDM can't afford for other people to learn about that, particularly for anyone to know there are two of you running around. It would be too easy then for someone to suspect he's an impostor."*

"Why not just keep Dubh prisoner here? It's not likely anyone would find him, any more than anyone is likely to find us," I thought.

"That's actually a good question…for a change," Old Dark Me conceded. *"Something must have happened while we were unconscious that would make sense of that choice. Ah, I have it!"* he thought triumphantly. *"He used the lyre to amplify his memory wiping ability to handle even someone like Dubh, so he wouldn't be able to remember the spell or that there are now two Taliesin Weavers. Then NDM would do the same thing I would do if I were the one in charge,"* continued Old Dark Me wistfully, *"I would take Dubh and the lyre back to the faerie authorities. They will be so glad the threat of Dubh is eliminated that they will be more than happy to let NDM keep the lyre as a reward. He will use the opportunity of all that good will flowing to try to provoke action against Nicneven."*

"So you don't think he'd try to form an alliance with her?" I asked.

"Only if he had no choice," said Old Dark Me slowly. *"Remember, they have the same end game, and Nicneven isn't likely to want to share power with him any more than he wants to share it with her.*

"I'll tell you who he will form an alliance with, though," Old Dark Me continued. *"Morgan le Fay."*

I jumped at that idea. *"Why would he trust Morgan, or she him?"*

"Honestly, sometimes you act so idiotically I almost forget you are as intelligent as I am," complained Old Dark Me. *"Nicneven could at any moment throw every faerie and every witch in Scotland at us, to say nothing of her own magic. It would be foolish not to want a caster as powerful as Morgan on your side, particularly one not as squeamish about entering our world as most faeries. Also, her end game is not about total control. All she wants is Lancelot—and New Dark Me can give him to her."*

I shuddered despite myself, knowing my shadowy alter ego would feel it and laugh at it. *"Surely he won't do that to Dan?"* While my mom still had her abilities as a seer, she had discovered by accident that Dan was Lancelot reincarnated. I should have wiped that memory when I had the chance. If Morgan found out, Dan would never have a normal life again, not until Morgan was dead, or at least imprisoned forever.

Old Dark Me laughed almost maniacally at my desire to protect Dan. *"He will do that to Dan, as you should have long ago. Dan betrayed you. He kept you and Eva apart! He kept…me and Eva apart!"*

"He was thirteen, and he's apologized a thousand times since then," I pointed out. *"I'm over it. Besides, I'm with Carla now."* I shouldn't have said that last part. I knew that my relationship with Carla was a sore point with Old Dark Me.

He laughed again, even harder and more abrasively this time. *"Dumb ass! You're only with Carla because she cast a spell on you."*

I tried to stay calm. *"You know that love spell of Alcina's is so disruptive anyone who's even half paying attention will be able to spot it from a mile away. Besides, that spell produces amnesia, and I haven't forgotten anything."*

"I don't know how she did it," admitted Old Dark Me after a pause, *"but I know she did. When you were at your weakest, she did something to you, something subtle but potent. Mark my words, though: she will pay for it one day. I will see to that!"*

If Old Dark Me felt that way, I was certain New Dark Me felt the same way. The difference was, New Dark Me was running loose, perfectly capable of acting on his impulses. Dan was definitely at risk, but Carla could be in even greater danger—and I was stuck here, with no way to help her. I spent a couple frenzied minutes ridiculously trying to break the chain, giving Old Dark Me his loudest laugh yet.

"Taliesin, I had heard you were heroic," boomed a deep voice behind me, "but can you really break heavy chain with your bare hands? If so, I did not need to come."

I turned and stood as quickly as I could. Though I had one leg chained, I could still at least move my arms, and Shar had taught me some unarmed combat, but I realized immediately the stranger was not hostile.

Despite my magic senses being blocked, I could tell he was a faerie, an Irish one judging by his speech, and, like Gwynn ap Nudd, a particularly tall one, nearly seven feet. Although he wore a sparkling breast plate and carried a round shield, both bearing complicated Celtic designs and somewhat obscuring his body, I could tell he was muscled like a body builder. Actually, he made even Shar look like a lightweight. In his right hand, he clutched an enormous club, certainly bigger than what any man or ordinary faerie could wield, yet the massive muscles in his right arm did not appear to be exerting at all.

The original Taliesin had never met him, nor indeed any of the *Tuatha de Danaan*, the faerie race once worshiped as gods by the Irish, but I had no doubt I was in the presence of the Dagda, former high king, long presumed dead, and (though I had forgotten about her in all the subsequent turmoil) grandfather to Doirend, whom I had saved earlier.

"Your Majesty!" I exclaimed, making a somewhat awkward bow."

"Majesty no more," said the Dagda casually, looking around at the pulsing, multicolored disaster that had once been Hy-Brasil. "This place has suffered much since Braseal ruled it."

"Indeed it has, but my lord—"

"Not really that, either," replied the Dagda somewhat wistfully, "but let us dispense with ceremony. My granddaughter owes you a debt I intend to repay."

With that, the Dagda brought his gigantic club down on the chain with a resounding crash, breaking some of the links and cracking the great stone beneath them in the process. Getting the shackle off my ankle took somewhat more subtle tactics, but finally the last vestige of the chain was off of me, I felt my magic return, and together the Dagda and I made much quicker work of freeing Nurse Florence.

The gigantic former god made a quick bow to both of us and seemed ready to leave. "Wait!" I said quickly. "Oh Dagda, we appreciate this rescue more than we can say, but our world and Annwn both face a great threat from the north. Will you aid us in that struggle?"

The Dagda looked back at me sadly. "The time is not yet quite ripe for me to reveal that I am still alive. That time will be soon, but until then, I must remain in the shadows. I will return to aid you if I can, but I cannot pledge to do so." I thought about pushing harder on him, but I knew it would do no good. His mind was made up. He had rescued us here only because no one else was around, and, since Hy-Brasil was its own little world, it was unlikely anyone would detect his presence. I thanked him again, and he was gone as quickly as he had come.

"Nurse Florence, are you all right?" I asked, registering for the first time all the blood on her face.

"I need a few minutes to heal and clean up," she replied. "Then we should be on our way as fast as possible. There's no telling what Dark Me is up to now."

While she healed her damaged nose, I filled her in and all that Old Dark Me had said. When I got to the part about Carla, she looked at me very strangely.

"Tal, I promised I wouldn't say anything about this, but Stan and Dan had suspicions about Carla, too."

"Stan told me...yesterday, I think. I'm still a little fuzzy right now. My question is, why didn't you say anything about it?" I asked with just a little edge in my voice.

"I didn't see the need. I couldn't find any evidence you were under a spell."

"You shouldn't have scanned me without telling me." I was beginning to get a little irritated. She really should have told me everything.

"I'm sorry," she said apologetically. "The guys, Stan in particular, didn't want you to think they distrusted you—"

"Even though it seems they did," I interrupted.

"They were concerned for you," Nurse Florence said. "I think Dan at least wasn't convinced, though, even when I assured them that all was well."

"I'll have a talk with him when we get back," I said quickly.

"Tal..." she started hesitantly.

"Yes?" I asked. I should have known better than to think any potential problem could be easily dispensed with.

"There is one thing that troubles me. Tal, Dark Me has been more active lately. I mean in you; I know why he was able to take control of Robin so easily."

"So what?" I asked, just a little defensively.

"Someone whose mind is controlled or unduly influenced by another becomes more susceptible to further interference. Dark Me's greater activity is evidence that something is wrong. Your moods have seemed a little off to me as well."

"I told you," thought Old Dark Me loudly. I suppressed him as roughly as I could.

"I'm sure it's just coincidence," I assured her. "As for the moods, I've been under a lot of stress lately. Anyway, I'm a teenager. Aren't I entitled to a little angst now and again?"

Nurse Florence smiled just a bit at that. "Well, I suppose so. Just to be on the safe side, though, I want to do a more in-depth scan when the opportunity presents itself, just to be sure."

"I *am* sure," I replied, "but if it gives you peace of mind, yeah, you can do it—when we have time. I'm not sure exactly how long we were out, but New Dark Me has a considerable head start on us, and if Old Dark Me is right, his newer alter ego might even try to spring Morgan. After all the trouble we went through to keep her locked up, I really can't let him succeed."

"Agreed," said Nurse Florence quickly. "The first priority is locating and restraining...what did you call him? New Dark Me? If Old Dark Me isn't manipulating you for purposes of his own, it sounds as if Annwn is the best place to look. Gwynn's court, perhaps. Now that we're unchained, I can get us there in minutes."

It was good to be free and have a solid plan.

I just hoped this wasn't a case of too little, too late.

Chapter 20: Hanging with an Archangel (Khalid)

I was happy to see Israfel, so I couldn't quite figure out why no one else was. The Olympians had a wide range of reactions ranging from confusion to fear. As for Alex, he looked like he expected the angel to grab him and throw him into hell with one toss. I don't know if Alex knew what he was doing, but he had started to back away.

"Great Raphael," said Apollo solemnly, falling to his knees, "you honor us with your presence." The other Olympians followed Apollo's example, and so did I. Alex kept standing and looked ready to bolt at the slightest excuse.

"Rise, please," said Israfel gently. "I did not come to demand your attention. I came because Khalid and Alexandros need me, and I did not think it wise to wait until they returned to Earth. Events are moving too fast."

"You did not come then to punish us?" asked Hephaestus as he rose unsteadily. With one bad leg, he had a hard time kneeling and then getting up.

"Punish you?" asked Israfel, confused. "No."

"But then, you did not come to free us, either?" asked Athena. Every Olympian in the room looked at Israfel expectantly now that punishment was off the table.

At first Israfel did not seem to know how to respond. Finally he said, "The Almighty will enable you to travel from realm to realm again if and when He will. He has not sent me with a message for you." I couldn't read minds like Tal could, but I didn't have to; obviously the Olympians were disappointed.

Israfel saw it, too, and he smiled at them reassuringly. "I should not go beyond what my Lord has instructed me to do, but He has noticed your attempts to atone for your earlier sins, and He is pleased. I do not know whether your state will ever be exactly as it was, for humankind has changed much in the centuries in which you have been cut off from it. I think, though, that the day may come when your punishment shall be lifted."

"They have helped me and all my friends very much," I said. Everyone else seemed surprised that I had spoken. Maybe it was because I had djinn blood in me, but I didn't think of Israfel as someone to be afraid of.

Israfel smiled even more broadly. "I know they have, Khalid. So does the Almighty."

"They've been very sad, thinking that perhaps nothing they could do would ever get Allah to forgive them," I added. "If He has been pleased, why did He not send an angel to tell them so? It would have helped them to…keep up the good work."

Israfel chuckled, and his laugh sounded like bells ringing. "Khalid, Allah has to be careful. Everyone, even the Olympians, has the opportunity to do the right thing…and the wrong thing. Without that chance, there could be no free will, and if everyone was…getting a score report, let us say, from Allah all the time, people would gradually do the right thing not because they truly chose it, but only because they knew they would get in trouble with Allah otherwise. Do you understand?"

"I guess," I said reluctantly, and Israfel chuckled again. "It is said in the Hebrew scriptures that Abraham bargained with God in an attempt to save as many of the people of Sodom and Gomorrah as possible. Khalid, you have the same spirit as Abraham, and in your life you *will* save as many as possible." I couldn't help but be a little proud of Israfel's praise, but I tried not to show it.

"Time is short. Though Allah restrains Himself, His angels, and His other servants in the interest of free will, there are times when the Evil One does something that requires a little more direct response from us. I am here to give you a little help in the battle to come. Not as much as I would like to give, please understand, but enough if you use it wisely."

Israfel raised his arms, and his light shone even brighter. As he did that, my arrows sparkled even more than they had before. He was giving them the blessing Hephaestus thought they needed.

The archangel looked me in the eye. "You have the blessing you sought, Khalid, but you need to do one thing to make it work."

"What do you want me to do?" I asked eagerly.

"You know in your heart what it is," he said calmly.

Damn! Suddenly I did know.

Israfel wanted me to forgive Alex.

"I don't know how to do that," I said simply. All the pain Alex had caused me flashed through my mind. I was willing to give him a chance, but shouldn't he have to prove himself before I forgave him?

Israfel looked a little sad, and I could have sworn his light faded just a bit. "You do know how to do it, Khalid. And the moment will come when you will need that blessing on your arrows to work. You have until then to do what your heart tells you is right."

"Aren't you placing a great deal of responsibility on a child?" asked Aphrodite hesitantly.

"I am," replied Israfel sadly. "But that is at it must be if he wants Allah's blessing. So it is with the help that angels give: the person to whom we give it can either use it or throw it away. The choice is always there." He turned to me again. "Choose wisely, Khalid. Be like Abraham and save as many as you can."

"Oh, Alexandros!" he said, turning to Alex. "Your Olympian friends have already cautioned you to provide as much help to Khalid as you can. You may be in a position to protect him when nobody else can."

"I'll do whatever it takes," Alex mumbled, not looking the angel in the eye, "but what about Apollo's prophecy that the day Khalid smiles at me may be the day I die?"

"'May' is not 'will,'" replied Israfel. "There are dangers, Alexandros; you know that without my telling you. You will be safe if you remain on Olympus…but if you do that, the Olympians will never be able to trust you to leave hereafter, and you know that, too." Alex hung his head but said nothing more.

"Now I must leave you all," said Israfel, turning back to the rest of us.

"Can you not go with Khalid yourself?" asked Athena. "That way we would know no harm could befall him."

"I will be with him as much as I can," said Israfel, again sounding a little sad. "I have rules to abide by, too." His light intensified to a blinding brilliance, and when it subsided, he was gone.

"Rules!" scoffed Athena.

"Careful, sister," cautioned Apollo. "We have come too far to risk offending God now."

"Most people don't get a blessing from an archangel," I said happily, putting the whole forgive Alex thing out of my mind as much as possible. "I'm sure everything will be all right."

Then I thought of something else. "I didn't realize all of you spoke Arabic."

The Olympians looked puzzled again. "We do not," replied Apollo.

"Then how did you understand Israfel?" I asked.

"He spoke Greek," replied Athena.

"No, English," said Alex.

"Interesting," said Hermes thoughtfully. "Each one of us heard Raphael in our primary language. I wonder what he was actually speaking."

"That is a question for another time," said Athena, shifting into strategy mode. "Time is running out in Khalid's world. We must decide how best to send him back. We know of the strange magic covering Santa Brígida, and it will prevent us from sending him back there directly."

"Send us to Tal," I said without really thinking. Who else could put my information to better use?

Athena looked uneasy. "We have...lost track of him. He is in a world with which we have no experience."

"Then send us to where Shar told the guys to meet him," I suggested.

"Godric Grove? Have you ever been there?" asked Aphrodite. I shook my head sadly, realizing that meant we couldn't get there directly from Olympus.

"I've been there," offered Alex.

"Then we can use your connection with the place to send both of you there," said Athena quickly, "and indeed that seems the best plan."

"Beware, though, of poor Shahriyar," Aphrodite reminded me. "Until you break the spell, he will think you are his enemy."

"I'll break it as soon as I see him," I reassured her, "and I'll stay invisible until then. Oh," I said, looking at Alex. "Can you give him something to make him invisible? The guys will find his presence...distracting."

Hephaestus looked hesitant. "I do not think I have any articles on hand that endow the wearer with invisibility, and crafting one will take time."

"I will cast an invisibility spell on him," suggested Hermes. "It won't last long, but it should hold long enough to give Khalid time to explain the situation to Taliesin's other men."

"Yes," agreed Athena, "that will work. However, Asmodeus will be able to see either of you if you get too close, and if he suspects someone is present. I suggest both of you hover well above the ground until the moment when you strike. None of the people Shahriyar has called can fly, so I doubt Asmodeus will be watching the skies very closely."

"Uh, when the invisibility spell wears off, how am I going to be able to move around if I need to?" asked Alex. Not being used to the way Tal's guys did business, he naturally wondered what would happen if he had to walk down the street carrying a sickle and wearing winged sandals.

"We have seen enough of the enchantments on the equipment of Taliesin's men to copy them," replied Hermes quickly. "Ordinary mortals will see your garb as regular clothing and your weapon as fencing equipment."

"We need to get started, don't we?" I asked anxiously. "We have to beat Shar to the park."

"Indeed!" said Hermes. "Brothers and sisters, let us open the doorway to Godric Grove." The Olympians were getting a lot better about working with portals; they had one open in less than a minute.

I waved good-bye and flew through. Alex followed, somewhat clumsily.

"This flying is awkward," Alex complained. He looked unhappy, and I felt just a little sorry for him.

"Even Tal had trouble with flying at first," I said. "Right now, though, all you have to do is get up high enough that Asmodeus won't notice you. As soon as we have time, I'll give you some pointers."

"Thanks," he said, sounding as if he meant it, but I couldn't be sure.

Alex could really be a big help—or he could stab me in the back at the first opportunity. Only time would tell.

Chapter 21: Making the Team (Alex)

I thought flying would be a real rush, but instead it felt as awkward as my first day in freshman PE. All I needed now was a bully to laugh at me. Fortunately, there was no one flying above the park except me and Khalid. He still didn't trust me—that was painfully obvious—but at least he wasn't laughing, even though he could fly as if he had been doing it all his life.

He picked the right altitude: high enough hopefully to go unnoticed by Asmodeus, but low enough to see the guys when they arrived. Unfortunately, I didn't stop fast enough and almost ran into him. Since no one was around, he took the time to show me how to change direction, change speed, and stop more easily. For a little kid he was very skillful. I guessed he had to be in order to survive.

That thought brought on a major guilt attack. I had almost killed the little guy. I could tell myself I hadn't really meant to do it, that Ares had been manipulating me, but those defenses didn't take away the pain in my heart or the shadow of fear in his eyes when he could bring himself to look at me.

"Khalid," I began, throat tight with embarrassment, "I know it sounds lame to say, but I really am sorry."

For a long time he didn't speak or even look at me. Finally he said, "Sorry doesn't fix everything, you know."

"I know," I replied, mouth dry, skin clammy.

Finally he looked at me. "You help me save Shar and everybody else, and we'll be even, OK?"

"Thanks," I said, not knowing what else to say. I almost wanted to hug him, but I knew instinctively he'd cringe, and I couldn't take that right now.

Instead I looked below us. I know people say not to look down if you are very far up, but the sensation is a little different if you're flying. I found myself stunned by the view. I could see the ocean glistening to the south, and below us the browns and greens of Elings Park, with Godric Grove right underneath us. Just as I wondered if we were too high up to really see the guys arrive, Khalid said, "Look! They must have come together." Squinting, I could just barely make out a group entering the area. Then they snapped into sharper focus, and I realized that my Olympian transformation must have given me sharper vision than I realized.

"I don't see Shar or Asmodeus yet," continued Khalid. "With a little luck, we can get everybody else out of here before they get here. I'll go down first. You go a little lower but stay in the air. I need to explain your presence before you appear, or the guys might think you're attacking."

"OK," I said quickly. I knew he was right, but it hurt a little to think how hostile the other guys would be. Khalid was not the only one I had injured, though. I had to expect they weren't going to want me around at first.

He shot down, and I descended more gradually, drawing Harpe, just in case. Actually, I went down farther than Khalid probably wanted me to, but I figured I'd better be as close as possible if something went wrong. I had seen how fast some of these supernaturals could move, and I was pretty sure someone like Asmodeus could act fast if he wanted to.

Khalid landed on the raised area used for weddings. Though I had not seen them in months (my time), I could instantly recognize Dan, Jimmie, Stan, Gordy, and Carlos. To my surprise, there was also a girl with them. The strawberry-blond hair told me she was Eva, Tal's ex-girlfriend, but what was she doing here? I wasn't eager to see her, since I had revealed Tal's feelings about her to Oberon and gotten her kidnapped as a result. Of course, I had broken Stan's ribs and very nearly gotten him and the rest of Tal's friends killed too. I was also the reason they survived, but that was only because I was such a screwup that I had ruined Oberon and Ares's plan.

"Guys!" yelled Khalid, whose sudden appearance had startled them. "Get out of here now! Carla's possessed, and she's cast a spell on Shar."

"What?" asked Dan in obvious disbelief.

"Let me finish!" insisted Khalid. "Shar got you here so a demon called Asmodeus could send you to another world, one where nobody will be able to find you."

"How did Carla get possessed?" asked Stan.

"I think…oh, I don't really know for sure," said Khalid hesitantly. "I know she is, though; I heard a conversation between her demon and Nicneven."

"Nicneven?" echoed Gordy skeptically. It was clear the guys thought Khalid must be mistaken somehow. I wanted to back up Khalid's story, but I couldn't very well appear now. He hadn't even mentioned me yet.

"I'll explain later," Khalid replied impatiently. "The demon isn't in Carla right now, at least as far as I know, but I bet it will come with Shar. You all have to leave before they get here."

"Khalid, Shar told us to come because we needed to deal with an emergency," begin Stan.

"The only emergency is the one Carla and her demon are stirring up!" insisted Khalid. "Please believe me!"

"What's up, bro?" asked a voice I recognized all too well. I saw Shar walking toward the others even before Khalid did. The little guy spun in Shar's direction while simultaneously launching himself into the air to keep out of Shar's reach.

"Run!" Khalid shouted, but the others had known Shar for too long to really be frightened, even after what Khalid had told them.

Shar looked at the group and pretended to be puzzled. "I don't know what your problem is, Khalid, but we can talk about later. Right now we have bigger issues to discuss."

Wasting no time, Khalid threw the vial with the green potion in it at Shar—who caught it one-handed, his hand moving so fast it blurred.

I knew that Tal sometimes sped his men up to faerie levels, but Tal wasn't here, and Shar couldn't do magic himself. That could only mean one thing.

Asmodeus was already here!

I don't know if it was another result of my transformation to an Olympian, but by squinting I could make out a vague form next to Shar. The demon was invisible, but I could see through its concealment if I concentrated, just as he could see through mine if he had reason to suspect I was there.

I couldn't tell whether Khalid could see him or not, but Khalid was focused on Shar and clearly not looking around for anyone else yet.

"What's this?" asked Shar, looking down at the vial.

Rather than answering, Khalid shot one of his arrows right through the vial, shattering it and sending the potion flying in all directions. Some of it hit Shar, but whether it was enough I couldn't tell. A lot of the stuff ended up on the ground.

"What the hell?" asked Shar weakly, staggering back a step. At least enough of the green fluid must have hit him to have some effect.

The shadowy form next to him moved quickly, and a portal opened behind the group of stunned friends. They were focused completely on Shar and Khalid, oblivious to the danger behind them. All Asmodeus needed to do was cast a spell to force them backward, get them to stumble through, and then close the portal before they could recover.

Khalid hadn't had the chance to explain me to the group, but if I was going to help, I had to move now. I shot downward, aiming for Asmodeus, ready to do some damage with my sword, and hoping the demon was too preoccupied to notice my approach. I couldn't be sure he was physical enough at the moment for the sword to even touch him, but perhaps I would surprise him out of invisibility. Surely the sight of the demon would get the others to realize the danger.

A good plan—except that I hadn't had the time to really internalize Khalid's pointers about flying, and in any case the transparent demon didn't make the best target. I ended up slamming into Shar, and though I managed to avoid cutting him, I didn't strike quite far enough to hit Asmodeus, either. Well, so much for the element of surprise!

Shar couldn't see me, but his combat reflexes took over, and he threw me down hard enough to rattle my teeth, then kicked hard, hitting me in the shoulder and causing me to let go of Harpe as pain rocketed down my arm. Shar's glance suggested he still couldn't see me, but as lucky shots go, that last one was pretty good.

Weakened as I was by human blood, I was still stronger and faster than normal, and I managed to fly up, though without my sword, which now lay visible on the ground.

"We're under attack!" yelled Shar. The other guys drew their swords.

"The only danger here is Shar!" Khalid yelled back. "Watch out for him!"

"Khalid must be enchanted!" shouted Shar. "Restrain him, but don't hurt him!"

For someone who was supposedly such a good strategist, that last suggestion was actually pretty stupid. Khalid was airborne, and he was the only one there with a long-range weapon; a fighter on the ground had no hope of stopping him. I wished somebody would question whether Shar was the one controlled by magic, but everyone's eyes focused on Khalid.

"Khalid!" I yelled. "Asmodeus is to the right of Shar!" Again the kid was amazingly fast, firing another of his special arrows. Unfortunately, Asmodeus was fast too, and, warned by my shout, he jumped out of the way. The arrow exploded with bursts of love, sunlight and hearth fire when it hit the ground, but not close enough to Asmodeus to have the intended effect.

"That voice!" exclaimed Gordy. "That scumbag Alex is loose!"

My presence, which Khalid still hadn't had time to explain, was enough to convince the others that Shar's assessment was correct. However, they couldn't see me, and so the best they could do was back together, swords facing out, making themselves a more difficult target. Eva, unarmed, they placed in their center, as far away from harm as possible.

"Hermes sent Alex here to help me," said Khalid belatedly, but I read in the frightened eyes of the others that these words were too little, too late.

I think the sudden arrival of Khalid and me must have surprised Asmodeus, but he had not been idle during the last few minutes. He might have been able to shove the guys through the portal one at a time, but their current defensive posture effectively prevented that. Instead, he had raised a wind that came from nowhere and almost immediately started ripping leaves from the nearby trees. His aim had to be to force Tal's fighters through the portal. At the same time I could feel myself getting inconveniently...excited. I remembered from somewhere that Asmodeus was the demon of lust, so he must have been launching a distraction to further increase the possibility of getting everyone through the portal before they knew what hit them.

"Portal!" I screamed, buffeted by the ever growing wind that was now closer to ripping off tree branches than leaves. The group had stumbled closer to the magical doorway, oblivious to my warnings.

I struggled to come up with some way to stop Asmodeus. At the moment I couldn't see where he was, I didn't have Harpe—or any other weapon, for that matter—and the wind was making it hard for me to hover above the area.

There he was! He was still relatively close to Shar, who was looking a little dazed and hadn't yet joined the others. That partial blast of potion must have had some effect, but not enough yet to be really useful. I couldn't see Asmodeus very well, but I had to believe he was preoccupied by the dual attacks with wind and lust to be paying much attention to me.

Taking a big chance, I landed right next to Shar and used my shield to hammer the space where Asmodeus was standing. I don't think he had much material form at that point, but at least the power of the Ancile was enough to hurt him and break his concentration. The wind began to slacken, the sexual stimulation to abate—and then I got knocked aside by something that felt like claws hitting my armor. I staggered, almost fell, and Asmodeus was on me, ripping away my invisibility.

My sudden appearance caused almost as much confusion as Asmodeus's earlier tactics had. The demon withdrew from me, but the others were on me in seconds. Since they all knew me as evil, and since some very strange things had been happening, they naturally blamed me and were not about to be gentle with me. I doubted they would kill me unless they thought they had to, but they would do what they needed to do to restrain me, and then I couldn't help Khalid.

Damn it, I was not going to fail my mission in its first few minutes!

Still feeling fast and strong as an Olympian, I maneuvered my shield expertly to deflect first Dan's sword stroke, then Gordy's, then Stan's. I dodged back, forcing them to follow—and, not coincidentally, move farther away from the portal. My one problem was that I couldn't tell where Asmodeus was or what he was doing.

Khalid thudded down in front of me, putting himself between me and his friends. "Stop! Stop!" he pleaded. "He's on our side!"

I noticed Stan taking in the scene. He had as much reason to hate me as anyone, but he was also probably the most quick-witted among them. Did he realize something wasn't right?

"What's happening?" said Carla's voice, but a quick glance told me it was Asmodeus in the shape of Carla, or at least I thought it was. I could see just a little bit of shadow outlining her and a hint of hellfire in her eyes. Both of those signs could also indicate possession, but there was also something off about the appearance, something I couldn't quite put my finger on. Ah, her breasts were just a little too big, not that I would have complained under other circumstances. (I know that sounds strange, but a guy notices things like that—particularly a guy like me who had fantasized about Carla so often.)

I didn't know whether Khalid's partly supernatural heritage let him see what I was seeing. I didn't even realize until now that I could see signs of demonic presence. Just to make sure he knew what was happening, I shouted, "That's Asmodeus!"

I had maneuvered close enough to Harpe to pick it up. Gordy charged me, and our blades clashed, sending sparks shooting in all directions. I didn't want to break his sword, and fortunately its faerie nature prevented that, but I did manage to tear it out of his hand. Dan was trying to circle around behind me, so I backed up against the nearest tree to make that kind of maneuver more difficult. Since I hadn't pressed my attack, Gordy retrieved his weapon, and then all of them advanced on me. Well, all but Shar, who was still looking dazed. It was getting harder and harder to defend myself without hurting one of them and complicating the situation even more.

At that moment fake Carla used a little burst of hellfire to set the tree behind me on fire and force me into a more vulnerable position. Stan's eyes widened; he had finally put two and two together.

"Carla doesn't have fire magic!" he shouted to the others, who halted and looked at each other in confusion.

"That's not her!" I yelled, hoping that someone might listen to me now.

If no one else believed me, Khalid certainly did. One of his special arrows hit Asmodeus in the chest. I could feel the love burst even from yards away, and everyone could see the twin explosions of sunlight and hearth fire.

Asmodeus screamed and dropped the pretense of being Carla. Instead he stood before us taller than Goliath, with three heads (a bull, a ram, and a man) all of them red-eyed from the flames of hell, and all of them spitting fire. I could just make out the serpent tail behind him.

Unfortunately, Khalid had not yet activated Raphael's blessing, and so the arrow hurt Asmodeus, but did not drive him back to Hell. He yanked it out of his chest, and threw it aside, but Khalid kept up the barrage, scoring a hit with each arrow.

I had to give the guys credit for responding quickly to the new situation. They charged at the demon, busy with the arrows that were now raising clouds of smoke from its flesh. Asmodeus was tough, reputedly one of the most powerful demons, but he had made the mistake of becoming physical to impersonate Carla, and Khalid's attack had weakened him enough to hinder his shedding physicality entirely. Even so, Asmodeus looked as if it could easily slaughter virtually any group of humans. Fortunately, our specialized equipment could hurt him as no ordinary weapon could. Not only that, but, if the conversations I had overheard on Olympus were correct, Asmodeus was contractually bound not to physically harm any of Tal's men. That should put the demon king, who had expected to take them by surprise and instead had been surprised himself, in a pretty tight spot. Of course, if his survival were threatened, he might release Carla's soul to save himself, but he wasn't going to do that except as a last resort, giving us an advantage.

Asmodeus did manage to spray enough fire around to keep the guys at bay, but he could only do that in one direction at a time, so by unspoken agreement we split up. Stan, who from the gleam of his sword was now in King David mode, stood directly in front of Asmodeus, far enough back to avoid the fire, but close enough to keep drawing it. Asmodeus did not want whatever holy power entered that sword whenever Stan was David getting anywhere near Asmodeus's demonic hide, and so David kept the demon's middle, human head occupied. Carlos and Gordy drew the attention of the ram's head, Dan and Jimmie preoccupied the bull's head, and I flew around behind. Despite Asmodeus's stripping me of my invisibility, he was too preoccupied to notice my movements.

No one had told me Harpe's full history, but I had more than enough Greek myths to know that it was not just the sword that had severed the head of Medusa. Before that, it had been the sword given by Gaia, Mother Earth, to Chronos, her son, so that Chronos could defeat his oppressive father, Uranus. If this blade could wound a ruler of the gods, surely it could wound the demon king—if only I could get close enough.

The combination of distractions served me well, especially as Khalid hit the ram's head in the eye while I was sneaking up…uh, well, as effectively as one can sneak in armor, but at least the armor created by Hephaestus was much lighter than normal armor. Anyway, while the ram's head was screaming, I charged up behind Asmodeus and struck at the neck of the bull's head, cutting clear through it and causing the other two heads to scream with such intensity I feared the sound would deafen us all. The bull's head flopped to the ground, blood bubbled from the demon's neck, and he swung around to face me, spraying fire I only barely managed to deflect with my shield. His serpent tail struck at me, but the fangs bounced off my armor. However, I was less lucky with his right arm, which hit my shield with such force I fell backward.

It was then I realized I probably wasn't covered by the pact's protection of Tal's men. Fortunately, I managed to keep on my feet, shield up, as another fire blast came my way. Apparently, Asmodeus was breathing regular fire, not hellfire, at least right now, but either could burn me if I wasn't fast enough on the defensive.

The surviving heads screamed again as David's sword plunging into its back, piercing its heart. Asmodeus's momentary focus on me had given the King of Israel an opening, and he had taken it.

Asmodeus did not die immediately, but we were all over him now, and even if he had wanted to start killing the other guys, it was too late for that strategy. I took off the human head with one stroke of Harpe. Dan's sword bounced off the ram's head's neck, but Jimmie, with a skill I didn't remember he possessed, managed to shove his ice blade down the thing's throat. Blood sprayed out, the head fell sideways, the body staggered and fell, and the fight was over.

I wondered what we were going to do with the god-awful mess left over from the battle. Yes, that was a better problem than wondering how to reattach a severed arm to one of our guys, but a problem nonetheless. I knew enough about the supernatural world to know that we were supposed to keep a low profile on Earth. Glancing around at the massive carcass, severed heads, and pools of demon blood, not to mention the burned tree and the wind damage, I didn't think this was going to be an easy cleanup job…unless we could enlist the help of someone with magic.

Fortunately, part of the problem solved itself; the demon's remains dissolved quickly, leaving only a hint of sulfur to remind us that they had ever been there. The damage to the landscaping, however, remained, and the destroyed tree was one that appeared in every picture of the wedding venue, so it was not as if no one would notice.

"Is it dead?" asked Khalid as he landed.

"The body is," replied Stan, "but demons are like Olympians: you can't really kill them. If they take physical form, killing that form does slow them down, though. It will be a while before Asmodeus reenters our world."

"When did you have time to switch from physics to demonology?" asked Dan, halfway between joking and admiring.

"I made time after our close encounter in Annwn last month," Stan replied. Then looking around, he asked, "Where's Eva?"

The question hit us like a bomb. I remembered seeing Eva up until the guys moved to attack Asmodeus. I couldn't remember seeing her after that. Nor could anyone else, apparently, since something close to panic ensued. Calling Eva's name produced no answer. Looking for her produced no results, either, even though Khalid and I did a quick aerial search.

Eva was not supernatural in any way and could not possibly have gotten out of the park that fast, even by car, much less on foot.

She hadn't gotten close enough for Asmodeus to have done something to her, and we would have seen if he had. That left only one possibility: the portal.

It must had closed with the death of Asmodeus's body, but in the confusion, Eva could have stumbled into it first. We had no idea where the portal had led; based on Asmodeus's plan, we were unlikely to be able to figure it out, and at the moment, we had no one around with magic who could attempt a rescue anyway.

At first, it looked as if panic would really take over, and I realized suddenly that this must be the first major battle the group had fought without Tal. Well, for that matter without Shar, who was still standing nearby in a daze, caught between the spell and its cure.

Part of me wanted to try to calm them down, but I had the feeling they were not in the mood to listen. Fortunately, Stan took the lead.

"The important thing now is to keep calm," he said loudly enough to get everyone's attention. "None of us can open a portal, right?" He looked at me uncertainly, and I shook my head. "Then we need to find someone who can."

"Asmodeus sent Eva somewhere none of us have ever been," said Khalid quietly. "Even if we had someone who could open a portal, there'd be no way to open one to where she is."

Khalid paused for a moment, allowing his stunned friends to catch up—an astute move for such a young guy. "Even if portals worked differently, and someone could open one to a place none of us have ever been, we don't know where the portal should lead," He continued. That was a pretty good summary of how thoroughly screwed we were.

"At least she isn't in immediate danger," I pointed out.

"What do you mean?" asked Gordy in a belligerent tone. He didn't add the "scumbag," this time, but it was clearly implicit.

"On Olympus Aphrodite let Khalid view Shar and Carla, and we learned quite a bit."

"How—" Khalid started to ask.

"I was eavesdropping then," I admitted.

"Creeper," muttered Gordy.

"He was on our side," said Jimmie.

"Yeah, this time," replied Gordy pointedly.

"We don't have time for this," snapped Stan, with more command in his voice than before. Perhaps he was channeling David a little bit. "If Alex and Khalid have relevant information, let's hear it."

I looked at Khalid, who nodded to me. He had been a little overwhelmed by the whole Carla situation, and the Olympians seemed to make a point of being overprotective with him and not telling him everything. Being a smart kid, though, he knew he had some gaps, so he let me tell the story.

"Asmodeus didn't just take Carla's form. He has possessed her actual body before. That's the way he got control of Shar; while he was in Carla's body, he used Alcina's drastic love spell on him. That potion Khalid splashed on Shar was supposed to cure him, but he may not have gotten hit with enough of it."

"How was she vulnerable to possession?" asked Stan. "To take somebody with the willpower of a major sorceress would not be easy."

I cleared my throat nervously. "While Aphrodite was monitoring Carla, we got to hear a conversation between Asmodeus and Nicneven. They're working together, but what's relevant right now is that the conversation suggested Carla has sold her soul."

"Why would she do that?" asked Dan, dumbfounded.

"At a guess, Tal," I replied, trying to keep my voice neutral. "Even I know they had a big fight before you guys left Olympus. She made the deal in exchange for Tal's love. Asmodeus mentioned placing a subtle spell on him—"

"I told you!" Dan said sharply to Stan.

"We can chew on that later," said Stan nervously. "All right, Alex, how does any of this tell you that Eva is safe?"

"Carla apparently had the presence of mind in negotiating her pact to put in language preventing physical harm to any of you," I said. "To me that suggests that Asmodeus couldn't risk sending Eva to someplace dangerous. If anything happened to her as a result, couldn't that be treated as a breach of the agreement?"

"It could," conceded Stan, "though that kind of contract is notoriously tricky, and none of us actually know what it says. Where's the real Carla? When she knows Eva is at risk, she might tell us what we need to know."

"The real Carla won't do you any good," I pointed out. "Apparently she also negotiated language that caused her to forget what she had done. Aphrodite and the other Olympians believe she has no conscious knowledge of any of it. She just thinks Tal loves her."

"She's damned and doesn't know it!" said Dan. I'd never seen him look horrified before, not even when Asmodeus revealed himself, but he looked horror stricken now.

"If any of this is true," said Gordy, glaring at me.

"It is," said Khalid. "I didn't understand everything when I first heard it, but even Shar told me Carla was possessed, and I remember hearing a lot of the other stuff Alex said."

"And what's he doing here?" asked Gordy suspiciously.

"I asked for him to come," replied Khalid, surprising me a little, since I had begged him to let me come.

"Hermes told me he was making progress in getting Alex back to normal, and I figured I might need the help," continued Khalid in a solemn tone. That kid could lie like a rug, but I was grateful to him. He glanced at me, and I couldn't see the shadow of fear as much in his eyes.

"Progress!" scoffed Gordy.

"He did as much as anyone else to defeat Asmodeus…well, more actually," Stan pointed out.

"Look, I don't expect any of you to trust me right away…or ever, maybe," I said. "I don't know. I don't deserve anything from you. All I ask is that you let me help. I really want to help…and you have to admit I can. The Olympians have a way of reeling me back in any time I don't act in your best interest." Everyone looked to Khalid for confirmation, and he nodded.

"All right, so Alex is part of the team…provisionally," said Stan.

"Who died and made you king?" asked Gordy, clearly bent out of shape.

"No one…yet," said Stan. "Look, Gordy, we can't turn down the help of someone who can bench-press any three of us and hack off demon heads with the flick of a wrist. If Khalid vouches for him, that's good enough for me. Everyone OK with that?"

Even Gordy nodded reluctantly. I tried to be nonchalant, but inside I was jumping up and down.

All I had wanted before Ares corrupted me was to be part of this team. Maybe, just maybe, that could still happen.

"Let's prioritize," Stan said. "As I see it, we have four problems right now. Tal and Nurse Florence have been out of contact for hours. Shar is…well, whatever Shar is right now, and Zom is missing, so I assume Asmodeus has stashed it somewhere. There is still that thing over Santa Brígida right now that will keep us from going back and that seems to be making Vanora sick. Oh, and Carla is no longer reliable."

"She made her own bed," said Gordy. I always thought of him as more a happy-go-lucky type, not as judgmental.

"She is Gianni's sister," said Khalid. "We need to find a way to get her soul back," he added with finality.

"Uh," began Stan, with a grim look on his face.

"We'll do what we can, Khalid," cut in Dan smoothly. "Assuming she doesn't die, though, she's in no immediate danger. Eva, on the other hand, we don't know about. I say we see what we can do about her first."

"Don't we need to find Tal and Nurse Florence first?" asked Stan. "We don't have any magic, Vanora is halfway to coma, and without magic we can't recover Eva anyway."

"Perhaps the Olympians can help," suggested Jimmie. "I know they can't act in this world, but maybe they've seen enough to know where Tal is or where Eva is, or both."

Since the group had no easy way to get to its faerie allies but an expressway to the Olympians, that suggestion met with immediate approval. Implementing it, however, was a little trickier. The one with the best connection to Olympus was Shar, and he was still incapable of invoking the Olympians on his own. Any of the others, having had the hospitality of Olympus, might have made the connection with a little magic boost, but we had no magic.

"Alex, you basically are an Olympian, right?" asked Stan finally. "Can you get through?"

"Absolutely!" I said. Some of the others were nervous, but they had no real alternative at this point. Within a minute I was back on Olympus, with the others following, Khalid and Gordy bringing up the rear, steering a zombielike Shar in their wake. The same

Olympians who had sent Khalid and me off were all there, watching us anxiously.

I let Stan do the explaining, since the others had accepted him as leader in Tal's absence. The Olympians were eager to help, but their ability to do so was more limited than we had hoped.

The good news? Aphrodite applied some of her tears to Shar's eyes, and he was immediately restored. That, however, raised its own problems, since he tried to kill me the moment he saw me, and even after Hermes explained what was going on to him, he was even less willing to trust me than Gordy. Only Khalid's gentle intervention caused Shar to give grudging agreement to my presence, at least until the group could restore itself to full strength. "Then we'll see," he added in a tone that suggested he already knew what he was going to see. Well, if I could barely look myself in the mirror because of what I had done to Khalid, I could hardly blame Shar for hating me. That didn't stop me from praying to be able to change his mind, though.

With the other items on the to-do list we had much less luck. Aphrodite, who had been watching anxiously, had indeed seen Eva stumble into the portal, but she had no idea where she had gone.

"Yet all is not lost," said Hermes thoughtfully. "Apollo, surely you can offer some guidance about how the young lady can be found?"

"So far I have no insight," said Apollo sadly, "but I will continue to ponder."

"Dan, when Nurse Florence was using you as a clandestine way to communicate with Tal, she reconnected with you in a few minutes after we had been abruptly pulled into Annwn," said Stan, looking at Dan.

"True," replied Dan, "then there was a *tynged* connecting us, though."

"As, from what we have been told, Hecate can send power to Nicneven, even across worlds," observed Athena. "If anyone is magically connected to Eva, you should be able to find her through that bond, regardless of where she is."

"Yeah, but who has that kind of magical bond with her?" asked Shar.

Aphrodite glanced up quickly. "Perhaps Taliesin does."

"Wife, what do you mean?" asked Hephaestus.

"We have never been told of such a tie," Hermes pointed out.

"Men!" said Aphrodite dismissively. "Young warriors, did you not tell us the tale of how Eva was used as the focus to break that earlier love spell upon Taliesin?"

Stan nodded. "Yes, my lady, but we weren't trying to create a permanent magic bond."

Aphrodite smiled in a way that would have made roses bloom in Antarctica. "Often we do what we do not intend. All that friendship and other emotion sent to Taliesin, reinforced by the power of a Lady of the Lake and two faerie rulers, and received by his own buried love for Eva—how could that not create a permanent bond, however tenuous? To save Eva you need only find Taliesin and break the spell upon him. Once he is himself again, he will be able to find his way to Eva. Asmodeus, who understands only lust, would never realize how strong true love can be."

That brought us, however, to the final roadblock. The Olympians had no idea where Tal was, either.

"It is odd," admitted Apollo. "I see inconsistent images, not just in the future, but now as well, as if there is more than one Taliesin.

"Someone is trying to keep us from finding him!" exclaimed Gordy.

"Possibly," replied Apollo. "Certainly my vision is not clear in his case, either for his current location or his immediate future. All I can say with certainty is that finding him is crucial to your success against Nicneven."

"That answers our question about what our first priority is," observed Stan decisively.

"I agree completely," said Shar, "but is there a quick way to find Zom? I feel like I'm missing an arm when I don't have it."

Apollo chuckled. "Shahriyar, I wish I could help, but objects with that powerful an antimagic field are especially difficult to find with magic...or even with the visions of an oracle. If you know it is in a general area, you can get someone with magic to scan that area. Find a...blank spot, I think you would say, and you have found the sword."

"Thank you, my lord," said Shar, trying to keep his disappointment from showing.

"Husband," said Aphrodite, "surely we have something for this brave warrior?"

Hephaestus grinned broadly. "Shahriyar, until you find Zom, would the sword of your past self, Alexander the Great, do? We retrieved it from Babylon after his premature death. In my idle time I have added a few features."

Shar beamed. "Thank you, my lord!"

Hephaestus hobbled off, returning with surprising speed with a sword that shone like gold. "I fear this is not as great a protection as your own sword, but I have done some work with Alexander's sword in what spare minutes I have had. It has been recently blessed by Apollo, so its light will give you a greater resistance to hostile magic, though not complete protection. Like the arrows of Apollo, it can bring disease upon those you strike, and I have further enhanced it so that it can bring healing to those you tap gently. In that way it can work something like the great club wielded by…what was his name? A former Irish god, I think."

"The Dagda," said Stan, who had doubtless been reading up on Irish gods as well as on demons. If research was the answer, Stan was clearly the go-to guy.

"Yes, the Dagda," said Hephaestus with a smile, handing the sword and scabbard to Shar.

"Perhaps it would be more fitting if Shar and I traded gear," I suggested. "It seems wrong for me to carry a sword used by his ancestor, Perseus, and armor worn by his past self, Achilles."

I was trying to be nice, but Shar looked at me as I had defiled the gear by my touch. "No, keep them," he said coldly.

"Yes, keep them indeed," added Hephaestus, perhaps trying to smooth over the tension. "Shar is a great enough warrior to wield any weapon. You could use a bit more practice, and you are already accustomed to Harpe. As for the armor, I have more if any of you have a need."

Stan considered that idea for a moment. "We're really more used to the dragon armor, lighter even than that from your forge, but at the moment it's all magically cut off from us at Tal's place; only he can get to it. Well, actually, even he can't right now, because of the spell blocking us from the whole town. If we cannot recover our own, can we take advantage of your kind offer later?"

"You can indeed," replied Hephaestus. "I made a great deal over the years, and much of it we recovered in the old days, when we still could, if the original family to whom we gave it died out or became corrupted."

"What if we can't find Tal?" asked Khalid. "We don't have anyone left in our world that can do magic, and he could be anywhere, maybe even in another world."

"There is the woman called Vanora, is there not?" asked Athena.

Stan shook his head. "She's nearing exhaustion from trying to keep our town safe. I don't think we can count on her."

"We will keep looking for him," said Apollo reassuringly. "Shar and…Alex, you two are the most able to reach us, so one of you should check back every couple of hours to find out what we have seen."

Before we left, Stan made a few other arrangements, including getting a sapling to replace the tree in Godric Grove. Blessed by Persephone, it would grow to full size as soon as it was planted. Aphrodite also insisted on blessing it when she heard it would be planted right next to where marriages were performed. Though we could not restore the place to exactly what it had been before the battle, we might in some ways make it better.

I breathed a sigh of relief when we finally returned to our world. Olympus was more beautiful, but, having been pretty much a prisoner there for months, even being able to spend a little while back home felt like heaven.

We stopped first at Godric Grove to dig up the burned remains and plant the new tree, which, true to the promise of Persephone, grew immediately into a tree more or less the same size as the old one. It would not be identical of course, but the good feeling it radiated would probably be enough to distract people from looking too closely.

"Well, what's next?" asked Shar. "Wait for Apollo to find Tal for us? I've never been good at doing nothing."

"Unfortunately, we can't just do nothing," replied Stan. "We have to decide what to do with Carla."

"Save her is what we do with her!" insisted Khalid. I recalled how the little guy had pleaded for me when the Olympians had wanted to throw me into Tartarus and forget about me.

"Perhaps there is a way—" I began.

"You don't get a vote!" snapped Gordy. Shar nodded but said nothing.

"I thought we'd agreed to table arguing about Alex," said Stan slowly. "For now, he's on the team." Both Shar and Gordy looked unhappy with Stan, but apparently they were willing to swallow their discontent for the moment, since they didn't press the point.

"But," Stan said, looking at me, then at Khalid, "I don't know of any way to save someone who has sold her soul to the devil. We need to wait until we can consult someone with more direct knowledge than I can get from reading old tales. Those, as you know, aren't encouraging."

"I just did a search," said Jimmie, his face lit by the glow of his cell phone. "There are over 193,000 results for 'breaking a pact with the devil.'"

"Why go to church when you can go to Wikipedia?" said Carlos in a mock-serious tone.

Stan rolled his eyes. "These days, who knows? Maybe there could be something useful. Jimmie, will you take point on that? But what I actually meant was figuring out how to restrain her. We can't just let her run around loose if Asmodeus could take her over at any time."

"We can't exactly hold her prisoner, either," pointed out Shar.

"If she truly doesn't remember what she's done, maybe the first step is telling her," said Carlos. "If she's conscious of what's really going on, perhaps she can resist Asmodeus. She could also help us find Tal."

Stan turned to Shar. "Do you know where she is?"

"Not for sure," replied Shar. "I left her on Butterfly Beach, but I doubt she's just been standing there this whole time." He glanced quickly at his phone. "Several missed calls from her. She must be really worried by now."

"Call her back," suggested Stan. "Clearly, no weddings are scheduled here today, so let's get her to join us. This is a quiet place to talk, and if she won't believe us, we can take her to Olympus and let them straighten her out."

"Well," began Shar, "unless Asmodeus bounced back faster than we thought, in which case she could take all of us over with irresistible love spell."

Stan sighed. "That's a fair point, but I think we may have to risk it. I don't see any other alternative. As I recall, Khalid is immune, so if worse came to worst, he could fly away and get help. Alex, how about you?"

I shrugged. "I don't have any idea. As a full Olympian, I could probably have resisted for a little while, anyway, but Hermes has human blood pumping through me to keep me in this world, so it's hard to say."

"Why so glum, chums?" said a voice we had all been hoping to hear. We all turned to see Tal walking up the path toward us, confident as always, with White Hilt hanging comfortably at his side and the lyre of Orpheus in his hands. At least one of us was having a good day.

Everybody else was elated to see him. I knew his return solved a lot of problems, but I wasn't really looking forward to having another round of explanation, yet another chance for everyone who felt like it to vent about my still being evil.

Tal was smiling, but sure enough, when he saw me, his smile vanished. Shoving the lyre into his backpack, he drew White Hilt, which obediently burst into flames at his touch.

Why was nothing ever simple?

Chapter 22: Working the Con (New Dark Me)

That stupid Amadan Dubh had made a complete mess of Hy-Brasil, but using the lyre I could put enough power behind some old druidic spells to cleanse a bit of the land and cause the areas where Tal and Nurse Florence lay to produce enough clean food and water to keep them alive until I could figure out what to do with them. That task could have been complicated, but the lyre made it surprisingly easy.

Dubh I took with me. He might prove useful, and keeping him asleep through the power of the lyre was no problem. Breena was annoyed by his presence, unconscious though he was, but I assured her he would not interfere with the fulfillment of my agreement.

Satisfying Robin's contract with Breena, not to mention satisfying Breena herself, really the same thing, was a great release. I didn't want Tal to end up with Carla instead of Eva, but how I had ached for him to do Carla, or at least do someone. Damn his morality! Well, I didn't have the same constraints, and I had the wildest sex with the faerie woman that I've had in several lifetimes. Well, actually in several of Tal's lifetimes, but now that I really was Tal in more ways than one, I wasn't about to quibble over the distinction.

When at last Breena was exhausted, I had no problem persuading her to sail me back to Ireland. Opening portals in the western isles was a little tricky, and I figured there was no point in hassling with those complications. Then I bid her good-bye, making a promise to return some day. I had no intention of doing that, of course, but I got tired of hearing her pleading.

From Ireland I took Dubh via portal to Alcina's island, where I put him into what amounted to suspended animation and then buried him beneath the sand, putting wards over him powerful enough to make him undetectable to even a fairly powerful spell caster. Eventually I wanted to hand him over to Gwynn ap Nudd, but first I wanted to check on things back home, and since no one but Tal's little group and Morgan, who was still in jail, knew how to get to the island, it was a good location to stash him.

From the island I returned to Santa Brígida. Well, really I opened a portal just outside and checked. Sure enough, Nicneven's spell still shrouded the town, and I had no time to waste right now in trying to break through. I had more urgent concerns.

I wasn't sure exactly how long Tal's blood would hold up, but I was certain it would run out soon. I supposed I shouldn't have spent so much time in lovemaking, but find me a guy who wouldn't have done exactly the same thing, and I'll buy you a beer.

I should have given more thought to bleeding Tal before I left Hy-Brasil, and returning now would be tedious. Fortunately, I remembered Tal had just given blood during a blood drive at school. It wasn't hard to find the local clinic where it was being stored temporarily. Since it was Sunday, I only had to magick a couple of people to get past them and into refrigerated storage. I was drawn automatically to Tal's blood, naturally enough, and once I had that pint, I was good to go for a while, since the spell only required a few drops each time. By the time I ran out, I would have figured out a way to copy his blood accurately, eliminating the need to keep going back to Hy-Brasil—or so I hoped.

Storing it was a little more complicated, since it needed refrigeration and was kept in a relatively fragile plastic bag. With a little work, though, I managed to craft a spell that both shielded the bag from damage and kept it cold enough to preserve the blood properly. Once that was done, I slipped it into the backpack I'd shoplifted earlier—shoplifting isn't hard when, like the comic book character, The Shadow, you have the power to cloud men's minds.

The next step was finding Tal's merry little band and making sure I could fool them. I wasn't about to go to Gwynn's court, for example, if my disguise wouldn't hold up even against nonmagical people. I feared they might still be in Santa Brígida, and I would have to scheme to get them out. Fortunately, I reached out with my mind and found most of them in Elings Park for no apparent reason. Carla wasn't with them, which was fine by me. I would deal with her later, though—count on it.

The Prius was still in Santa Brígida, but who needed it? I turned invisible and flew to near where the gang was. I had been using magic pretty heavily, but with the lyre to boost my efforts, I felt far less tired than I would have ordinarily.

As I approached the gang I could sense their tension, but I wasn't worried. When they saw their fearless leader, their confidence would be restored.

"Why so glum, chums?" I said, ready to start pouring on the comfort.

Then I saw *him*—that worm, Alex. I had no idea how he had escaped from Olympus or why the guys weren't trying to fight him, but this time I wasn't going to repeat Tal's earlier mistake and let that miserable piece of garbage live.

When I was finished with him, there wouldn't be enough left to scrape off the sidewalk.

I drew White Hilt, noting with satisfaction how fast it flamed for me. Clearly Robin's spell was good enough to fool the magic within the sword.

To my disgust, Khalid threw himself in front of Alex. "Tal!" the little brat yelled. "It's all right! He's different now." Knowing Khalid was fireproof, I was sorely tempted to just blast away. Enough of the flames would lick around the kid and get to Alex. However, if I was going to steal Tal's identity, I knew I had to act like him, at least when people were watching. The Boy Scout would wait to find out what Alex was doing before killing him, so I had to do the same. Hell, the Boy Scout would find every possible reason not to kill him anyway, but I knew the guys in general hated Alex enough that I could get away with a little mayhem in this instance.

"What's he doing here?" I said, letting my voice sound suspicious, because Tal too would not have understood his presence.

"Shar got me to Olympus to save me but couldn't get away himself," explained Khalid. "He was in danger, as was everybody else, and I needed help. Hermes and Asclepius had found a way for Alex to visit our world temporarily, and they believed he had changed."

"None of us liked the idea at first," added Stan, "but Alex really did make the difference in the battle against Asmodeus."

"Asmodeus?" I said, lowering White Hilt. "I've barely been gone a day, and you had to fight a demon king. You'd better fill me in quickly. It sounds as if events are moving even faster—and in far crazier directions—than I expected."

"In order for you to understand the story," said Shar, "there is something we need to tell you...something you definitely aren't going to want to hear and may not even believe."

Stan started to object, but Dan put a hand on his shoulder. "He needs to know, Stan. Even you must see that now."

"He's not going to believe us," muttered Stan. "I tried to tell him already."

"We've got better evidence now," Dan muttered back as if I couldn't hear every word they were saying.

"Know what?" I asked. An uncomfortable silence followed, making me wish someone would man up and tell me. From Stan's comment I knew they were talking about Carla, of course, so maybe I just needed to tell them I knew already—anything to speed up this stupid conversation and get it over with.

Then I noticed Khalid pulling out a vial of clear liquid, and that seemed strange.

"What you got there, Khalid?" I asked, trying to sound as much like Tal as possible, which in case meant sounding less annoyed with the kid than I actually felt.

"It's a potion Hermes gave me to take a spell off you," the half djinn replied nervously.

Bingo! So it wasn't just Stan and Dan anymore; the whole gang that couldn't shoot straight had finally figured out about Carla. I couldn't see why they hadn't reached the conclusion I was under a spell a long time ago. Clearly, they weren't as talented as Tal thought they were.

"Guys, I already know about Carla," I said, partly for the pleasure of seeing their amazement.

"But how—" began Carlos.

"Nurse Florence noticed the spell on me while we were away," I lied. "Once she knew it was there, it was easy enough to remove. I'm free again."

"Where is Nurse Florence, by the way?" asked Dan.

"She's at the headquarters of her Order," I lied again. "There was a big problem. Nicneven had one of her witches infiltrate, and the Order is weaker than we thought these days. Nurse Florence is helping Coventina, the leader over there, strengthen the defenses."

"I hope she comes back soon," said Jimmie sadly. "I think we're really going to need her."

"Especially without Carla," agreed Dan. "By the way, Tal, we were just discussing what to do with her."

"Take her to Olympus and let the Olympians throw her into Tartarus," I suggested without thinking. After all, the bitch had betrayed me. As soon as the words were out of my mouth, though, I realized had badly I had screwed up. The Boy Scout wouldn't want Carla in Tartarus —or Hell, for that matter. I'd bet he'd even find some way to make the situation his fault.

I looked around at their shocked expressions. Even Alex looked shocked, and he certainly didn't have a right to be.

"I…I'm sorry," I said, feigning confusion. "I'm still a little raw from the removal of the spell. Nurse Florence said I might be pretty emotional for a few days, maybe react too strongly." That explanation would hopefully give me a little latitude, at least for a short time. The goody-two-shoes routine was already giving me a headache. God, I needed a beer! Of course, the Boy Scout didn't have a fake ID or anything, but when you can control people's minds, you don't really need one.

"Are you going to be all right?" asked Stan sympathetically. I wanted to smack him. Clearly, he was implying that maybe I wasn't able to take the lead. I'm sure the little nerd was getting off on being in charge and didn't want me back quite so soon.

"Stan, I'll be fine. If I can handle Dark Me, I can handle this." Yeah, I smirked inwardly over the nice irony.

"The question remains," nagged Dan. "What do we do with Carla?"

The gang proceeded to give me an overly long-winded explanation of how Carla could be possessed by Asmodeus.

"Nicneven could attack any day," I pointed out. "The move against the Ladies of the Lake suggests she intends to come after us soon. She wouldn't have attacked anyone so directly if her plans weren't about to come to fruition. If, as you say, Asmodeus and Nicneven are working together, then we have to get Carla away from us. Otherwise, she could turn on us at any moment."

"Just until we find a way to save her, though, right?" asked Khalid. I swear, the kid was so sweet, he was making my teeth decay.

"We'll do our best, Khalid," I said, trying to imitate Tal's reassuring older-brother routine. "Right now, though, we need to prevent her from being used as a tool by our enemies. She doesn't know I'm free of her control—"

"She doesn't even know you're under her control in the first place," Shar reminded me.

"All the better," I said. "Get her here, and I'll put her to sleep." I held up the lyre for emphasis. "Now that I've recovered this little trinket, she won't be able to resist my magic."

They had to agree that plan sounded reasonable. Of course, if Carla were to mysteriously disappear while we were out fighting evil, they couldn't very well blame me, could they?

Shar got Carla on the phone, told her where he was, and asked her to meet him right away. She sounded frantic, which meant she would be hurrying and making mistakes. Good—all the easier to capture her.

Since Shar had made the situation sound urgent, I knew Carla wouldn't take the time to drive here. She, too, would become invisible and fly, so I kept watching toward the south east. Sure enough, in just a few minutes I could see something, and as she got closer, I knew it was her, even though I had to focus hard to be sure.

She landed and became visible, clearly surprised to see the rest of the group, to say nothing of me and Alex.

"Tal, Shar, what's happening?" she asked, voice filled with concern.

"We've been betrayed," I said casually. While she was absorbing that comment, I pulled out the lyre and started to play, directing all the force of my magic at her. For a second I had toyed with the idea of putting everyone out, but I still needed the guys to help me defeat Nicneven, and possibly some of them would be useful later as well.

Carla had all the willpower of her earlier self, Alcina, and my magic alone could not have overcome her quickly, but with the power of the lyre, she sagged and fell almost immediately. She hadn't even really had time to realize what was happening. Still playing, I took her from sleep to suspended animation.

"Tal, she's not breathing!" said Stan, who had bent over her to make sure she was out.

"She's breathing, just very slowly," I reassured him. He did have a tendency to be a drama king, and that was the last thing I needed right now. "A sleep spell, even one reinforced by the lyre, might not keep Asmodeus from taking over. This kind of enchantment will make it harder for him to use the body and easier for us to hold Carla without making her uncomfortable. Shar, I assume Vanora has covered for her, right?"

Shar nodded. "Vanora cooked up some story to explain our absence from town, so her family isn't going to be looking for her right away."

"Excellent!" I replied. "We can find some place to stash her for a while, then we can figure out how best to defend ourselves against Nicneven."

"There is something you may want to address first," interrupted Stan. It would figure the dweeb had yet something else to prattle about.

"What's that, buddy?" I asked.

"Asmodeus was trying to send us by portal some place we couldn't be found. During the battle Eva must have stumbled through the portal, and when Asmodeus's physical form was destroyed, the portal closed."

"What?" I almost shouted. "Why was she here in the first place?"

"Take it easy—" began Shar.

"Don't tell me to take it easy," I snapped. "It was irresponsible of you guys to bring her."

"We didn't exactly know we were walking into a trap set by a bewitched Shar, much less a demon king," explained Dan calmly, "and when she heard Shar needed our help, she wanted to come."

I had an almost overwhelming urge to punch him in the mouth and knock all his teeth down his throat. After all, he had stolen Eva from me four years ago, and even though she now knew the truth, she couldn't recapture her old feelings. Grudgingly, I had to admit I still needed Dan for the upcoming battle, but as soon as that was done, he would pay for that past betrayal, every bit as much as Carla would pay for her more recent one.

Forgiveness was such an overrated quality!

"I get that you didn't think the situation was dangerous," I said, feigning calmness, "but what are we supposed to do now? Even I don't know how to search for someone in another world—particularly when I don't know *which* other world."

"Well, we now know that supernatural bonds persist across worlds," said Stan. I was so goddamn sick of his being Mr. Expert on everything, even on magic, about which I knew far more than he ever could. Still, maybe he would finally get to something useful.

"So…" I prompted.

"Aphrodite suggested you and Eva have such a bond as a result of the role she played in the ritual that broke that first love spell on you. If she's right, you could connect with Eva and figure out where she is. Probably Aphrodite could help you design a spell to activate that bond—"

"No!" I cut in quickly. "The Olympians have helped enough already. Let's try to solve this on our own first."

The sad part was that Aphrodite could almost certainly have worked out a spell in minutes. I just wasn't ready to test my disguise against someone like Apollo yet. It should hold up, but it would be safer to give it a milder test first, not one that could involve eight or so ex-gods. Even armed with the lyre, I wasn't eager to have to fight all of them at once. No, better to find an occasion to see if one supernatural being could tell before exposing myself to a whole pantheon of them. They couldn't exactly read minds, but Apollo had that unpredictable seer ability to receive little bits of the present and future. Walking into his presence was too big a risk.

"What can we do to help?" asked Gordy.

"Why don't all of you keep watch? I need time to concentrate, and I can't do that if I have to worry about someone unexpected popping up." The guys could see I was a little touchy and were more than happy to give me some space. As soon as they were gone, though, Carla's comatose form distracted me. I thought about how hard the Boy Scout had worked to bring her out of a coma, and how thoroughly she had betrayed him. I also thought about having sex with her. She was a backstabber, but she was also smoking hot. As long as she thought I was Tal, I was pretty sure she'd consent if I woke her up. I'd have a hard time explaining to the guys what was happening if anyone came back to report, though. Anyway, I really didn't have an hour to kill with Carla if I wanted to rescue Eva as fast as possible.

I spent a long time trying to activate the bond Aphrodite thought was there, but I made no headway. Just as I was developing a splitting headache from all that concentration, the truth struck me with stunning force.

Robin's spell let me pass as Tal even with someone who could read minds, even with someone who analyzed my body all the way down to the genetic level. One difference still remained, however, and though it was not something anyone else could readily discover, it was enough to thwart my efforts.

Tal long ago realized that two minds sharing the same body were not impacted the same way by mind-affecting spells, which normally only reached the mind actually in control at that particular moment. My situation proved that point: Carla's love spell had captured Tal but missed me, which was why I still loved Eva even when Tal thought he loved Carla.

Unfortunately, it was Tal in control when Eva and the others freed him from Alcina's love spell, so if Aphrodite's theory was correct, it was Tal, not I, who had a world-crossing bond with Eva.

Now I realized just exactly how big a bind I was in. I couldn't risk letting Tal's mind take over this body; he might be able to keep control, particularly if he, and not Robin, was the one doing the driving. No, I had to go back to Hy-Brasil to get the original Tal to help me find Eva. I could count on the Boy Scout to save her. However, he couldn't do that if he were bound with that magic chain, and setting him free meant making him a threat again. I knew that with the lyre I could beat him easily, but I couldn't just control him, because I couldn't be sure exerting that kind of power on him would enable me to access his bond with Eva. If I didn't control him completely, I couldn't be sure he wouldn't somehow manage to broadcast a message to someone like Gwynn ap Nudd, and suddenly I would have a whole new range of problems.

I actually considered letting Eva stay where she was until Nicneven had been defeated. If what the guys had told me was correct, Asmodeus wouldn't have sent her any place dangerous, because that would have risked voiding the contract with Carla. However, conditions could always change, and anyway I didn't want to think about Eva in some strange world, alone and frightened. Also, the sooner I could be the hero who brought her back to safety, the sooner I could finally bed her. I would have to chance the trip to Hy-Brasil. The guys would never know what I was up to.

I was portal lagged, and it took me a minute to figure out what day it was. Back in Ireland, it had been relatively late at night on Sunday when we caught our ride to Hy-Brasil, but Santa Barbara was eight hours earlier. I glanced at Tal's cell phone. It was already after 4:00 p.m. on Sunday, February 17. By the time I got back it could be some time on Monday. Would Nicneven try to attack in the meantime?

The attack on the Ladies of the Lake indicated that Nicneven could come after us for vengeance against Tal any time. Coventina would doubtless get word to the faerie authorities, who would have no choice but to mobilize against Nicneven. The wintry queen would then have no choice but to spend most of her energy defending herself and very little leisure to worry about Tal.

On the other hand, I had seen faerie justice in action, and it was sometimes glacially slow. That could give Nicneven a few days before the other faerie rulers posed a serious threat.

Why would she wait? Because the Ice Moon fell on Monday, February 25, and she would be more powerful then than now. Given the forces at her command, that might make no difference, but she knew Tal had defeated some pretty powerful enemies in the past and might just delay if by doing so she could have more assurance of defeating him. Her actions up to now, like the isolation of Santa Brígida beneath several layers of magic and her attempt to knock out the Ladies of the Lake, suggested a desire to weaken Tal as much as possible before striking. Waiting until her own power waxed as far as it could this close to spring would be consistent with that strategy.

Damn it! I could stand here forever speculating. The reality was I couldn't know for sure. If I could recover Eva fast, though, I could almost certainly be back and ready before Nicneven struck, and that was the important thing.

I assembled the guys and told them I thought I had found Eva, but that I needed to do some intelligence gathering, and I needed them to stay here for a variety of reasons: watching Carla, whom I didn't want to have to drag with me, keeping Vanora posted, helping with the evacuation that was almost bound to occur in a day or so.

They weren't happy; in fact, they were irritatingly eager to go with me, but in the end my reasoning prevailed. Somewhere along

the line Shar had lost Vanora's illusion that made him look thirtysomething, so I restored it for him, with instructions to get the gang
set up in the Biltmore, on the assumption they needed to get rested
up when they weren't actively involved in some necessary job. Again,
they bowed to my wishes, though I could tell they worried about me
being off somewhere alone. Their concern was touching…in a sickening kind of way.

I finally flew away, glad to be free of them. I was especially
eager to get away from Alex. I knew the Olympians were watching
him, and I wanted their focus somewhere I wasn't, just in case.

Once I had Eva back, I was confident I could defeat Nicneven. Then there would time for getting laid, and time as well to
plan my revenge against all the people who had crossed me.

Chapter 23: Poison (Vanora)

Too late I realized why I was having so much trouble maintaining my energy: the shadows in the dome around the city were subtly hostile to anyone with magic. I should have been protected in Awen: it and Tal's house were by far the best-warded points anywhere in town. Unfortunately, the malign influence got to me through my security men, and if I disconnected from them, I could no longer efficiently protect the city. Of course, that problem would be moot when I collapsed, perhaps only a few hours from now. Staying awake virtually all the time would wear me down pretty quickly anyway, but under these circumstances, none of my Lady of the Lake regenerative tricks seemed to work anymore.

Those punk teenagers had all abandoned me. Perhaps Shahriyar did need them, but I needed them as well, and their loyalties could not have been any more clearly displayed. I was convenient to have around, and that was all. One word from him, and they all left, despite my protests.

For some time I had been unable to reach Shahriyar or Carla. Probably something was happening outside, but I would like to know what, so I could help. Oh, who was I kidding? I had already been so weakened by Hecate's magic, delivered via Nicneven, that I could barely protect Santa Brígida. Doing anything beyond that would be more than I could manage.

I reached out to the Order for help, but it offered me none. Short-handed and under attack, it could have allocated research personnel to examine the spell that surrounded me, but the backup I really needed was an impossibility. Tal and Viviane had already tried, apparently, and failed. Viviane had at least called to tell me that, but I hadn't heard from her or Tal in hours.

Maybe they were all ignoring me on purpose. Maybe they were all dead. If the worst had happened, I feared I might be joining them.

One of my aids just told me Santa Brígida was experiencing its first snowfall ever. The mayor, in a moment of independence more rare than the snow, resisted my insistence on evacuation, and I was spread too thin to apply any magical persuasion, especially from a distance.

Wouldn't it be ironic if the mayor's discovery that he had a spine proved to be the ruin of us all?

Chapter 24: Destiny Calls (a watcher upon Snowdon)

I expected to be dead by now. I thought that all I had to do was end the spell that had been keeping me alive, and nature would take its course, freeing me to proceed to my next incarnation. I was just being foolish, though. My life has never been as simple as that.

I looked into the cold depths of Glaslyn, a lake more than halfway up Yr Wyddfa, or Snowdon, as modern people called it. It is said that after most of the remaining Knights of the Round Table died in the battle of Camlann, Sir Bedivere, at the request of the gravely wounded Arthur, hurled Excalibur into this supposedly bottomless pool, from whence it was retrieved by the Ladies of the Lake. For a while I contemplated following Excalibur in, but I had stayed out of Satan's clutches all this time, and I feared suicide would finally make me his prisoner.

There was a timeless quality to this place on this early morning, as if the whole world had been frozen with me in this moment. A giant slain by Arthur was buried nearby, and the body of a water monster lay somewhere in Glaslyn's own depths. Some of Arthur's men were also nearby, on Y Lliwedd, slumbering until the day when Arthur would return. The place had otherworldly ties as well. Once there had been a fixed portal into the realm of the Tylwyth Teg, and I could have slipped through for a little visit with Gwynn ap Nudd. Perhaps I would try to find it later, but that wasn't really why I had picked this particular mountain. No, I had come here because its storied past had left enough magical residue to obscure my presence. Someone was looking for me, you see. That old crone Nicneven had gotten a whiff of me and now seemed determined to seek me out. I could tell she was both more evil and more powerful than when we had last met, and I had no more desire to be in her clutches than in Satan's—if indeed there was still a difference. I looked in the general direction of Scotland and shuddered, though not from the cold.

I had spent most of yesterday trying to see what lay ahead, but the possible futures were even more tangled than usual, and also more shadowed.

The one element that seemed common to most of the tangled threads of the tapestry of time was the sense of imbalance, of wrongness, brought about by too much meddling with the universe, too much effort to pull it away from God and reshape it. No one could truly beat God at that game, of course, but that never seemed to prevent anyone from trying, and as of old, God oft left the resistance of such plans to us poor mortals.

I suddenly knew why I was still alive. God wanted me to take up this one last task, to join in one last battle before finally I could rest. Had I followed my impulse to throw myself into Glaslyn, it would have spat me up on shore instead of drowning me.

I would in any case have had to leave Snowdon soon, for I could feel Nicneven's piercing gaze nearby, but now I knew the direction in which I must travel. Before I left, I would pay an invisible visit to Hafod Eryri, the new visitor center at the mountain's summit, and I would read again the inscription, the English part of which says, "The summit of Snowdon: Here you are nearer to Heaven."

Then I would wonder whether my journey would take me nearer to Heaven...or to Hell.

Chapter 25: Unpleasant Surprises (Tal)

Nurse Florence and I stood on the beach below Shoreline Park, feeling afternoon slowly morph into evening and wondering what to do next.

I had been sure we could surprise New Dark Me. After all, unless he had gone back, he would think we were still trapped on Hy-Brasil. Unfortunately, most spells designed to locate a person would fail in this case because I was essentially trying to locate myself. Consequently, the spell would just point out my current location and end. It was also possible New Dark Me was masking his presence somehow, in which case the only hope of finding him would be a slow, painstaking examination of the area, one grid at a time. If my mind touched a spot with magic concealment operating, that would be a pretty good clue, since there were only a handful of people who could do such a thing in the whole county.

However, that assumed New Dark Me was even in Santa Barbara. My gut told me he would come back and try to assume my identity, though Old Dark Me disagreed loudly, insisting that he would go to Annwn and try to free Morgan le Fay.

Neither one of us had tried to get in touch with anyone yet, but I began to think it would be best to get help, given the size of the task. New Dark Me had relieved us of our cell phones and me of my wallet and ID, but he had not thought to take Nurse Florence's purse, and she had bought us both burner phones at a drug store as soon as we arrived in town.

She started by calling Vanora, and I started with Carla, whose voice I really needed to hear anyway. Her number went straight to voice mail, though. At that point a horrible thought occurred to me.

"New Dark Me probably shares Old Dark Me's attitude about Carla having somehow bewitched me. What if he's hurt her?" Old Dark Me started to protest, but I muzzled him as thoroughly as I could.

"It's a possibility," admitted Nurse Florence, "but would that really be his first move?"

"I don't know. It depends whether he can get her alone or not. If he's pretending to be me, though, nobody is going to expect that to be his first priority, and he'll have to spend a little bit of time dealing with what's happened since we left."

"Speaking of," said Nurse Florence, "Vanora is maybe only minutes from collapse, and the mayor isn't yet convinced the situation requires evacuation. I told her she should call the people Nicneven could most easily use as hostages, suggest they get out, and then get out herself."

"Give up the town to Nicneven? But I thought you said—"

"I know what I said," cut in Nurse Florence, "but Vanora can't defend the town if she collapses, and she believes that spell around town is...poisonous to anyone with magical ability. She could conceivably die, Tal."

"Of course we can't risk that," I agreed, "but that means we need to get the guys together quickly, find New Dark Me, capture him, and then get ready to deal with the situation in town. I'd better try Carla again."

I did, with no results. She could still be with Shar, but he wasn't picking up, either. My uneasiness grew steadily.

Well, if I couldn't find the only other person who could provide some magic help, the next best bet would be Stan, so I punched in his number.

"Hello," said his familiar voice. I could have jumped for joy.

"Stan, Nurse Florence and I just got back, and things are looking bad. Dark Me is actually running around loose in a body just like mine."

"What?" asked Stan tightly.

"It's a long story," I said rapidly, hoping he wouldn't ask too many questions. "The important thing is we need to get everyone together, and I can't raise either Carla or Shar, but at least you can help gather anyone who's still in Santa Brígida."

"We aren't in Santa Brígida anymore," said Stan emotionlessly. "We're at the Biltmore in Santa Barbara...where you told us to go. Or at least, I thought it was you. How do I know it wasn't? How do I know you aren't Dark Me?"

Stan had a point...and even if he had magic, he probably wouldn't be able to tell who was who. Fortunately, I was able to put Nurse Florence on, and she vouched for me.

"Convinced?" I asked him as soon as I got the phone back.

"Yeah," said Stan. "He was acting a little strange, but he told us it was because…"

"Because what?" I asked impatiently.

"I…better tell you in person. How fast can you get here?"

"Wait, where is he? Not with you, I take it?"

"No," said Stan, voice tight again. "He had a few things to take care of, or so he said. He'll be back, though."

"Then the Biltmore is the last place any of us want to be. Stan, you know how to get to Shoreline Beach from the Biltmore, right?"

"Yeah, get on East Cabrillo Boulevard, stick with it until it becomes Shoreline, and take Shoreline to Santa Rosa. The park closes at sunset, though."

Stan always had been the practical one. "I'll take care of the park personnel," I reassured him. "Those who are still on duty won't notice you. Just take the staircase down the bluff to the beach and Nurse Florence and I will meet you. Everyone with you at the Biltmore?"

"Not exactly," said Stan nervously. I must have gasped audibly, because he continued, "Don't worry; nobody died or anything. I'll explain what's up when we meet."

"OK, and be sure to explain to the guys what's happening…but don't take too long, all right? I don't want Dark Me getting back before you leave."

"I'll move as fast as I can," Stan assured me, immediately hanging up to emphasize how well he understood me.

I walked back up to the park, made sure that the park employees would indeed not notice the guys (or me and Nurse Florence, for that matter) and then walked quickly back down to the beach.

The sunset was fading by the time the guys arrived. I could see them heading down the stairs…with swords drawn. I guessed I really couldn't blame them.

When they reached the bottom of the stairs, they came over to where I was standing and silently encircled me. I adjusted my eyes to the growing darkness and quickly took roll: Stan, Shar, Dan, Gordy, Jimmie, and Carlos. Khalid, who apparently now had a bow, floated in the air above us, arrow ready.

"Where's Carla?" I asked quickly. "And...what's he doing here?" I continued, shocked to see Alex.

"*Déjà vu*," replied Carlos. "Dark Me asked the same thing...if that's who it was."

"Nurse Florence is here to vouch for me," I replied. "She's been with me the whole time."

"How do we know that's really Nurse Florence?" asked Gordy. Given the number of shape-shifters we'd met in the last few months, that was a fair question, and for a moment I was at a loss to figure out how to prove my identity.

"Shar, ask the Olympians to open a gateway to Olympus. Apollo can clear me. Whoever I am, I can't fake Olympus for you."

Actually, if I were a master illusionist, I probably could make them think they were on Olympus, but I hoped none of them would realize that. We needed to end this impasse and get to work.

"The other one didn't want to go to Olympus," said Khalid thoughtfully. "There was a time when he could have used Aphrodite's help, but he didn't seem to want to ask."

"Probably because he was afraid his disguise wouldn't hold up," I said. "I, on the other hand, have nothing to hide. In fact, I'm eager to go to Olympus."

Shar stared at me, then said, "Maybe that won't be necessary. The other one was acting strangely. He said a couple of things...and he was just about ready to explode at us. I could tell. I've never seen you like that before, Tal."

"He did explain why he was acting differently," Dan reminded them.

"And I didn't really buy that, either," said Stan. "Is that a subject you can imagine Tal being so matter-of-fact about?" I saw heads shaking.

"Maybe I can talk to whoever hears my invocation," suggested Shar. "Maybe we don't all have to go to Olympus."

"Worth a try," agreed Stan. Shar sheathed his sword and stood a little away, concentrating. At that moment I realized he had been using a sword with a faint yellow-white glow rather than Zom's emerald green one. I would have to ask about that later.

In a few minutes Shar spoke to us, though his eyes remained closed. "Aphrodite and Apollo both vouch for this Tal as the real one."

"Just to be clear, how do they know?" asked Stan. He already seemed convinced, but I assumed he was clarifying for any doubting Thomases in the group.

"This Tal is still under the spell," said Shar slowly. Then, with a smirk, he added, "and the other one is at this moment making furious love to a faerie woman somewhere off the coast of Ireland. That's proof to Aphrodite, because she knows the real Tal would be faithful to the woman he loves. However, even Apollo couldn't tell you apart otherwise. He says he's never seen a spell result in two such identical people before. Anything else?"

"No, but thank them for us, Shar," said Stan. "Are we all satisfied?" he asked, and this time everyone nodded. Despite knowing for sure I was the real deal, they seemed oddly grim.

"Now, why is Alex here?" I asked, eager to clear up that riddle.

"Tal, you were the one who made this possible," began Alex. My face must have betrayed my shock that he was the one speaking, because he asked, "Is it OK if I talk?" I nodded, tight-lipped, and he continued.

"Hermes and Asclepius have been trying to heal me, just as you asked, and they made progress. I'm more like I was before Ares got into my head. They also gave me this," he said, holding his hand up so I could see the throbbing red gem on his ring finger. "It does something to my blood so I can stay here longer to help out."

"He's proving himself," added Khalid.

"It's a little like probation," put in Stan.

"That seems risky," I said, looking hard at Alex. "I know I should be happy to be proved right, but you said, 'made progress,' didn't you, Alex?"

"I still have problems," Alex replied, looking me straight in the eye. "A time came when Khalid needed help, and I was the only one the Olympians could send to help him. The ring will kill me if I betray Khalid, if that makes you feel any better." There was almost a feeling of accusation in his tone.

"I'm sorry if I'm suspicious," I said. "You can understand why I'm a little reluctant to accept a miracle cure. Hermes told me it might take months."

"It has been months on Olympus," Alex reminded me.

"Even I can't complain so far," said Shar. "He helped Khalid when I…wasn't able to."

"Which brings up a lot of other questions," I said, figuring I wasn't going to get any more satisfaction on the subject of Alex right away. "Why couldn't you help Khalid yourself, Shar? Where's Zom? What aren't you guys telling me? And where's Carla?"

Silence descended like death itself. "Guys, come on!" I said, as encouragingly as I could. "What could be so bad you can't tell me?"

"You don't really love Carla," said Dan, rushing his words as if he wanted the whole thing out in one breath. "She sold her soul for a lot of stuff, but primarily for a subtle love spell no one could detect. She cast it in Annwn when you were recovering from your fall." The rush of words over, Dan looked at me as if expecting my head to explode. Instead, I just laughed.

"It's a little early for April Fools', isn't it?" I asked.

"He's serious, Tal," said Stan. "I didn't want to believe, either, and you had me almost talked out of it that time I raised our suspicions with you, remember? There's really no other explanation that works anymore, though."

"No other explanation for what, exactly?" I asked. "I know our lives are pretty crazy, but how does anything that happened prove my love for Carla isn't real?"

"It happened too fast," suggested Dan. "You went from furious with her to in love with her in like seconds."

"It wasn't seconds, and I forgave her first," I clarified. "I've been over this with Stan already. Maybe I'm finally growing past my inability to forgive easily. That's a good thing, isn't it?" Dan looked down and wouldn't meet my eyes.

"A love spell would explain your mood swings and the activity of Dark Me," said Nurse Florence. "It's the only theory we have for his sudden strength inside of you."

"Just because we haven't thought of anything else doesn't make the only theory we have right," I pointed out.

"A few days ago I would have believed you," said Shar slowly, "but Aphrodite is the one who told me the truth about Carla. I saw Carla possessed by the demon Asmodeus. He got Zom away from me. He cast Alcina's ultimate love spell on me. That's why I couldn't protect Khalid. Tal, Asmodeus almost got Khalid because of Carla!"

"From what we know now, though," cut in Stan, "part of Carla's bargain keeps Asmodeus from physically harming us."

"Don't make excuses for her," snapped Shar. "It wouldn't have prevented Asmodeus from sending all of us to a different plane of existence from which we couldn't get back and in which no one could ever find us! Oh, Tal, that's what happened to Eva, by the way. Dark Me evidently can't find her, but Aphrodite thinks your bond with her will make it possible for you to do it…once the spell is gone."

Anticipating New Dark Me's return, I was keeping myself at faerie speed, which is the only reason I was able to dodge the potion Khalid tossed at me. It struck the sand with a thud, still unbroken, sparkling in the moonlight.

"What the hell, Khalid!" I didn't quite shout, but I did raise my voice.

"I'm sorry. That's the potion Aphrodite and Hermes gave me to take the spell off you." His tone was apologetic, but his eyes told me he would do the same at the next opportunity, so I stamped on the vial with all my strength, shattering it and letting the glowing fluid leak harmlessly into the sand. Khalid and others looked horrified.

"Would you guys pull yourselves together?" I asked irritably. "A couple of hours ago, you were ready to think Dark Me was me. Now you're ready to believe some fairy tale about Carla casting a spell on me. This is obviously someone's trick to cause friction among us. Nicneven's, probably."

"Even if everything that's happened, including a fight with Asmodeus, by the way, is some kind of elaborate trick, why is Aphrodite so convinced? Who would know a love spell better than the ex-goddess of love?" asked Carlos.

"She's not omniscient, now is she?" I asked, trying to keep my tone reasonable. "Even Apollo isn't. Khalid, when you were on Olympus, did anyone mention Dark Me impersonating me?"

"Not in so many words," admitted Khalid, "but Apollo did say something about it being as if there were two of you. He said the future was hard to make out, I think."

"Not quite the same thing, is it?" I asked them all triumphantly. "They were mistaken then; they could be mistaken now. Where's Carla?" No one answered.

"Where's Carla?" I said again, getting angry for the first time.

"Back in her room at the Biltmore," said Shar finally. "Dark Me put her to sleep with the lyre of Orpheus to keep Asmodeus from using her body anymore."

"I'll be breaking that spell," I said firmly. "We'll need Carla when Nicneven attacks."

"Man, aren't you even listening?" asked Gordy.

"Longer than I should have," I replied, trying to look as grim as they did. "That you guys would believe Dark Me over me hurts…but regardless of what you believe, I'm not going to allow Carla to remain under a spell of his contriving for something she didn't do."

"We can't allow you to do that," said Shar in a determined, no-nonsense tone. "She poses a threat to all of us right now." To my surprise, he drew his new sword, which gleamed softly in the night.

"Stand down, Alexander the Great!" I said, somewhat mockingly. "I'm speeded up; you're not…and all I have to do is fly away."

"I can fly, too," said Khalid. I was shocked he again had an arrow aimed at me.

"I can fly as well," added Alex, soaring up overhead and brandishing a curved sword.

I raised my empty hands. "Dark Me has White Hilt, and however misguided you are, I can't believe any of you would actually use your weapons on me, even if I were armed."

I had them there, and dark as it was, I could see it in their eyes, even Alex's. They might threaten, but they would never hurt me. I had only to take off and head for the Biltmore. I had no doubt Alex and Khalid would follow, but I was safe from the sword and the arrow.

It was a good thing I had kept my senses sharp as well as my speed up, because even as it was I almost missed the sound of music in the distance. I cast my deafening spell just in time to keep New Dark Me from putting all of us to sleep with the lyre of Orpheus.

"Now you've got a real target. Hit him hard, guys!" I thought loudly, *"Try not to kill him, though. A helpless Robin Goodfellow is trapped in there!"*

Khalid shot an arrow at his usual half djinn speed, and having had it already nocked was handy, but New Dark Me was also operating at faerie speed and managed to dodge. Khalid kept up the barrage, and Alex headed straight for New Dark Me, sword raised.

Having seen the Amadan Dubh perform the spell to reverse deafness, I knew New Dark Me could probably cast it, but facing two attacks at the same time gave him no opportunity. Instead, he turned and sped out to sea. Alex and Khalid followed without hesitating, and that gave me another dilemma.

We had to capture New Dark Me, but I suspected he would try something as soon as he got Alex and Khalid alone and unsupported. Much as I wanted to leave his capture to them and go free Carla, I couldn't allow them to face New Dark Me alone, and no else could follow except me. Even if it had only been Alex, I wasn't about to just sacrifice him. Carla was safe for the moment, so rescuing her would have to wait.

They had a head start on me, but I did what I could to catch up. Alex, a less experienced flier than Khalid, was lagging behind, so I caught up with him first. I extended my levitation around him to steady him, and then I accelerated both of us as much as I could. I could barely make out Khalid in the distance.

We had to catch up!

The direction New Dark Me was flying suggested that he was heading for Santa Cruz Island.

"Painted Cave," muttered Old Dark Me from deep inside me.

Painted Cave, one of the largest sea caves, was said to be home to an entrance to the lower world of Chumash myth. If I knew that, then obviously New Dark Me did as well. Clearly, he wanted to escape, and a fixed portal would be faster to use than one he needed to conjure up himself, but was he really stupid enough to blunder into a gateway to another world without having a true sense of what was on the other side? All I knew was the Chumash belief that the lower world contained the two giants serpents on which the world rested. Obviously, the earth didn't really rest on two serpents in the physical sense, but what if we encountered beings tied to Earth in some way? And what if New Dark Me interfered with them somehow? What if they attacked both of us as intruders, and we had to defend ourselves? Nurse Florence had suggested that a disruption on Olympus or some other plane could affect Earth if it was bad enough. Could a disruption of the Chumash lower world have the same effect? If there was even a chance, I had to stop Dark Me from ever reaching it.

He was far away from me, though, and even had he not been, it'd be pretty difficult to hit someone with magic who was flying as fast as New Dark Me. On the plus side, he couldn't make very effective use of his own magic or of the lyre, either, though I suspected he might have figured out how to speed up with his own flight with a strum or two. He certainly seemed to be traveling even faster than faerie speed.

Fortunately, my family had vacationed on Santa Cruz Island when I was younger. Using my memory of the place, I opened a portal in front of me, and through it I steered myself and Alex. Khalid was too far ahead of us to pull back, but having him continue to pursue New Dark Me would help to camouflage the fact that Alex and I weren't there any longer.

We appeared on Alcina's island momentarily, then, as fast as I could open a portal back, we emerged on Cavern Point, where my parents had hiked with me when I was a kid. More important, we were now in front of New Dark Me, and if we proceeded skillfully enough, we should be able to catch my alter ego between Khalid and us.

Unfortunately, Alex panicked. "Where's Khalid?" he almost shouted. "I have to protect him!"

"Easy!" I said, putting a hand on his arm. "I wouldn't do anything to put Khalid in harm's way. I just brought us out in front of New Dark Me so we can surprise him."

A quick mental scan confirmed New Dark Me hurtling toward the island at surprising speed, with Khalid still on his tail.

"Let's go get him," I said to Alex, pulling him along as I rose into the air. Alex nodded, but he was still clearly worried about Khalid.

Could he really have changed so much? Well, curing him had been my idea in the first place, so I guess I shouldn't be so resistant to the possibility that the idea had actually worked.

We soared into position just in time to intercept New Dark Me as he slowed to change direction. He was just surprised enough that I managed to levitate the lyre out of his hands. Unfortunately, he was still moving at amazing speed, and he managed to grab the lyre again before I could pull it into my own hands. However, he was off-balance, and Alex got close enough to bring his shield down on the lyre, tearing it out of my evil twin's hands. The instrument started to fall, but again I grabbed it with my mind and pulled it toward me.

I had to admit that Alex was now following orders and showing common sense. Instead of hacking at New Dark Me with Harpe, which might well have killed him—and Robin—Alex grabbed my dark side in a bear hug. Alex's nectar-and-ambrosia amplified strength was far more than New Dark Me's, though the body thief might have been able to shape shift his muscles to compensate if given a chance. To prevent exactly that kind of move, Alex gave him a stunning head butt, and New Dark Me lost consciousness. By now Khalid had joined us, and the three of us easily flew our captive back to Shoreline, though I was feeling a little dizzy from having to fly so far and so fast.

Once back on the beach, I helped Nurse Florence bind New Dark Me with enough magic to ensure he wouldn't pose a problem before we had a chance to remove the spell sustaining his impersonation of me.

"Wow, you got him!" said Gordy enthusiastically. "I can't believe it was that easy."

"Not exactly easy," I corrected him. "With just a little luck, Dark Me could have zapped all of us with the lyre. Once we were deafened, and he had three of us able to fly attacking from different directions, he couldn't use the lyre effectively, but he did almost manage to get away, and that would have been bad.

"Alex did a good job," I added, surprising him by patting him on the back. "I don't think Khalid and I could have managed to capture Dark Me by ourselves. Alex did exactly the right thing at exactly the right time." A smile flickered across his lips. I couldn't help feeling it might be his first smile in a long time.

"Maybe he just got lucky," muttered Shar. I thought it best to ignore him, and Alex didn't seem to mind. I didn't have to read his mind to see how much my acknowledgment meant to him.

"Well," began Stan, "now you have Dark Me corralled and White Hilt and the lyre back. Nurse Florence was suggesting that as soon as you guys returned, we should connect with Vanora to make sure she was all right."

"Great idea," I replied, "as soon as I free Carla." Everyone else immediately became quiet.

"And," I added quickly, "the subject is not up for discussion."

The guys all froze for a second. I had already called their bluff, but I could see they were pondering whether or not to draw their weapons again, even though it was obvious they weren't about to use them.

What they might have done next I was never to find out, because at that moment I felt an enormous build-up of magic power above us. Looking up, my adjusted vision enabled me to see several figures flying toward us through the night sky.

I had only a few seconds at most to assess the threat. From what little I could tell with a cursory scan, some of the intruders were faeries, but some were human witches. That mix definitely sounded like some of Nicneven's followers. How they had been able to find us wasn't clear, nor was how they had gotten to Santa Barbara so quickly. Perhaps they had used some poor tourist's memories to get here, just as we feared they might.

"Incoming!" I yelled. The guys snapped out of their paralysis and readied their weapons. I accelerated them to faerie speeds and adjusted their eyes to be able to see in the dark while Nurse Florence prepared what defensive magic she could.

Lacking Carla, we were short on magic. I was particularly going to miss connecting to her and using White Hilt or the lyre of Orpheus through her hands. As it was, I had to pick one or the other. Lacking Zom, we were short on protection, though at least Shar's new sword looked formidable.

Drawing White Hilt, I created a flaming dome to cover us—my go-to ploy these days when facing superior forces. While my shield wouldn't block spells, it would make the more physical ones damn hard to aim. The same could be said for faerie arrows. Our foes would doubtless start some kind of counter move, but at least we now had a few second longer to prepare.

In that time Nurse Florence managed to get a deflection field up to make hitting us with arrows even harder. Once I felt that defensive layer in place, I risked dropping the fire shield to hit our opponents with a burst of pure fear powered by the lyre. Back on Olympus the same strategy had driven away hundreds of faerie archers.

This time? Not so much. In fact, that powerful magic produced almost no effect.

Clearly, I wasn't the only one to realize that deafness would protect against the lyre's power. Having seen the Amadan Dubh counter that spell, I was pretty sure I could as well, but that would take time to figure out exactly how he'd done it, and our enemies were now upon us.

Faerie arrows rained down with vicious intent. Nurse Florence's spell helped some, but they were still getting uncomfortably close. Meanwhile, the witches were circling above us, gathering power for what looked like a cold blast of Arctic proportions. If they could pull that attack off, they would freeze us to death right where we stood.

Khalid opened fire, and though he was shooting well, the faeries were shooting even better, using their arrows to deflect his and give the witches the time they needed to ready their kill shot.

I could see Alex hesitating, and I wasn't sure what to tell him to do. We were facing a large number of flying opponents, and he was one of the only three of us who could fly, so it might make sense to send him up. On the other hand, Nurse Florence's deflection spell wouldn't cover him if he soared too high, and he didn't have the ability to sense magic, so he had no way of knowing when to stop. The number of faerie archers in the air suggested he could be very badly wounded, maybe even killed.

"Stay put!" I thought at him.

I had been considering how to remove the deafness effect from Nicneven's troops so that I could hit them with fear again, but it was possible they might have additional protection against that effect, since Nicneven obviously knew from her spies what I could do. I needed an unexpected tactic, something they couldn't possibly have prepared for.

I knew both from the ancient stories about the lyre and from the way that the Amadan Dubh had been using it that it could manipulate natural forces just as powerfully as it could manipulate minds. I hadn't really practiced that part of its power, but there was no time like the present.

I strummed the lyre and sang, focusing all of the music's power on the nearby ocean. At first little happened, but as I became more used to what I was doing, I pulled a mighty wave out of the Pacific and sent it hurtling skyward, shaping it into a blast at the witches that might disrupt the spell-casting, perhaps even knock them right out of the sky.

The witches had enough magic accumulated to blast waves of cold at my waves of water. It tried to keep the fury of the sea moving in their direction, but as the water froze it became heavier and started falling to the earth in great icy chunks.

Had I been fighting the witches with my own druidic spells, they could have easily brought my casting to a frosty end, but with the strength of the lyre behind me, I could drain their power with continuous attacks until, dry of magic, they would drown in midair.

The faeries were now making a concerted effort to shoot me down, and the more arrows they shot at me, the more strain was placed on the deflection spell, which might eventually collapse, after which we would all be sitting ducks. I could easily have reinforced the protection, but that would have taken my focus off the witches. Perhaps the risk would be worthwhile, as their magic was clearly already much weakened, but we couldn't afford to have them decide to retreat and get away. Now that they had been to Santa Barbara, they could all open a portal to it without needing to trap some random Californian to do it. The protection we had from distance would be erased if even one witch or faerie escaped this battle.

Nurse Florence was trembling a little as the sky became a faerie cloud that rained arrows on us incessantly. The protection was getting thinner, thin enough for lucky shots to breach especially worn parts of the deflection spell.

Khalid was the first hit, just a flesh wound on his left hand, but enough to focus Shar entirely on him. Fortunately, a tap from Shar's new sword was all it took to heal the injury. Clearly there was more to that weapon than I had thought.

Alex too reacted to Khalid's wound, crying out as if he himself had been shot. Like me, he watched Shar heal Khalid, but then Alex took off before I could stop him, drawing the faerie fire away from the rest of us, but clearly risking his own life.

I switched over to defense and tried desperately to extend the deflection field around Alex as he rose, but I was not fast enough. The armor of Achilles caught a lot of the arrows, which bounced off harmlessly, and Alex deftly used the shield of Ares to knock away others, but then he started taking damage. He was just getting small nicks at first, but he began to lose blood, which fell in small droplets on us, a blood drizzle in the dark night.

Above us the witches, no longer on the defensive, were readying themselves for another cold blast, and the arrows kept right on coming. Both groups were much larger than I had suspected at first, or else fresh troops kept arriving. Now I could count hundreds, not just a cloud of opponents but a whole storm front, ready with a downpour that would create a flood to rival Noah's.

Made faster even than the faeries by the winged sandals of Hermes, Alex shot toward the bluff, trying to draw at least part of the force after him. He succeeded, but only with a small part. The rest went back to firing on me.

Gordy took a hit to his right arm, not a serious one, but a foretaste of what would happen when the deflection spell caved it, which it might almost the moment I stopped concentrating on it. Shar healed Gordy as he had healed Khalid, but the new sword could touch only one person at a time, and that would not save us when the arrows were hitting all of us more or less simultaneously.

Then the answer came to me: wind.

My ocean attack wasn't fast enough because of how easily the witches could draw on Nicneven's mastery of cold to freeze water. The gases in the air, however, had a much lower freezing point.

Magic was limited partly by what the caster could visualize. Something told me that witches, even in the modern world, probably didn't have graduate degrees in physics or chemistry. Frozen water was easily visualized, but frozen air? They might get to liquid nitrogen, and then we'd have to deal with that raining down, but it might boil back to gas before it hit us unless the witches pulled enough juice to lower the ambient air temperature tremendously, and that would freeze their faerie allies just as fast as it would freeze us. I doubted most of them could really accurately visualize a temperature that low, which meant they probably couldn't produce it, no matter how much raw power they got through the bond with Nicneven.

Wind had another advantage, of course: it would blow the faerie arrows away from us. I could use it to attack and defend simultaneously.

Shoreline Beach occupied a long stretch of coast north of the sea, so I started playing like mad on the lyre, conjuring up a powerful south wind that took both faeries and witches completely by surprise.

The guys would have some trouble with the wind, too, but they weren't up in the air. Nicneven's minions would take it much, much worse.

If enough of the faeries had managed to connect and focus their power, they could probably have countered the wind, but they didn't organize themselves rapidly enough. A few tried to accumulate magical force, but others kept right on shooting arrows, though with steadily diminishing result. Still others tried to fly above the wind or out over Shoreline Park and away from it. Those who went too far that way ran afoul of Alex, who was far enough away not to be too bothered by the wind yet and who flew straight at any faeries that got too near him. At close range, the faeries had no way to counter Harpe, and though Alex struck to wound and not kill, the blood raining down from the sky was now far more fey than human.

I couldn't spare too much attention for scanning the area, but I did notice some of the witches had gotten above the winds, by now gale force, and they were again trying to gather their power for some kind of strike. In an attempt to counter them, I changed the melody to transform the gale into a hurricane. To think some people questioned the value of the study of meteorology!

Many of the faeries and witches were trapped as the gale winds began to speed up still further and to form a funnel around us. Careful to keep the guys in the eye and to maintain as much control as I could, I kept pushing for higher and higher air speed. The winds pulled beach sand upward, not only dizzying our opponents but sandblasting them as well. If anyone managed to pull free, Alex was waiting for them.

I worried a little about the repercussions of using all this magic in my own world. Creating a storm of this magnitude in Annwn would have been one thing, but on Earth the possible damage, if not the storm itself, would certainly be hard to conceal. Much as I hated to think about it, there were bound to be corpses as well, both witch and faerie, scattered on the beach, at the southern edge of the park, and in the northern part of the nearby ocean. Could we possibly clean up all evidence of the carnage before dawn, when it would become far more visible? I doubted it.

However, Nicneven's invasion of our world was even more unprecedented. Our best hope was that the wrath of Annwn would turn on her instead of on us. After all, no large group of faeries had invaded the human realm since the days of King Arthur, and we could hardly be blamed for defending ourselves.

Even more important than the public relations, however, were the implications. If Nicneven was ready to defy the laws made by her fellow faerie rulers, she must be confident in her ability to defeat them, but that did make me wonder. What trick could she possibly have up her sleeve that would overcome the united forces of Annwn?

The wind—and its victims—howled in my ears. I still had trouble counting, but the force sent against us was larger than I would have thought possible. Would Nicneven have sent her whole army without coming herself? Or did she have an even larger force in reserve for later? As always, I had far more questions than answers.

Despite the power of the lyre, I could feel myself tiring. The guys would let me borrow some energy if I needed it, though. Nurse Florence was still recovering from trying to maintain deflection against so much opposition, and Alex was out of reach, but everyone else was just standing around, frustrated by their inability to join the battle.

Then I suddenly felt much worse for no obvious reason. Using magic normally caused fatigue gradually. It never felt like a vampire draining me unless I had to put out a tremendous amount of power in a short time. I guessed technically I was doing that, except that the lyre was providing most of the power. There had to be some other explanation for the weariness that gnawed at me.

"Tal!" cried Nurse Florence, trying to make herself heard over the storm. "Tal! Above us! Like the dome over Santa Brígida."

Well, there was a dome surrounding us now, but not exactly like the one over Santa Brígida. That one was hard to sense from inside, at least at first. This one was very blatant. I guessed the witches didn't have the time for subtlety.

Also, the spell that shrouded Santa Brígida had been toxic to spell casters, but very slowly. This one seemed crafted to be much more potent and faster-acting. It was what was draining my strength. In a couple of minutes I wouldn't be able to sustain the hurricane. While that storm had done a lot of damage to Nicneven's army, it had by no means eliminated it. Once Nurse Florence and I collapsed, the guys would be almost defenseless against renewed attacks from the air, both physical and magical.

My head ached, my vision started to blur, and my increasingly numb fingers began to falter. One minute more, and I would be unable to keep playing. I wished I had some brilliant strategy to save us, but my brain was running in low gear.

My friends were all going to die, and there wasn't a thing I could do about it.

Suddenly Alex was beside me. He must have flown back before the dome had blocked him completely, and he must have risked flying right through the funnel to get here, or else it was so weak now that there was no risk.

"Tal, I…I just knew something was wrong!" he shouted over the storm. Perhaps his enhanced abilities included some sensitivity to magic after all.

"I…feel sick," he continued. Evidently, his enhanced Olympian ancestry made him vulnerable to whatever the witches were doing. That could mean that Khalid as half djinn was also affected…but since we'd all be dead in a couple of minutes, it didn't matter.

"Is this Hecate's magic?" he asked. My hands felt like those of an arthritic old man. I was now striking wrong notes, each one sending a shock through my nervous system.

"It's…it's not Nicneven's winter…stuff, so…probably." By now I could no longer play, and I could focus only with difficulty on what I was trying to say to Alex. He was looking pale, but at least he was still standing. Maybe he could still do something.

"It's…a…little like…the spell over Santa Brígida. Dark…there's dark in it." The lyre slipped from my nerveless fingers. I tried to pick it up and fell, though I was still clinging to consciousness like a drowning man clinging to driftwood.

Dan and Jimmie helped me up, and Stan put the lyre back in my hand, but the gesture was futile. No longer manipulated by magic, the winds were dying rapidly. Soon we would feel the full force of the faerie archers.

Nearby Alex and Shar were arguing.

"Let me fly you up, or give me the sword!" demanded Alex shrilly.

"You aren't touching me or the sword!" insisted Shar angrily. "I don't trust you. Back off, or I'll do to you what you did to Khalid."

What was there about Shar's sword? It wasn't Zom anymore, so it couldn't…

Then a thought occurred to me, perhaps one of the last I would ever have.

"Stan," I rasped. "David played the harp, and this lyre is a lot like his harp."

"On it!" responded Stan quickly. In about half a second, David had taken over and was lifting the harp out of my hands.

"I will play," said David, "but I do not know if the Lord would approve of me using something with…magic." I couldn't fault David for wanting to avoid betraying God again, but at this moment the attitude might have been damn inconvenient…except that he wouldn't need to use magic if my idea worked.

"Just play," I whispered, my vision going completely out of focus, my legs now so weak that Dan and Jimmie had to hold me up. "Play as you did when you sought to worship God through music."

David played a melody much less strident than the one I had used to raise the hurricane, but infinitely more sweet. There was longing in it, desire to be united with God. Just as I could see light on David's sword in combat, I could see light radiating from the lyre as he played it, and the light spread outward with the sound. As it touched me, I felt immediately better.

I had long known that God lent David a certain amount of power without David's even realizing it. I had seen evil things retreat from the glow of David's sword, and I had hoped that his music might have a similar effect. I must have been right, because the only way I could be recovering so fast would be if the power radiating from the lyre was divine protection drawn from the king of Israel's music. Shielded from Hecate's darkness that was shrouding us on all sides, I seemed to be recovering quickly.

Now, however, we had a strategic dilemma: I had no reason to think the music would protect us from arrows, and I could see the surviving faeries regrouping. If I took the lyre back from David to raise another storm or other defense, we would lose the protection his music afforded, and I would quickly fall victim to the poisonous magic. If I didn't, we would all be filled with arrows in about two minutes. Either way, we would lose eventually.

Unsheathing White Hilt, I raised a flame barrier around us to buy a little time.

Now that I could think better, I turned my attention to the continuing argument between Shar and Alex.

"Shar, I thought you were telling me Alex had done a good job protecting Khalid," I said in a calm tone, trying to get Shar to chill out.

"That was before he ran," said Shar, glaring at Alex, who looked stricken but didn't immediately respond. "He ran at the first sign of trouble, like the coward he is!"

"He wasn't running!" I answered, exasperated. "He was risking his life to draw fire away from us. If he'd drawn more, he'd be dead right now." Shar looked first shocked, then chagrined.

"Shar, quick, tell me about your sword," I continued, ignoring his obvious discomfort. Arrows began to hit the flames, and though the first few incinerated, a heavy enough barrage would get some through for sure.

Shar opened his mouth but didn't start talking, so Alex filled in, quickly and quietly. "It's blessed by Apollo. It gives the wielder some magic resistance, so I thought maybe it could break whatever spell seems to be around us."

"You said there's darkness in the spell," added Khalid. "My arrows have some sunlight from Helios, among other things. Maybe while Shar or Alex hacks at the dome, I can shoot at it."

"It's a good idea," I said, "except that neither Alex nor Shar can see what we're dealing with, and Khalid, I'm not sure how well you can see. Let's link up more closely, and I'll try to lend you my ability to see magic. Wait! You still won't be able to work through the fire, and if I release it, we'll all be pincushions in about a minute."

"If Dan and Jimmie lend me some strength, I can sustain deflection for a few minutes," offered Nurse Florence. "Longer maybe. There don't seem to be as many archers in action."

"Do it," I said to them, and each of them took one of Nurse Florence's hands without question. It took a couple of minutes, but then I felt a deflection field rising around us. I had already established appropriate psychic links among Shar, Alex, Khalid, and me, so I let the flames die away and showed them what I was seeing around us. That wasn't as good as their being able to see it for themselves, particularly with regard to aim, but I hadn't yet developed a way to allow others to perceive magic on their own.

I added that to the to-do list, looked at Shar and Alex, and said, "OK, Shar, Alex is much better armored than you are, and to go high enough to get at the dome, you'd have to be exposed to the full power of the faerie archers. Swap swords with Alex."

"Sorry," muttered Shar to Alex, not meeting his gaze. "You can take the sword." He handed it over without another word, and Alex handed him Harpe.

Arrows were coming down fast and furious, reminding me we had to get a move on. Khalid cleverly had started to shoot his own arrows at the side of the dome near ground level. The archers, not realizing what he was doing, did not try to counter him at first, and the triple magic bursts from each arrow wreaked havoc on the barrier.

Alex shot up past the deflection field and started taking damage again, but he ignored his own wounds long enough to take several good swings with the gently glowing blade. Each strike caused the shadowy veil to shudder all around us, and cracks began to appear in it, but the abomination was stubbornly still holding together, probably reinforced by the witches, and now I could see some of the faerie archers unsheathing swords. Alex was well enough protected to have kept going a little longer despite the arrows, but if attacked from all sides by close-combat weapons, he was going to be in trouble.

Using White Hilt to throw bolts of fire, I kept the faeries at bay, but I couldn't shoot bolts in several different directions at the same time, so inevitably some of the faeries slipped through and struck at Alex with their swords. One succeeded in cutting his sword arm.

"Send me up!" demanded Shar. "Levitate me, and I'll cover him."

I could understand Shar's desire to make up for his false accusation, but that kind of move could be suicide, and if I had to focus on levitating him, it would prevent me from covering Alex myself.

Khalid, however, picked up on what was happening and began shooting at the faerie archers. After he hit a couple, they tried to take him out, but the deflection shield held, and he remained safe...at least for the moment.

Our situation was still far from ideal. David's playing seemed to have created an antimagic zone that baffled the witches and whatever spell casting faeries might be present. One witch even tried hellfire, but it dissipated when it reached the area David's music was affecting. That was something I hadn't expected, but it was a welcome relief. The deflection shield was keeping us similarly safe from most arrows.

However, we still faced forces that were far superior numerically. So far the faeries were staying airborne, probably to neutralize most of our fighters, but at some point they would have to realize that if they landed and tried to fight us in close combat, they could eventually overwhelm us. A lot of them would die, but if they were willing to sacrifice themselves for Nicneven, they would wear us out sooner or later. Alternatively, they could just keep firing at the deflection field until it collapsed and then keep up their fire until we all dropped. I could retake the lyre and resume the wind attack, but the witches were now above my reach, and without David's protective music, they would start attacking us with heavy-duty magic. Not only that, but Nurse Florence and I would start being poisoned again by the spell dome.

Great choice, huh? We could die by arrow, die by sword, or die by magic.

Our situation might be a little better if Alex could knock down that barrier, and he was dealing it damage, but Apollo's sword was just not as good in that respect as Zom would have been, and the witches kept repairing the cracks and openings Alex's blows created. Despite my and Khalid's efforts, Alex was taking more damage than the barrier. In the long run, he would have to retreat or die, and either way, the barrier would still be there.

"Is there any way of winning this?" asked Gordy. Just a few months ago, he would have had no clue, but now he had enough combat experience to realize we were losing.

"I'm not sure," I muttered.

"Perhaps it's time to retreat," suggested Carlos.

"And leave Nicneven's minions to run loose in Santa Barbara?" I asked.

"If we're all dead, they'll be free to run loose anyway," argued Gordy.

"Only two of us can open a portal," I pointed out, managing somehow to keep shooting fire bolts despite the distraction of the conversation. "You know how hard it is to multitask with magic. I need to keep Alex from getting killed, and if he comes down, the faeries will be able to attack us much more effectively. Nurse Florence needs to keep the deflection going, or a lot of arrows will hit us really fast."

Until I said it out loud, I hadn't really thought about the fact that we probably couldn't retreat fast enough even if we wanted to. Like it or not, we were stuck here.

Well, unless of course someone else opened a portal for us, like the Olympians, for example. I began to think about asking Shar to connect with them. I still didn't like the idea of leaving Nicneven's forces at large in Santa Barbara, but Gordy was right: we weren't going to do the people of Santa Barbara or anyone else any good if we let ourselves be killed.

At that moment Alex changed tactics. Hacking away at the dome spell as the witches renewed it wasn't getting him anywhere. I didn't know what prompted him to change strategy, but he seemed to be trying to take the fight to the witches. At least, he flew much higher, and that was the only reason I could think of for moving beyond the spell—and further away from any ground support.

The dome itself stood between him and the witches, but fortunately he was smart enough not to fly right through it. Perhaps, like me, he knew instinctively how dangerous that could be. Instead, he accelerated to the top speed his sandals could produce and crashed into the dome at its highest point, leading with Apollo's sword and Ares's shield. The two Olympian artifacts smashing into the magical barrier didn't destroy it, but the collision did create enough of a hole for him to fly through.

By now the faeries had realized what he was up to, and the closest ones rose as rapidly as they could, then swerved to intercept him, creating a solid mass that blocked his path to the witches. Others moved in behind him to block any downward escape route. He was high enough up now that it was difficult for me to provide much coverage with fire bolts; he had gone beyond what White Hilt's effective range was, or anyway what I had stretched it to be. The sword had not been crafted to do anything other than surround itself in flame, the rest being druidic improvisation on my part. I guessed Alex was out of range of Khalid's arrows as well, though I noticed Khalid was trying to shoot that high.

I reached out with my mind to check Alex's wounds and was shocked to discover how few he had, certainly not enough to account for all those arrow strikes. Then I remembered seeing Shar heal Khalid and Gordy by tapping them with the new sword.

"The sword you lent Alex has more than just protection against magic, right?" I asked Shar.

"The wielder can bring disease with a strike or healing with a tap," Shar replied, his attention also focused on Alex.

"That explains why he's still holding together," I said, and Shar sighed with what could be relief.

Alex was now wreaking havoc in the ranks of faeries, wounding with every sword swing, sometimes cutting multiple faeries with one stroke. Apollo must have added some arms training to his healing efforts, and the fact that Alex was Olympian strong didn't hurt. The combination of strength with a blade forged by Hephaestus was enough to hurt an opponent even through faerie armor.

I kept sharpening my vision to follow Alex's upward progress. Sure enough, he was tapping himself every so often to heal his wounds. That ability plus his magic resistance might just get him close enough to the witches to give them a major headache. Perhaps the situation was not as hopeless as it had seemed only moments before.

Then I saw the sickening flash as hellfire streaked toward Alex. Had he been on the ground with us, David's music would have protected him, but I doubted Apollo's blessed sword was strong enough to keep him from taking damage on a direct hit.

Alex dodged the first one, but two more were coming at him from different directions. Fast as he could fly, if there were multiple damned witches—damned in the literal sense—he would eventually get hit. Having the Olympians open a portal now might save us, but it would not save him.

Nurse Florence understood the growing fear on my face. "Witches who have bargained away their soul for the ability can use hellfire, but not as well as demons; the effort will exhaust a witch much more quickly than it would a demon."

"Which would be comforting if we had any idea how many of them there were," I replied worriedly. I still hadn't been able to get an accurate count on the shifting mass of enemies above us, and the witches were too distant for me to sense accurately how many of them might be readying hellfire.

"*Alex, retreat!*" I yelled to him mentally, but if he heard me, he gave no sign.

He had been dodging with surprising skill, but finally a burst of hellfire struck, and I could hear his scream. He had used his shield to deflect the blast, but some of the heat must have gotten through and burned his arm. Nor was that his only problem. The faeries had pulled away from him when the hellfire barrage started and were now shooting at him with wild abandon. Alex tapped himself with his sword, but with four blasts of hellfire now heading his way, he was soon going to reach the point at which he couldn't heal the injuries as fast as they happened.

It was at that moment I knew I couldn't just let him die. Yeah, he had broken Carla's nose, Stan's ribs, and practically every bone in Khalid's body, but that psychotic bully was not the same person risking his life to save us. I had to believe that...which meant I had to save him.

If I tried to fly to him, though, I could very well die myself. As soon as I got beyond the reach of David's music, the dome spell would start poisoning me, and when I got above it I would face faerie arrows, since I would also be above Nurse Florence's deflection, and witch spells, including some hellfire blasts. If I took the lyre up with me, I could play protection around myself much more successfully than I could do unaided, but then the guys on the ground would be exposed.

I tried desperately to think of another strategy. There had to be some way to save him without sacrificing someone else.

Alex took another hellfire hit, again on the shield, and again he screamed. I tried to reach out to him, but his nerve ending were screaming louder than he was, and I couldn't connect.

Then Khalid took off, and in a second I knew why: he wanted to save Alex.

"Khalid!" I screamed at him mentally. "Your fire immunity doesn't work against hellfire!"

"Then I guess I better move fast!" he replied solemnly, right before he severed our connection.

He managed to make it through the dome right before the witches sealed the gap Alex had created. It was just as well the little guy made the attempt in time, because he might have been impulsive enough to try flying right through the spell, and I hated to think what effect that might have had on his half djinn nature. Unfortunately, with that route closed and at least a hundred faerie archers between us, how was I going to get him back?

Moving with the speed of panic, Shar was at my side. "Tal, do something!"

Much as I hated my life sometimes, being constantly threatened with death, whether my own or that of a friend, had developed my ability to stay calm under pressure. A few months ago this kind of situation would have caused me to freeze, and I never would have remembered the flute.

Yeah, Robin Goodfellow's flute, blessed by Hermes and Apollo, was right there in New Dark Me's belt. I had forgotten all about it until this minute.

It wasn't as strong as the lyre of Orpheus, but it did pack a pretty good wallop. The faeries were probably still deafened against an emotional attack, but in order to free Merlin, I had learned how to weaponize sound—and then I was using only my voice. If I could amplify bursts from the flute, backed up by the instrument's double blessing, I could do quite a bit of damage whether my opponents could hear sound or not. That just might be enough to keep me from getting shot down right away.

Unfortunately, sonic energy probably wouldn't affect the dome, and flying straight through it would almost certainly kill me— or worse. Given time, I knew I could figure out how to counter that spell, but I had at most minutes before Alex and Khalid would be killed, and that would never be long enough.

Despite being used to danger, I began feeling more than a little desperate. Just in time I remembered a detail that might help me save Khalid and Alex.

Khalid had done some pretty good damage to the dome with his arrows. Examining the spots near ground level where his shots had hit, I could tell that the witches had not finished making repairs, and gaps large enough for me to fly through still remained. Probably they had been too busy repairing the damage created by Alex, and now his move in their direction had been even more distracting. Possibly they had forgotten these holes, or they figured the damage wasn't significant. Either way, these gaps were exactly what I needed.

Grabbing the flute, I stated playing for all I was worth, directing the sound upward so as not to shake my friends. As soon as I could, I flew sideways toward the nearest gap in the dome. The faeries realized what I was doing, but wave after wave of high frequency sound hit the nearest ones, pushing them out of my way and shaking them too much to get a clean shot at me.

Khalid had already bought me a little time by distracting the witches. I was pretty sure there were four of them on hand who could shoot hellfire, and now two of them were targeting Khalid, who so far was able to avoid them. With only two targeting Alex, he too was able to avoid the attacks, though only barely.

I ramped up the sound attack as far as it would go, sending faeries screaming away from me, in some cases bleeding from their ears. Then I reached Alex and began to weave a song of protection around us. He had managed to tap himself with the sword, but his wounds took a little time to heal, and I could smell his burned flesh.

"Alex, get your butt down to the ground!" I ordered. "Get inside David's music."

Shar, if he could have seen us, might have been cursing me for going to Alex first, but I knew if I could get him down, Khalid would follow.

A burst of hellfire hit both Alex and me, and what protection the flute added to the blessing on his sword enabled us to escape with only minor burns…this time. If the witches still had several hits in them, I knew they would eventually burn through the protection and fry us. We might both be able to evade, but if we separated, I couldn't extend my protection to him very effectively.

I think Alex was about to follow my order. The fact that Khalid was also risking getting fried shook him up; I could tell. Unfortunately, just as he was about to agree, the witches found a new way to make life difficult for us.

I felt the magic intensifying below us. Then, looking down, I could clearly see a new layer of shadow forming over the dome, stronger and far more deadly than the one Alex had successfully breached before. A quick scan told me that the witches had also filled the gaps near ground level, leaving us no way to rejoin our friends and get back within David's protective music. There was no way we were getting back the way we had come. We couldn't keep taking hellfire hits either, but if we flew away, our friends on the ground would all end up dead.

Alex's earlier impulse to take out the witches might have been the best bet even then—but right or wrong before, it was our only course of action now.

Some of the faeries had regrouped after Alex's earlier onslaught and were opening fire. It would be hard to dodge the arrows and the oncoming hellfire as well, but we had no choice, at least not for a few seconds.

"*Evasive action!*" I thought to Alex. He nodded, and we did the best we could…which meant I took one arrow, he three, and a hellfire burst came close enough to singe my hair.

I heard Khalid scream in the distance and knew that he had taken an arrow.

"*Khalid! It's not safe to go straight down, but fly over to the park!*" I mentally yelled to him.

"Not until you do!" he replied defiantly. As things stood, I couldn't really do anything to make him retreat, and Alex and I couldn't retreat either. We needed a better strategy, though, or we weren't going to last five minutes.

"Alex, we have to neutralize the—" I started to order, but then I heard Khalid yelling in the distance, "Alex, I forgive you!"

Did Khalid think he was about to die, or that Alex was? If so, he was probably right.

Another arrow hit me. Man, did I ever miss my dragon armor! I could stop the bleeding without using much power. The rest would have to wait.

At that moment I was too slow dodging hellfire and almost certainly would have been badly injured, even through my musical bubble of protection, but at the last second the blast dissipated. What could have been strong enough to do that?

Suddenly, Khalid was at my side. The arrows in his quiver had always been vaguely luminous, like Alex's sword, but now they sparkled with a pure light even beyond the radiance of Apollo's blessing.

"Israfel's blessing," he shouted. "Explain later."

Yeah, an archangelic blessing would stop hellfire. I got firsthand evidence when I actually saw Khalid shoot the next blast, dissipating it in a flash of holy light that made the arrow's other three bursts of magic force pale by comparison.

"Guys, let's kick those witches clear back to Scotland!" I yelled in their minds. I switched the flute to offensive sound bursts again, forcing the faeries to pull back and sparing us any further arrow fire.

I led us higher and in the general direction the witches were. We had to weave back and forth, but Khalid's arrows kept us from taking any more direct hellfire hits.

By the time we approached, the witches had surrounded themselves with a darkness far greater than the night. They must be drawing very heavily on Hecate's magic. We couldn't see them, and flying blind into those writhing shadows wasn't a good plan. They could see us, however, and only moments remained before they targeted us with more aggressive magic.

Without my having to ask, Khalid shot one arrow after another into the darkness. Each burst of divine aid came close to ripping the darkness to shreds, and when I glimpsed the witches' faces, I could see their shock. They probably knew we didn't have Zom, and they had not expected such an effective antimagic response. At this rate we would wear them down in short order.

Too late I remembered that some of the hellfire casters had shot from different angles; they weren't hiding in that one special patch of darkness, but somewhere else. I managed to dodge when one of them struck again, but Alex was not so lucky. The sword prevented him from being incinerated, but he suffered third degree burns on his sword arm. He managed to tap himself nonetheless, but the damage was healing slowly. The sword was being pushed to the outer limits of its power by the repeated attacks and healings in such a short period of time.

Khalid focused his attention on the hellfire witch and managed to hit her in the shoulder with an arrow. Its various bursts of power knocked the witch unconscious and sent her tumbling from the sky. He moved farther away to look for other stray witches, not a bad idea. However, now we had no easy way to dispel the darkness.

I could have tried shattering their concentration with sonic attacks, or I might have used White Hilt to blast through the shadows with fire in a wide enough pattern to make it hard to evade. Either approach could well have succeeded, but I had an even better option.

For a long time I had been good at getting magic swords to exceed what their makers had intended. I had used first White Hilt and then Zom as ray weapons. Surely I could do the same with the antimagic effect on Apollo's sword. Letting my fingers come to rest on the hilt, just above Alex's shaking hand, I reached out with my mind and felt the magic of the sword. Unlike Zom, which had been reluctant to obey at first, this sword almost immediately responded to my psychic command and shot a ray of purest light into the heart of the clotted darkness.

The shadows did not yield at first; even at thirdhand, Hecate's magic was formidable. However, the witches were already approaching exhaustion, and soon enough they could not maintain the spell against the unrelenting assault I had drawn from the sword.

By the time their concealment and whatever trap lay within it faded completely, they were too weak to mount much of an attack, and the continuous doses of antimagic seem to have slowed their attempts to fly away—a good thing, since there were at least a dozen of them, and if they had scattered, most of them would have gotten away. As it was, before they could flee, we were upon them.

There was no easy way to capture or subdue an opponent in midair, since any serious injury would cause them to lose concentration and fall, and rescuing them would mean letting others escape or even attack from behind. I wasn't anywhere near as keen on killing as I had been in earlier lives, but I had prepared myself for the fact that some or all of these witches would die...and I was kind of OK with that.

Apparently, Alex was more than OK with it. I didn't know if it was the pain from his wounds, his exhaustion, or some kind of weird flashback in which the witches had the faces of the bullies who had once tormented him, but he went medieval on them—literally. I couldn't look away, because I might have made myself vulnerable to attack, but watching him hacking off limbs and lopping off heads, even peripherally as I fought a witch myself, was almost more than I could take.

Two magically armed fighters, both of them faerie fast and one of them demigod strong against a dozen almost exhausted witches? Not even close!

I just wished I could feel better about this victory. I wasn't used to being covered in blood spray, most of it from Alex's new slice-and-dice fighting style.

Fortunately Alex stopped swinging when the last witch was dead. I was afraid he was so far out of control that he would just keep going, chopping up me, Khalid, anyone in reach. At least in that respect I had been overly pessimistic.

We looked at each other, and I could see his eyes were slightly unfocused. I did a superficial mental probe and found a red, swirling mess. Alex had been trying really hard to hold together for us; I knew that. Unfortunately, the stress of so much desperate combat, particularly the threats to Khalid, had exposed some of the damage Ares had done to him.

Hermes and Asclepius might have been wrong to let him out so soon.

As Alex's eyes focused, he must have been able to read the horror in mine.

"Tal...Tal, I didn't mean..."

I couldn't help but be repelled by the new Alex Witch Slaughterer, but I knew that wasn't all that was inside him. Once before I let him be rejected, and that had driven him right into Ares's arms. I would not make the same mistake again.

"Alex, it's all right," I said, trying to mean it. "We need to work on emotional control during combat, that's all."

"I look in your eyes, and I see it again. I see Khalid beaten to a pulp. That's the only way you'll ever see me, isn't it? As the guy who did that...who could do it again."

"No!" I insisted. "You aren't that anymore."

"Tal!" shouted Nurse Florence in my head. *"We need you, Alex and Khalid right now!"*

"Alex!" I said quickly. "There's trouble on the ground. Are you OK?"

"In a serial-killer kind of way," he said bitterly, looking at his bloody hands.

"Tal!" This time it was Khalid in my head. *"Help us!"* He must have chased someone down and gotten caught in whatever was happening below.

"Alex, I need you. Khalid needs you," I added in the calmest voice I could manage. Khalid's name seemed to flick some kind of switch in his head. He nodded reluctantly, and we flew down together.

The dome's new outer layer had vanished, as had the dome itself. I guessed the witches hadn't had time to make it self-sustaining, and it had disintegrated once they lost the battle. Whatever might have happened to it, at least we could reach our friends fast.

Nurse Florence's deflection field was still up, but from what I could tell, the faeries had landed and were trying to overwhelm the guys with sheer numbers, just as I had feared they might.

As we got closer, I could see specifics. Khalid, who must have finished his witch hunting and realized there was a new threat on the ground before I did, had taken up a position in front of Nurse Florence and was shooting at the faerie mass to good effect, but he was also nearly out of arrows. David had dropped the lyre, which he had no idea how to use aggressively, and switched back to the sword, but he and the guys were pressed by a mob of faeries in the process of using their superior numbers to encircle them. Some had also broken away to charge Khalid, who held his ground but would have a hard time fending off several faerie swords, since all he had was the bow and a dagger, neither designed for that kind of job. Even with a sword, his reach would have been less than theirs. Nurse Florence couldn't drop deflection to aid him without risking the more distant faeries attacking again with archery.

Seeing Khalid threatened, Alex landed next to him and started hacking away, though with a little restraint this time. He had that group of faeries on the defensive, so I flew to aid the rest of the guys, grabbing up the lyre as I did so.

Jimmie had already fallen, his ice sword glowing frostily right next to him. He didn't seem wounded, but then I noticed some kind of magic on him. He was struggling to get up but seemed unable to do so, suggesting some kind of paralysis was at work. He didn't look as if he were dying or in pain, so I focused for the moment on the faerie attackers.

The guys had circled as well as they could and now stood back to back, with the faerie mass pressing them all around. They were all proficient sword fighters, and they were doing damage, but since the faeries they wounded were shoved out of the way by a fresh bunch, eventually the guys would tire, and finally the faeries would bring them down.

Outside the circle I was more vulnerable, so I used fire from White Hilt to create a fire shield around me. Then, hanging on to the sword in one hand, I managed to drop the lyre on the ground with the other hand. After positioning the instrument as well as I could, I used that same hand to strum awkwardly on it. I couldn't summon up much power with such inferior musicianship, but a little boost was better than none. Using the music to intensify the fire, I expanded the flaming dome as rapidly as I could, forcing the faerie mob to back off hastily.

Had the faeries been determined to kill us at any cost, even that powerful attack might not have been enough. Faeries might have thrown themselves into my protective flames until the sheer mass of burning flesh smothered the fire, and then their living comrades would have overwhelmed me by sheer weight of numbers. Fortunately, their orders must not have been for a suicide mission. A combination of my fire attack, the appearance of blood-spattered Alex charging them with murder in his eyes once he had defeated their comrades, and Khalid's magically explosive arrow fire convinced them that the battle could not be won, especially since the witches were nowhere to be seen. They broke ranks and started flying away in all directions.

Yeah, I know—any one of them could now travel by portal back to Santa Barbara, having already been here. The safety in distance from Scotland and Elphame was lost to us. There wasn't much I could do about that, though. Even with the power of the lyre, I had no way to bring down so many of them so quickly, particularly since they were flying in every conceivable direction. At least we had all survived, and that was more than I might have expected.

Well, sort of survived. Alex had apparently snapped again when one of the faeries had thrown a sword with enough force to graze Khalid's head. Then both Khalid and Nurse Florence had witnessed the new and not-so-improved Alex butcher that group of faeries with disquieting efficiency. When the battle ended, they both stood like statues, surrounded by faerie body parts scattered on the blood-drenched sand. Khalid was sobbing a little, probably more from shock than anything else.

Unfortunately, Alex had still been in kill-everything-and-ask-questions-later mode when he came charging in to help the guys. Help them he did, but he also treated them to the third episode of the *Alex Chops up Everyone in Sight* show.

Damn it! They had just begun to appreciate him. Even Shar was softening. Now I could feel the questions hanging in the air. What was wrong with Alex? Could they trust him? Honestly, I didn't know.

Since everyone—on our side, anyway—was in one piece, the first thing to do was see what was wrong with Jimmie. Nurse Florence and I both ran to him, though naturally Dan got there first.

"What happened, Jimmie?" he asked quickly. "What's wrong?"

"I don't know," said Jimmie weakly. "When the faeries started landing, I began having muscle spasms, and then I couldn't move at all. I'm so sorry!"

"There's nothing to be sorry about; you couldn't help it," said Dan reassuringly. "We'll get you fixed up right away."

I wasn't so sure about that. I was scanning Jimmie and seeing evil magic throughout his body. There was a central point in his chest, but from there it radiated out in all directions, gripping every muscle. I didn't have the first clue how to break that intrusive a spell. I'd never seen anything like it.

"Nurse Florence, what do you make of that?" I asked, knowing she was seeing the same thing I was.

"I can't tell what we're dealing with," she replied, attempting a neutral tone, though I knew she was as alarmed as I was. "There is some kind of spell on him that is preventing him from moving, but it's more pervasive than any spell of that kind I've ever seen. It will take some time to figure out how to free him."

She looked at me then. "I don't have a thermometer, but did you notice his body temperature? It's a little low, and the magic inside of him feels cold somehow."

"That sounds like Nicneven's handiwork, but how could she have gotten to him?" I asked. Then I noticed a hint of guilt in Jimmie's eyes.

"Jimmie, do you have any idea how Nicneven was able to cast a spell on you?"

"Of course he doesn't!" snapped Dan. "How could he?"

"There's metal in his chest," said Nurse Florence, startled out of her neutral tone. "A circular disk, with...with a chain around it that loops around his neck, but on the inside. It looks like...a saint's medal. It's the source of the magic."

Now Jimmie looked really guilty. "That can't be! I got that medal from—"

"Wait," said Dan, "you *knew* you had a saint's medal inside your body like that?" Jimmie nodded unhappily.

"Jimmie, who gave you the medal?" I asked gently.

"It wasn't Nicneven. I'm not stupid! It was...it was Gyre-Carling."

Nurse Florence and I exchanged troubled looks.

"Very, very beautiful girl, right?" I asked Jimmie. He nodded unhappily.

"Jimmie," I continued, "Gyre-Carling is another name for Nicneven. She sometimes uses it when she's in her beautiful maiden form."

"Why would you take a saint medal from a stranger?" asked Dan. Under other circumstances, I might have laughed out loud. That wasn't exactly something kids were warned against.

Now Jimmie started crying. "I...I didn't mean to cause a problem. I just...I wanted so badly to get physically coordinated, and she...she told me the saint would help me if I wore the medal, but I had to keep it secret. It worked, too," he added defensively. "It worked until just now."

"It's all right, Jimmie," I said. "It was an honest mistake."

"Wait, that's why you suddenly got so good in sports?" asked Dan, dumbfounded.

"Even I got that part," said Gordy, quietly but a little reprovingly.

"How do we cure him? Remove the medal?" I asked.

"I wish it were that simple," replied Nurse Florence. "It looks to me as if the grip on his muscles is not just magical. Somehow the metal has woven its way through his body in ways I've never seen before. Removing the medal now means ripping it out of every voluntary muscle. That's hours and hours of surgery...by a surgeon who knows the supernatural. I don't exactly know anyone who fits that description. You?"

"You mean...you can't get this thing out of me?" asked Jimmie, suddenly terrified.

"If it takes cutting, I think Alex is your guy," said Gordy. He had intended to be funny, but even he realized how badly he had misstepped as soon as the words were out of his mouth.

Alex, still smeared in blood more or less from head to toe, looked incredibly guilty.

"Man, I didn't mean—" Gordy began.

"Yeah, you did," said Alex tiredly, yet quickly. "I'm more broken than I thought...and you all know that. You really want me to just go away and never come back."

The last thing we needed right now was more drama, but I didn't see any way of avoiding it. "I don't want you to leave."

"Tal," said Carlos uncertainly, "I know Alex was brave today, and he's a great fighter, but he's…sort of out of control when things get tough."

"And we're going to help him learn control," I said in my most commanding tone. Then, more gently, I added, "We all have our issues. I've got Dark Me…now in stereo," I said, gesturing toward the still comatose New Dark Me. "I've lost control more than once. You guys didn't want me to leave, though. And then there's Jimmie, who just screwed up today. Anyone want him to leave?"

"That's not fair," said Dan defensively. "It's not the same thing at all."

"Alex gave in to temptation at one point, and so did Jimmie. So have I. So have you, Dan. So probably have all of us at some point. And you know what? I used to be the most unwilling to forgive of any of you. You know that, Dan, as well as anyone. Well, no more. I'm not about that now. *This team* is not about that, either. We will help Jimmie. We will help Alex. Clear?"

Alex looked uncomfortably at the group, and he could see as well as I that they weren't exactly ready to forgive and forget, though they almost all nodded at my words.

The exception, unfortunately, was Shar, hugging Khalid, who had just stopped crying.

"At the very least, he needs to go back to Hermes and Asclepius for more treatment," said Shar, one eye on Alex. "How many weeks is it going to take for Khalid to get over the nightmares he'll have from this day?"

"I'm not a child," said Khalid weakly. "I'll be all right."

"No, you won't," said Alex quietly. "I look in your eyes, and I see me beating you. That's what you fear is going to happen again, right?"

"No," said Khalid, but even more shakily than before. He was trying, but he just wasn't that good an actor.

"We need to table this discussion for the moment," said Nurse Florence. "We have to find some way to clean up the area before dawn. Even though we didn't start this fight, the authorities in

Annwn will still have our heads if we allow evidence of it to be discovered. Then we have to start studying Jimmie's condition. Oh, and we need to check on the situation in Santa Brígida."

"I can help with the beach," said a familiar voice. I turned, shocked to see Coventina smiling at me.

"My lady," I said with a bow, "I am immeasurably glad to see you, but how can you be here? I thought the Order's situation—"

"Became less urgent when I sensed your peril," she said. "I have been…restless. I knew things were amiss somehow. Nicneven's incursion into this world drew my attention, I suppose in part because two who are bonded to the lake were so close to it when it happened. Once I became aware, it was a simple matter to come to you through the bond. I had hoped to reach you during the battle, but having failed that, at least I can help you cleanse this land."

I noticed that the guys had stopped looking at Coventina and started looking behind us. Their expressions of amazement made me turn and look as well.

Behind us, partly on the sand and partly extending out over the sea, was an enormous castle, shifting as I looked at it. Sometimes it seemed a Roman fort, sometimes a much later medieval castle, but always oversize, always formidable, always feeling incredibly ancient.

Relocating a structure like that would have required incredible amounts of magic, at least the way Earth inhibited casting, but even in Annwn, such a feat would have been difficult. Looking closely though, I could see a vague aura around the edges of the castle, as if it were being superimposed on the landscape rather than being part of it. Of course it couldn't be part of it, anyway; if there were a huge castle on Shoreline Beach, we'd surely have noticed it a long time before. Either it was an illusion of some kind, or the castle was real enough, but it was located somewhere else, and we were being shown its image for some reason.

The door to the gatehouse was standing invitingly open, and beyond it the drawbridge had been lowered across the moat, and the inner gateway opened. Clearly, someone wanted us to pay a visit—though how we were expected to do that when the castle wasn't on our plane of existence I wasn't quite sure.

"Nicneven?" I asked.

"No," said Coventina. "Look at the banner the castle is flying." I did look, and on a field of brilliant blue was a luminous cup filled with a blood-red liquid.

"You mean—" I began.

"Yes," said Coventina. "This is Carbonek, the Grail castle. I saw it once, long ago," she said almost wistfully. "If it has appeared to you, you are being offered a Grail quest. Turning down such an offer would be folly."

"How do we accept?" I asked, watching the structure cycle through another round of architectural mutation.

Coventina smiled. "As I recall, all you need do is walk in its direction."

I thought about Saint Brendan's word of warning, but Coventina was right: refusing to enter would be folly. Even with the lyre, Nicneven's forces had nearly gotten the better of us—and that was without Nicneven. We needed the Grail if we were to win the inevitable battle.

"I don't mean to seem ungrateful, but why now?" I asked. "We have all these other problems…"

Coventina laughed. "And the Grail may well be the solution to all of them…if one of you can win it. I will stay here and cleanse the beach for you. Maybe I will have a little help," she said expectantly, looking at Nurse Florence.

"I know this isn't a one-person job, and the resources of the Order are not…what they once were," said Nurse Florence sadly. "I will stay and help."

"What about Jimmie?" asked Dan.

"Take him along," said Nurse Florence. "It is said there is no ill the Grail cannot heal, no spell it cannot break. If you win it, you can surely drive Nicneven's evil out of Jimmie."

"What about him?" I said, indicating New Dark Me.

"The Grail can surely break that spell as well and restore Robin," suggested Nurse Florence.

"Should we all go?" asked Gordy, torn between eagerness and reluctance.

"We probably should," I said. "I have it on good authority that I'm not the one who can win it." Everyone except Nurse Florence looked puzzled, but I wasn't inclined to elaborate.

"What about those of us who...aren't Christian?" asked Stan.

"Some of the old stories suggest that only a true believer can see the Grail, but we can't be sure even of that. If you aren't too uncomfortable with the whole thing, I say come on ahead."

"Jesus was Jewish," said Gordy, as if no one else would have remembered that.

"What about me?" asked Khalid.

"Jesus liked the innocence of little children, if I recall," said Dan. "For all we know, Khalid, you are the most likely to succeed."

"What about him?" asked Shar, pointing at Alex, who looked at the ground.

"Maybe the Grail can cure him," I suggested. "Either way, everyone comes. If the Grail quest was only intended for some of us, the castle would only have appeared to some of us." I had no idea if that was really true, but it sounded good, and everyone seemed satisfied with it—or at least, like Shar, willing to put up with it rather than let the opportunity pass.

"We could do with some cleaning up," said Carlos. We all had some blood on us, and Alex seemed to have it on every inch of his body.

"This is the Grail castle," I said quickly. "I think they know what blood looks like. In any case, in the old stories questers sometimes stayed there and received hospitality, even though the knights in question were relatively fresh from the battlefield. I'm sure they'll let us clean up."

It took us a few minutes to gather up our gear and conjure up stretchers on which to carry Jimmie and New Dark Me. Then, after thanking Coventina and Nurse Florence for staying behind to cleanse the beach, we turned and walked cautiously toward the gate house.

I thought about the many knights who had tried to find the Grail castle during the reign of King Arthur. Most of them had ended up dead, though they had more often than not died while still searching for the Grail. At least we didn't have to spend months trying to find the castle.

That didn't mean the tests inside wouldn't kill us, of course. Surely, though, God hadn't opened this door simply to let us die.

Well, at least it was comforting to think that. Whether it was true or not was a different matter.

Chapter 26: Unexpected Castle (Tal)

From what Coventina had told me, the castle was not just an illusion or projection, but more like the real thing, seen through some kind of portal. Whatever gateway had opened to let us see the castle was far different from the portals we were familiar with, though, since it showed us Carbonek superimposed on Shoreline Beach, with no hint of what its actual surroundings were like. Nor was there any obvious opening, but when we had gone a few steps in the direction of the castle, whatever gateway there was closed behind us with a resounding psychic thud. Committed as I was to finding the Grail if we could, I felt a little claustrophobic now that there was no turning back.

We could now see Carbonek was on a grassy plain, with rolling hills visible in the distance but no particularly distinguishing landmarks. The castle itself was certainly distinctive, but the constant shifting of its architecture from one type to another, from Roman fort to thirteenth-century castle with every imaginable variation in between, suggested a kind of infinite mutability I had never heard of in a building.

"Did the original Taliesin remember anything like this?" asked Stan.

"The original Taliesin never went on the Grail quest," I replied, "but I can't recall any stories about the Grail castle changing form like this."

"Remember how much the Chapel Perilous changed from what it had been in the time of the original Taliesin?" asked Shar. "Carbonek has had over fifteen hundred years to change as well. Perhaps the old stories aren't going to help very much."

"They probably wouldn't anyway," said Stan, shaking his head. "Each story describes the castle in completely different terms. Of course, it seems the castle isn't on Earth but opens portals when it wants to invite somebody in, which would certainly explain why different stories locate it in different places."

Gordy sighed loudly. "Not that this isn't absolutely *fascinating*, but shouldn't we get on with, you know, the quest?"

I chuckled a little. "You're right, Gordy. We have no idea how long this could take, or how the flow of time here relates to our own world. We do know that in our world we don't have long before Nicneven is going to attack again."

With Dan, Gordy, and Carlos carrying Jimmie, and Stan, Shar, and me carrying New Dark Me, we quickly covered the short stretch of dirt road to the castle, which as we approached settled on the form of an extremely elaborate thirteenth-century structure made from weathered stone that whispered of a much earlier era.

Two Grail knights in full armor—with what was obviously the Grail coat of arms (silver cup on a brilliant blue field) emblazoned on their shields—emerged from the barbican, gestured us across the footbridge, greeted us, and ushered us across the drawbridge over the moat. We passed additional knights in the guardhouse on either side of the gate, and finally we found ourselves in the oddly silent courtyard.

There were knights clinking in their armor, but little conversation. Thinking back on the medieval castles with which I was familiar, I could not remember any, not even Camelot, with such a solemn air about them.

To the north of us was an imposing keep with the Grail banner flying over it. Our two escorts guided us through the massive doorway and into the great hall. It was an impressive space, though more human than the comparable part of Gwynn ap Nudd's castle. The Grail castle didn't have its own luminescence, relying instead on the flickering torches projecting out from more or less evenly spaced sconces that lined each wall a little above eye level. The artwork was less spectacular than that of Annwn, but still enough to keep an art historian busy for months. Tapestries hanging from the walls depicted biblical scenes, beginning with David, the ancestor of the original Grail guardians, Joseph of Arimathea and his brother Bron. If one viewed these tapestries clockwise around the room, they showed the history of the Grail, from the last supper to the winning of the Grail by Galahad, also a descendant of David. How many ambiguities in the Grail tradition might they clear up? Sadly, I had the feeling I would never have the chance to study them in detail.

The great hall was much more animated than the courtyard had been, though it retained the solemn mood. Servants in Grail livery bustled around, preparing to serve dinner at a round table that could not help but remind me of the one at Camelot, though this one was somewhat smaller and seemed crafted from highly polished silver.

At the far end of the room I could make out two thrones, doubtless for the current Grail king and queen. Our escorts deftly maneuvered us around the table and led us to the royal couple, who leaned forward expectantly as we approached. They were comparatively young, midtwenties, I guessed. Both were black haired, brown eyed, and charismatic, though not strikingly attractive. Both were crowned in silver and wore white garments with the Grail emblem on their chests. To their left stood a figure whose appearance was in every way a contrast to them. The combination of his white hair, longish beard, wrinkled face, faded brown robes, and penetrating stare gave him the look of an Old Testament prophet rather than the adviser to a medieval king.

"Welcome, friends!" said the Grail king heartily. We set down our two stretchers and bowed to him and to the queen.

"Rise, please," he said, "for anyone who wins the Grail is truly our equal. Nay, more than our equal."

"As yet they have won nothing!" observed the old man sharply.

The king chuckled. "Eliezer, must you always be so pessimistic? They have only just arrived. The Grail may well find one of them worthy."

Eliezer snorted at that but said no more.

"Please allow me to introduce myself," continued the king. "I am Pelles, twenty-seventh of that name to lead the guardians of the Grail, and my wife is Helena, sixth of that name to be queen here. Both of us are ultimately descended from King David of Israel, I through Joseph of Arimathea, who first brought the Grail to Britain. Our trusted adviser, as you have no doubt surmised, is Eliezer. He is descended from Lazarus, he who was resurrected by Jesus and became a bishop in Cyprus."

"Actually, the name my parents gave me was Helaine," said the queen, "but since the Grail bearer is named Elaine, I chose to be called Helena both to avoid confusion and to honor the memory of the mother of Constantine, she who found the True Cross."

I started to introduce my party, but Pelles held up his hand. "Eliezer has been touched by God with the ability to see many things that would be unseen by other men. He is accustomed to introducing our guests to me."

Eliezer stepped forward confidently but then faltered a little when he looked at me. "Majesty, this is Taliesin Weaver, but he is older than he looks." Eliezer's eyes widened as he continued. "God has willed that his soul be in flesh many, many times. He knew the Grail questers in the time of King Arthur, and now he comes to win the Grail himself. I do not believe he will succeed."

"And why not?" asked Pelles.

Eliezer almost sneered at me. "There is a darkness near his soul. He has not given in to evil, yet somehow he still has evil within. Surely the Grail will reject him."

I tried hard to hide my disappointment, even though Saint Brendan had already told me the same thing.

"Eliezer," said Helena gently, "the castle would never have admitted him if there had been no hope."

"Unless," interrupted Eliezer, staring at me again, "it means to make an example of him."

"Please continue with the introductions," said Pelles calmly. "Our guests are tired and hungry."

Eliezer turned next to Dan, but at first he seemed even more puzzled than he had when he looked at me. However, eventually his expression became certain, almost triumphant.

"Lancelot!" he exclaimed. "Was not one failure to win the Grail enough for you?"

Now it was Dan's turn to look puzzled. "I'm not Lancelot! There are some members of our party," he continued, indicating me, Stan, and Shar, "whose past life memories have been awakened, but mine haven't."

"Nonetheless, you were once Lancelot," insisted Eliezer. "The memories slumber, but they are plain to me."

"If this is true," I interrupted quickly, "it puts my friend in great danger, for Morgan le Fay still lives, and she seeks the soul of Lancelot. I beg you not to speak of this to anyone."

"Do I look like a gossip to you?" snapped Eliezer, clearly insulted. "Besides, none of us who live in Carbonek ever leave it. Whom would I tell?"

"But guests do come from time to time, do they not?" I insisted.

"Very infrequently these days," replied Eliezer, "and I would say nothing to any of them about your friend."

Dan was looking in my direction. I knew he wanted me to confirm or deny Eliezer's story. I didn't return his glance. Because of my mother's vision, I had known for days that he was Lancelot, but, not wanting to worry him, I had never told him. Now didn't seem like the best time to give him one more thing to worry about.

Eliezer had already moved on to Stan. He studied him for a while, then looked alarmed and bowed quickly.

"King David, forgive me for not recognizing you sooner." Turning to Pelles, he said, "Now here is someone the Grail might actually accept. David returned again in the flesh, and carrying David's sword if I am not mistaken. A new Galahad if ever there was one!" Stan blushed but said nothing.

Well, Galahad, illegitimate son of Lancelot and Elaine, the daughter of Pelles I, had been a descendant of David and had carried a different sword of David. I could see where Eliezer was going.

"But I see I was too hasty," said Eliezer suddenly. "This one still follows the religion of Abraham. He will never achieve the Grail until he has become a Christian."

Stan went from blushing to pale in a second, and he practically started oozing guilt. I didn't need to read his mind to tell that he was already blaming himself for the loss of the Grail. Much as he wanted to help, I was sure he would never convert, and I would not have expected him to.

"That is for the Grail to decide, not for you," said Helena gently.

"The Grail has never chosen someone without faith," said Eliezer, clearly surprised by her response.

"The Grail has chosen exactly one person in the last two thousand years," said Pelles slowly. "And never before has a current member of the Jewish faith even been in the castle, at least as far as I am aware. You may be right, Eliezer, but I am content to let events unfold as they will. The castle would not have admitted him without some purpose."

Eliezer muttered a little at that, then looked at Shar. "Yet another soul several times in flesh," he said, scratching his head. "This one was Greek in the past, and now he too embraces the faith of Abraham." Eliezer had clearly dismissed Shar's chance at the Grail as well, and I could tell Shar was angry, but he said nothing.

Eliezer continued relentlessly down the line. Gordy and Carlos, he announced, were Christian, and hence at least technically eligible to win the Grail, but he clearly had reservations about both of them. I was happy he didn't share those reservations, however. It would be nice if he didn't destroy the morale of everyone in the party.

Eliezer stared longest of all at Khalid, amazed at what he saw. "This one is not fully human, and he is a son of Ishmael on top of that. If anyone is wasting his time here, it is he."

Khalid already had enough trouble dealing with his half djinn nature. Having Eliezer point it out and demean Khalid's Muslim faith had him struggling to hold back tears.

"How can you say something like that to a little kid?" demanded Shar, anger seething in every syllable.

"*Shar!*" I thought loudly to him, "*Please don't make a scene! I don't know what will happen if we offend our hosts.*"

"*No one speaks to Khalid that way!*" he snapped back at me. "*No one!*"

"I can say it because it is true!" said Eliezer, glaring at Shar.

We had barely been in the castle five minutes, and things were already going sideways. I couldn't defend Eliezer's attitude, which to my modern ears sounded pretty anti-Semitic, and I didn't want Khalid hurt for the world, but we needed the Grail. We needed it bad. I thought for a second about what Saint Brendan had said about choices. A second was about all I had. Shar was going to blow sky high any moment—and I couldn't really blame him.

"Your majesties," I said, addressing the king and queen. "My friend means no insult to you or to any in your court, but on his behalf I most protest Eliezer's manner. I know we come from a different society and have different customs. I know Eliezer does not understand our ways and believes what he is saying, but some of us would not agree. I must ask that Eliezer gives no further offense to the members of my party."

Eliezer looked completely flummoxed. "Majesty, these...people came seeking the Grail, one of the holiest artifacts of Christendom. Let them go seek relics of their own faith if they will not renounce that faith and accept the word of Christ in its stead."

"Majesties, are you familiar with a man named Adolf Hitler?" I asked the royal couple, ignoring Eliezer.

Pelles nodded gravely. "The devil's own spawn from what I have heard. Yet he sought the Grail!" The king shook his head in disbelief. "The castle never let any of his minions in, but it did occasionally open a gateway here and there, just long enough for people to see. I think it was taunting him."

"Pardon me for being so blunt," I said, "but Eliezer's thinking ultimately leads to Hitler's."

"Ridiculous!" scoffed the prophet. "I don't favor violence against the sons of Abraham or of Ishmael. I just do not think them worthy of the Grail."

"In our society we have found that it is easy to slip from thinking people aren't worthy to thinking they should be persecuted. Jesus criticized people for moral failings...including hypocrisy," I added, looking at Eliezer, "but, surrounded by people who believed differently from him, did he ever even once belittle someone because of what that person believed? Samaritans, Zealots, pagan Romans— a wealth of people to find unworthy, yet he didn't give into the temptation to demean them, not even once."

(Surprised? So was I! I guessed listening in Sunday school sometimes paid off.)

Eliezer was nearly apoplectic, but he could see Pelles was about to respond, so he restrained himself.

"Much of what you say is strange to us," admitted Pelles. "Here everyone accepts Jesus as the messiah. However, though the guardians of the Grail remain always at Carbonek, we do have ways of observing the world, and I cannot believe from what we know of history that religious persecution ever truly turned even a single heart to God."

"I never suggested—" began Eliezer.

"I know, I know, old friend," interrupted Pelles. "Your heart is pure. Yet young Taliesin is of good heart too, I think. In any case, the castle has opened its gates to men of different faiths. That has to mean something. I would ask you to pass no further judgment upon Taliesin and his men. The Grail will give itself to whichever of them it will...or perhaps to none of them. Let that be between them and God."

Eliezer looked disgusted but nodded in acknowledgment of the king's words. Shar caught my eye and whispered, "Thanks," then put his arm around Khalid. Perhaps the worst was over.

Unfortunately, Eliezer was not finished. Now he came to New Dark Me, still fast asleep in the grip of my spell, and again the prophet's eyes widened in surprise.

"This one is like Taliesin, yet somehow unlike him. Here evil rules. I cannot imagine why the castle admitted him at all."

"In truth there is someone else within, imprisoned by a spell," I explained. "We had hoped to free him with the Grail if we were fortunate enough to complete the quest."

"You speak the truth," conceded Eliezer. He clearly wanted to say more, but, glancing furtively at the king, he turned to Alex instead.

"This one smells of pagan gods!" Eliezer said in amazement. "He has also killed...and not always in a just cause. He comes to us smeared in blood. Surely this is a sign."

"Eliezer—" began Pelles, his tone full of warning.

"No, this is different," insisted the prophet. "This one forsook what he knew was right to seek personal gain, and other people died...many people."

"I will leave," said Alex quietly, not meeting Eliezer's eyes.

"You will not," I said firmly. "The castle admitted you as much as anyone else, Alex. In any case," I continued, turning to Eliezer, "there is no denying he has sinned, but he is also repentant. Jesus never turned away a repentant sinner."

Eliezer's stare made it clear he had absolutely no use for me, but instead of arguing, he turned to Jimmie, the last of us to be examined. Jimmie could barely raise his head but managed to get it up a little.

"Truly, this is the strangest group of Grail questers in the whole history of Carbonek," said Eliezer. "This one has been resurrected from the dead, and I might have been inclined to take that as an unmistakable sign of God's favor, yet a strange alien magic has taken root in him…by his own choice."

"He didn't know what he was doing!" protested Dan.

"He should have!" snapped Eliezer. "The signs were plain enough."

"As with all my men, he has risked his life for others," I said calmly, looking again at Pelles. "Yet he did not come seeking the Grail. We brought him in hopes the Grail might cure him."

"I'm afraid I must agree with Eliezer," said Pelles, much to my surprise. "At first I saw wisdom in following Carbonek's choices, but you have brought me not only unbelievers and infidels but murderers and traffickers in dark magic. I must ask that you all leave. Some of the guardians will escort you from this place."

Now Jimmie looked on the verge of tears. Even through the blood, I could see shame reddening Alex's cheeks. Khalid could no longer hold his tears in, and his whole body shook from his sobbing. I could argue that Alex deserved this kind of treatment, though even that didn't feel right, but Jimmie and Khalid? Never!

Shar and Dan both had one hand on their sword hilts, and in a few seconds the others would follow suit.

"Majesty, our need is great, our cause urgent," I said, choking down my anger. "I know we make an…unlikely-looking group, but this same group has fearlessly fought evil time and again. The castle has allowed us entry. Let it now propose an ordeal for me, so that I may verify our worthiness."

"The castle cannot be ordered about!" protested Eliezer. "It is not for you to demand trial by ordeal."

"However, there is a precedent," remarked Pelles, stroking his beard, "but be careful what you ask for, Taliesin, for a trial by ordeal may destroy you."

"I will undergo an ordeal," I pledged, "and if I emerge unharmed, it will prove the worth of all the members of my party."

"As you have said, so shall it be," replied Pelles, "but not as you imagine." He paused for a moment, then continued, "I think you were expecting trial by combat, but none of us doubt your courage in battle. Instead, you will face the same test Saint John was given by the Emperor Domitian: you will be boiled in oil. If you emerge unscathed, you will have provided your worthiness, and the worthiness of all you vouch for."

It turned out to be a lot easier to risk my life in the abstract that to submit to something that horrible. I opened my mouth to respond, but no words came out. In none of my previous lives had I been boiled alive, but even someone with a much less vivid imagination than mine would have had little difficulty visualizing what it might be like.

"I'll do it," said Khalid quietly, wiping away his tears.

I knew what he was thinking: his fireproof nature would enable him to pass through the ordeal unharmed. I had similarly thought for a few seconds that I could protect myself with magic. Somehow neither idea seemed that good. Surely beating the ordeal by anything but the power of God would only make things worse.

"No!" said Shar to Khalid. "I...I..."

He couldn't quite finish the sentence, either. Facing death in combat is one thing, especially when you know that you might win, and if you do die, the death is likely to be quick. Getting boiled in oil could be quick, but probably not the same kind of quick.

I didn't have to read minds to know that every single guy was ready to volunteer to take my place, but none of them could quite get the words out. I wouldn't allow any of them to do the ordeal for me, but I was still having trouble speaking.

"I'll do it," said Alex, winning the race and shocking the hell out of all of us. Yeah, I had begun to hope he could be redeemed, though my faith was shaken a little by his loss of control on the battlefield. Could he have come so far in such a short time?

"Hmmm...What do you say to that, Eliezer?" asked Pelles. "The one who stinks of pagan gods and murders people is willing to face the ordeal."

"No one will face it but me!" I insisted, finally finding my voice. I would have said more, but Eliezer started laughing heartily. Given his earlier grimness and meanness, that was the last thing I expected.

Then I realized that Pelles and Helena were laughing as well. Looking at my confused expression, Pelles got control of himself and said, "First and second tests passed, Taliesin."

"Huh?" said Gordy, speaking for us all.

"Surely you did not take us for such savages that we would actually boil you in oil," protested Helena, still smiling. "The castle does...speak to us at times, and it suggested offering the challenge to see how you and your men responded."

Helena hesitated for a moment. Her smile faded, and I thought maybe I could see a tear in her eye. "Taliesin, you didn't hesitate. Neither did your men...even the boy. Every one of them would have taken your place."

"I was afraid," I admitted.

"So was I," said Carlos quickly. The others nodded.

"Being afraid doesn't make you a coward," observed Eliezer. "Not being afraid does make you an idiot, however." Gone was the tone of the stern prophet, replaced by an almost friendly demeanor.

"Just because we never leave the castle doesn't mean our way of thinking fossilized hundreds of years ago," added Pelles. "The castle shows us what is happening in the world, and my ancestors and I have learned much in that way. Eliezer's pretense of a somewhat...less enlightened...attitude was designed to be your first test."

"You could have attacked us," Eliezer said. "Some of you dearly wanted to. That would have been a failure, but not the worst one possible. Taliesin, you could easily have decided to ignore the distress of your friends in the hopes of winning the Grail. That kind of compromise of principles would have doomed all of you."

Well, I dodged a bullet that time. Yeah, I had been thinking about that very kind of compromise. Shar would have been mad, but the guys would have swallowed the whole deal if I had asked them to. Good thing I didn't!

"Will all the tests be like that?" asked Gordy.

"The tests here take many forms. I fear some may be much more physical than that, though the castle tries to avoid killing someone whose intent is not evil," replied Pelles.

"I think perhaps it would be wise to reunite our guests with their friends now," suggested Helena.

"Friends?" I asked, having a hard time imagining who could have found us here. Perhaps Nurse Florence and Coventina had finished faster than they expected. I felt pretty guilty about leaving them behind to do cleanup.

"Yes," began Pelles, "the castle has never before admitted more than one party at a time, but a short while before you appeared, another group arrived, and the castle admitted them. They...they claimed to know you would be here."

"It was more than just a claim," said a familiar voice from the direction of one of the side doors. I looked over to see the elderly figure of Merlin striding purposefully in our direction, his staff tapping loudly upon the stone floor as he walked.

"Merlin," I said happily. "I'm so glad to see you. I thought you might be—"

"Dead?" asked Merlin, chuckling a little. "I did try to let go of life and return to the cycle of rebirth, but God would not let me. I think He had one more task He needed done," he added, winking at me.

"Because God naturally would need help from the prospective Antichrist," said Eliezer, mockingly but not maliciously. It took me a second to remember that his unbending contempt for all things unusual had just been an act.

"Long in the past," said Merlin dismissively. "Oh, as I was traveling here, Taliesin, I noticed how careless your men have become with their equipment." With a flourish he produced a green glowing sword from somewhere in his robes.

"Zom!" exclaimed Shar happily. Merlin, smiling broadly, handed the blade over to Shar. "I've also brought along all those sets of armor Gwynn so improvidently had made for you. Imagine being careless enough to leave all of them behind!"

"Merlin, they were stored in my house, behind spells that would admit only me," I protested.

Merlin shrugged. "You will need to restore those spells later. They were well crafted, though. It took me almost an hour to decide I just needed to break through them rather than trying more subtle methods. I did get the opportunity to meet your mother, though. Fine woman!"

"She's all right?" I asked quickly.

"Of course!" scoffed Merlin. "Did you think I had designs on her virtue?" We both had to laugh at that. Then he continued, "I will say though that she took surprisingly well to my being Merlin."

"Yeah, she's had some...experience in that area," I said, trying to hold back another laugh.

"I doubt it not, with you as a son," replied Merlin. "Be that as it may, my visit to your pleasant little town also gave me the opportunity to meet one of your Ladies of the Lake: Vanora, I think her name was."

"Is *she* all right?" I asked.

"How little faith in me you have!" said Merlin. "Yes, she is much better than she was. She collapsed from Nicneven's little area spell, but fortunately I hadn't had the time to be poisoned by it, so with the help of her men, I got her out. Then I got the evacuation she wanted rolling. You mayor was surprisingly resistant to the idea, but don't worry...he'll recover eventually." Merlin winked again.

"How did you get in, Merlin?" I asked. "None of us could."

"Yes," he said, stroking his beard, "I felt...resistance to my presence, but from what I could tell the magic was directed more against you and your company. Whoever crafted it was not expecting me to pay a visit, and the barrier did not block my path."

"My, you have been busy today!" I said jokingly.

"And you have been careless!" said Merlin. "Aside from leaving weapons and armor strewn about, you have misplaced a few women as well." As if on cue, Eva and Carla emerged from a side door. "I had quite a time finding the blond one," Merlin continued, "but fortunately I had been watching Asmodeus's little attempt to exile your men to another world, and I got enough clues from his portal to figure out where it led. In any case, demons are never quite as clever at hiding things as they fancy themselves. The other one was just a little sleepy, but I managed to wake her up."

The mere sight of Carla sent my heart racing. Unfortunately, it had a very different effect on the guys, who all drew their weapons, startling both the girls and making me downright angry.

"Are you going to start that again?" I practically barked. "I told you didn't sell her soul. She couldn't have."

"She did," interrupted Eliezer. "I could smell it on her the moment she arrived. Why the castle admitted her is beyond me, but at least her demon can't find her here."

"Tal, what are they talking about?" asked Carla, looking at them as if they had all gone mad.

"Dark Me was impersonating me for a while," I said. "He convinced them that you had made a pact with a demon."

"It wasn't just Dark Me, remember?" asked Shar. "Aphrodite warned me about this. We've already been over that."

"It's a trick!" I insisted angrily. "Nicneven is using this wild idea to rip up apart. What surprises me is that you are all falling for it."

I glanced at Merlin, who no longer had his playful look but had gone utterly solemn, much like Eliezer in the beginning. "Taliesin, I did foresee that something like this could happen. I brought the girl along because I knew a demon would eventually break that spell she was under, and I wanted to keep an eye on her."

"But you only see possible futures, right?" I asked. "You can't be sure that particular future happened."

"I can be much more sure of the past," replied Merlin. "Recall that I am half demon myself. No one knows the signs better than I. This girl has clearly trafficked with demons."

"You won't get through to him," said Dan loudly. "He's under a spell."

"I do not—" began Merlin.

"It's subtle," interrupted Shar. "Tal, let him examine you. Let us prove it to you."

"I'm fine," I insisted, "and so is she!"

I looked at Merlin, whose gaze was oddly fixed on someone behind me. I turned and saw a handsome man only a bit older than I and the guys were as he entered from another side door. He was oddly wearing only a loin cloth, revealing a muscular body marked by a number of small, bleeding puncture wounds. He looked strangely familiar, but I couldn't quite place him.

"Saint Sebastian?" asked Jimmie weakly.

Chapter 27: Saint Jimmie (Jimmie)

I had seen him once before, in a vision, tied to a fence, with the arrows of his martyrdom still sticking out of him. Now I knew too well what he had been trying to tell me, and I looked away from him, ashamed.

"James, it is a pleasure to finally meet you!" he said, walking right up to the stretcher on which I was lying.

"Saint Sebastian?" asked Tal, echoing my earlier question. "How can you be here?"

"Saints occasionally do visit," said Helena.

"Yes, Taliesin," he replied. "Saints do not usually show themselves in this way, but your friend there is a special case. When the forces of evil impersonate one of us, it is like...calling us out, I suppose you would say. The Almighty gives us a little more latitude to respond in such a case."

"When did a demon—" began Dan.

"Not a demon," I said. "Nicneven. She came to me as Gyre-Carling, remember? The thing inside me started out as a fake Saint Sebastian medal."

Sebastian was leaning over me, looking at me intently. "I had hoped to remove this curse from James here, but I cannot yet. I did not realize how it has woven itself into his body. I can cure plague, but I can't heal a body that has been ripped to shreds. I must summon one of my brethren with broader healing powers. Unfortunately, healing saints are normally extremely busy, so summoning one here will take time."

"Take it out now!" I said as loudly as I could.

"I dare not," replied Sebastian. "The process would be too painful."

"I could block the pain," Tal suggested.

"I do not doubt your abilities," replied Sebastian, "but as you know, magically induced pain cannot be blocked by deadening the nerves. What is in James will fight against being removed, and it will induce pain beyond anyone's ability to block."

"If one of us completes the quest, won't the Grail heal Jimmie?" asked Dan.

"Undoubtedly," agreed Sebastian, "but none of us can surely know whether you will succeed in the quest or not."

"I want it out now!" I insisted. Despite myself, a tear rolled down my cheek. "Please, please take it out!"

"It is not just the pain," said Sebastian in a voice that suggested he was humoring me. "The intrusion is partly magical, but partly physical. Your body will be badly damaged when I remove the curse. Without a healer, you may die."

"Taliesin could act as healer," suggested Merlin.

"I've tried, Merlin," said Tal sadly, "but I haven't had much luck. I can stop bleeding and stuff like that, but reconstructing damaged tissue has never worked for me, even though I theoretically should have been able to learn it; I've seen Nurse Florence do it often enough."

"That was before you were joined to the lake," replied Merlin. "Where do you think the Ladies gain their healing power?"

Tal hesitated. "Coventina only mentioned traveling by water, not healing."

"I believe the connection you have will allow you to tap the healing energy as well, but if you allow me to examine the tie, I can be sure."

"Don't you see?" I said to anyone who would listen. "This way I'm just a burden to all of you...and it's my fault. I did this. I did it because I wanted to be good at sports like the rest of you...and now...now I almost lost us the battle, just like Nicneven planned." By now the tears were flowing freely, and I was embarrassed. "I can't stand to be like this anymore."

"Jimmie," said Dan, bending over me, "making a bloody pulp out of yourself isn't going to help matters. We'll worry about you even more then. And it's not your fault anyway; none of this is." Dan looked as if he was tearing up too.

"It is, it is!" I insisted.

Suddenly Alex was looming over me. I cringed a little.

"It's OK, man," said Alex. "I just wanted to tell you whatever you think you did doesn't compare to what I did." He was crying too; I could tell because the tears was streaking the blood on his face.

"You didn't know who you were dealing with, Jimmie. I did. I tried to lie to myself about it, but I knew perfectly well what a bastard Ares was. I let him use me anyway. You'd have a long way to go to screw up as badly as I did."

"It is true," said Sebastian. "You thought Gyre-Carling was an emissary from me."

"I...I saw you in...a vision, though. You tried to warn me," I whispered, fighting back sobs.

"It was already too late then," said Sebastian sadly. "The cursed thing was already within you."

"Taliesin has the healing powers of a Lady of the Lake now," said Merlin, "and having watched Nurse Florence use those powers, he should be able to emulate her."

"'Should' doesn't reassure me," said Dan. "No offense, Tal."

"None taken," Tal replied, "but I'm scanning Jimmie's body now. I think I can put it back the way it was once the evil has been removed."

"You 'think'?" asked Dan. "That's not good enough."

"Dan, please!" I implored. "Please let Sebastian take it out of me!"

"We still can't do anything about the pain," insisted Dan. "I can't put you through that if there's another way."

"I've already died in a car crash," I reminded him. "How much worse could this be?"

"Much worse," put in Sebastian, "except you will not die this time."

I looked at him and choked down an angry response. "Sebastian, I want to do this! I've read about saints who have suffered far worse."

"But not at my hand," said Sebastian. "Even as a captain in the Praetorian Guard, I never tortured anyone, and I do not wish to start now."

"Would you deny a sinner the chance to repent?" I asked in desperation.

He frowned. "The Almighty does not require—"

"Saint Sebastian, sir," said Alex very tentatively. Sebastian looked in his direction but said nothing.

"Saint Sebastian, I know if I could get rid of the evil inside me by having it ripped out, I would want it, too."

"Ah, if only getting rid of evil were so simple," said Sebastian, who sighed and looked at me again.

"Nobody asked you!" Dan snapped at Alex. "Maybe you'd like to see Jimmie go through that pain."

"We can't block the pain," said Tal in his thinking-out-loud voice, "but could we share it? Divide it up among us, I mean."

Sebastian looked stunned for a moment. "I have never seen anyone do such a thing."

"I'm certainly not comparing myself to Jesus," said Tal nervously, "but don't some people think that when Jesus was sweating blood in the Garden of Gethsemane, it was because he was taking all the suffering of the world upon himself? Isn't there a prophecy in Isaiah—"

Sebastian held up a hand. "I have never thought to question the Lord on that particular matter. I cannot say."

"I can link all of our minds together," said Tal.

"You may all feel all of the pain in such a case," said Sebastian. "How would you divide it?"

"We have in the past divided strength, even life force among us," Tal replied. "Why not pain? Jimmie, can you wait just a few minutes? Merlin and I will try to work out something."

"Sure!" I said quickly.

"I don't like this," insisted Dan.

Carla walked over to join Tal and Merlin's huddle. Shar and the others were about to object, but Eliezer stopped them. "Her demon cannot reach her here, and she may perhaps help."

After what seemed an agonizingly long time, Tal, Merlin and Carla walked over. "I can do it," said Tal, "assuming it doesn't interfere with what Sebastian must do."

"I can remove the curse regardless of James's state of mind," Sebastian assured them.

"Then it's settled!" I said happily.

"It is profoundly not settled!" insisted Dan.

"I'll share the pain with Jimmie," said Alex immediately. Dan all but snarled at him.

"So will I!" announced Khalid, moving over next to Jimmie.

One by one all of them agreed, until Dan stood alone, not because he wouldn't share the pain, but because he wanted to spare me any at all.

"I'm his brother!" Dan almost shouted. "I do not give my permission!"

"But I give mine!" I said, looking directly at him. "Dan, I'm in more pain now than you can imagine. This can't be any worse."

It took a while longer for me to get Dan to relent, but in the end he reluctantly agreed. From that point it took Tal only a few minutes to wire us all together mentally in preparation for the shared pain.

"From what Sebastian tells me, everyone should lie down," said Tal. "Even with all of us sharing, the pain will be intense enough to knock you off your feet." Everyone except Sebastian lay down on the cold stone floor around me. That caused another delay, as Helena insisted that the servants bring mats for them to lie on. Finally, we were ready.

Sebastian held his hands over me and began to pull the thing inside loose from my body.

I often wondered later on if Tal had lied about being able to divide up the pain just to get Dan to withdraw his objection. I felt as if dull, rusty knives were tearing through every muscle. My own screams were quickly drowned out by everyone else's screams around me. After what seemed like hours in hell, I finally lost consciousness.

***

I came to once, just briefly. It must have been after Sebastian had finished. There was blood everywhere, and every nerve in my body was screaming. Tal, pale, sweating, and shaky, was bending over me, with Merlin right behind him. Tal put his hand on my forehead, and I said good-bye to both pain and consciousness.

***

I awoke to the sensation of being kissed and the smell of jasmine perfume.

Eva, it was Eva who was kissing me.

Wow! That almost made all the pain worthwhile. It also convinced me that at least one part of my body was back in working order, so to speak.

"Brave!" she whispered. "You're so brave!"

"What about you?" I said hoarsely. "What about everyone? You all went through the same thing."

"We didn't really have much choice," said Eva, "not if we wanted to support you...but you did have a choice. You could have waited for the Grail, for example. It might have drawn the thing out of you painlessly."

Suddenly, I realized I was wearing something around my neck. I jumped a little despite myself when I looked down and saw it was a Saint Sebastian medal.

"Do not worry," said the saint gently, "that one is, as you would say, the real thing. I thought you deserved something for enduring all that suffering. I'm afraid it doesn't automatically make you a great athlete as the evil one did. All it does is give you normal coordination. The rest will have to come from hard work...and a little faith, I hope."

"Thank you!" I said, blushing a little because Sebastian had seen Eva kissing me, though I wasn't quite sure why that should bother me. He didn't even seem to notice it.

"How is the patient doing?"

I jumped a little, suddenly realizing Tal was so near. Actually, everyone was gathering around me now.

"I feel a little sore," I said, pretty amazed, "but not too bad, all things considered."

"It will take a couple of days for your muscles to get back to normal, I think," said Tal. "You should be all right then, though."

"Better than all right," answered Merlin. "Tal did an excellent job putting you back together. There will not even be scars."

"Maybe I deserve some scars," I said softly, "you know, after all the trouble I caused."

"Man!" said Gordy. "Have you been taking lessons in the Taliesin Weaver School of Feeling Guilty about Everything in the Universe? Get over it! We all make mistakes."

"Hey!" protested Tal.

"You know it's true, man," responded Gordy. "I'm just saying!"

"Indeed, we all make mistakes," agreed Sebastian, "and the one mistake you made you certainly paid for. My own martyrdom was not that painful."

"Yeah, about that—" began Shar.

"Sorry," said Tal, who really sounded as if he meant it. "I guess the pain sharing ended up being more like pain multiplication."

"It did ease Jimmie a little," suggested Sebastian.

"It was worth it!" said Khalid. "Every second of it!"

"That's not exactly what you were screaming at the beginning," said Shar, looking at Tal suspiciously.

"I really did think it would work," said Tal defensively.

"As did I," said Merlin. "Still, one can appreciate the pleasures of life more after experiencing so much pain. That brings us, I think, to the subject of dinner," he said, looking expectantly at Pelles. "It must be hours since any of us have eaten."

"First," said Pelles with surprising grimness, "we must discuss the Grail quest."

Chapter 28: Change of Heart (Tal)

Something about Pelles's tone set off every alarm in my head.

"Majesty, is something wrong?" I asked shakily.

"I'm afraid your stay here at Carbonek will soon be over," he said, staring at me intensely. "I had hoped to have you and your party as our guests much longer."

"Was it something I did?" asked Jimmie weakly.

"Tell them!" prompted Helena.

"I'm afraid you must soon leave…for once you have attained the Grail, you will have no further reason to stay!" said Pelles, now smiling. Eliezer actually snickered.

"You mean…" I was shocked I couldn't finish the question.

"Yes, Taliesin," continued Pelles, "and, noble as you and your men are, I was still surprised to learn the Grail had made its choice."

I looked around stupidly. "How do you know?"

"Remember, the castle sometimes speaks to us," said Helena. "Really, we believe it to be the same divine power that dwells in the Grail. Over the centuries, it gradually radiated into the very stone of the castle as well. Be that as it may, we received word just a short time ago that no further testing is required. All of you have demonstrated your worthiness already."

"Many have been rejected rapidly in the past, but I did not expect such a rapid acceptance," said Pelles. "Your need seems both dire and urgent, however, so it gladdens my heart that you were able to complete the quest so quickly."

"All of us?" I asked, still trying to absorb our sudden good fortune.

"Yes, all of you…in the group you came with," replied Eliezer. I guessed that was a polite way of excluding poor half-demon Merlin.

"Even…the non-Christians," Eliezer continued with an almost Merlin-like wink. "I remember when we maintained higher standards!"

"You will need to select one of your number to be the Grail bearer," Pelles pointed out.

"Jimmie!" said Khalid loudly and little shrilly.

"But…but I screwed up so badly…"

"Join the club," muttered Alex. Then, much more loudly, he added, "Jimmie!"

"Jimmie!" agreed Eva, eyes sparkling. In a couple of minutes everyone joined the chorus, which then became a chant. "Jimmie! Jimmie!" By that point, Jimmie's face was bright red.

"Your choice is made," said Pelles. "Let it be so! One more point. The Grail is never given for more than a short time. You may take it with you to the battle with Nicneven, but it will return here after that battle ends."

"I expected something like that," I replied. Actually, I hadn't known what to expect, but I didn't really imagine I could just take the Grail home and keep it on the mantle or something.

"You must know what the Grail can do…and what it cannot," said Helena. "It can heal any injury, any illness, no matter how grave, but it will not raise a man from the dead. It can shield the bearer and those near him from any evil spell and break those already cast, but if someone strays too far, he will be outside that protection." Helena suddenly looked sadder. "The Grail was not really intended to be carried in battle," she said almost apologetically. "Had you an army, it could not shield so many at a time."

"Fortunately, we don't have one," I said, though I was realizing how that limitation would affect our logistics. Again I regretted that so few of us had long-range weapons. Still, having the Grail would be far better than not having it.

"Remember, too, that the Grail is not an offensive weapon," continued Helena. "It will not bear the touch of someone…or something…who is evil, but it will not smite an evil being who is nearby. However, some evil beings may become frightened and flee at the sight of it.

"Finally," she continued, "it can nourish you, either by creating actual food and drink, or, if you prefer, by passing energy directly into your bodies. Anyone within its area of protection can be sustained in this way, not knowing tiredness or hunger, but be aware that it can only provide so much support without some kind of respite. The protective aura will never fade, but the Grail's ability to heal and to nourish can be exhausted for a time. That time will be short indeed, but in the middle of a battle it is best to be cautious."

"Thank you, Majesty," I replied, bowing. "I will remember all that you have said."

"Bring forth the Grail!" ordered Pelles loudly. A door behind the thrones opened, and from it walked an amazing, beautiful woman carrying a silver cup from which flowed a brilliant light.

"Elaine of Carbonek, mother of Sir Galahad, kept forever young by the Grail," Eliezer explained.

When Elaine of Carbonek had nearly reached us, Merlin walked over to her and said, "Dear lady, may I have the honor of carrying the Grail the rest of the way?"

Eliezer immediately adopted an air more like the one he had acted for us originally. "Merlin, what are you thinking? There is an old story that you once tried to become the bearer and guardian of the Grail yourself."

Merlin looked annoyed. "I mean to do no such thing now. Think of it as merely an old man's last request. Even if I survive the battle, I do not believe I will last much longer than that."

I had a sudden flashback of the time a demon impersonated Merlin and tried to kill me. Surely, though, this was the real Merlin. He couldn't have gotten into the castle otherwise...could he? And if he were someone in disguise, wouldn't the Grail reject him? Helena had certainly suggested that.

Confusion crossed the lovely face of Elaine of Carbonek, and she glanced at Pelles for guidance. After a moment he nodded, and Elaine handed the Grail to Merlin, though with clear reluctance.

Carla had walked over and put her arm around me. "What's happening?" she whispered.

"I only wish I knew," I whispered back.

Merlin turned away from the Grail bearer and walked toward Jimmie, who shakily rose to meet him. At the last minute, though, Merlin veered in my direction. I raised an eyebrow. Merlin tipped the Grail toward me as if he were aiming it at me. I blinked as the sparkling light surrounded me and Carla.

"Break all evil spells," Merlin said solemnly, almost in the way he would order someone to do something. Could he have been addressing the Grail?

In a split second, my life changed forever.

First, I heard Old Dark Me's voice, which had been raised in protest, fade away. The Grail had cured the damage I had inflicted on myself with dark magic. I would still have to avoid dark magic, but as long as I did, I knew instinctively that Dark Me would be gone for good.

If only the Grail's effect had stopped there!

Instead, I started feeling strange, the way you feel when you have almost awakened but have that momentary confusion about whether what you were dreaming was real. I had that moment, and then reality settled upon me like a shroud.

The guys had been right. Everyone had been right.

My love for Carla was only a spell…again.

Falling out of love is one thing; it's gradual, and it's voluntary. This was more like having my still-beating heart ripped out of my chest, leaving a jagged, hollow space behind and nothing else. In that instant, I was like an addict craving a fix; I would have done anything to have the spell put back, to forget the last couple of minutes, to go back to an illusionary heaven instead of having to deal with real-life hell.

Now I would have to face the reality of having been betrayed by Carla for the second time…or was it the third?

It took my old feelings for Eva less than half a minute to reassert themselves. Yeah, Eva, who insisted she no longer loved me.

Eva, who had just been…kissing Jimmie?

I still had my arm around Carla without even realizing it. She pulled away from me, and I glanced reflexively in her direction.

I had seen many things in recent months, but few of them rivaled the expression of absolute horror on Carla's face. It wasn't horror over the fact that I now knew the truth. It was horror because she knew the truth, because the spell Asmodeus had woven to suppress her own memories was gone as well.

To say my feelings toward her were ambivalent at this point would be a colossal understatement, but she was so obviously in pain that sympathy momentarily trumped anger.

Carla tried to speak, to apologize perhaps, or at least explain, but, overcome by the magnitude of what she had done, she turned to flee, cheeks burning with shame.

"Restrain her!" commanded Pelles, and his guards were on the move, but Stan and Dan were closer, and they successfully grabbed her, though not without a struggle on her part. She fought like a woman possessed. Uh, well, that was a poor choice of words.

"Let me go!" she pleaded. "I just want to leave!" The guys, confused, looked to me for direction.

"Hold her...gently," I managed.

"Gently... is... going... to... be... hard... to... do!" gasped Stan as Carla continued to struggle.

"Carla!" I commanded, trying for emotionless, but the words came out ice cold instead. "Stop that!" To my surprise, she suddenly went limp in their arms and switched from frenzied struggle to uncontrollable sobbing.

With an effort, I squeezed my boiling emotions down far enough to think and turned to Merlin.

"Are any spells on her gone completely?" I asked.

"As you can see, her memories have been restored," replied Merlin, "and I do not think Asmodeus now has a way to possess her, though he may try to rebuild that route into her head later. Finding the original pact and destroying it, followed by the right rituals and prayers, will probably free her soul. She is practically free anyway. I cannot see any future in which Asmodeus can now fulfill the terms of the pact. Still, we want to make sure Asmodeus does not try to interfere with her—or you—again."

Focusing on acting rather than thinking, I walked over to the table, picked up a chair, and carried it over to where Carla was hanging limply between Stan and Dan. "Put her in the chair," I ordered quietly. Then I knelt next to her.

"Please go away!" she said, not taking her weeping eyes from the floor. "I can't bear to look at you!"

"You think he wants to look at you?" muttered Shar angrily.

"She's Gianni's sister," Khalid reminded Shar loudly enough for Carla to hear. "She did a bad thing, but we said we'd save her, right?"

Shar didn't answer.

"I'm not worth saving," Carla said quietly, more to herself than to Khalid, but I was close enough to hear it.

Things had gone about as sideways as they could get now. Part of me could barely look at Carla, but there were other parts of me that were not ready to just throw her away. That was pretty much what I had done when she had tried to trick me into marrying her by disguising herself as Aphrodite and giving me a false prophecy. How had that rejection worked out? Not well. Apparently she had run off in such despair that she had been an easy mark for Asmodeus.

I could not see possible futures like Merlin or even my mom, but I had the feeling that I was standing at the crossroads, that what I did in the next few minutes would change everything…probably for the worse, given the way my life normally worked out.

What was it Romeo had said? Oh, yeah: "my mind misgives/Some consequence yet hanging in the stars…" I wasn't much like Romeo, and I didn't believe in astrology, but that sense of foreboding? I could relate.

"I know that face, Tal," said Gordy. "You're figuring out how this is all your fault I bet."

"Shut up, Gordy," I snapped.

"It isn't!" Gordy protested, ignoring my last sentence. "It just isn't!"

"I said shut up!" I almost shouted. Gordy looked hurt, but he backed off. I heard Dan whisper something about giving me some room.

How much room do you need when your insides have been ground into hamburger?

It almost seemed as if time had stopped. Elaine of Carbonek looked like an expression of shock was permanently etched into her once untroubled face. I wondered if she was doubting the Grail's choice. Hell, at this point I wouldn't have been surprised if the Grail flew out of Merlin's hand and disappeared.

As for Merlin, I think he had forgotten he still had the Grail. His grip on it seemed uncertain as all his attention focused on me.

The Grail knights stood close, awaiting further orders, but neither Pelles nor Helena seemed inclined to give any. In fact, they looked as if they wished they could find a discreet way to extricate themselves from this train wreck. Eliezer stood there with a now-I've-seen-everything expression on his face. The guys and Eva all looked as if they wanted to do something, but they had no idea what. My chewing Gordy's head off seemed to have paralyzed them all. Even Sebastian appeared reluctant to approach me.

I was alone in a room filled with people. Alone...and desolate.

The only good thing I could see about this situation was that everything now such a complete mess that I couldn't make it any worse.

"Merlin?" I asked. He knew what I wanted without my having to elaborate.

"Everything is in flux," he answered. "I cannot be sure what your best course is. It does seem, though, that you must do something soon. Nicneven is readying another attack, and if we are not there to stop it..."

"I know," I said. "I know. Carla," I turned, turning to her, "we need to talk...faster than I would like, but we need to talk a little."

"What is there left to say?" she got out between sobs.

"I'll talk. You just listen," I replied, though I still didn't really know what I would say. What does one say to someone who is simultaneously a traitor and a friend?

"Do you remember the conversation we had on Olympus when I caught you pretending to be Aphrodite?" I asked. I was still trying to be emotionally neutral, and my words were still coming out pretty frosty, but I just blundered on ahead.

She nodded, but she didn't even look up.

"You asked me then why I could give Alex a second chance and not you. Carla, you were right to ask."

"Here it comes!" muttered Gordy.

"Gordy!" I snapped. I knew he wanted to say more, but he saw something in my eyes that stopped him.

"I should have been willing to give you that second chance then. Because I wasn't, you...you sold your soul."

Finally she looked me in the eye. Despite how puffy she was from crying, she still looked beautiful. "Don't make it worse. Gordy's right—this is my fault, not yours."

"It took both of us," I said, pushing forward. "I didn't give you the second chance then, but I'm giving it to you now."

"What the hell?" asked Shar. I glared, and he, too, subsided, though I could feel his anger without even trying to read him.

"I have to be honest, Carla," I said slowly. "I don't know how I feel about you right now. I know I don't love you. Right now I can't let myself feel anything, one way or the other. I'm afraid of what will happen if I do." She sobbed again at that but remained otherwise silent.

"What I do know is this," I said, finally managing something approaching gentleness. "Despite what you did, I know there is goodness in you. I know you, like everyone else here, has risked your life for me more than once. And I think I know something else: given a little time, we could be friends again. I can't promise that, but I won't reject that idea the way I did last time. I won't reject you."

"She put us all at risk!" protested Shar angrily.

"We've all done stupid things, Shar," I replied. "But we're…we're all a kind of family now. We know that some of us were connected in past lives. I'd be willing to bet we all were. And I'll bet you something else—that connection won't end with this life."

"But…" Shar began.

"Shar, channel Alexander for a minute. There are few enough of us as it is. From a strategic standpoint, can we really afford to lose someone with Carla's magic ability?"

"No," admitted Shar grudgingly, "but how can we be sure we can trust her, or, if we can, that she's in a fit condition for battle?"

Given the fact that Carla was barely choking back her sobs, that was a reasonable question. Magic required focus, and right now hers was pretty much shot to hell.

I looked at Elaine of Carbonek. She knew my question without my having to ask it.

"The Grail can cheer the heart, but it cannot wipe away guilt. Carla must atone and seek God's forgiveness…and her own as well." I saw her point. Probably God would forgive her before she could forgive herself.

"I wouldn't even know where to start," muttered Carla, obviously having trouble speaking at all.

"The road to repentance is sometimes a long one," added Sebastian, "and I doubt she can travel it before your next battle."

"The Ladies of the Lake have always been able to bring emotional tranquility," suggested Merlin.

"But we don't have one—" I started automatically, then remembered I was now bonded to the lake. "Uh, I don't know how to do that, though. I've seen Nurse Florence do healings, but I've never seen what you describe."

"I believe it is a simple matter if she is willing," said Merlin, gesturing toward Carla. "Focus on her and visualize a calm lake with nothing stirring its surface."

"Carla?" I asked quickly.

Carla continued to look down at the floor. "If you can help me get enough control to help in the battle, do it."

I knelt next to Carla, took her face in my hands, and gently got her to look me in the eye. Then I called on the power of the Lake and visualized a surface so unmoving it seemed to be ice rather than water. After a minute, I could feel calmness caressing me, and I broadcast that unshakable stability into Carla.

When we finished, Carla remained just as miserable as she had been, but I had managed to endow her with a kind of clinical detachment. Outwardly, she showed little emotion, but she had her focus back. I would have to settle for that right now. True healing—even magic healing—would take longer than we had.

That left us with some very large logistical problems. Though we had killed a number of Nicneven's minions in our earlier battle, Merlin assured us that she had more than enough troops to send an even bigger force against us if she chose. He retired for a short time to meditate, then returned with the announcement that Nicneven was even now marshaling her forces in Elphame. That much we might have expected, but Merlin revealed an even more chilling possibility: she appeared to be planning another incursion into our world, this time to attack all the evacuees from Santa Brígida—including our families.

"To what end?" I asked.

"To draw you out," he replied solemnly.

"How can you be sure?" I pressed, hoping Merlin was wrong. "Surely she would not make her deliberations easy to spy on."

"And indeed they are not," agreed Merlin. "I see what she intends from the way the possible futures are converging. In most of those I can see, we have to fight her again in Santa Barbara, but this time with a large number of innocent bystanders to inhibit us."

"That seems risky on her part," said Shar. "She won't be as powerful on Earth."

"Her army seemed plenty powerful last time," pointed out Dan, "and that was without her."

"I fear I must agree," said Merlin. "Nicneven is strong enough to be a threat even in an atmosphere that somewhat hinders magic."

"So what's our best move at this point?" I asked. "We can't allow her to threaten innocent civilians."

"We can't let her choose the battlefield," replied Shar. "We need to strike first, when she isn't expecting it."

"Attack Elphame?" Dan asked, shocked. "Isn't that where she's going to be strongest?"

"David likes the idea of surprise," Stan said, "and she doesn't know we have the Grail, correct?"

"As far as we know, what happens here cannot be viewed through magic," said Pelles, "so I do not see how this Nicneven or anyone else can know."

"From what I can tell, Nicneven has at least one extremely inspired seer," said Merlin thoughtfully. "However, based on my own visions of the future, the Grail creates a blind spot for seers. Zom and other antimagic artifacts have a similar effect. Futures involving them and their wielders are much harder to see. In truth, even certain spells can make it hard to see the future of who or what they are cast on."

"Then Nicneven really isn't going to know what hit her!" said Stan happily. "We have the Grail, and—what the hell?"

"Stan!" I said automatically, worrying about our hosts. Then I looked in the direction he was pointing and almost unleashed a whole string of expletives.

New Dark Me—now the only Dark Me since the Grail had wiped out the one within me—was gone!

Pelles immediately questioned the guards and determined that Dark Me had left at some point during Sebastian's surgery on Jimmie. All of us had been too focused on the pain to even notice. Pelles told us that he, Helena, Eliezer, and all the Grail knights in the main hall had been in almost constant prayer for us, and our agonized cries would have distracted them from any noise Dark Me might have made on his way out. As for the Grail knights he would have had to pass, they had no orders to prevent anyone from leaving, and in any case they thought he was me.

"My spell must have worn off, and Dark Me took advantage of our distraction to escape," I said, trying not to betray the frustration I felt.

"Didn't you say the spell that transformed Robin would wear off when the blood that fuels it runs out?" asked Carlos. "We've been here for hours. Isn't he nearly out?"

"I do believe he is somehow carrying your blood, Taliesin," said Merlin quietly.

"Yeah," I replied. "When I searched his backpack, I found the blood I donated to the blood bank, preserved by one of his spells. I didn't think to take it out. After all, he wasn't in any position to use it then. That blood gives him a supply for days."

"I'm afraid it's worse than that," said Alex grimly, holding up his hand. It took me a second to register on his bare ring finger.

"Hermes's ring?" I asked, already knowing the answer. Alex nodded stiffly.

"Before Dark Me left, he must have looked around and noticed that ring! Now we really are in trouble," I said. "Uh, I mean more trouble."

"What's the big deal?" asked Gordy. "The ring turns Alex's ichor to blood, right? What can Dark Me do with it?"

"It uses blood magic," said Stan patiently. "Yes, it turns ichor to human blood, Gordy, and no one right now needs that capability except Alex. But to Dark Me, with all of Tal's cleverness, even something as seemingly useless as that could be exactly what he needs. If he studies how the ring works, it won't be a big jump from there to adapting it to a different purpose. What's to prevent Dark Me from getting it to transform something else into Tal's blood? Then he can remain an almost exact replica of Tal forever."

"I doubt that even someone with Taliesin's wits can accomplish such a thing over night," said Merlin, "but he might do it before the blood supply he has is exhausted."

"Then we need to go after him," said Alex.

"No," I corrected. "Nicneven is still the priority. Even Dark Me doesn't want her to win, so at the very least he won't interfere with us until we've dealt with her."

"I don't like this one bit!" said Gordy.

"None of us do," I assured him, "but it could be worse."

I should never say that, because almost immediately the universe proved me right, as things once again got worse. A quick inventory revealed that Dark Me had gotten away not only with my blood and Alex's ring, but also with Black Hilt, Jimmie's sword...and with the lyre of Orpheus.

Talk about armed and dangerous!

"I was going to tell you to rid yourself of that blade anyway," said Merlin. "It clearly belongs to Nicneven."

"But we won it in battle with Morgan!" I protested. "Wait! I always did wonder where it came from. Morgan was allied with Ceridwen at one point. And Ceridwen had contact with Nicneven. I think Ceridwen might have been her ally."

"Pawn is more likely," suggested Merlin. "Either way, it confirms what I had begun to suspect. Nicneven has been interested in you for some time, much longer than you realized. I would guess one of her seers must have long ago identified you as a possible threat."

"Just as Ares did!" said Alex.

"I noticed a lot of Ceridwen's magic seemed very un-Celtic!" I exclaimed, light bulbs flashing on in my head. "She must have been trading magic with Nicneven...and through Nicneven, with Hecate herself!"

"That would explain the development of new magic like the awakening spell," said Stan. "Ceridwen couldn't bond with Hecate directly, but she could learn some of her lore from Nicneven, who bonded with Hecate before the Olympian world was sealed off."

"The union of different styles of magic can have very unpredictable, but very powerful, results," observed Merlin.

"Uh, don't we have a battle to plan?" Gordy reminded us.

I was sure Gordy was bored with the conversation. However, he was also right. I could puzzle out the role Nicneven might have played in my earlier life later.

Merlin conferred with Pelles and determined that Carbonek could connect to any world at practically any location. As a result, we could arrive in Elphame where the troops were massing. There were a lot of little details Merlin couldn't pick up, but assembling so much faerie and witch power in one place was difficult to conceal.

That took care of picking the battlefield. Strategy was the next topic, but our equipment more or less dictated that for us. In his role as Grail bearer, Jimmie would be in our midst. We had to stay close so that Nicneven's magic, as well as that of her various allies, couldn't touch us, though Shar, because of Zom's protection, could stray a little if he needed to, as could Gordy. (We all agreed that the sword Apollo had given to Shar should become Jimmie's now that Shar had Zom again, but Jimmie wasn't recovered enough for heavy sword fighting, and in any case he had to hold the Grail, so Gordy, whose fear-inducing sword didn't do much against supernatural opponents anyway, got Apollo's sword temporarily.)

I would use White Hilt and other magic to blast away at Nicneven's forces as needed. Carla would do the same, as would Merlin. Khalid would fire his four-times blessed arrows, at least while they lasted. The guys in general would cover us, since the Grail would not shield us from physical injury, though it could heal the damage.

At least this time we had our dragon armor, which would both protect us from harm and endow us with the additional powers Govannon had crafted into it at Gwynn ap Nudd's request. Only Khalid had been able to wear his last time.

While we changed, two more visitors arrived at the Grail castle: Nurse Florence and Coventina, having finished the beach cleanup.

"I didn't expect you'd be able to join us," I said happily, "but the more, the merrier."

"I didn't expect to be able to, either," said Nurse Florence, "but it is said you can only find the Grail castle when you aren't looking for it, and certainly I wasn't."

"Nor I," said Coventina, "but this will make it much easier to join you in battle with Nicneven."

"I'm very grateful," I said, "but I would have thought you needed to return to headquarters."

"Headquarters is well hidden," she said dismissively, "and I do not think we have any more spies. Besides," she continued, "if anything happens to you, the Order will almost certainly die out anyway." I knew she was exaggerating my importance, but who was I to quarrel with the addition of an ex-goddess to our ranks? Perhaps she was powerful enough to rival Nicneven herself, but at worst she was formidable enough to increase our power substantially.

There still remained one logistical problem: Alex. With ichor fast rising in his bloodstream, he would almost certainly vanish back to Olympus before the battle was done, perhaps before it had started.

He looked somber when I mentioned the problem. "Yeah, I thought of that. I can feel the pull of Olympus already. Perhaps Hermes is fast at work making another ring and will be able to send me back quickly."

"Perhaps the Grail can help," suggested Khalid. "It can heal anything, can't it?"

"I am not sure the Grail would regard Alex's Olympian nature as a disease or injury," said Merlin. "After all, Khalid, it did not change your half djinn nature."

"Then again, he didn't ask it to," said Alex. "Nothing ventured, nothing gained," he added, stepping toward the Grail.

"It might go all the way," I warned. "Alex, you might not lose just the ichor, but the extra muscle and whatever else Ares gave you. We have no way of knowing."

Alex paused and looked me in the eye. "Would that mean I'd be out again? Out of the group, I mean." He was trying not to look nervous, but I could tell he was shaking inwardly at the idea of being tossed aside like last time.

"We aren't a group anymore," I told him. "I said it before: we're a family. And you're part of it, Alex, regardless of how the Grail changes you."

"You can get the muscle back if you work out enough," pointed out Stan, "and anyway, even in battle, muscle isn't the only thing that counts."

"That's lucky for you!" said Dan, poking Stan affectionately. I was reminded of the days when they could barely tolerate each other.

"Well, then I'm willing to take the risk," said Alex. Maybe that's what's supposed to happen. Having me here, even if weaker, is better than not having me, right?"

"Stan's right," I said reassuringly. "Maybe you won't be able to swing a sword as well for a while, but there are plenty of ways you can still help us."

Without any more hesitations, Alex took the Grail from Jimmie, knelt, and prayed. For a moment the Grail's radiance engulfed him, then just as quickly receded.

"Well?" I prompted.

"My blood feels like blood again," he said, and smiled. "I still seem to be as strong, though." He acted casual, but I knew he was happy not to have suddenly been "re-nerded." Still, I was all the more impressed that he had been willing to risk even that just to be able to help in the upcoming battle.

"How about the…uh…" I began.

"Yeah, I remembered the…anger management issue and prayed about it, too, but I think that part I have to fix on my own," he replied.

I could see Carla looking at the Grail. Alex's ability to touch it must have gotten her thinking. It didn't reject his touch. She must have been wondering whether it would accept hers as well. I knew her well enough to guess that she wanted to try and see what happened, wanted it with all her heart, but she was too afraid. Just as well, probably, at least right now. If the Grail refused her as too evil, I didn't know if I could raise her morale again before the battle.

After the battle? Then it might be worth the risk.

Chapter 29: Surprise Attacks and Reinforcements (Tal)

Now that we were ready for battle, it didn't take long to depart from Carbonek. Sebastian beat us to the door. Apologetically, he explained that he could not join us in battle. Really, I hadn't expected him to, given the kind of restrictions God seemed to maintain in the interest of free will. Sebastian did bless all of us, though, and I felt a little extra tingle beyond my usual precombat adrenaline.

"This will be farewell for all us," Pelles pointed out. "No one has been able to find the Grail castle twice." He, Eliezer, Helena, and Elaine all made a point of saying good-bye to each of us, even poor Carla, who I knew didn't want attention from anyone right now. Despite her feelings, she maintained a stoic exterior; the calm I had projected into her remained in place, at least superficially.

No, Carla was not a problem at this point...but Eva was. I wanted her to stay at Carbonek until we were gone, after which Pelles could arrange her return to Santa Brígida.

"Tal," she said, speaking calmly but giving me the evil eye big-time, "I'm going with you."

"Eva..." I started, then hesitated, not sure how to frame an argument in a way that would get her to accept it. Well, that and I was having a really hard time keeping my resurgent love for her from short-circuiting every rational thought in my head.

"Surely you wouldn't send me away just because I'm a girl, Tal," she said, almost as if daring me to do it.

"You know me better than that, Eva. You don't have armor, though, or even a weapon."

"Jimmie doesn't have armor, either," Eva pointed out.

Having been a ghost when Gwynn had given us the dragon armor, Jimmie hadn't needed any at the time. Now, though, Eva had a point.

"You're not sending me home!" Jimmie said immediately. "I'm the Grail bearer."

"And I am part of the Grail company," Eva quickly reminded me. "We all won the Grail together, if you'll recall."

"She speaks the truth," said Pelles, "though it is not right for women to go into battle."

"Majesty, I am afraid you will not win that argument with this group," said Merlin grimly. "Neither will you, Taliesin," he told me. "I do not approve of women in battle, either, but unless you intend to force Eva to return to your world, all you will accomplish with this argument is to delay us further."

I had expected Eva to react in some way to the obvious chauvinism of Pelles and Merlin, but she kept her eyes fixed on me with single-minded determination.

"Eva, be reasonable," I pleaded.

"I am going with you," she insisted, and I was frankly stumped. Any logical argument I had could also be applied to Jimmie, and I couldn't possibly send him home.

"What Tal is trying to get out is that you won't be helping if you come along with us," said Shar, obviously trying to rescue me from an awkward situation.

Eva looked shocked, but Shar just kept going. "The truth is that we all have some role to play in the battle, except for you. And don't start rambling on about your self-defense training. It's not going to help much against the kind of opponents we'll be facing. If you go, you'll just be forcing us to build our strategy around defending you."

"Jimmie—" she began angrily.

"Isn't armored and can't wield a sword well right now," interrupted Shar. "Yeah, but we do need someone to carry the Grail."

"So you'll need to defend him anyway," Eva pointed out. "I'll stand right next to him, and you won't have to go to any extra trouble."

"Why do you want to go so badly?" I asked. She looked at me as if I had just disproved the old adage that there is no such thing as a stupid question.

"Because all of my best friends are going to risk their lives, and I...I want to do something!" she snapped, eyes blazing. "There must be something I can do," she added, voice still fierce but eyes looking desperate. I knew how badly she wanted to help, and I wanted to let her with all my heart, but what if she died because I let her come with us?

"She can have my bow," said Carla quietly.

"What?" asked Shar, clearly irritated.

"She can have my bow," Carla repeated, somewhat more loudly. "I'm going to be spell casting pretty much the whole time. I won't be able to aim arrows properly and use magic at the same time."

Based on my own experience with simultaneous sword play and magic, I thought perhaps she could have done both, but I had been forced to learn how, while she had never had to both before.

"Eva can't use a bow," said Shar quickly.

"Excuse me, but how do you know that?" said Eva angrily. "I've had the same kind of summer camp experiences with archery that Carla had. I'll admit I'm not a crack shot, but one more archer still has to help a little…right?"

She was asking me rather than Shar. I looked at Merlin, who shrugged unhelpfully. I took that as Merlin for, "I do not really want her on the battlefield, but the future is too unclear to be sure. She might be of some help." OK, so that was perhaps reading too much into his shrug, but if he had something more definite to share, he would certainly have done so.

"All right, Eva, you can go with us," I said reluctantly. Shar opened his mouth, but I continued before he could say anything. "Shar, you've got to admit we have a pretty small force. It's hard to believe Alexander would have thrown away an extra archer under such circumstances."

"I guess he wouldn't have," grumbled Shar, "but Eva, you have to stay right next to Jimmie and the Grail. We can probably protect both of you as you suggested, but only if you stick together like glue."

"I can do that easily," said Eva, smiling at Jimmie. His return smile looked almost as if…

Sure enough, Jimmie was crushing on Eva…big-time! Well, I guessed I couldn't blame him for that, given how beautiful Eva was and how gentle she had been with him.

Certainly Eva couldn't feel the same way…could she?

Of course, I could easily have found out what her feelings for Jimmie were, but not without violating my own rules about using mind probes. Anyway, the idea was certainly too ridiculous to worry about, so I forced it out of my mind and made ready to leave Carbonek.

Our immediate logistical issues finally taken care of, we were all eager to reach Elphame as fast as possible. Pelles told us to leave the castle but then to stop just outside the guardhouse. From there the castle would dispatch us to the very spot Nicneven was assembling her army. Not that we really needed to be told this, but he reminded us we would need to strike quickly to make the most of our surprise.

Making our final thanks, we proceeded quickly to the gatehouse as Pelles had instructed. Jimmie was carrying the Grail, and the Grail knights bowed as the sacred chalice glowed past them.

"How is the future looking?" I asked Merlin quietly.

"In flux," he replied cautiously. "We will definitely disrupt Nicneven's plans. Whether we will prevail or not I cannot tell; there are just too many changes happening too quickly."

As soon as we stepped out the gatehouse, we could see a different landscape in front of us: no longer the green hills surrounding the Grail castle, but a great icy plain with an enormous mountain behind it. For a second I thought it was Ben Nevis, but something about the vividness of the scenery told me we were seeing a twin of that great mountain in Elphame. Just as well—if we had to fight near the real Ben Nevis, towns like Fort William and Glen Nevis would be at risk. This way we could throw everything we had at Nicneven's army and not worry about bystanders.

We surged forward and into Elphame, much to the shock of the faeries who were assembling on the plain. I did not need to look to know that the path to the Grail castle had already disappeared behind us.

The faeries initially tried to resist. After all, we were a small number of intruders, and they were a mighty army, larger than the group we had faced at Shoreline Beach. Spells crackled all around us, but none got past the nimbus of light created by the Grail. Our spells, not inhibited in the same way, hit our opponents full force. I seared them with White Hilt; Merlin unleashed storms nearly as strong as those I had conjured with the lyre of Orpheus; Coventina struck with her high-pressure fire-hose water attack.

While some of us attacked, Carla and Nurse Florence wove about us a defense against the faerie arrows that whizzed our way, and initially all were deflected. The faeries were not so lucky; they were too numerous and too spread out to use the same defensive strategy we were executing. Conceivably they could have created several small deflection fields, but they were clearly more used to archery than defensive magic, and before they could shift gears, Khalid let his arrows fly and explode on each target with four different kinds of anti-evil power, invariably knocking the unlucky faerie from the sky. Eva's attacks were not as effective, though she had not lied about having had a little archery training, and the bow of Artemis was strong enough to wound anyone who got hit, even if the victim was wearing faerie armor.

Did some faeries die? Yes, and I wasn't happy about that, but it didn't sicken me as it would have a few months ago. Part of me remained horrified, though—at the deaths, and at the fact that the rest of me wasn't feeling anything about them. Don't get me wrong; I would have avoided this carnage if I could have, but Nicneven was never going to stop coming at us…unless we stopped her.

Our initial attack cost Nicneven's forces dearly, but, realizing they couldn't stop us, they flew away in droves, withdrawing toward the mountain. Khalid and Alex wanted to follow immediately, but I insisted they stay put. The retreat could be a way of luring some of us away from the Grail, where we would be vulnerable. Instead we moved forward in tight formation, protected for the moment from both magical and physical attacks.

The fixed portal to the real Ben Nevis lay somewhere nearby I was sure, but I was confident Nicneven's army wouldn't flee through it and leave us here to wreak havoc in her kingdom.

Still, it was unfortunate we couldn't move faster. While preparing for battle, I had boosted all of us to faerie speed, but we were moving at a fast walk at best, and faerie walking couldn't compete with faerie flying. The ground was too slick to run easily, and though the casters in the group could probably have gotten everyone in the air, keeping everyone in a tight formation near the Grail would have been more difficult, and at the very least powering levitation would have limited what offensive spells the casters might otherwise have used.

I was beginning to see why Helena had commented repeatedly that the Grail was not intended for battle. It gave unmatchable protection and stamina, but at the cost of rapid mobility and flexible deployment. Not only that, but by now the element of surprise was gone as well, and Nicneven was doubtless scheming some way to destroy us.

All things considered, though, I still felt confident. We were shielded from any long-range attack, magical or physical, and we had ample resources to defeat anyone who got close enough for hand to hand combat.

Yeah, I felt confident. As always, that proved to be a mistake.

As we approached the mountain, the ground started shaking. The earthquake must have been magical, because it didn't shake us, but it shook the mountain, creating a hail of stones and loosening enough big rocks to start a landslide.

The Grail would protect us from the magic itself, and probably from someone magically flinging a boulder at us directly. But would it ward off the boulders loosened by the earthquake but rolling toward us under the power of gravity, not magic? I guessed not, and clearly Merlin agreed, because he at once started an effort to levitate away from us what was by now an avalanche.

I could feel his mind buckle under the tons of rock he was trying to move. He had levitated Stonehenge once, but that was like comparing swimming in the kiddie pool to swimming across the English Channel. I linked with him, offering him my strength while simultaneously reaching out to the Grail to renew our energy. The boulders kept coming, though. Coventina, Nurse Florence, and Carla all joined us, and we managed to deflect the first barrage of boulders, but just barely. The earthquake was continuing, as if Nicneven was trying to throw the whole mountain at us.

"I thought Nicneven did ice and stuff like that," said Gordy, looking with disbelief at the boulders landing dangerously near us.

"Hecate has power over the air, sea, and *earth*," I said through clenched teeth. "Nicneven is drawing on her."

By now we were all getting hit with pebbles, but we managed to deflect yet another avalanche. We burned through power fast to bend the laws of physics that far, but the Grail's supply seemed to be holding, at least for the moment.

I could feel a third avalanche forming, but Nicneven must have realized that strategy might not pay off, so she added another prong to the attack, or perhaps what happened had been her strategy all along. All I knew was that suddenly the ground beneath our feet collapsed. Nicneven must have shifted away some of the underlying soil and rock, and the Grail did not automatically float us above the chasm that opened beneath us. Instead, we fell with bone-jarring force, in most cases losing our balance. Jimmie fell harder, and the Grail went flying out of his hands, hitting the shattered soil some distance away. The surrounding ground tried to swallow the Grail, which defeated such a direct use of magic, but now we were too distant from the Grail's protection, which meant the earthquake hit most of us with full force and kept us off our feet.

Shar, Gordy, and Stan (who was, to judge by the glow of his sword, clearly David again) could get up because of their varying types of protection against magic. Unfortunately, before any of them could close the distance between himself and the Grail, the ground beneath us dropped with a sharp jolt, and then repeated the same drop twice, leaving us in what amounted to a deep pit, with sides too steep to climb and the Grail still at ground level and thus effectively out of reach. Alex or Khalid, or for that matter any of us spell casters, could have flown up to get it, but we needed to be able to stand up to launch ourselves, and at the moment none of us could.

The spell casters among us did manage to stay linked to each other and to surround the group in a repulsion field designed to keep boulders from smashing into us or the sides of the pit from collapsing inward and burying us alive. However, if Nicneven could keep up the avalanches, now that we were not being refueled by the Grail, eventually she would crush us all. She had to burn through magic to keep the quake going, but gravity did the heavy lifting after that, while we had to fight against gravity to keep from dying.

Above us I could sense Nicneven's faeries grouping for an attack. They couldn't position themselves to fire arrows at us without being in the path of the next round of avalanche debris, so I suspected their real purpose was to make a pincushion out of anyone who tried to reach the Grail. Our dragon armor would protect the parts of us it covered, but let enough faerie archers open fire, and some of them were bound to hit us. The earlier deflection spell wouldn't cover a very wide area effectively, so I doubted it would stretch far enough to cover someone making a grab for the Grail.

Great! Now even if one of our fliers managed to launch, he or she still probably couldn't get the Grail.

I thought of retreat, but opening a portal would take time and concentration. Nicneven might try to collapse the walls on the pit if we didn't put all our strength into repulsion, and I doubted I could focus with enough precision to open a portal while my teeth were being jiggled out of my head.

For someone supposedly caught by surprise, Nicneven's speed in trapping us was remarkable. All I could think was that, unable to get a clear reading of the future, she must have kept herself in a state of perpetual watchfulness. Even such constant alertness, however, couldn't explain how she had such a precise plan to knock the Grail out of our hands. She didn't even know we had it. She couldn't have known that...unless...

Dark Me didn't know we had won the Grail, but he did know we had been in the Grail castle and might conceivably get it. It didn't make sense for him to side with Nicneven, though. Dark Me always wanted to be at the top, and he had to know Nicneven would settle for nothing less herself.

Of course, he did have a sword that Merlin had suggested was under her control. Could she have dominated him somehow?

I could ill afford to spare any attention from the protective spells, but I detached myself just enough to search for...well, basically myself. That took some doing, but once I finally got the searching part of my mind to stop pointing back at me and began to search the surrounding area, I found an uncomfortably large number of faeries, as well as a smaller, but still threatening, number of witches. Forcing myself to look beyond the power they possessed, I pushed further, further, until I thought I could sense Nicneven. She was naturally shielded from any deep mental probing, but there was definitely someone with an incredible amount of power positioned on the other side of the mountain. Near her was someone else I couldn't probe mentally, but I got enough of a feel of the physical body to know it was me...Dark Me, that is. I could also read Black Hilt's power, added confirmation since Dark Me had left with it.

"*We are in big trouble!*" I broadcast to the whole group.

"Are you only just now realizing that?" asked Shar humorlessly, moving quickly in my direction.

"Nicneven's whole army is pretty much right above us, so even if Nicneven runs out of juice, we'll be at the wrong end of a shooting gallery," I said, ignoring Shar. "Not only that, but it looks as if Dark Me has joined forces with Nicneven, whether voluntarily or involuntarily. That means she can use Dark Me's insights to guess our next moves…oh, and it means she has access to all his magic, and the lyre of Orpheus."

"One problem at a time," said Shar insistently. He thrust Zom into the ground with an emerald flash, and the shaking stopped in that immediate area, giving me the chance to get to my feet.

"It's time to use your little trick to spread Zom's love to all the evil magic in the ground," said Shar with a smile. His hands remained on the sword to steady himself, but there was enough room from me to touch the hilt, and Zom cooperated quickly, until the ground beneath and around us glowed a dull green, and Nicneven's hold on it disintegrated.

"Next moves?" I asked, figuring it was better to stick to mental communication with so many sharp-eared faeries nearby, and now that the shaking had stopped, at least for the moment, linking the spell casters to everyone else was no problem.

"Nicneven's forces have us too well covered to levitate out of the pit," thought Merlin. "I suggest we move quickly by portal to someplace else, then back here, but above ground. They will not know exactly where to look until we reappear. That will buy us a few seconds anyway, time enough to snatch the Grail. You and I will handle the portals, while the lovely ladies prepare a spell to keep the ground from collapsing under us again."

"Let's do it," I thought. If we waited too long, some other attack was bound to start. We had disrupted the local part of the earthquake, but the mountain was still being shaken apart, and I could already hear the roar of the next avalanche.

Once we started to open a portal, I felt Nicneven and Dark Me trying to counter our efforts, but they were too far away. Under Merlin's direction we stepped through the portal and on to Snowdon, which Merlin had picked because of the amount of ambient magic around.

"We should be safe here for a few minutes," he said to everyone. To me he said, "There is a fixed portal nearby to take us to

Gwynn ap Nudd. It will not attract the attention of Nicneven as much as using a newly made portal or traveling Lady of the Lake style would. Given the numbers arrayed against us, we need an army...at least a little one, if we hope to prevail."

Merlin knew Snowdon well and had brought us out literally only a few steps from the portal, so it was easy to run through it. I was surprised to find that it opened directly into Gwynn ap Nudd's great hall. So was he, apparently, for the large, dark-skinned faerie jumped up, sword in hand, before he realized who we were.

"Forgive the intrusion, old friend," said Merlin quickly, with a deep bow to Gwynn, "but our need is great."

"So it would seem, Merlin," replied Gwynn, "to bring you back from death itself, and through a portal I forgot about a thousand years ago."

"It was my fate to die much earlier," agreed Merlin, "but that destiny was superseded by another, and death eluded me...though I think I may well catch it soon. Today we fight Nicneven, and we entreat you to provide what help you can."

"That may be less than you imagine," replied Gwynn sadly. "The faerie rulers have met in council at my urging. That Nicneven threatens the balance of the universe can scarcely be doubted by an-yone...or so I foolishly believed. My request that the united lords of all the faerie realms declare war on Nicneven and strike her down before it was too late failed. Finvarra stood with me, as did Manann mac Lir, king of the Manx faeries—he said something about you showing exceptional honor while near his domain, Taliesin. Against me stood the Korrigan; Tanaquill, who calls herself Gloriana now; Joan, queen of the Cornish pixies; the Xana Mega, queen of the Ga-lician faeries; Auberon, Oberon's distant cousin and king of the French faeries outside Brittany; the Cailleach, Nicneven's proxy, and Jamshid, king of the Persian Peris, a group with mixed faerie and djinn ancestry, who have not sent a representative in centuries."

As always, faerie politics made me just a little sick to my stomach. "Why does Nicneven get a proxy?"

"She is still faerie queen of Scotland and thus entitled to a vote," grumbled Gwynn. "I did not dare to hope for her support, but I was expecting Tanaquill to side with her mother, not her mother's enemy. I fear the daughter may seek to replace the mother and rule England permanently."

"Such a thing would not surprise me," said Merlin, shaking his head sadly.

"Auberon I fear may be in league with his cousin, who could see Nicneven's triumph as a way to return to power himself, and it would not surprise me at all if Nicneven were using the opposing ambitions of father and daughter to her advantage. The Korrigan appears to be motivated primarily by dislike of you—I'll wager there is a story there, if ever there is time to tell it," said Gwynn with a wink. "As for the others, I was surprised to see any of them, for they seldom come to such assemblies. Had they stayed away, and had Tanaquill voted with us, we could have carried the day. As it was, we are powerless to act without risking the ire of our fellow rulers."

"Surely your fellow rulers would not be offended if you lent us some troops," suggested Merlin. "If they were attached to us and not officially representing you—"

Gwynn sighed loudly. "My ties to Taliesin are well known, and now it is equally well known that Nicneven is hostile to him. After my demand for war was defeated, my fellow rulers voted, with exactly the same people on each side, to forbid any of us to attack Nicneven unless she brought an army against one of us or into the mortal realm."

Now it was my turn to sigh. "Majesty, we believe she was about to lead just such an army against our fellow humans; we struck first in Elphame to preempt such an attack."

"Great strategy," conceded Gwynn, "but at this time, not the greatest politics. Nicneven can easily paint you as the aggressor, and she has done nothing yet to violate the rules laid out in council, so I cannot act without risking uniting the other rulers against me."

"Majesty," said Sir Arilan respectfully, "My men and I would be willing to accompany Taliesin, if you will release us from your service." Arilan had led the security detail that had protected us during a trip through Annwn, and we had profound mutual respect. I would have loved to accept his offer, but I figured Gwynn could still get into trouble for it, especially if Sir Arilan returned to his service later.

"Though I appreciate the offer," I said as politely as possible, "such a small force would not really help. You and your men are too far outnumbered by Nicneven to provide much cover. You would just end up dying in the attempt, and neither I nor my men wish to see such an outcome." Sir Arilan looked shocked by my refusal, but he nodded, accepting my decision as stoically as possible.

"Would you also refuse my help then?" asked a sweet and familiar voice. I turned to see Queen Mab, darkly beautiful as always and wearing her gown that looked like the night sky, walking rapidly in our direction.

"Majesty," I replied with a deep bow, "I cannot guarantee your safety. Besides, will not your fellow rulers be as angered by your joining as they would by Gwynn doing the same?"

"Our stature is not the same," she replied. "Gwynn is an independent ruler. I am queen of Connacht, but I am subordinate to Finvarra, high king of Ireland. If I am caught aiding you, it is he who will…punish me," she said in a manner suggesting her punishment would be light indeed.

When I seemed hesitant, she continued, "You accepted Coventina's help, though she is in as much danger as I would be. What does a faerie queen need to do to join this party, offer to marry you?" I blushed a little at that, and Gwynn chuckled.

"Another story I see!" he added almost merrily.

I glanced at Merlin quickly. "You would do Queen Mab a great discourtesy if you were to reject her help under these circumstances, Taliesin. Besides, turning down the aid of a spell caster of her power would be nothing short of madness when faced with such mighty opponents."

I turned back to Mab. "Welcome, then, to our army."

"Thank you for so graciously accepting my aid," replied Mab in a tone that had just a slightly ironic edge to it. "However, it would not do for the queen of Connacht to ride into battle unescorted, and I have brought insufficient men with me for a suitable escort. Gwynn, may I prevail upon you to lend me a few of your own men? Sir Arilan and his team perhaps?"

I saw Gwynn smirk for the first time. "Yes, Mab, I will lend you Sir Arilan and his company, though with the understanding that they are as of now under your command, not mine." Evidently the concept of plausible deniability had found its way into the faerie realms. If Gwynn was happy with that arrangement, the only polite course of action was to accept the help; Mab had cleverly arranged the situation so that I couldn't refuse to take Sir Arilan and his men. Well, we desperately needed their help anyway. We would just have to do what we could to make sure they came back alive.

Between Queen Mab and Sir Arilan we now had thirty-six faerie archers, hardly a match for the hundreds Nicneven had, but possibly significant if we found the right way to deploy them.

"I have one more matter to discuss with Gwynn," I told everyone else. "Shar, why don't you take charge of working out the best way to deploy our troops so that we can avoid problems like last time's earthquakes?" He nodded and led everyone else over to the spot where Merlin began the spell to activate the fixed portal and take us back to Snowdon.

When he turned back to Gwynn, he had raised an eyebrow. "Keeping secrets from your men now, Taliesin? That may not be wise."

"I'm just saving time," I reassured him. "Majesty, I have promised Titania to investigate Oberon's case, and I have done little to do so."

"Surely even Titania will understand that," pointed out Gwynn.

"I'm sure she will, but as a matter of honor, I should do what I can…and I'm not sure whether I will survive this battle." Gwynn started to protest, but I raised a hand to ask for quiet. That was presumptuous of me, but Gwynn knew me well enough not to be offended.

"Just in case," I continued, "I have a theory that could conceivably prove Oberon's innocence. Please let me pass it on to you in case…in case I'm not around to follow up on it." Gwynn looked unhappy but nodded. I knew not being able to go into battle with me was gnawing at him.

"Recently I learned of the existence of a spell that creates a whole new kind of shape-shifting, one that makes the shifter indistinguishable from the subject whose likeness the shifter takes on, and all the shifter needs is a few drops of the subject's blood."

Gwynn scoffed at that. "Spell casters who are not natural shifters have used spells like that for centuries, but their deception can also be detected by any reasonably powerful spell caster"

"I know that, Majesty, but this spell is different. I have seen it used to create a double of me, one that even I can tell only with great difficulty is not me. The spell duplicates the body to such a degree that human science cannot distinguish it from mine, but it also duplicates the mind in such a way that even someone who can read minds would have to dig very, very deeply to find any trace of the original shifter."

Gwynn's eyes narrowed. "That would explain some of the odd visions my seers have been having. One claimed you were in two places at once, another that you had turned evil, though yet a third disagreed."

"Yes," I said, "others have told me that the presence of two of me in the universe is wreaking havoc on the seers' predictive abilities."

"But how does this spell have anything to do with Oberon?" asked Gwynn.

"It only just occurred to me that the...being you have in prison may not be Oberon at all."

Gwynn looked tempted to laugh, but if so, he restrained himself. "Surely the jailers would have observed closely enough..."

"They probably can't read minds," I interrupted. "They could have spent hours and hours with the false Oberon and never realized what was happening. Any normal magical test would confirm that a shifter using this spell with some of Oberon's blood *was* Oberon."

He shook his head. "How can such a thing be?"

"Does it really make that much less sense than assuming he just randomly turned evil or assuming that some greater power had twisted his mind in a way completely undetectable to magic?" I asked. "Those are the only two theories we've had so far, and neither one of them makes a lot of sense."

"That is true," admitted Gwynn. "Something is not right. But how could someone have cast such a spell on him without being observed?"

"I can only speculate," I said, "but Robin Goodfellow told me Oberon was having a lot of secret meetings. Robin assumed they were all about the development of the spell, but Oberon wasn't telling him anything, so really Oberon could have been lured somewhere after the spell was created and then become its first subject."

"If what you say is true, who is responsible for this outrage?" asked Gwynn angrily. "To kidnap and impersonate a faerie king…that would be a great crime indeed!"

"The logical choice would be Nicneven," I suggested. "I now have evidence that she was working with both Ceridwen and Morgan. You will remember that Morgan convinced Oberon she was the reincarnation of his mother. From what Robin told me, I suspect it was Morgan who convinced Oberon to seek the spell, perhaps as a way to aid her escape if need be. For all we know, the spell already existed, and a false quest for it was the way Oberon was trapped in the first place. Perhaps Morgan knew the real Oberon would never go as far as she truly wanted, or perhaps Nicneven was manipulating her in some way.

"Nicneven has been engaging in subversion for weeks now in preparation for some kind of attack. Some of my own men have been affected, and we know she has sown confusion in faerie ranks by disrupting the government of England."

"Aye, that she has!" agreed Gwynn.

"Well," I continued, "inserting a false Oberon as the English leader would certainly have helped her plan. He nearly tipped the balance of power far enough to thwart our efforts on Olympus and get us all killed. When he failed, I believe Nicneven switched plans, finding some way to get the new shifting spell into Robin's hands, knowing he would botch things up, and so he has, for he has inadvertently made himself into an evil version of me and is now allied with Nicneven. I doubt that's coincidence."

"If you are right, the situation is worse than I feared!" said Gwynn. "Have you proof?"

I shook my head sadly. "If I survive, I will need you to arrange a way for me to visit Oberon and reveal the deception. Right now I can but speculate. Based on what I know, what I have told you is the most logical possibility."

"I believe you," said Gwynn slowly, "but at least some of the other faerie rulers will require proof."

"I will get them proof if I can," I assured him. "If I should fall to Nicneven, that task will become yours."

"I cannot read minds as you do, yet I will find a way," he assured me.

"Then I can go to battle knowing I have done my best to honor my bargain with Titania," I said. "I wish there were more time, but we must rejoin the battle with Nicneven before it is too late."

"Go then, and I will...pray...yes, pray for you," said Gwynn, more accustomed to being on the receiving end of prayers.

"I thank you, Majesty," I said, and then I raced over to activate the portal. In less than three minutes, I was with the guys on Snowdon.

"Have you arrived at a good battle plan?" I asked.

Shar nodded. "How could you think otherwise?"

"Just checking!" I assured him. "So don't leave me in suspense. What's the plan?"

"We spare some of the magic for floating those of us who can't fly, and we come at Nicneven from the air."

"She can use Hecate's power over the sky as well," I reminded Shar.

"Yes, but we stay in tight formation within the Grail's aura. She can't use magic on us or aim wind or lightning at us with magic. She can't throw rocks at us, either. When we are on the ground, something could get broken loose and fall toward us through gravity, but none of us could think of an air attack that Nicneven could set in motion by magic that wouldn't also require magic aiming. As long as we hold on to the Grail," said Shar, with a pointed glance at Jimmie, "we should be safe."

I wasn't thrilled with that plan, but I had to admit traveling by ground was no longer a viable option, so we had little to lose by giving air a try. "Arrows?" I asked after thinking for a minute.

Shar laughed. "We have good deflection spells, and we have enough archers of our own now to have them surround us. They'll be firing constantly, and just as before, the enemy archers will be spread across too wide an area to be protected from our shots as we are from theirs; there are just too many of them to group tightly enough. Merlin confirmed that."

Merlin nodded. "The plan is sound, and even if the archers are somehow protected from our arrows, the best outcome that gets them is a standoff."

"We will appear in the air at the farthest point we could see from our last position," added Coventina. "It will take Nicneven's minions time to orient themselves to our new position. If Nicneven hasn't moved, we can fly to her in a minute or two, and if our luck holds, we can overpower her before her forces can converge upon us."

"Job assignments?" I asked Shar.

"Jimmie will be at the center, holding the Grail, with Eva by his side to shoot any enemy who gets close enough, and with Carlos and Dan guarding both of them in case close combat is required. Gordy, Stan, Alex, and I will stand ready to join that close combat if the faeries realize their arrows are ineffective and charge us with swords; we'll intercept as many as we can before they even get to Carlos and Dan. Carla and Nurse Florence will maintain a deflection spell. You will attack with fire, Coventina with water, and Merlin with air, though he can switch to a different element if need be. Queen Mab will use her power over dream and illusion as circumstances permit. The faerie archers and Khalid will keep shooting as much as they can, with Khalid aiming for the most powerful targets, since he has by far the most effective arrows.

"We should be able to cut through any opposition that can gather in front of us," Shar continued. "We land as close to Nicneven as we can, and we hit her and Dark Me with everything we've got while the archers cover us from behind."

"Try not to kill Dark Me," I cautioned. "Remember, Robin Goodfellow is still in there somewhere."

"We'll keep that in mind," said Shar, though he didn't look particularly happy about it. He had a point, actually. It could be that Dark Me would be the strongest caster present, next to Nicneven herself. Still, Robin had gotten into this mess trying to help us, and I still wanted to get him out of it in one piece if I possibly could.

It took a while to double-check spells like faerie speed, and to get everyone positioned properly in the air. (Since we would be under attack the moment we reappeared, we had to be ready to hit the ground running…or in this case, hit the air flying.) When all was finally ready, I nodded to Merlin, who was going to open the portal, and in less than a minute we were soaring over the quake-wracked landscape of Elphame.

For a few seconds I allowed myself to hope that we were actually going to win.

Chapter 30: Repentance or Hellfire (Carla)

It was too bad Tal's effort to deaden my emotions didn't work as well as he thought it would. I guessed I must have seemed calm enough to fool him. I had pretended, but the truth was every part of my mind was still screaming as if my skin had been ripped off…and then I'd been buried in salt.

To find out suddenly that for weeks I had been living a lie was bad. To find out that I was the one who created the lie was far, far worse. To realize I had put people I cared about, including Tal, in jeopardy? I couldn't think of anything that would make me feel lower.

Tal's efforts to reassure me made me feel even worse. I knew he meant what he said about trying to restore our friendship, but his willingness to forgive made me feel worse for betraying him than if he'd blown up like the last time. I actually preferred Shar's wordless contempt, or the way Gordy refused to meet my eyes, or even Dan's expression. Since he had screwed up pretty badly once, he looked as if he was trying to understand me…trying, but failing.

Who was I really kidding? I had been a comrade-in-arms to all of these guys, and now all of them had to make themselves tolerate me, not because they wanted me around, but because they needed my magic for the battle. Khalid still smiled at me, but probably only because my little brother was his best friend.

Well, actually there was one creepy exception: Alex. His being in league with Ares and trying to kill Khalid and Stan with his bare hands might even qualify as worse than what I'd done, and he kept going out of his way to smile at me and put out an encouraging vibe.

It was a mark of how low I had sunk that my only real fan had been, and perhaps still was, a violent psycho—and I wasn't even sure he actually wanted friendship. Based on what I'd accidentally seen in his mind when we first met, it was far more likely he just wanted sex.

The worst part was that some day I might feel desperate enough to give it to him.

With a shudder I banished that thought and tried to focus on the battle ahead.

Merlin brought us back into Elphame as far from our previous location as he could, and the tactic seemed to be working. The faeries and witches had spread themselves pretty thin in order to catch us when we returned, and they had a hard time regrouping fast enough. Of course, they had to cope with pretty significant wind resistant generated by Merlin while dodging Tal's fire bolts and Coventina's water blasts, to say nothing about volley after volley of faerie arrows, an attack they couldn't return because Nurse Florence and I were keeping the group so well shielded.

Of course, that advantage would not last forever. Even with our reinforcements, Nicneven's troops had an overwhelming numerical advantage. Given a little time, they could still overcome us if they were willing to sacrifice enough of their number to do so. Our best hope was to get Nicneven and Dark Me. That should put a dent in the enemy's morale and give us the aggressive magic of the lyre of Orpheus.

As fast as we could, we flew around the mountain. Nicneven had been on the far side, and every one of us with magic could still feel her there. The faeries confirmed our feelings by making a concerted effort to block us, but our combination of physical and magical firepower cut through their ranks like a sword cutting through rice paper.

When we finally saw the queen of Scottish faeries and witches, though, I began to wonder if she had lured us to her.

For one thing, she had a full-scale blizzard going above her. It took a couple seconds for me to figure out why she was wasting so much magic energy on a storm the Grail would protect us against. Then I realized the storm could still shelter Nicneven and the troops clustered around her from our arrows. That and the magical shielding around them, which would probably deflect much of our magic, would force us to land and engage Nicneven's troops up-close-and-personal. As I realized what Nicneven had for ground troops, I began to understand exactly how tough that would be.

I had no special knowledge of Scottish magical creatures in my current life, but Alcina, the evil sorceress I had been centuries ago, would have known perfectly well what I was looking at, and so I did as well.

It was no surprise to see Dark Me standing right next to Nicneven, sneering and brandishing Black Hilt. Him we could take. I was much more concerned with the abomination that stood at Nicneven's other side.

The Nuckelavee, something like a giant centaur, but several times the size of one, with shadow black skin and blazing red eyes, stared at us with pure hatred, eager to snack on us. The Grail might protect us from its poisonous breath, which could bring plague, but it would not help against physical dangers, like being crushed beneath its hooves.

The Nuckelavee would have been a formidable opponent all by itself—but it was not alone. Nearby stood the Uilepheist, a dragon-sized lizard with sickly blue-green scales. Like the Nuckelavee, it was capable of inflicting massive physical damage from which the Grail could not shield us. Unlike a dragon, it couldn't fly, but if we landed, it could swallow one of us whole without even straining.

To make matters worse, Nicneven and Dark Me were surrounded by several ranks of each-uisge, shape-shifters even more vicious than kelpies. At the moment they were deceptively appearing as handsome and not terribly warlike men, but some of them had telltale bits of seaweed in their hair. Like kelpies, they were accustomed to drowning their prey before eating it, but based on what Tal had told me of the encounter he and Stan had with a kelpie, I was sure the each-uisge would skip the drowning and just rip us to shreds if the opportunity presented itself. For that matter, they could also assume a horse shape and trample us to death in a stampede. Yeah, there were that many of them, an odd thing all by itself, since they were typically solitary creatures.

It hardly seemed to be a coincidence that someone with magic as formidable as Nicneven's would have gone to such trouble to assemble an overwhelming physical force designed to neutralize the advantages possession of the Grail gave us. After our first appearance, she knew how absolutely we were protected from magic, but how could she have assembled this freak show so fast?

Not surprisingly, Tal had already figured out the answer. *"Dark Me!"* he thought through our links. His alter ego must have figured we'd get the Grail somehow and been able to warn Nicneven in time for her to strengthen her defenses against us.

"The blizzard—it's made of sea ice!" thought Coventina, who sounded unable to believe it.

"The Nuckelavee and the each-uisge are creatures at home in salt water," observed Merlin. *"They aren't especially vulnerable to cold, and as the ice melts, the sea water will continuously refresh them—and I suspect blunt your ability to attack with fresh water, my lady."* I could feel Coventina cursing silently. The sea-ice blizzard and Nicneven's magic shielding together would probably make Coventina's signature attack ineffective. Too bad, since from what I'd heard, even a little splash of fresh water might send the Nuckelavee running.

"It's another deadlock," thought Shar. *"They can't attack us while we're in the air, but we can't attack them from the air very easily, either."*

"What are our chances on the ground?" asked Stan.

"What do you think?" asked Tal. *"She's got two giant monsters, either one of which might beat us on its own, plus a whole army of creatures stronger than any normal person. The Grail won't stop a physical attack, so if we land, I'd say we're done for."*

"There might be a way," I thought suddenly, *"and we might not have to land to do it, though we'd probably have to get uncomfortably close."*

"If we're going to do something, it should be quick," observed Gordy. *"Pretty soon we won't be able to retreat."*

I barely had to look around to tell he was right. The faeries couldn't get too close to Nicneven's position without being hit by the blizzard themselves, but they could encircle us from behind, and clearly they were doing that. Our archers and spell casters could make them keep their distance, but there were too many faeries to be driven off easily, and soon they would have blocked any physical exit route. Then they would probably start hitting us with enough concentrated arrow fire to crack our protective spell, and we would be in trouble. Fortunately, a mental discussion of my idea would take only seconds, not the minutes we would have wasted if we were speaking.

"What's your idea?" thought Tal impatiently.

"You'll recall that one of Alcina's specialties was control of sea creatures, and she could control masses of them at once. If you can get me

close enough, I think I can get at least a portion of Nicneven's army to switch sides."

"*That could create some confusion,*" admitted Shar, though he clearly wanted no part of any plan I suggested. "*But can you do it?*"

"*We aren't talking about getting dolphins to do tricks,*" Merlin thought. "*I know about Alcina's magic from the days of Camelot. Her spells are formidable, but creatures like the Nuckelavee are much stronger than ordinary creatures of the deep. Even the each-uisge, because of their supernatural nature, would almost certainly be resistant.*"

"*What would be the harm in trying?*" asked Coventina. "*As long as we have the Grail with us, Nicneven can't use her magic, no matter how close we get. If we can stay out of the reach of the larger creatures, why not make the attempt?*"

"*I sense a possibility here,*" added Queen Mab. "*This magic of Alcina that Carla controls might not in itself be enough, but what if I add my strength to hers? I have no touch with sea creatures, but my control over what the modern mortals call the unconscious mind is formidable. It might be possible to blend my ability to influence thoughts with her specific skill at influencing sea creatures. At the same time, Coventina's ability to summon the power of the lake, which is after all the ultimate fresh water power, might weaken Nicneven's monsters and give our efforts the ability to wear through their resistance.*"

"*What you propose is little short of madness,*" insisted Merlin. "*I'll concede the merit of the idea, but your suggestion is not like mere power sharing in which you each channel power to Carla. Instead, you want to blend three separate kinds of power from three separate casters who have never worked together before. Had we months, or perhaps even days, I do not doubt that you could do what you advocate, but in the next few minutes? No one can do that.*"

"*Tal can,*" suggested Nurse Florence. "*If he orchestrates the blending, I think it can work.*"

"*I...I'm not sure,*" thought Tal slowly. "*I've never tried anything like that before.*"

I felt a headache beginning to throb. Nicneven's faeries were taking wounds so that some of them could get close enough to shoot at us. With more evenly matched forces, that tactic would never have worked, but we had thirty-eight archers, counting Eva and Khalid, while they had pretty close to a thousand, and now they were using their numbers in an attempt to overwhelm us, just as we had feared might happen.

"*If we move under Nicneven's blizzard, it will be harder for her faeries to shoot at us,*" I pointed out. "*We're starting to take heavy fire.*"

"*The casters should concentrate on the archers again,*" countered Merlin. "*We will drive their casualties high enough to keep them back.*"

"*Say that works,*" thought Nurse Florence. "*Say you knock all of them out of the air. That doesn't get us any closer to beating Nicneven.*"

"*Free from other distractions, the casters can then break through whatever shielding against spells she has,*" thought Merlin triumphantly. "*Then we can hit her effectively from a distance, and from what I can see, we should be able to command more magic than she is able to.*"

"*I am not at all sure that is what would happen,*" replied Coventina. "*Nicneven has faerie casters and witches in abundance to draw power from. At best, we would have another deadlock that still requires us to face her monsters…unless we find a way to overcome them, and Carla's plan offers the best chance of doing so.*"

"*I'm not as knowledgeable as all of you,*" thought Stan, "*but wouldn't the magical protections Nicneven has in place prevent Carla's plan from working?*"

"*In theory,*" replied Tal, "*but Nicneven is trying to ward a large area with an impromptu shield. We know that the bigger an area magic protection covers, the more likely it is to weaken and develop holes. Let me see if I can work this out. If Merlin hits Nicneven's defenses with everything he has, he will draw her attention toward the spot he is attacking. At the same time, we get close enough for Shar, Gordy, and Stan in David mode to hit Nicneven's protection in different places. I'll broadcast what I'm seeing, so they'll know where to aim. Zom will cut right through, David's sword seems to have some kind of holiness when David wields it, and Apollo's sword should make a dent, maybe more. At close enough range, Khalid's blessed arrows should be able to at least hit Nicneven's shield even if the blizzard prevents anything requiring sharper aim, and they too should pierce her defenses. Nicneven now has intense pressure from Merlin and possible holes in four other spots. If the whole thing doesn't collapse, or at least become very unstable, I'll be extremely surprised. Meanwhile Carla, Coventina, Queen Mab, and I will focus everything we've got on Nicneven's marine monsters, starting with the ones farthest from her; they'll be at a spot where the protection is at its weakest to begin with. Nurse Florence will maintain the deflection of arrows as best she can, while our remaining archers keep Nicneven's archers back as far as possible. We'll probably take some hits from arrows, but all we need to do is pull the arrows out and let the Grail heal us. To me that plan sounds reasonable."*

"To me it sounds like risking us all on a very iffy strategy," thought Shar loudly. *"We don't know how many casters Nicneven has in the area to draw power from, and what about Dark Me? What's to prevent him from using the lyre to reinforce Nicneven's defenses?"*

"He hasn't so far," pointed out Khalid, but that argument sounded lame even to me.

The links among us were designed to allow us to receive and broadcast mental messages and nothing else, but they weren't perfect, so it wasn't surprising that I picked up emotional nuances from some of the guys. It was because of that I knew that Shar's reason for opposing the plan was not Alexander the Great's battle acumen but plain old distrust for me. I couldn't really blame him. Asmodeus had used me to take control of him and jeopardize Khalid and everybody else. Nor could I blame Gordy, Dan, Carlos, Stan, and even poor Jimmie for feeling pretty much the same way. I didn't have any kind of vibe from Merlin, but I guessed his attitude toward me was a factor in his opposition as well.

Here it was: an opportunity to redeem myself by helping to win the battle—only I wasn't even going to get a chance to try. I could feel the growing tension through the links. Tal might want to give me a chance, but I doubted he would try to force the guys into following a strategy most of them disagreed with. Probably Coventina and Queen Mab wouldn't insist over Merlin's strenuous objections, either.

I wanted to find some way to convince the doubters to go along, but how could I argue forcefully when I had betrayed them all? What could possibly make them trust me in the next five minutes? Nothing.

"Carla, it is time to honor your agreement," said a deep, utterly inhuman voice in my head.

Asmodeus!

"You can't...you can't..." I stammered mentally.

"*Can't what? Can't reach you while you are under the protection of the Grail? The Grail only wards you against uninvited evil. You voluntarily signed a pact with me, and even the Grail cannot protect you from that.*"

"*I knew it!*" thought Shar. "*She's still under the demon's influence!*"

It was then I realized everybody else was hearing Asmodeus through their link with me. Whatever chance I had of executing my plan had just gone up in smoke—and hellfire!

"*I am not under anyone's control, least of all his!*" I insisted.

We all got treated to Asmodeus's blood chilling laugh. "*How would you even know? I used you for days, with you none the wiser. The pact gives me that power. The Grail did break the connection, but once you were outside the castle, I had no trouble restoring your tie to me.*"

Everyone was looking at me, even Alex, even little Khalid. Asmodeus had shaken any trust in me they might have had.

"*To be on the safe side—*" began Nurse Florence.

"*No!*" I thought emphatically. "*This is what Asmodeus wants. He wants to derail my plan, which means he knows it could work.*" Shar was staring at me with an incredulous, give-me-a-break look, but I pressed on. "*He doesn't control me. Tal, Merlin, you can look inside and see he doesn't.*"

"*These things can be deeply hidden,*" thought Merlin. "*It might take hours—*"

"*I can prove it!*" I insisted, my panic mounting. "*Could a tool of Asmodeus do this?*" I had been maneuvering myself closer to Jimmie as I continued the conversation, and at that moment I reached out to touch the Grail.

I had no idea what would happen. For all I knew, the Grail would burn my arm off. I knew what I said was true, though. Asmodeus picked this particular moment to jump into my head because he wanted to stop my plan. I had to take the risk.

Unfortunately, Jimmie, caught by surprise, yanked the Grail away from me. I tried to follow, but Dan blocked me. "*Back off, Carla!*" he thought-shouted at me, probably because he perceived me as a threat to Jimmie.

I wasn't sure whether momentarily stunning Dan with just a little magic would be viewed by the Grail as a hostile sorcery and blocked, so I settled for kneeing him in the crotch and dodging past him before he could recover. Never let anyone tell you those self-defense courses don't sometimes come in handy.

"Jimmie, give her the Grail," Nicneven stage-whispered in his head. Apparently his accepting the bogus saint medal from her had given her the ability to speak to him despite the Grail. As with Asmodeus's conversation, everyone heard Nicneven speak to Jimmie, which I was sure was exactly what she intended. Jimmie turned white and trembled. I could feel his determination not to do what she wanted.

My one advantage was that the magic keeping the nonfliers in the air required everyone to stay in relatively tight formation, so Jimmie had very limited space to evade me.

However, before I could reach him, Shar got between us. *"I don't want to hurt you, Carla, but I will if I have to,"* he thought, raising Zom, which blazed emerald, as if matching his determination to hold me back.

"Carla, Shar, everybody, stand down!" ordered Tal. *"Fighting each other is just playing into our enemies' hands!"*

"Whereas letting our enemies know our plans isn't?" demanded Shar sarcastically. *"If we can hear them, can they hear us…through Carla?"*

The moment he had that thought, I realized it was probably true. However brilliant my plan was, however well it might have worked, Nicneven, Dark Me, and Asmodeus could now design countermeasures. I hadn't meant to, but once again I had threatened everybody else's safety.

For the first time in my life, I had absolutely no idea what to do. That's how badly broken the situation was. I'm ashamed to say suicide actually flashed through my mind, but that would hurt my former friends even more. Anyway, if I was going to do that, the time would have been before I sold myself to Asmodeus and caused all this chaos, not now.

Selfishly, I also didn't want to be remembered as the girl who threw away her soul for a guy, and that's exactly how people would remember me if died before I at least tried to salvage something from the utter mess I had plunged everyone into. Hard as it would be for most people to believe at the moment, I wasn't one of those girls who had to have a guy to complete her. Independent women fell in love, too, though. If I had to take the advice Artemis had given me and forget all about men in general and Tal in particular, would I have done it? Even now I didn't see how I could do that and still be me.

Of course, right now it would be good to be someone else...anyone else.

With considerable exertion, I managed to pull myself out of the self-pity I had been wallowing in. I wasn't going to get near enough to the Grail to touch it; that was excruciatingly clear. How could I find some other way to prove myself? With Nicneven's archers pushing us and her ground troops ready to exploit even the slightest mistake, there was no way anyone was going to have time to examine me and pronounce me demon free; Merlin was right about that. What else was there?

My mind drifted back to how others had tried to redeem themselves. When Tal blamed himself for my coma, he had put himself on the line, even risked death, to heal me. When Dan lost Tal's trust, he had kept right on risking himself by Tal's side until his and Tal's common love for Jimmie had resurrected their friendship. When Jimmie realized how Nicneven had tricked him, he had faced unbearable pain, perhaps even death, to get her foul, magical hold ripped out of him by force. There was an obvious common thread here: self-sacrifice. Tal, Dan, and Jimmie had all felt the guilt of letting other people down, though they had erred far less grievously than I had. They were very different people, but each reacted to letting people down by risking whatever the situation required to undo the damage or at least to atone for it. I didn't know if what I had done could possibly be undone...but I was damn well going to try.

Suddenly I knew what I had to do. As much as they now distrusted me, the guys would never have agreed to my plan, so I didn't ask them. Instead, I levitated straight up and then flew with all my might away from them and over Nicneven's army. Tal demanded I come back, so I just broke my links to him and the rest of the group. If nothing else, they could now plan without our enemies overhearing.

My move had been unexpected enough that Nicneven's forces didn't know how to react. In seconds I was outside the arrow-deflecting field I had helped to create, but the faerie archers didn't fire on me. Nor did any of them pursue me, though they probably could have outrun me. They likely had orders to focus on the group, and Nicneven hadn't had the time to alter those mandates. Either that, or she figured I wasn't a threat and could safely be ignored. Hopefully, I could prove her wrong.

Once I got going, I was moving too fast to be an easy target for hostile magic, so, even though I was outside the Grail's protection, any casters around didn't even try. Again, they probably didn't have any idea how much potential damage I could do to them. Dark Me could have figured it out if had enough time to think about it, but I had no intention of giving him that time.

Nicneven or Dark Me could have flown after me, but they didn't, presumably because the rest of the group was still close at hand and might have had an easier time picking them off if they became airborne. The rest of Nicneven's army was not capable of flying, so at least in that respect I was lucky.

Before long I had flown past Nicneven's whole army—and a disturbingly big one it was. This far back, though, I could sense how weak Nicneven's protections were. Given just a little time, I was confident I could rip through them. Not only that, but the blizzard didn't extend back this far, either, so the each-uisge here would be far weaker than the ones in the front ranks.

I slowed my flight and positioned myself to hover just out of reach of the many each-uisge who were starting at me. This would be a bad time to find out that they had a flying form, but fortunately, though some of them became fierce-looking horses, none of them showed even the hint of a wing or a feather anywhere.

While they were trying to figure out a way to attack me, I reached out with my mind and felt the wards experimentally. Definitely as weak as I had hoped! In about half a minute I ripped a hole large enough to work some magic through, and then I tried to take control of the nearest each-uisge.

As Merlin had warned, the creatures had strong wills and a certain amount of magic resistance. I could probably tear down that resistance, but I began to worry I might not have enough time. I wasn't sure if Nicneven would realize what I was doing, but she would certainly know I had broken through her protection, and she was bound to react in some way. At this point she could thwart me with even a dozen archers: I couldn't protect myself from arrows and bend the each-uisge to my will.

Suddenly, Alex was at my side.

"What are you doing here?" I thought to him.

"I could ask you the same question."

"Executing my plan," I thought. Asmodeus presumably already knew what I meant, but at this point I wasn't about to remind him.

"Tal's mad," Alex thought, *"but he doesn't want you to die. No one does. By the way, Khalid would have tried to fly here as well. Shar had to hold him back by force."* There was a long pause, at least by the standards of mental dialog. Then Alex continued, *"I didn't exactly ask to come, but you'll notice no one tried to hold me back."*

I suppose I should have been pleased someone cared, but I was trying to find a polite way to get Alex to stop trying to think at me. I needed to focus every ounce of concentration I possessed if this was going to work. Besides, I still had the sneaking suspicion that Alex was just trying to get into my pants.

I had spared just enough attention to monitor the nature of the forces around me, and I could feel magic surging in this direction like a tidal wave. Best-case scenario: Nicneven was reinforcing her wards. Worst-case scenario: Nicneven was coming with a dozen or so hellfire-flinging witches to finish me off. Being more precise would have been too distracting…

I could sense a portal opening nearby. That couldn't be good news. I could feel my magic having some effect on the nearest each-uisge, but getting a significant number of them to actually side with me? I was minutes away at least.

"Carla!" yelled Tal. It took me a second to realize I was actually hearing his voice. Was he projecting it somehow?

I spared a glance in the direction from which the yell had come and was surprised to see Tal and everybody else floating just a few feet away. The power surge I had felt hadn't been Nicneven at all; it had been the cavalry coming after me.

"Don't look so surprised." Tal said. "I told you I wouldn't turn my back on you."

"Never mind that you had to remake your strategy to her liking," said Shar acidly, giving Tal the evil eye big-time.

"We have seconds before Nicneven realizes where we are, and maybe another minute before she arrives herself," thought Merlin forcefully. *"Let us try this girl's plan if we must."*

I felt pressure to link with someone and realized it was Tal, Coventina, and Mab trying to sync with me. I could hardly believe it. They were going to give my idea a chance! Well, in that case I had better make sure it worked.

I quickly joined my mind to the three with whom I would be working. Asmodeus would be aware, but I hoped he wouldn't have time to do anything about it. I was dimly conscious of the archers moving in front of me, including me in their protection. Although I couldn't feel the Grail's aura, I was sure I was encircled by it as well and once again shielded from any magical attack.

I had felt Tal's mind before, and I tried to keep the link as narrow as possible. His support now probably had nothing to do with any feelings for me, and certainly they weren't an indication of some sudden realization he loved me...but I had no desire to get confirmation of my assessment straight from his own mind.

Coventina and Mab were a different matter entirely, for I had never linked with either of them, and both were faerie rather than human. From Coventina I could feel the power of the lake, vast, cold, tranquil, and primal. From Mab I picked up the even greater vastness of the human subconscious, deep as an endlessly rippling ocean, familiar somehow yet completely unfathomable.

I knew Tal had the ability to comprehend unfamiliar magic quickly, and not so long ago I had seen him rebuild Jimmie's broken body flawlessly, even though he had only seen healings and never actually performed one. This attempt to merge three dissimilar magics into one powerful spell must be pushing the envelope even for him, though. To perform such a feat before Nicneven could interfere? No wonder Merlin was skeptical.

My power to command sea creatures became the center of the force we strove to create. To this base Mab added depth, allowing my control to seep into parts of the each-uisge mind I had never imagined even existed. Coventina added an edge, an ability to cut through each-uisge mental resistance better than I could ever have managed on my own. I had imagined such a blending, but even I was amazed as Tal steered the energies involved, pulling them into a new pattern the three of us could not on our own have managed, at least not in so short a time.

As we worked, I became uncomfortably conscious of the arrival of Nicneven's faerie archers, who approached from above and started raining arrows down on us. Our far less numerous archers would counter as best they could, and Nurse Florence would try to deflect the arrows alone, since I had no energy to spare, but now only Merlin remained to keep the archers at bay with magic. The rest of us were all occupied, and almost immediately I could feel the pressure against the protection Nurse Florence was generating escalate to dangerous levels.

"*Focus,*" Tal reminded me gently, and I tried to shut out the growing chaos around us.

The new force we had made began to radiate out toward the each-usige, but I could feel an awkwardness in it, a subtle dissonance, and it did not seem to be working.

I had more or less forced everyone else into this battle plan, and now it was going to fail.

"*Have faith!*" Tal demanded. I tried to suppress my fear of failure, but suddenly the idea that had seemed so great only a few minutes before now had the feeling of death about it.

I could sense the sea-ice blizzard shifting in our direction. I could feel the barrage of arrows nicking into our protection, wearing it away one layer at a time.

"*Carla! You must end this attack now! Our pact forbids you to interfere with my plans,*" hissed Asmodeus.

Now that I could remember our deal, I tried to recall the details.

"*The pact is broken,*" I replied, straining to keep the power flowing to my spell as Tal worked feverishly to make adjustments. "*You failed to keep Tal in love with me.*"

"*The pact can still be fulfilled; therefore, it is still in force and still binds you,*" the demon prince asserted angrily. "*Obey me at once, or forfeit your soul.*"

"*He's bluffing!*" said Tal. "*Just as you said, he knows your plan can work, and he'd do anything to break your concentration.*"

In seconds Tal was proved all too right—at least about the concentration part—when a hell gate burst open below us, spraying sulfurous fumes in all directions. The glow from the flickering flames of Hell on the other side drew my attention despite myself. Asmodeus had already shown he could get inside my head even while the Grail was protecting me. Could he literally drag me to Hell while I was under that same protection? I couldn't imagine how, but there was no way to know. I'm not sure if even the Grail king and his retinue could have figured that one out.

In fact, I was sure of only one thing: I needed to get Asmodeus out of my head.

Chapter 31: Demons and Darkness (Jimmie)

I was feeling pretty useless. Don't get me wrong. The Grail provided crucial protection, and being the one who got to hold the Grail was certainly an honor, but pretty much anyone could have done that. It didn't exactly take any special talent. Even so, I'd managed to drop the Grail once already and kinda wished I could Super Glue it to my hands. Anyway, you can imagine how much fun it was to be the person who screwed up the job a trained chimpanzee could do. No one said anything to me about it, of course, and they never would…but I still knew I screwed up.

Yeah, that was me: Jimmie the screwup. The best that could be said for me was that I hadn't sold my soul to the Devil or made a deal with someone like Ares. Pretty much anything else I could screw up though, I had. At first being part of winning the Grail had made me feel much better, but now, with the battle looking more and more difficult, I would have given anything to be able to swing a sword like Shar or cast spells like Tal—or at least not need babysitters, otherwise known as bodyguards, whose chief function was to protect me, because unique among the whole group, I couldn't protect myself. Yeah, I had no armor, and my arms were still healing, so I wouldn't have been very good with a sword, but that didn't prevent the situation from weighing on me a bit. Even the girls contributed to the battle in ways I couldn't.

I could see Nurse Florence trembling and going pale again, and I knew what that meant: she couldn't keep deflecting arrows much longer. Carla seemed to be having a bigger problem, though, and I knew that meant everyone was having a problem, because Tal needed her for whatever magic they were trying right now. His face betrayed the fact that something wasn't working, and I certainly noticed the opening of what appeared to be a doorway to Hell. I'd never seen one before, of course, but if the sulfur smell and the flames hadn't given it away, the expression of horror on Carla's face would have confirmed where that door led. My mom would say that Carla was getting what she deserved, but I wasn't so sure. Regardless, we were running out of time, and I figured someone needed to stop Asmodeus from interfering with Carla so that whatever she, Tal, and the faerie women were doing would have a chance to work.

I wasn't sure Asmodeus was even physically present, but then I spotted him near the opening to Hell. This time he was disguised as an ordinary man; maybe he still remembered the butt-kicking we gave his three-headed form at Elings Park, or maybe he was still weak from that encounter, and a regular human form took less effort. If he was trying to pass for an ordinary human, though, that hell-fiery glow in his eyes gave him away.

Looking around, I didn't think anyone else had seen the demon yet, or at least my bodyguards hadn't. Eva, brow wrinkled in concentration, though closer to me than the other archers, was using the bow of Artemis to pick off what faeries she could. Dan and Carlos were standing really close to me, as if they thought I might break or something, but their attention was up, from where faeries might attack, not down, where Asmodeus was.

"Guys, there's Asmodeus!" I said, pointing. "I'll bet he's causing problems for Carla. We should do something." Eva kept shooting in the other direction, but Dan and Carlos both looked down, and Carlos crossed himself.

Dan looked unnerved by the appearance of yet another problem. On the athletic field, he was in charge, but in battle he usually followed Tal's lead. This time Tal was still trying to make the magic work, and Shar, his self-appointed second-in-command, was on the front line with the archers, using well-placed sword thrusts to fend off what faeries tried to get to close quarters.

Like the rest of us, Dan was used to combat, but I suddenly realized he was more like the brave soldier leading the charge than the strategist. Anyway, he didn't have the first clue what to do about the appearance of the hell gate and Asmodeus, and neither apparently did Carlos, who raised his sword as if he thought Asmodeus would fly up and attack but didn't offer any suggestions.

Of course, Carlos could have been right. I knew Asmodeus couldn't use magic against us if we hung close enough to the Grail, but he was capable of a considerable physical attack, and it occurred to me he might try to fly up and grab Carla or do something else that would disrupt our defenses. That made it all the more important to do something about him, but what?

Aside from Merlin, who had seemingly lapsed into a trance, I didn't think anybody in the group would know much about Asmodeus. Then I remembered that Carlos had said something about Asmodeus being in the Bible.

"Yeah," said Carlos in answer to my question, eyes still focused on potential incoming threats, "in the Catholic Old Testament, specifically a book called Tobit. Asmodeus keeps killing the husbands of a woman named Sarah, because he wants her for himself."

"I presume he must have been stopped somehow," prompted Dan.

Carlos wrinkled his brow for a minute. "One of the characters burns a fish's heart and liver, creating fumes that drive Asmodeus away."

Dan looked around doubtfully. "Unless an each-uisge's organs will do—"

"Wait!" interrupted Carlos. "It was the archangel Raphael who suggested the method of driving away Asmodeus, and then Raphael bound the demon after he fled."

"The same Raphael who blessed Khalid's arrows?" I asked hopefully.

"The very same!" said Carlos with a smile. "I bet those arrows are just what we need."

"Khalid, Asmodeus is down there!" yelled Dan. "Shoot him!"

Khalid was nothing if not fast. It took him only seconds to find Asmodeus and open fire. Unfortunately, Asmodeus was fast too and managed to dodge. Probably if all of our archers had focused on the demon, they could have hit him, but I doubted any arrows except Khalid's would really work.

At that moment Merlin came out of his trance, looked around, and said loudly, "Asmodeus must be stopped!" I could actually have figured that much out without the sorcerer's help.

Apparently, Khalid thought as fast as he moved, because he abruptly diverted his attack from the swiftly dodging demon to the stationary hell gate. Hitting what would have been the door frame on a physical door, his first arrow exploded against the evil surface, causing the fiery opening to shudder. Asmodeus turned his angry gaze on

Khalid and snarled, but the little guy ignored him and kept lobbing arrows at the hell gate; each of them caused the gate to shudder more than the preceding one, and now what was visible through it was more smoke than fire.

Asmodeus was boiling mad and actually tried to breathe hellfire at Khalid, but the Grail's protection held, which didn't surprise me at all. What did surprise me was that demon managed to fend off what looked like a pretty powerful bolt of raw magic force Merlin threw at him.

"You are only half a demon!" Asmodeus shouted. "And less than half a man! You will never stop me." Undeterred, the air crackled as Merlin sent one magic attack after another in Asmodeus's general direction. The demon apparently couldn't turn back that much hostile energy at once. He still dodged successfully, but Merlin's attack gave Khalid time to get a couple more arrows into the hell gate, which collapsed in one final surge of hellfire. Asmodeus shouted angrily, but he was still unwounded and could always open another gateway if given enough time—and Khalid would eventually run out of arrows, as the quiver couldn't make them fast enough to keep up with constant shooting.

"Carla! Head in the game!" I heard Tal demand. Glancing over, I could see that she was watching Asmodeus as someone would watch an auto accident. Unable to tear her eyes away, she must not have been concentrating well enough to do the other casters any good.

Now I could see two figures flying toward us, and I did not need magic to know they were probably Nicneven and Dark Me. The each-uisge noticed also, and some of them smiled evilly. We were running out of time.

I knew that Tal might be able to succeed if only Carla could get her mind off of Asmodeus. I could think of only one way to do that and perhaps undo one of my earlier screwups at the same time.

"Carla, take the Grail!" I said, moving in her direction. It was hard to move evenly in a situation in which I was being levitated by others, but the spell was designed to allow for some movement, so I took advantage of that.

Carla looked startled, and even Tal seemed uncertain.

"Are you sure about this?" asked Dan.

"It's not like she can hurt it," I replied, holding it out to her.

"I think you should take it, my dear," Coventina offered. Carla was mirroring Tal's uncertainty, however, and we were running out of time. I knew Nicneven was approaching, with her blizzard not very far behind.

"You were right the first time," I insisted. "Touch it, and you will know." Again I held it out toward her. Slowly her right hand reached toward it.

Unfortunately, at just that moment Nurse Florence's arrow deflection collapsed. Our faerie archers took the hardest fire, but an arrow scratched my hand, and I nearly dropped the Grail a second time.

"Pull the arrows out of yourself or anyone near you," Tal reminded us. *"The Grail will heal any wound."* The scratch on my hand had already healed by the time he finished broadcasting.

Again Carla reached toward the Grail. This time I heard a bone-chilling shriek and knew that Asmodeus was flying toward us, just as I had thought he might in the first place. We had been defending against attacks from the side and from overhead, not from below, and apparently he caught both Khalid and Merlin by surprise, their latest attacks hitting where he had just been rather than where he now was.

Asmodeus might have killed me, except that his magical ability to fly must have faded away when he entered the area the Grail protected. However, momentum carried him far enough to grab one of my feet, and his weight was enough to pull me downward before anyone could reinforce the spell holding me up. I could feel his claws sink into my ankle, and I screamed, but I also clutched the Grail so hard I bruised my hand. I was not going to botch that job again.

Once Asmodeus hit the ground, he threw me down so hard that I could feel bones breaking. Still I held on to the Grail, and the bones began pulling back together. Asmodeus raised another hand to strike me, but Dan, who had come screaming down after me, sliced right through the demon's wrist, and the hand flopped to the ground. Asmodeus stopped the spraying blood almost at once, but Dan nicked his arm, and now Carlos was with us, too, swinging his sword for all he was worth. He too managed to nick Asmodeus, this time in the other arm. The demon was too powerful for the sword wound to cause him to drown, as Carlos's sword would have done with a lesser opponent, but fighting the drowning effect did cause the demon to hesitate; he was slowed just long enough for one of Khalid's arrows to pierce his chest. The blessing of Raphael surged from the arrow into Asmodeus, ripping him apart like a nuclear blast. I knew he was not banished forever, but at least his current body was torn apart, and even the fragments were seared from within by the power of Raphael, until nothing but ashes remained. If our previous experience was any indication, this was one demon king who would be sitting out the rest of the battle.

Unfortunately, beating Asmodeus had come at a cost. Dan, Carlos, and I were all on the ground, and the each-uisge, once they recovered from the shock of our sudden arrival, were converging on us rapidly. As none of us could fly and had dropped below the range of the levitation spell, we had to be rescued by the spell casters in the party.

I looked up quickly and realized we were far enough below our airborne friends that the Grail's protection no longer extended to them. The blizzard had reached the area and hit them with full force, making it difficult for any of the spell casters to concentrate. At the same time, all of them were taking damage from the arrow fire that the Grail was no longer close enough to heal.

Even I knew enough to realize that they had only one move they could make: straight down. I knew Tal too well to think he would consider the death of any of us acceptable losses, and there was no way our friends could protect us where we were as long as they were under such intense attack. Nor could they survive long without the Grail's protection. Even with Asmodeus gone, Nicneven and Dark Me would be powerful opponents, especially since Dark Me had the lyre of Orpheus.

Just as I predicted, I could see our friends coming down to us. However, the each-uisge got there first.

The three of us would likely have died if Alex and Khalid, moving much faster than the gradually diminishing levitation spell, had not flown down to our rescue. Since I was unarmored, and the other four had either dragon armor or Olympian armor, they circled around me and tried to hold the each-uisge back long enough for everyone else to reach the ground, or at least be close enough to help.

Our enemies were so fierce and so numerous, even that short a delay might be impossible, though once again the healing power of the Grail helped a lot, sealing up more than a few claw wounds, mostly on the guys' hands.

Actually, holding back the each-uisge in Alex's case was a polite way of saying chop any of them who came within sword range to bits. Even the each-uisge themselves seemed frightened by his savagery, though they kept pushing forward. Evidently, they feared Nicneven more than death. Dan and Carlos inflicted somewhat less mayhem, though I was grateful for their blades flicking back and forth, doing enough damage to the each-uisge to keep them from overwhelming us.

Khalid was the weak link, mostly because he couldn't fire arrows as fast as the others could swing swords. He should have stayed in the air, but he wanted to help shield me, forgetting how vulnerable he'd be if the enemy could get within arm's length. The each-uisge on his side managed to grab the bow and pull it away from him, after which they could have torn his head off with their bare hands. Without a weapon, I was helpless to save him, and the others were pinned down by the each-uisge on their sides.

Talk about dilemmas! The other guys might have abandoned their current positions to try to save Khalid, but that would have left me exposed. They could not hope to save both of us, and shifting positions would have made them more vulnerable to attack as well.

That's how the situation looked to me anyway, but battle-crazed Alex apparently had other ideas. Giving the winged sandals another workout, he shot like an arrow through the each-uisge ranks, swinging his sword at faerie speed as he went. It took him thirty seconds to reach Khalid. By that point the air was filled with the sound of each-uisge wailing over lost limbs, and the ones about to tear Khalid to shreds turned to face Alex, a meeting that did not work out well for them.

By now the air was foul with the smell of blood, and I really wanted to vomit, but I knew Alex was doing the only thing he could do to save Khalid. I truly didn't care what Alex had to do, as long as it worked.

Right about that time, though, Carlos fell, slashed across the throat by each-uisge claws. He would have bled out rapidly, except that the Grail started healing him immediately. However, that healing wasn't happening fast enough to keep him on his feet, and he and I would both have died if the rest of our group hadn't arrived at that point. Tal managed to raise one of his signature fire shields, burning through a number of the each-uisge in the process. That gave the other guys time to deal with the creatures inside the shield when it went up. A few flashes of emerald light from Shar's blade, of sunlight from Gordy's, and no more attackers remained inside the shield.

It was then I realized how badly beaten up our friends were. The vast majority of them had taken arrow wounds, though these would now heal through the power of the Grail. Several of the faerie archers, however, were dead already, and we had been warned that the Grail could not resurrect the fallen.

"We have something in common," said Merlin to me. I jumped a little, because I hadn't realized he was right next to me. It took me a few seconds to realize that I was seeing, not Merlin, but his ghost.

I know I should have been more manly and not cried, but the nine-year-old part of me started, and the rest just went with the flow.

"Do not weep for me, Grail bearer," he said gently, "for I well knew that coming here would probably mean my death, and at least in dying I managed to save Stanford, who will perform many great deeds in the future. Most of his life is still yet to be lived, while mine has gone on far longer than it should have. I come to you now not to bring you grief, but because only you can see me, and I have a message to convey."

I looked around quickly, wiping my tears, and realized he must be right about no one else being able to see him, since no one was paying any attention to him. Of course, Tal was too busy maintaining the fire shield against a massive barrage of arrows, some of which came flaming through despite him. Judging from the screams all around us, he must be keeping the heat at maximum to prevent the each-uisge from breaking through by sheer weight of numbers. If only he had been able to look around, I was sure he could have seen Merlin that one last time.

"I'm not manifesting myself," explained Merlin in response to my thoughts. "You can see me because you were once among the dead yourself."

"The others will want to say goodbye!" I protested.

"The others are either too busy to afford me that attention they would like to give me, or too stunned by what is happening. If I try to draw their attention, I will only reduce the likelihood that they will still win."

"Can we win?" I asked, glancing around. "We needed to stay in the air, I thought."

"Oh, indeed, it would have been better," said Merlin, "but all is not lost…yet. Victory can still be drawn even from such a grim situation as this one. Whether it will be, I cannot surely say."

I found myself unable to stop crying. "My death is what must happen," Merlin continued in what he probably imagined was a comforting tone. "My destiny lies elsewhere. Tell Taliesin when the battle is over that I have left for him a message on Snowdon, disguised so only he can read it. As for you, James Stevens, I give you one last prophecy: we shall meet again, possibly even in your current life, possibly in a future one. Until then, have faith in yourself. Farewell."

Merlin was gone before I could respond to him. I looked back at Taliesin, and now I could see that he was crying too, partly for the fallen faeries, but mostly I thought for Merlin.

Looking around, I counted the people who had been wounded but were now nearly recovered: Nurse Florence, Carlos, Stan, Coventina, Sir Arilan, and about a dozen of the remaining faeries.

Then I realized Alex and Khalid weren't with us. That could only mean they hadn't been inside when the shield came up. They were still outside and unprotected.

Then I noticed that Shar was in the process of chewing Tal's head off over that very issue.

"I had to put up the shield quickly," Tal said tiredly, trying to hold everything in place, "and I tried to include the area where everyone was. I didn't realize at first that Khalid was outside the boundary I created, but even if I had, I couldn't have extended the

Hiatt 404

shield much farther without risking having it collapse once Nicenven's troops started attacking. We'd all be dead if that had happened. I care about him, too, you know." Tal added.

Shar was not having any of it. "We risked a lot to shift our position and save Carla. Are you telling me you couldn't have done *something* for Khalid?"

"I did what I could, Shar. You know me well enough to know that's true."

"I'm going out to look for him," said Shar coldly, not acknowledging Tal's last statement.

"He's nowhere close, Shar," interrupted Nurse Florence before Tal could say anything else. "A half djinn and a former Olympian both have pretty distinctive signatures. I could tell if either was anywhere within a few miles."

"They both have equipment that lets them fly," said Carlos. "Maybe they flew away."

"Alex is...a little crazy, and you know Khalid," protested Shar. "How often has he endangered himself for others? I can't see him just flying away and leaving us."

"Can you see him flying a safe distance and waiting for an opportunity to surprise Nicneven later?" asked Nurse Florence. "That's what I'd bet happened."

"But you don't know—" began Shar angrily.

"I know he's not anywhere close...and, to be blunt, neither is his body," replied Nurse Florence calmly. "I can't see what else to think but that he is alive. Oh, and he's with Alex, who, whatever his faults, has gone to phenomenal lengths to protect him."

"Alex could have gone over the edge. We've seen how he acts in battle. What happens if he reverts to...to what he was like before?"

"Shar, Khalid's safer than we are at this point," insisted Tal. "If he hasn't reappeared by then, we'll hunt for him as soon as we get out of this mess."

I knew Shar well enough to tell that he wasn't happy, but from a practical standpoint he must have realized there was no point in searching for someone who simply wasn't there. However, without saying another word, he stalked off, unwilling to admit Tal might be right.

At this point everyone except Shar gathered around Tal to discuss our next move. Clutching the Grail, I joined them. Dan put a brotherly arm around me, but I wasn't as comforted by that as I would normally have been.

I had a hard time saying goodbye to Merlin, whom I barely knew. What would happen if I had to say goodbye to Khalid, who had gotten himself into a bad position because he wanted to defend me? I prayed that he was all right, because if he wasn't, it would be Jimmie the screwup's last screwup. I could never live with the guilt.

At the beginning of the meeting, Tal explained that he, supported by Carla, Coventina, Queen Mab, and now Nurse Florence as well, was keeping the fire shield at maximum. The each-uisge had tried to break through several times, but the fire was too hot for them to survive, and the bodies incinerated too quickly for them to be used as a way to make a hole in the shield.

"*However,*" he thought, "*Queen Helena told us the Grail's resources are not infinite. It can keep the spell protection up regardless, but healing and replenishing are both dependent on a power that can be temporarily exhausted. Keeping the shield at this level burns enormous amounts of power. If that power runs out, the spell casters among us will wear down, and once the shield begins to fade, the each-uisge, perhaps by now the larger monsters as well, will have us for breakfast. Actually, Nicneven could have finished us already, except for the fact that Grail's protection prevents her blizzard from affecting us or the shield.*"

The earth shook violently at that moment. "*Unfortunately,*" Tal continued, "*we have already seen that she can start a landslide and let gravity deliver it to us. The Grail won't prevent that. She can also move away earth that is somewhere below us but not directly beneath our feet. Eventually, we will have another cave-in.*

"*We can open a portal and escape,*" Tal continued. "*The power of the Grail will block any interference with that on her part. However, if we do that, it seems likely that she will go back to plan A and come after our families. If we try to fight her in our world, she will be at a little bit of a disadvantage, but there will be civilian casualties…lots of them, I'd guess.*"

"*How about leaving for a few minutes, as we did before, and then coming back with reinforcements?*" asked Dan.

"*Reinforcements from where, exactly?*" countered Tal. "*Potentially sympathetic faerie rulers are prohibited from supporting us directly. Gwynn lent as much aid as he could already. In time I think the faerie rulers will understand what a danger Nicneven poses—but that time is not yet.*

"*As of now, we have lost…Merlin, and you know how much he contributed.*" Tal seemed about to choke up, but he continued. "*We have also lost several of our faerie allies—*"

"*Fine men, all,*" thought Sir Arilan.

"*Given time, I might be able to bring more men,*" said Queen Mab.

"*We have no way of knowing when the Grail's power will run out,*" thought Tal grimly. "*I'm not at all sure how much time we have. You could come back with reinforcements and find us all dead. We can't go with you without risking Nicneven bringing her army into our world while we're gone.*"

"*In other words, we're damned if we do, and damned if we don't,*" thought Gordy sullenly.

"*We need to find a way to change the situation,*" thought Shar, finally rejoining the conversation but still sounding a little cold. "*Why not get into the air again? That way Nicneven's ground troops will once again be useless.*"

"*Floating up the people who can't fly was always challenging,*" said Tal after a moment. "*Doing it while keeping everyone from getting burned up by our own defenses would be trickier. Also, the Asmodeus incident demonstrates that we need to be covered from below, which means adding a flaming floor, at least until we get back into position. It could be done, but it would involve certain risks.*"

"*More than doing nothing?*" Shar asked. Another fairly powerful earthquake answered his question. An avalanche would hit us at some point if we remained on the ground.

"*Perhaps we could leave for a few minutes, just to reposition ourselves,*" suggested Dan.

"*That would buy us time,*" agreed Tal, "*but by itself it won't be enough to enable us to win.*" I could tell from the glum look on his face that he was beginning to doubt our ability to beat Nicneven.

"*Merlin told me we could win,*" I thought quietly.

"*Merlin? When?*" asked Tal quickly.

"After he...you know. His ghost told me."

In any other group, people would be wondering if I was still sane, but in this group, talking to a ghost was just business as usual.

"What else did he say?" asked Tal.

"He wasn't specific about strategy," I thought, half wishing I hadn't started this conversation. *"But before, when he was still...when we were fighting Asmodeus, he said that Asmodeus must be stopped, and he was. I think maybe Merlin saw that eliminating that demon gave us a chance to win."*

The ground shook again, and I thought I could hear a rumble in the distance.

"Avalanche," said Gordy loudly.

Tal nodded, and I figured someone was going to open a portal and get us out. Before that could happen, however, we heard lyre music.

The lyre of Orpheus! But what was Dark Me doing with it?

"He's...I don't believe it! He's deflecting the avalanche!" exclaimed Tal.

"Does that mean he's now on our side?" asked Carlos. "This doesn't make any sense."

Sensible or not, in a short time we heard a shower of stones and at least one large boulder crashing all around us, but none of them actually hitting near enough to be a problem.

"Why would that bastard help us?" asked Dan.

"I really prefer the term, 'savior,' and a thank-you would be better than a question about my motives," said a voice remarkably like Tal's in a tone totally different from his.

I did not need to turn in the direction of the voice to know that Dark Me was somehow with us.

Chapter 32: Captured (Tal)

"How can you be here?" I asked, realizing almost immediately that it was a stupid question, or at least not the first one I should have asked. Everyone else had drawn their weapons. Dark Me snickered loudly.

"I'm not really here! Asmodeus could communicate with Carla despite the Grail, and Nicneven with Jimmie, so I figured I probably could communicate with you, Tal. Everyone else being able to see and hear is just an added bonus."

Coventina nodded. "He is just an illusion."

"Indeed, my lady!" replied Dark Me with a little bow.

"What do you want?" I asked impatiently.

"What I want is to save your sorry ass, if you'll let me."

"By joining Nicneven?" I countered.

"If you can't beat 'em, join 'em," Dark Me replied lightly. "It's because I joined her that I can offer you such a good deal."

"Not interested!" I responded immediately. Shar and several others nodded.

"Why so hasty?" he asked, smiling mockingly. "Merlin is dead." I wanted to slug him, but since he was just an illusion, what would have been the point?

"Several of your faeries are dead. Two of your men are missing. Two are…compromised," he added, looking first at Carla and then at Jimmie. "You've inflicted heavy casualties, but Nicneven still has over a thousand troops in the field, and you have a handful at best."

"We're willing to take our chances," I said.

Dark Me sneered. "You mean you're willing to die. You can't think there's any real possibility of victory any more. Besides, if all of you end up dead, Nicneven can do whatever she wants. The deal I got her to agree to constrains her in ways you are going to like."

I would rather have crawled naked for three miles over broken glass than make a deal with Nicneven and Dark Me. However, if I knew what they really wanted, maybe that would help me find a way to beat them.

"All right, describe the deal," I said with feigned reluctance. *"I'm just figuring out what their endgame is,"* I thought to everyone else, assuming the Grail would not let someone who was hostile read our minds. Besides, Dark Me probably knew I wouldn't seriously negotiate with him.

"What Nicneven wants is to be high queen of all the faerie realms. She is willing to leave you and your world alone if you let her rule the faeries in peace."

Shar snorted. "You don't really expect us to trust either of you, do you?"

"You don't have to," replied Dark Me. "Everyone involved will be bound by appropriate *tynghedau*."

Given my past luck with *tynghedau*, I was pretty sure Nicneven would find a way to leave herself loopholes, but I didn't comment on that. Instead, I asked, "You expect me to abandon my allies among the faeries?"

Dark Me laughed loudly and abrasively. "You mean Gwynn ap Nudd? Where is he, Tal? Where are his troops?"

"Some of them died her today," said Sir Arilan tightly.

"Ah, so the king with an army the size of Nicneven's sends…how many exactly? Twentysomething?"

"Two of us faerie rulers came in person," observed Mab, her voice betraying no emotion.

"And you will still retain your domains, as will all the current faerie rulers," replied Dark Me. "All Nicneven asks is that you swear allegiance to her as high queen."

"Never!" said Coventina firmly.

"What do you get out of this?" I asked. "Honestly, I expected you to fight against Nicneven."

"Unlike those of us with a martyr complex," began Dark Me sarcastically, "I know when continuing the fight is the same thing as suicide, and Nicneven, powerful as she is on her own, knows a live ally is better than a dead enemy."

"In other words, you're her bitch!" said Shar mockingly.

"Actually, I will be high king of the faeries and rule at her side," replied Dark Me, though I could tell Shar's taunt bothered him.

"But don't worry!" Dark Me said, looking right at Eva, "ours will just be a political marriage, and she has no problem with my keeping a mistress, as long as I'm discreet."

Irrational as the gesture was, I just couldn't avoid it any longer; I threw a punch at the Dark Me illusion. My fist naturally passed through, but as I pulled it back I exerted a little magic and caused the illusion to dissolve. I tried to make it look as if that had been my goal all along, but I could tell nobody really bought that.

"Well, did he give away any useful information?" asked Dan.

"In that load of crap?" I said angrily. "No. I have no doubt Nicneven is ready to buy us off using some kind of agreement with a hidden flaw the size of Texas, but I could have guessed that before he started talking. As far as his own motives, he's lying."

"How do you know?" asked Carlos.

"Because I lived with him in my head for weeks," I pointed out. "His ambitions were always focused on our world. He could have cared less about something like being high king of the faeries...especially when the most Nicneven would ever allow him to be would be a figurehead. Had she wanted a king, she would have taken one hundreds of years ago."

"Could Nicneven have gotten control of him somehow?" asked Stan.

"Yeah, maybe," I said slowly. "That would account for his buying into her whole agenda. It would have been hard for her to do, though; he's got all my willpower and the lyre of Orpheus."

"Why would either one of them want to make a deal now?" asked Carlos. "They have the upper hand."

"Easier to trick us out of the way than get more of her followers killed in order to kill us," suggested Nurse Florence. "If her agenda is really to become the ultimate ruler of all faeries, she's going to have a lot of tough battles ahead of her."

"But doesn't Dark Me want us dead...you especially?" asked Gordy.

"Oddly enough, no," I replied. "He's not totally evil, just incredibly selfish. I think he'd rather have all of us on his side if he can somehow manage that. Anyway, he needs me alive until he can successfully replicate my blood."

"He seemed willing enough to let us die at first, though," said Gordy. "So did Nicneven, which makes me think something changed."

"If that's true, we need to find out what," said Nurse Florence. "It would help to know why our safety suddenly became more important to either of them."

It occurred to me that one of the things that could have changed would have been Dark Me finding out Eva was with us. He wouldn't automatically have expected her, and I was willing to bet he still wanted to end up with her. I kept that idea to myself, though, to avoid embarrassing Eva any further.

"How do we do find out what's really going on?" I asked. "I can read minds, but probably not easily at this distance, and both of them are likely to be well shielded."

"There's always the old druidic trick of sending your consciousness out through some bird or animal to be your eyes and ears some distance away," suggested Nurse Florence. "You used to do that more often before you figured out how to read minds, but I'm sure you haven't forgotten how."

"That might be hard to do while I'm maintaining the fire shield at the same time," I pointed out, "and anyway Dark Me would be sure to notice something like that."

"Taliesin, all you need to do in provide direction," said Mab, "and let us furnish the power for a few minutes, so that most of your concentration could be devoted to spying. Surely someone as accomplished as you are could manage such a feat."

I blushed a little at that and hoped Mab didn't notice. "Majesty—" I started, only to be cut off by Nurse Florence.

"There's no harm in trying, Tal. If the shield becomes unstable, you can always pull back, and if Dark Me does notice, we're still no worse off than we are now. He may not, though. You don't use animals like that very often anymore."

I could see her point, and anyway the attack seemed paused at the moment, probably to give us a chance to accept Nicneven's terms, so I could devote a little less attention to the shield for a few minutes. I was still skeptical about such a ploy working, but Nurse Florence was right about the plan being low risk.

I reached out with my mind, careful to avoid the spot nearby where I sensed Dark Me and Nicneven lurking. However, at first my search turned up nothing. What wildlife there was seemed to have fled from the ferocity and clamor of the battle. At last I found a solitary tawny owl, gray like so many of the creatures in Nicneven's domain. On the whole, I could not have been luckier. Owls had only slightly better vision than humans had, but they had far better hearing, so I might be able to pick up something from conversation that would tell me what I needed to know.

We had only a few minutes at best before either Dark Me, or Nicneven, or both would become impatient for our answer. Unfortunately, I had to take most of that time setting up the shield up so that the others could keep it up with only minimal intervention from me. Then I lost almost all of the rest trying to get my mind to synchronize with the owl's. The wildlife in Elphame seemed resistant to the magic of anyone but Nicneven. However, Nicneven's hold on any one specific creature could only be so great, given the thousands that must exist in this realm, so I was able to take control…just not fast enough to suit me.

I kept the owl flying high enough to be inconspicuous, but close enough to verify that Nicneven and Dark Me were indeed below me. Then I just circled, hoping neither one of them—or anyone else, for that matter—would be watching the sky when the natural tendency would be to keep an eye on my party to make sure we weren't trying anything unexpected.

I started listening and was immediately rewarded by an argument between one of Nicneven's advisers and the queen herself— not what I had expected, but I'd take it!

"Majesty, this course of action makes no sense!" protested the adviser. Faeries did not show their age the way humans did, but there was about this one an air of dignity even in anger, and his willingness to be so blunt with Nicneven suggested a much longer association than his youthful appearance ever would have.

"Eacharn, had I wished your opinion, I could certainly have asked for it," replied Nicneven calmly, almost blandly. Given the savagery of her strategy, her tone surprised me.

"And had you wished to demote me," Eacharn replied, "you could have done that as well, yet you still acknowledge me as your *ceannard*, the commander of all your forces. Never before have you demanded of me that I wait until asked before warning you of a military problem."

"You have done nothing but warn me these many hours, my *ceannard*. What new warning have you left to offer?" I would have expected more anger, but if anything, she sounded more tired than anything else.

I didn't want to come too close, but I looked at Nicneven as carefully as I dared. She was in her young maiden form, probably as a concession to Dark Me, and she wore the same gray robes Jimmie had described, was just as alluring as Jimmie had claimed. For a moment I wondered if she had seduced Dark Me, but he was too into himself for that to have been an easy thing to do, and it was hard to imagine him changing his long-term goals for a woman, unless perhaps that woman was Eva. Anyway, there was something repellent about Nicneven. Even from a distance and in owl form, I couldn't help being creeped out a little. Then again, I suppose it would be surprising if she didn't seem cold, given the region she ruled and the way in which she ruled it. If ruling the Underworld had made Hades dark, why wouldn't ruling the cold North with an icy fist make Nicneven lose whatever warmth she might once have had?

Eacharn was clearly about to explode. "My queen, you force us into war with your fellow rulers too soon, and you take risks I have never known you to take. You yourself told me of the seer's prophecy that this Taliesin would be the ruin of your plans, yet you offer to spare his life and make an ally of his…what is this creature exactly?" asked Eacharn, waving his hand at Dark Me.

"This creature is your future king," answered Nicneven with a touch of anger, "and you will show him the proper respect!"

"I like to think of myself as an improved version of Taliesin," cut in Dark Me cockily. "You may address me as King Lamperó Métopo, or just as Majesty, if you prefer."

It took me a moment to realize that the name Dark Me had chosen meant "radiant brow" in Greek, just as Taliesin meant "radiant brow" in Welsh. At least at some point he had given up on the idea of replacing me and seemed intent instead on creating his own identity, but it was disquieting to realize that he thought he could hold on to Robin Goodfellow indefinitely.

"Only someone of faerie blood may be king!" shouted Eacharn. "If you choose to take a lover, Majesty, that would be your concern, but trying to crown this...whelp will just make the other faeries fight harder to keep you from becoming high queen."

Now at last Nicneven appeared on the verge of losing her temper as well. "Eacharn, you will treat my future husband with respect, or I will remove you as *ceannard* and exile you."

"I meant no disrespect to you or your authority, Majesty," said Eacharn slowly, managing to sound calmer despite what must be going on in his head, "but think of what you do. You keep alive the boy Taliesin who may be destined to bring you down because your...future husband asks you to, for his own obscure purposes...and you do this after attacking in a way that risks war with at least some of the faerie rulers before we are adequately prepared. If you intended to offer the boy such a generous peace, why not do so in the beginning? This kind of sudden and ill-thought-out change of strategy is so unlike you that it forces me to speak."

Eacharn was raising good questions, but I could tell from Nicneven's expression that she wasn't buying anything he said. I could see wanting the lyre, but, surrounded by her own guards, she could easily have worked out a plan to kill Dark Me and take it. All she needed to do was catch him by surprise. She must have wanted something else from Dark Me, but what could have been worth all the political trouble she was stirring up for herself? It made no sense for the careful planner who had so thoroughly disrupted my group to act so rashly.

"My love," said Dark Me, completely ignoring Eacharn, "the moment I promised you has arrived. Seize the body of the owl above us, and I will seize its mind."

I felt myself grabbed by magic so instantly that Dark Me must have been communicating mentally with Nicneven, planning almost the whole time I was in the air above them. Before what was happening could fully register on me, I felt the owl body break out of the circling pattern I had made it assume and fly rapidly toward Nicneven below. At the same time, I felt Dark Me grab the part of my mind that inhabited the owl and try to keep me from returning to my body. He shouldn't have been stronger than I was, but he was now playing the lyre to reinforce his efforts, and the part of my mind in the owl's body suddenly seemed chained to it.

Both Nurse Florence and I had foolishly assumed that, as long as my physical body was still under the Grail's protection, magic would not work on the part of my mind I used to see and hear through the owl. Clearly, we had been wrong.

I might have fought back more successfully if part of me wasn't still maintaining the fire shield, but I didn't dare withdraw that power, or all my friends could be slaughtered by Nicneven's forces. With my concentration divided, and at the additional disadvantage of having to face the lyre's power as well as whatever bonds Nicneven had with the wildlife in her kingdom, this was not a battle I could win.

I landed on the icy ground at their feet and stood frozen, not by the cold but by the paralyzing weight of Nicneven's magic.

"Ah, Boy Scout, you've arrived at last!" said Dark Me in his usual mocking tone. "Something tells me your friends will now take any deal we choose to offer them." He continued to strum on the lyre, sapping my will to resist.

"Of course, if they don't," he continued ominously, "I've always wanted a pet."

Chapter 33: That Plan Could Have Gone Better! (Tal)

"You are sure this is really him?" asked Nicneven, eying me with interest.

"Oh, it's him all right," Dark Me assured her.

I wanted to...well, peck his eyes out, but I couldn't move anything except my head. My claws felt as if they had taken root in the ground; my wings felt as if they were encased in concrete.

I made one more shot at pulling my consciousness out of the owl and returning it to my own body, but Dark Me had my mind locked into the owl so firmly that the effort was like trying to tear my arms and legs away from the rest of my body. In seconds I was in agony. A few seconds more, and I had to stop.

Dark Me laughed at my predicament. "Sorry about that, Boy Scout, but it was a pretty stupid plan." I felt him loosen his hold just enough to let me respond, though not enough to communicate with my allies.

"Just for the record, what makes it stupid?" I thought. I wanted to hear what he had to say about as much as I wanted to gargle with hydrochloric acid, but he was so full of himself now that he might just let something slip.

Dark Me laughed again. "You ought to have known I'd be on the lookout for some kind of spy attempt, and have you ever seen an owl keep circling repeatedly over an area for no reason? It wasn't hard to figure out you must be controlling it somehow, and the easiest way to do that would be to have part of your own consciousness in it. Risky, don't you think? Why would you assume that just because your body was cozy inside the Grail's little force field you could send your mind wherever you wanted and still have that magic immunity going for you?"

When he posed the question that way, I had to admit it did seem stupid, but since part of my consciousness was still in my body, it wasn't unreasonable to assume I might be protected. That was the problem with trying to use the Grail in a combat situation: it had never been tested.

"Well, are you ready to surrender?" asked Dark Me. "I don't know how you managed to split your concentration up enough to maintain the fire shield and see through the owl at the same time, but

I can see from here the shield is becoming unstable now that most of you is cut off from your friends, and you know they won't last ten minutes once that shield goes down."

"You may have me, but retreat is still an option for them," I pointed out.

"Ah, but that's the beauty of the situation you've so thoughtfully created. I'm about to pay them a little mental visit and point out just exactly what will happen if they try to leave with you in your present condition. They don't have any place they can go in Elphame, and if they try to open a portal and flee back to our world, they will tear your mind in two."

"You don't know that for sure!" I protested.

"No, I don't," admitted Dark Me, "but I do know your friends won't take the chance."

Without giving me time to reply, Dark Me sat down on the ground, and I felt his mind shift, creating a projection of himself for the benefit of my friends and allies.

He was right: they would never risk ripping my consciousness in half. Since they couldn't hold off Nicneven's forces indefinitely, they would have no choice but to take her deal. That gave me just minutes to find a way out.

This would have been a good moment for another saint or angel to pop up, but I knew that wasn't how things worked. If there was a way out of this mess, I was going to have to find it on my own.

My body—or the owl's body, I should say—was almost completely paralyzed, but Nicneven had left me neck movement, which at least gave me a chance to look around quite a bit, especially since owls can rotate their heads almost 270 degrees. I could see easily enough that Dark Me slouched over in his trance, but I kept glancing back to make sure. The rest of the time I focused on Nicneven and Eacharn, looking for something, anything, that I might be able to use to escape from this situation.

Nicneven and Eacharn were speaking in low tones, but that was no problem for my owl hearing, which enabled me to pick up more than the nearby guards could. However, all that conversation did was reaffirm what I already knew: Eacharn didn't trust Dark Me and didn't understand Nicneven's actions.

I studied her closely. I had never met her—in any life—so I didn't have a baseline to judge by, but there was something off about her. For a formidable leader who presumably expected to be feared and obeyed, she wasn't handling Eacharn at all well, although it was clear from the context she had known him for years. At times she seemed to overreact, at others to underreact, as if she wasn't feeling the underlying emotions but was only acting them, and not acting them well.

The fact that Eacharn, clearly sympathetic to her goals and loyal to her personally, was not falling into line and kept complaining that she was not herself made clear that I wasn't wrong; Nicneven really wasn't acting normal for her. Taking a quick glance around at the guards I could see, I noticed that some of them looked nervous; they too had picked up on the wrongness of the situation.

Eacharn kept harping on how much Nicneven was changing her strategy in response to Dark Me's whims. What could make her change course so dramatically? Sure, Dark Me was potentially a decent ally, but if the price of that alliance was alienating her own men, why was she so willing to pay it?

I could only think of two possibilities, the first being that the woman I saw was not actually Nicneven, but the only way Dark Me could pull that kind of scam off would be if he had an accomplice and had used the blood spell to enable that accomplice to pass for her. Possible in theory, I decided, but highly unlikely. How could he have gotten a drop of blood without making Nicneven suspicious? Besides, the spell took a while to cast. He would have needed to be alone with Nicneven for at least a short time, and I couldn't see any way he could plausibly have gotten her to agree to that. Nor could he have prevented Eacharn and her other advisers from noticing her absence, but Eacharn had not mentioned any suspicious times during which the queen was nowhere to be found.

That left only one possibility: Dark Me had used Alcina's love spell, not the watered-down version Carla used on me but the full blast, wipe-out-everything-else-in-Nicneven's-head-except-Dark -Me version. I knew how to cast it, which meant he did as well, and it would have required very little time. In fact, if he had caught Nicneven by surprise, the effect could have been nearly instantaneous.

The spell's existence wasn't widely known, so Nicneven would not have realized she needed to ward herself against it.

The circumstances were not hard to imagine: Dark Me popped up with an offer of alliance and got into Nicneven's court under a safe conduct guaranteed by *tynged*. Nicneven presumably wanted to get the lyre one way or the other and didn't necessarily trust negotiations to produce that outcome. She would have left loopholes so that she could ensure Dark Me would never become an enemy if he didn't become an ally. Dark Me, having my memories of being cheated on *tynghedau* in the past, would have examined the pact closely and either taken advantage of her loopholes or somehow managed to introduce some of his own. Either way, he had a moment alone with her, he looked into her eyes, and zap, she was in his complete control.

Because the spell worked partly by blasting many of the victim's memories of people away (to eliminate any possibility of a competing loyalty to someone else), the spell could explain Nicneven's inability to placate an old supporter and the way she sounded like a mediocre actress reading her lines with the wrong emotions. She really didn't know the people around her. Dark Me must have filled her in, possibly on the fly. Since most supernaturals were not telepathic, no one would have noticed if he sent Nicneven mental messages, getting her to correct any noticeable mistakes.

And he said my plan was risky! There were dozens of things that could have gone wrong with his. It was a dark miracle that he had managed to play this kind of game as long as he apparently had.

Typically, powerful supernaturals, though they might not be able to read minds themselves, could instinctively defend against that kind of intrusion, so I didn't even try to read Nicneven's mind. I didn't need to. The spell left a very distinctive residue on the affected person, and now that I was this close, I could feel those distinctive traces even in my impaired condition.

Sure enough, Dark Me had used the ultimate love spell on Nicneven, and it had worked!

Of course, as a paralyzed owl with my mind split between two different locations, I couldn't do much about that, but I knew someone who could...and would, if I could just make him believe me.

"Eacharn!" I thought as loudly as I could, hoping the wiggle room Dark Me had given me to respond to him would enable me to communicate with someone else who was close enough. *"Eacharn! Heed my warning! Your queen is in dire peril."* I saw him start to look around, and I couldn't have that. *"Pretend you hear nothing, but answer me with your thoughts. If Her Majesty realizes I am communicating with you, we could both be done for."*

Eacharn deftly cut off his conversation with Nicneven by feigning agreement. It took him longer than I would have liked, since if Dark Me got back, he could overhear our mental conversation.

"Who are you?" he thought at last.

"At the moment, most of me is trapped in the owl in front of you," I replied.

"Taliesin Weaver?" he asked, the expression of amazement too apparent on his face.

"Keep your face as expressionless as you can." He gave me an almost imperceptible nod.

"Why should I trust you?" He asked. *"Even before that scoundrel, Lamperó Métopo, first appeared at court, the queen knew you were her enemy."*

"Lord Eacharn, you know something is wrong with your queen. I tell you now there is an incredibly powerful spell upon her that compels her to love Lamperó Métopo and to do his bidding."

Eacharn raised an eyebrow at that. *"Such a thing is impossible! She is too powerful."*

"As is the spell that was used on her. Can you not sense something different?"

"There is a strange magic upon her," he admitted slowly, *"but she explained that as a new protective spell she was trying."*

"Think, Eacharn! If you value your queen's safety, you must ask yourself one question: can a protective spell account for the way in which she now behaves?"

At that moment Dark Me awakened from his trance. I risked a quick, *"Say nothing more; he could hear us,"* and then I stopped broadcasting to Eacharn. I had to hope he would see the truth before it was too late.

"Well, Boy Scout, your people want you back in one piece. In fact, they want it enough to agree to Her Majesty's terms. I think

Mab and Coventina are inclined to quibble about the form the new high queenship will take, but I'll leave the queen's advisers to work out the specifics."

Glancing over to where my team was, I could see the shield had come down, but the each-uisge were not advancing, so apparently Dark Me had agreed to a truce.

Eacharn kept giving me covert looks, as if trying to decide whether I spoke the truth or not, but I couldn't afford to wait for him to make up his mind, and the truce opened up another possibility.

I had divided my concentration originally in order to maintain the fire shield while I scouted, but now I no longer needed to split myself that way. Checking the bonds Dark Me had placed on me, I could see they prevented me from reuniting with my body. They did not, however, prevent me from pulling the part of my mind still in my body into the owl's. I had to move fast, though, before Dark Me realized what was up.

Actually, most of the consciousness was with the owl, but much of the spell casting muscle was still with my body. I had needed to divide that way to maintain the fire shield and to keep the owl from radiating too much magic, though that hadn't saved me. One good strong pull, and I felt all that power flow into me.

I was still an owl, and I was still paralyzed by Nicneven—but I was now a pretty badass owl, magically speaking, and the binding Dark Me had placed on my magic snapped with one mental tug. I turned my head and stared straight into the eyes of the Scottish faerie queen. She looked back, and suddenly her impassive expression shifted to one of ice-cold, calculating rage. Dark Me, no doubt psychically linked to her, caught the shift a second or two before Eacharn became aware of it.

"What—" he started, confused by the sudden disappearance of his spell.

"*Now who's stupid?*" I said mockingly. "*Haven't you noticed how spells and even seers confuse the two of us? Didn't you realize I could lift the spell you placed on Nicneven?*"

Dark Me looked almost as furious as Nicneven and would cheerfully have stomped on the owl body, but he had bigger problems, the first being Nicneven pointing at him and screaming, "Seize him!" Dark Me picked up the lyre, but Eacharn, evidently stronger than a typical faerie, knocked it out of his hands. Dark Me then drew Black Hilt, forgetting it was under Nicneven's power. In seconds she sent a burst of freezing through it that frostbit his sword hand and forced him to drop the blade.

By now he was facing not only the outraged faerie queen and Eacharn, but all of her nearby guards as well. He might have flown away at top speed and had a chance of escaping, but his attempts to recover the lyre were his undoing.

Dark Me was as strong a caster as I, but surrounded by faeries and facing Nicneven, one of the strongest spell casters around, he didn't stand a chance. Her guards had him subdued in seconds, and Nicneven, surrounded now by flashing knives of ice, seemed ready for an on-the-spot execution.

"Don't kill him!" I thought to her as emphatically as I could. *"He is just the product of a spell. There is a faerie, Robin Goodfellow, within him, and Robin has done nothing that would deserve death."*

Nicneven looked at me with gray eyes as deep and cold as glaciers. "Who are you to give me orders?"

"I gave no order, Majesty, but merely made a humble request from one who has done you the service of freeing you from a dire spell."

I could see from Nicneven's expression she didn't want to be in my debt. Then I felt her grip me, not quite as mentally as Dark Me had earlier, somehow gripping me through the owl body, holding me in it as securely as he had, and I realized her idea of disposing of her debt was not what I had expected.

"Kill this…whatever he is," she said in a tone like an echo from an icicle, "and kill that vile bird as well."

I wasn't sure if I would actually die if the owl died or simply revert to my own body—and I didn't really want to find out. Unfortunately, her grip on me, though unreinforced by the lyre, made my mind feel as if it were buried under tons of ice, and digging my way out seemed impossible.

It was then that I heard the incongruous sound of harp music in the distance.

Chapter 34: Deus Ex Machina…Sort of (Tal)

"What is that sound?" asked Eacharn as if it hurt his ears.

Nicneven's rage at Dark Me was obscured for a moment by her surprise. "I…I have not heard it in centuries and did not think to hear it again. Surely it cannot be what I think…yet it has power. It is stilling my sea-ice blizzard!"

I could feel the same power she was talking about, a sense not only of enormous strength but of…rightness…a cancellation of a blizzard that had no place in nature. But whose music could reinforce the natural order in such a way that even Nicneven's undeniable mystic muscle could not resist it?

Then I heard commotion coming from the west of us. Each-uisge screams? I couldn't turn my head enough to see, but someone else had joined the battle—and very successfully to judge by the number of howls. I could also make out a thudding sound, like the noise a very large club might make by hitting flesh and bone.

"We are under attack!" said Eacharn. "Your orders, Majesty?"

Nicneven squinted for a moment toward the sounds, then turned back to Eacharn. "Kill these two, as I have already commanded, have any troops nearby kill the other followers of Taliesin, and then sound retreat. The each-uisge should hold our new guest off long enough."

I wondered how the each-uisge felt about being cannon fodder, but I wondered more about Nicneven's choice of the singular. One opponent was doing all this damage?

"I could help you!" pleaded Dark Me.

Nicneven's laugh was like the sound of an ice pick striking metal. "Or you could die, which is what you deserve, dog! Your offense is beyond pardon, beyond reprieve!"

Great! I had defeated Dark Me's scheme only to ensure my own death and the death of my friends! Well, and his, too—but that I could live with. I still wanted to save Robin Goodfellow, though.

In this life I had always been a little phobic about shape-shifting, but I had done some minor shifts, so it wasn't too difficult for me to give the owl body a reasonable approximation of human vocal chords.

"Hear me, oh Queen!" I hooted. "We may yet prove of more worth to you alive than dead."

Nicneven looked disdainfully in my direction and tossed one of her flying ice daggers my way. Unable to dodge, I felt it take my head off in one smooth but painful slice.

The good news? I was right. I didn't actually die. My consciousness could return to my own body.

The bad news? Nicneven obviously realized that my soul wasn't moving on and held my mind in the owl body, preventing me from returning to my friends.

At first I couldn't figure out how she was doing such a thing, but then I realized her grip on me must owe something to Hecate's magic. I wasn't dead, but my mind was in a dead body and had experienced that death. Perhaps that was enough to allow Nicneven to use the kind of compulsion Hecate could use on the spirits of the dead.

Under less serious circumstances, I would have had a giggling fit over the possible horror movie titles that could come from this mess, like *Headless Zombie Owls from Another World,* but now I needed a way to break Nicneven's hold on me, and I had to do it without having a working body, not even an owl one.

Magic was mostly a mental process, but I'd never tried to cast a spell before in a disembodied state. Well, semidisembodied. I was still technically inside a body but no longer really attached to one.

Equally disconcerting was the way I was losing touch with the physical world. With no functioning sensory organs, I found myself in a lightless, soundless void. In theory, I should have been able to see my surroundings magically. I was still able to feel Nicneven's psychic grip on me; those kinds of perceptions had nothing to do with a physical body. However, I'd never had to use my powers to replace my senses, just enhance them or complement them. I was confident I could learn, but the each-uisge could already be attacking my friends, and if so I had to be able to know what was happening in order to help.

I tried lashing out at Nicneven, but she was surprisingly adept at locking down my magic, leaving me with little beyond the sense of my own captivity and a vague hint that she was still able to use her ties with Hecate to good effect. Only moments ago she hadn't seemed able to interact with my mind in this way.

Damn! It wouldn't matter why she could do what she did if I couldn't get free of her and back to my body.

I thrashed around for what seemed like hours, but was really probably just seconds; the only result was a momentary connection with my body. That should have cheered me up a little, since it showed me I might be able to rejoin my flesh if I just kept trying. Instead the experience horrified me, because I could feel my body shutting down. I was still connected to it, but the unnatural way Nicneven was holding me must be making it difficult for it to realize I was still there.

My own body had lost faith in me. It thought I was gone, and it was following its programming, as Stan would say, moving into coma, maybe even into death.

I would have expected the Grail to prevent my death, but perhaps the fact that my mind was elsewhere caused the Grail to see me as already dead and therefore outside its ability to help.

If Nurse Florence and Coventina were not fighting for their lives already, they would do what they could, but for all they knew, I was dead. I doubted if either of them could sense my spirit across the distance between us, and even if they could, I was not sure they would be able to tell I was still clinging to life. What I needed was someone who could specifically sense the dead, and we didn't have—

But wait! We did! Jimmie told me about his conversation with Merlin, whom he could see when the rest of us could not. If Nicneven was using magic on me as if I were dead, then it was logical to assume that I might be able to get a message to Jimmie because of his sensitivity to the dead. (And yes, thank God for Stan; he was the one who had gotten me to think of magic in more "scientific" terms, and the resulting insights had been helpful more than once. I prayed this time would be one of those times.)

Again I explored the way in which Nicneven was holding me. Ordinary psychic contact seemed to be blocked by her grip, but based on past experiences, communication with the dead seemed to be on a somewhat different frequency than regular psychic experiences. I tested a little, and I seemed to be able to get past Nicneven's grip that way, so I tried. I used my "ghost voice" to shout to Jimmie for all I was worth, but if there was a response, I couldn't sense one. Perhaps he was too far away. My physical voice wouldn't carry that far, so perhaps my ghostly one didn't, either.

"My, what a great deal of commotion!" said the last person I would have expected to hear from at this point.

"Merlin?" I asked, knowing it was him but not quite believing it. Of course, he had died nearby just recently, and I was broadcasting on "ghost frequency," so perhaps I shouldn't have been surprised.

Not only could I hear him, but I began to see a misty version of him surrounded by clouds. Then he became more solid, though he also looked as if glitter had been sprinkled all over him.

Merlin sighed in a very human way. *"I thought I was done with this life, Taliesin, but I couldn't leave without seeing the outcome of the battle. That decision may have been a most fortunate one."*

"Be careful!" I warned. *"Nicneven may find a way of trapping you."*

"I have been cautious," said Merlin. *"I know she can coerce the dead, so I have kept myself at a distance until now. At this moment she has too many other problems to notice me."*

"What's happening?" I asked, wishing I could just read his mind.

"The each-uisge seem to be mutinying. Why I cannot say for certain, but I suspect the shifts in Nicneven's state of being may be the reason. Remember, they are solitary creatures. She would have to have exerted enormous amounts of mental control to bring this many of them together and force them to work in unison. I think it likely she cast her compulsion upon them after Dark Me had already used Alcina's love spell upon her. Perhaps the breaking of the spell on her undid some of the magic she performed while under its influence. Or perhaps I am just rambling like the old man I am. By the way, did you know the Dagda still lives?"

"That's a pretty random question," I replied, not sure whether telling Merlin about the Dagda at this point would break my oath of silence.

"Not entirely random when one considers that it is he who is Nicneven's unexpected guest, and perhaps the each-uisge discipline is

breaking down because they do not wish to face someone who can kill eight of them with a single blow of his club."

Then I realized I'd been a big idiot. The sound I had heard earlier could only have been the Dagda's club making mush out of the each-uisge. The harp music should have been a bigger clue, though, since the Dagda had a harp that could play itself and that reinforced the natural order of things, so a deviation like a sea-ice blizzard would be hard to maintain against the harp's music.

Why he had picked this moment to go public I had no idea, but I wasn't about to look the proverbial gift horse in the mouth. Besides, I had more pressing concerns.

"*Merlin, are the guys safe?*"

"*They are strong enough to handle what's left of the each-uisge, and Nicneven's big monsters look as if they might go after the Dagda. Your allies aren't in immediate danger.*"

"*Dark Me?*"

"*Still alive. Nicneven didn't have any musicians handy and needed a way to combat the Dagda's music, so she gave him a choice: be bound to her by a tynged, or die instantly. He chose the tynged, as you might expect. He's busily trying to play enough chaos into being to counter the order radiating from the Dagda's harp.*"

"*Can you break me free of Nicneven's hold long enough for me to get back into my body?*"

Merlin nodded. "*I cannot use my magic in the living world in the same way I could before my death, but through Jimmie I let Viviane, Coventina, Mab, and Carla know what was happening. While the others vanquish the remaining each-uisge, the four casters are readying an attempt to bring you back to your body. I think I may be able to support them by using Jimmie as a channel. Among the four of us, we can probably break Nicneven's hold before she can reinforce it.*"

Merlin paused for a moment as if listening. "*They are ready.*"

"*Can I do anything to help?*" I asked.

"*Pray...hard,*" replied Merlin. "*None of us have ever faced exactly this situation. We have the power, but whether we will be able to use it effectively in this situation remains to be seen.*" With that less-than-comforting assessment, Merlin faded away, leaving me in the void again, feeling only the cold sensation of being in Nicneven's steely grip. I prayed as he suggested, and I waited.

A jolt hit me as fast as a lightning strike, and I knew my friends were making their effort to break me loose. I flexed what little muscle I had, and I could feel the constriction around me shudder.

Then a flood of sensations washed over me. I must have slipped far enough out of Nicneven's grasp to "see" some of what was going on psychically, but not yet enough to make it back to my body.

Much to my surprise, though the group I had come with was safe for the moment, the Dagda was in big trouble. As far as I could tell without having witnessed the event, the Uilepheist had circled around and used its enormous maw to swallow the Dagda's harp. The dragon could not destroy the instrument that way; indeed, from the expression on its lizard-like face, the harp's music was doing horrendous things to its innards. Still, as long as the harp was within the beast's gullet, its sound was muted at best and could not restrain Nicneven's disruption of the natural order. Not only that, but the discordant jangle Dark Me was extracting from the lyre of Orpheus seemed to have weakened the Dagda's charge. He might have fended off the few each-uisge that had the courage to get close enough, but the Nuckelavee attacked, and its poisonous breath seemed to have dazed the former high king. He still managed to swing his club just enough to keep the Nuckelavee from grinding him beneath its massive hooves, but the combination of the chaotic music and the poison were clearly taking its toll. His swings were far weaker than they should have been, his skin had gone pale, and his hands shook. I doubted he could keep up his defense very much longer.

I turned my attention back to my friends, the only possible source of aid for the Dagda. Nurse Florence, Coventina and Carla seemed ready to make another try to free me, but my warriors were not as occupied, having put down any each-uisge in range—a considerable number, judging by how high the corpses were piled. I thought about trying to signal some of them to go to the Dagda's aid, but the Grail could not be in two places at once. Shar could have left the Grail's protection because he would have been shielded from magic by Zom, but I couldn't ask him to face the Nuckelavee by himself. I realized what I had to do.

"*Merlin! Jimmie!*" I called out in my ghost voice. This time I could put some real energy behind my cry, and they both heard me.

"Tell the ladies to hold off," I said to them. *"The group needs to aid the Dagda before he dies...for real this time."*

Merlin, whose spirit floated like a gentle mist above the group, frowned at me. *"Taliesin, right now your bond with your body is fragile. If we are going to succeed, we have to try again immediately."*

"You can try again in a few minutes. Too much else is at stake now."

"I will not tell them to stop," replied Merlin firmly. I couldn't believe it—Merlin was going to ignore my wishes completely.

"Jimmie, tell Nurse Florence what I said!" I demanded. Jimmie looked about to cry, but he shook his head emphatically.

I should have been pleased my friends put such a high value on my life, but I could not be the cause of the Dagda's death. I looked in his direction and saw him stagger. Some of the nearby each-uisge, heartened by his obvious weakness, looked as if they were about to attack. I could also feel Nicneven unleashing a spell of great power, though I couldn't be sure of its type.

I felt another jolt as my friends tried again, and Nicneven's grip loosened a little more, but still not enough. The Dagda staggered a second time and came much closer to falling.

At that moment I was distracted from the Dagda's plight by Nicneven. I suddenly understood what she was doing. Channeling the power of Hecate again, she was raising an army of the dead. Such a force would be no use against my friends as long as Jimmie had the Grail, but it could be enough to crush the Dagda.

I could feel the tortured spirits appearing in greater and greater numbers from the shadowy gateway Nicneven had opened. I screamed to my friends, bracing for yet a third attempt, but the four women who might conceivably have heard my outburst were so focused on pulling me back into my body that they were blind and deaf to everything else.

Nicneven's faerie forces, confused at first by the lapse in the command structure when Nicneven was released from Dark Me's control and by the arrival of the Dagda, were regrouping in preparation for what I was sure would be another attack on my friends, who if they were still focused on me would not have enough magic left to deflect arrows that would shower them less than a minute from now.

The Dagda would die, and my friends would die—all because of me! I could not allow that to happen.

I started thrashing futilely against Nicneven's control again, working myself into such a frenzy that I almost missed the arrival of Alex and Khalid. The AWOL duo just suddenly appeared near the rest of our party. Since neither one of them had magic, they must have had help. It was hard for me to see details, but I thought I saw Alex bending over my body. For a second everything went black, and then I opened my eyes…my real eyes! I was back in my own body!

I sat up so fast I almost gave myself whiplash. "What happened?" I asked shakily.

"When Khalid and I got separated from you guys, I called out to our Olympian friends," said Alex. "They rescued us from getting captured…or eaten, or whatever, by the each-uisge. We've been on Olympus since then, waiting for the right moment to come back."

"But how did you revive me?"

"We and the Olympians were watching," said Khalid excitedly. "We saw you get trapped outside your body. Well, Hermes helped us see. We could tell you couldn't get back, so Hermes worked with Persephone to create a spell that would cleanse you of the vibes you picked up from the owl body's death. He thought that might break Nicneven's hold."

"He was the guide of souls to the Underworld," Alex reminded me, "so he knew enough about the problem to fix it."

"Thanks, guys," I said awkwardly. "You may just have saved us all. I'll thank you properly later. Right now, though, I'm switching to mental so we can have a quick strategy conversation." With that, I plugged back into the links among us I had created earlier.

"We have to move fast. I think we're about to get another aerial attack from the faeries, but that's not the only problem. The Dagda has come, I think maybe to rescue me, and he's about to get killed. We need to help him if we can. We also need to stop Nicneven, who looks as if she's putting together an army of the dead to throw against the Dagda or maybe us. Such a force couldn't get close to the Grail, but the very raising of it poisons this realm in ways we can only begin to imagine. The only way I can see to handle all of that is get some deflection going again to minimize damage from the archers, head for the Dagda and save him, then hit Nicneven and Dark Me as hard as we can. Questions?"

"By air or ground?" asked Mab.

"Ground I think this time. Nicneven is too focused on calling up the dead to waste energy on the earthquake strategy, and we'll be too far away from the mountain in a minute for it to work anyway."

We moved out as fast as we could, again in tight formation to make sure everyone was protected by the Grail. We did indeed start taking arrow fire in a minute or so, just as I thought, but with no other distractions, we had little problem fending it off. I saw some witches lurking quite a distance away, but none of them tried a magic attack, probably knowing it would be useless. They were, however, standing by in case someone dropped the Grail or something like that, so we had to be extra careful.

Even from a distance, we could see that the Dagda had fallen, but the Nuckelavee had not crushed him with its hooves. Perhaps the monster believed the former high king was dead. Perhaps it was waiting for a specific kill order from Nicneven, who was preoccupied. The Uilepheist was nearby as well, but its blue-green scales had gone so pale they looked almost white, it was shaking violently, and dark blue blood was streaming from its convulsing mouth. Apparently, swallowing the Dagda's harp had not been the best idea. Certainly, the creature no longer looked like much of a threat.

The Nuckelavee was a different story, though. The Devil of the Sea, as he was called, reared as we approached, threatening us with being crushed under his massive hooves. Terrifying as the sight of the creature was, he was no strategist, and his first move enabled both Eva and Khalid, as well as at least five of the faeries, to plant arrows in his stomach; Khalid's set off the usual holy fireworks display, and the creature howled in pain and rage, then started to gallop in our direction.

Coventina, knowing the creature's fear of fresh water, unleashed a powerful spray of it right in the thing's face, but it kept coming, the only time on record in which it ignored its fear. Coventina switched tactics, spraying the water sideways into the Grail to create instant holy water, which she then blasted at it with fire hose strength. It howled again as its black demonic flesh began to bubble from the holy water, but still it staggered forward, determined to have vengeance for our attack. Even two more of Khalid's arrows and ten faerie arrows did not bring it entirely to a halt, and now it was nearly upon us.

I raised a wall of fire, but the thing jumped through and landed nearly on top of us, red eyes flashing. Not expecting any of us to fly, it was taken by surprise when Alex shot upward and thrust Harpe into its stomach, wringing a scream from the beast but getting himself sprayed with digestive juices in the process. Now it was Alex's turn to scream as he fell, but as soon as he was back in the aura of the Grail, his pain faded, and his burned skin began to heal.

The Nuckelavee was staggering now and filling the air with a nonstop shriek—but it was big enough to kill us just by falling on us. As it started to teeter dangerously, we spell casters put everything we had into holding it up. We knew we couldn't stop it from falling any more than we could stop a full-scale avalanche, but we did manage to keep it upright until we got everybody out from under it. Then we let it thud to the ground with enough force to produce a minor earthquake. Though not yet dead, it was clearly dying, or at least badly incapacitated enough that it would not be any more of a threat than the Uilepheist.

By the time we reached the Dagda, he was so close to death Nurse Florence could barely find vital signs. However, his heartbeat became much stronger after less than a minute in the Grail's healing field. His progress after that seemed frustratingly slow, though.

"It takes a lot to kill someone that powerful," explained Nurse Florence, "so it will take the Grail a while to heal the consequences of all that punishment. Cleansing him of all the Nuckelavee's poison is a major task all by itself."

"You look worried, though," I pointed out.

"The Grail has been recharging us and healing us for hours now. Another possibility for its slow action is that it now needs time to recharge."

"It will still protect us from magic, though, right?" asked Carlos nervously. In the distance we could all make out a few gray-robed witches, just waiting for us to make a slip that would enable them to bombard us with magic.

"Helena was pretty clear on that, I thought," said Eva. "The protection against magic works regardless."

"We've tested the Grail in ways it has never been tested before," said Dan, clearly getting a case of the jitters himself. "I wonder if she really knows for sure we can't drain even that magic protection if we give it enough of a workout."

"The Grail only works if you have faith, remember?" I reminded them, perhaps more loudly than I needed to. "We don't want to all stop believing right now. We're so close to getting through this."

The truth was I was almost as nervous as they were, but for somewhat different reasons. Helena was one of the world's greatest experts on the Grail, so I believed her if she said we couldn't exhaust its magic protection. However, I was concerned by the fact that the Dagda was taking so long to heal. He was breathing, and his heart was beating, but he still looked white as snow, and he showed no sign of regaining consciousness. We couldn't leave him in that condition, but every minute that passed allowed Nicneven to summon up more of the dead and Dark Me to create more chaos to strengthen her constant bending of reality.

I thought about freeing the Dagda's harp from the Uilepheist's digestive system. I could still feel the instrument creating vibrations somewhere deep within the dragon's corpse. Left to its own devices, it would free itself eventually, but it might counteract Dark Me's playing better if we cut it out of the beast now. However, aside from the risk involved in exposing someone to the creature's digestive juices, Nicneven's faerie archers were hitting us with a more or less continuous stream of arrows. Our deflection was holding nicely, but no one could venture too far from where we were standing without basically painting a target on his or her back, and the Uilepheist was lying some distance away. Our archers and I tried driving the enemy archers back with arrows while I used fire blasts, but there were still too many of them, despite the earlier casualties, for us to force them completely out of range. Whether because of genuine loyalty to Nicneven or simply fear of her, they seemed willing to take more casualties to keep us pinned down.

Then I noticed something else: as the Grail labored to heal the Dagda, I felt progressively more tired. Of course, I'd been through a lot, as had we all, but up until now, as long as I was close to the Grail, I wasn't feeling any of that. I discreetly questioned Nurse

Florence, Coventina, Mab, and Carla; all four were beginning to feel worn out.

Nicneven, by contrast, seemed to be getting stronger. I noticed the lurking witches had retreated. Nicneven must have been drawing power from them to fuel...what exactly? Building up an army of the dead was a neat trick, but I couldn't imagine how undead soldiers conjured up by magic could reach us while the Grail protected us. Unfortunately, the enormous energy she was putting into summoning them couldn't be good for the barriers between realms. I could almost feel the fabric of reality crying out in protest. Even if the damage didn't initially affect our world, it could easily contaminate Annwn, other faerie realms, and possibly even some of the Norse ones; some of the Alfar had tried to settle Elphame long ago, and I had heard rumors at least one fixed portal between Elphame and Alfheim still worked. In the long run I knew there could be negative consequences for every world.

Then I realized the dead army was on the march—but not toward us. Instead, it was heading toward the portal Nicneven had just opened...a portal to our world.

Yeah, she knew she couldn't use those troops to attack us. What she could do was threaten helpless civilians with them in order to force our surrender.

I couldn't tell from this distance, but I would have bet five years of my life the portal connected to the Santa Barbara area, particularly the part where our families now were.

"I need volunteers to attack Nicneven right now," I thought with so much urgency Nurse Florence looked shocked.

"If we leave now, the Dagda may die!" She protested.

"Which is why I'm asking for volunteers. The Dagda came in the first place to save me—long story," I said, deflecting Stan's question. *"I can't let him die. But we can't wait until he's healed to go after Nicneven. She's been raising the dead to send them against our world, and they're getting reading to leave."*

"If we levitate him—" started Nurse Florence.

"We've got too many archers on us to travel by air...now that they've figured out to attack from below anyway. We'd be taking fire from all sides, and it's hard enough to fly this many people under the best

of circumstances. We already found that out. A few of us could slip away under cover of a spell, though—"

"And face Nicneven and Dark Me without magic protection? No way!" protested Dan.

"We take a small party," suggested Shar, "small enough for everyone to be able to touch Zom. That would be enough to shield us. If we get close to Nicneven, she's going to have to be more worried about our swords than we are about her spells."

The women were unanimous in disagreeing with my plan, but when I showed them a vision of the first of the dead emerging in Santa Barbara, they gave in. Then I suddenly had the opposite problem: everyone wanted to be part of our small group.

I had only seconds to make decisions, and they were not universally popular, but they were the best I could do. The other spell casters had to remain behind to keep the deflection going and to help the Dagda as needed. Jimmie looked daggers at me when I announced that he too had to stay, but being unable to wield a weapon well at this point made that decision an easy one for me. I also made Dan, Carlos, Alex, and Eva remain behind. Eva was an archer, after all, and some of the guys needed to stay back if the faeries tried to get up close and personal.

Khalid? Shar and I both wanted him to stay behind, but it was hard to refuse the power of his arrows, and if Shar and I both left, he would follow anyway unless we chained him down. Stan went too, because he could switch into David mode, which always seemed to result in a blessed field around his sword. Gordy was wielding the Apollo-blessed sword, which I was sure would be handy against the dead if they turned on us, so he went, too, even though the party was at least one larger than Shar would have preferred.

The other casters set an illusion to make the hostile archers believe we were still with the group, Khalid became invisible, and I cast invisibility around the rest of us. None of those spells would hold up against someone like Nicneven or Dark Me; if either was watching for us, we would be spotted before we could get close enough to attack. We had to hope that each was too preoccupied with the magic to really be looking for us, and once we reached them, the invisibility would no longer be necessary.

Quite aside from stopping the dead army, some of which was already through the portal, we had to make quick work of defeating both Nicneven and Dark Me. The archers would realize pretty rapidly what we had done once we attacked their queen, and they would turn on us. I could probably do a passable deflection spell, but not if I had to fight Dark Me, and if I had to surround us with fire, I could protect us for a while, but we would have a harder time stopping the dead if we had to assume such a defensive position.

We took off at a run, with Khalid protesting having to ride on Shar's back. Yeah, Khalid could fly, but there was too much risk of him getting separated, and by myself I couldn't get everyone else into the air very efficiently.

Luck was with us at first: none of the archers pursued, which meant none of them had seen through the illusion. I kept enough of my attention on the rest of our party to tell that they were still holding their own as the archers continued their bombardment. They would remain so as long as the deflection held, and with four of them sharing their power, that could be some time, even if the Grail was no longer refueling them very efficiently.

We came close to falling on the icy ground a couple of times, but we managed to stay close together and make reasonably good time. We had no choice; every second let a couple more of the dead slip into our world. I could only hope they wouldn't move until the whole army was through, or at least that they hadn't come pouring out right on top of our families.

As we got closer, I became even more concerned about the state of reality. Dark Me's playing had torn away at the natural order, creating ideal conditions for Nicneven's work but threatening to tear the barriers between worlds to shreds in the process. Dark Me was focused on his playing but looked profoundly unhappy now that he was bound by a *tynged* to obey Nicneven. The combination of the work and discontent made him unlikely to see us. Nicneven was wholly engrossed in the continuing stream of the dead still coming forth at her bidding, and she too would probably miss us until it was too late. She was ringed with faerie guards, but they were so disconcerted by Dark Me's playing and by the army of the dead marching all around them that they weren't really looking for any kind of attack.

Eacharn, however, was another matter. He was looking in the direction from which we had come, clearly expecting us to make some kind of move. I would have been disappointed in his military skill if he hadn't been, but if he saw us too soon, he could sound the alarm.

We were only yards away when I saw the expression of surprise on his face and knew that he had perceived our approach, at least well enough to know someone was coming.

"Guards!" he yelled. "Attackers are approaching from the west."

"Kill them all," said Nicneven emotionlessly, directing her command at Dark Me.

"Everybody touch Zom!" I yelled in their minds. *"We are about to get hit by everything Dark Me can muster!"*

Everyone having to keep contact with Shar's sword was going to hinder us considerably, especially with the faerie guards and Eacharn now running to intercept us, but we had little choice: the chaos Dark Me was stirring up with the lyre of Orpheus could easily destroy us if he aimed it at us instead of just using it to amplify Nicneven's ability to reach across realm boundaries.

Knowing we couldn't sword fight very well in such an awkward position, I used White Hilt's fire to shield us against the advancing faeries, but that was only to give me long enough to think. Adopting a strictly defensive option was self-defeating in this situation. What we needed was a way to fight without exposing ourselves to hostile magic from two very powerful casters.

"Shar, I'm going to try to channel Zom's energy in a burst style. Think good thoughts while I'm doing it."

I had learned from trial and error that directing Zom's antimagic energy in a beam focused on a caster temporarily disabled that caster's magic ability. A burst might be enough to buy a few seconds free of attack from either Nicneven or Dark Me, and once they were in the reach of our blades, it would be a very different battle. Unfortunately, Zom was a pretty temperamental sword where I was concerned and didn't particularly like my efforts to use its antimagic power in other ways, but it did seem to like Shar. If it knew he was on board with the plan, it would be more likely to cooperate with the speed we needed.

I deafened all of us first because I wasn't sure whether the lyre of Orpheus would be out of commission for long, even if Dark Me's own casting ability was. Then I caused White Hilt's flame to flare to blinding brightness for a few seconds, hopefully slowing our enemies enough to let me stop concentrating on White Hilt long enough to concentrate on Zom. I heard the shout of the faeries as their eyes hit overload, firmly grasped Zom's hilt, and sent out a burst I hoped was strong enough to take every nearby spell caster off-line. Zom cooperated, and I sent out two more bursts just to be on the safe side.

After that I figured we might only have a couple of minutes, so I hung as close as I could to Shar, just in case I needed to renew the effect.

The faerie guards and Eacharn were still blinded, and the loss of magic was definitely a shock to their nervous systems, so it didn't take much to overpower them without having to kill them. We just plowed into them like we were tackling them in a football game; the fact that Shar and Gordy were actually football players helped, but all of us except for Khalid had the bulk to knock down a typical faerie, even a warrior. Once they were down with the wind knocked out of them, I placed a binding on them to keep them down. The spell wasn't designed to last long—there was no time for that—but it should hold them long enough for us to finish with Nicneven and Dark Me.

My heart jumped when Dark Me's identity theft was disrupted by Zom's burst, and for just a few seconds I could see a dazed Robin Goodfellow looking around. Unfortunately, the spell apparently had enough power to reassert itself, and Dark Me reappeared, though dazed himself and without magic. As for Nicneven, she had nearly fallen after the third burst, and though she managed to stay on her feet, she didn't seem to know what to do without her magic to blast us.

As soon as we were past the faeries, Khalid, remembering how he had closed the hell gate, started shooting his powerful arrows at Nicneven's already flickering portal, and in a couple shots he closed it. That was a mixed blessing, because I hadn't had time to find out where the portal exited, but it was better in the short term to stop more of the dead from crossing over.

Unfortunately, closing the portal also canceled the orders Nicneven had given the dead, who up to this point had been ignoring us. The ones closest to the antimagic bursts had simply disappeared, but it took us just long enough to get the faeries out of the way that a large part of the remaining ghostly soldiers had managed to flow like mist into the gap between us and Nicneven.

By that point Nicneven had recovered her wits enough to whisper, "Kill them!" Her whispered command echoed through their ranks, and they were upon us in seconds.

Despite the impression you might get from horror movies, I'd rather fight zombies than ghosts any day. I'd never seen a zombie, and it was actually possible they didn't exist, but if they did, they were slow-moving, unthinking creatures who could be frightened by fire; armed with White Hilt, I could have easily cut through them. Ghosts, on the other hand, could move almost as fast as thought if they really knew what they were doing. They could have the same intelligence they had possessed in life, at least if enough power was put into their summoning, and fire meant nothing to them. Though by nature immaterial, strong ghosts such as these could become physical enough to attack, and they could easily repair any "wounds" to their fake physical presence. Worse, they could become like a gas and force themselves into a mortal's lungs, as some had tried with me in the Underworld. Enough semimaterial ghost in the airway or lungs could suffocate a person fast. Even worse than that might be the psychic poison created by the presence of so many of the dead in a place not really meant for them. Exposed for long enough, we would be pushed toward fear and even despair.

My whole strategy had been based on getting quickly to Nicneven and Dark Me. If the ghosts could hold us back until either or both of them started to recover their magic, we would probably lose.

"Don't try to wipe out all the ghosts," I cautioned the guys. *"The priority is to put Nicneven and Dark Me out of action. Just concentrate on getting through to them."*

Shar could best follow my advice, because every ghost he hit with Zom vanished in an emerald flash. Khalid's arrows caused the ghosts he shot to explode. Gordy had almost as much luck with the sword blessed by Apollo, though the ghosts had time to scream and writhe a little and usually had to be hit two or three times. Stan let

David be in charge in this kind of situation, and whatever blessing God granted to David's sword caused some of the ghosts to flee.

Had the ghosts stuck to being physical enough to fight us, most of us would have broken through in a couple of minutes. However, they realized our weapon strikes were too powerful to overcome, so instead they began to form clouds of deadly mist and try the suffocation strategy on a large scale. Their ability to be gaseous one minute, solid the next, and then completely immaterial the one after that, made them extremely hard to shake off. Those who couldn't try squeezing down our windpipes formed hands to grasp at us, and occasionally even teeth to bite at us. The idea of struggling through something that looked like fog but grabbed, punched, kicked, and bit when it wasn't trying to suffocate us was almost too much to bear, and on top of everything else the ghosts could make us feel both cold and afraid. Fortunately, we were all in one way or another able to resist the fear part: Shar was protected by Zom, Gordy by his sword and a special property of his dragon army, Stan/David by God I guessed, and Khalid by his half djinn nature. As for me, I had enough willpower to resist for a little while. What would happen if this battle took hours, I couldn't tell. Long before that Nicneven and Dark Me would have revived and killed us all.

As for my brilliant strategy of staying close enough to Shar to touch Zom if need be and send out more antimagic bursts, his earlier progress against the ghosts, much faster than mine, had separated us enough to put Zom well out of reach, and the ghosts clogged the space between us so efficiently that there was no hope of pursuing that strategy unless I told Shar to turn around and try to head back to me, something I didn't want to risk. After all, he seemed the one of us most likely to break through.

I spared a little concentration to see how the rest of the group was faring. As far as I could tell, the Dagda was a little better, but not much. I estimated conservatively it might be another half an hour before the others could try to join us. Not only that, but by now some of the archers were realizing their queen was under attack and flying to defend her. In seconds we would have to deal with arrows as well as ghosts.

I felt power surge nearby and realized that Nicneven was coming back on line. I glanced her way and saw her chilling triumphant smile.

Then I realized that, though the ghosts ignored my fire or became immaterial enough to be untouched by it, Nicneven, a physical being and long accustomed to her icy realm, was far more vulnerable to it, and I didn't need to be right on top of her to hit her.

From White Hilt I projected the strongest blast of concentrated fire I could manage. It shot right through the unsuspecting ghosts and hit Nicneven on the chest, burning through her gray gown in seconds and igniting her white skin. She screamed in panic and pain, but she still had the presence of mind to throw herself down and roll in the snow. A few ghosts shifted back to wrap her in their cold embraces, while the ones nearer me encased my sword arm in a semisolid mass, throwing off my aim and making my second shot go wild.

At that point an arrow hit the back of my dragon armor and bounced off. A few inches higher, and it would have been buried in my neck.

I had only one play left, but it was a risky one. I still had the vial of blessed water from Saint Brendan's well, and I knew it had the power to vanquish one evil enemy. The question was, how could I use it on Nicneven from this distance? In theory I could levitate it across the distance between us, then throw it at her by sheer force of will, but if the ghosts blocked me, or if I missed, the vial would be gone—as would our hope.

I looked over to see if Khalid might be able to grab it and fly with it, but too many ghosts were clutching him. He was using one of his arrows like a dagger, and each ghost scratched with it dissolved, but another immediately took its place, and he could only take out one of the several ghosts who gripped him at a time.

"Alex, if the others can spare you, fly over here as fast as you can!" I mentally shouted to him. If the group was not under too serious a physical attack, he might be able to break away, and the sandals of Hermes would give him a decent shot at dodging the faerie archers if too many of them didn't move to block him. The odds still weren't great, but they were better than nothing.

In seconds I could sense Alex approaching. I gave him a thought message explaining what he needed to do, and then with a little telekinesis, I lifted the vial out of my pocket, at the same time cloaking it in enough magic that the ghosts might not see it. That wouldn't fool them long, but it didn't need to. Another three seconds, and Alex was above me, so I telekinetically tossed the vial up to him. He grabbed it before any ghosts could rise up and entangle him, and then he shot in Nicneven's direction so fast he was like a blur.

She was still partially wrapped in the soothing ghosts who had come to her rescue, but Alex had an unobstructed shot at her head, and he broke the vial right in her face.

The queen of faeries and witches shrieked so loudly that she might have been voicing the agony of her whole people, not just herself. There was such indescribable pain in that sound that even the ghosts stopped and shuddered. Then she tried to rise and flee, but that blessed water was to her a thousand times more powerful than any acid, eating away not just at her face but at her entire being at the same time. Even someone as powerful as she could not resist that overwhelming force for more than a minute. I thought I caught a glimpse of the eyeless skull that had once been her face. Then it too was gone. In seconds not even any identifiable dust was left.

The ghosts, so mighty a force only moments before, were stricken with terror as if reliving their own deaths. A few of them feebly tried to continue the struggle, but with the destruction of their summoner, some of them were already fading, and those who did not immediately succumb were now easy marks for Shar, David, Gordy, Khalid, and Alex. As for me, I threw enough fire around us to slow down the archers, tore away from the now feeble grasp of ghostly hands and found Eacharn. He was still on the ground, but only a minute or two from escaping my spell.

"Lord Eacharn, your queen is dead, but there is no reason for more of your people to die. Give the order for them to break off the attack."

"Nicneven should have been the queen of all the faeries," said Eacharn sadly, "but she was too easily exploited by others…that foul twin of yours being the least of them. Still, you are right; there is no death more hollow than that for a cause that is already lost. Free me, and I will order a ceasefire."

I should probably have bound him with a *tynged*, but there was no time, and so I gambled on his honor, and for a change I won that bet with myself. Once free, he flew quickly into the sky, shouting orders, and the arrows ceased flying. In another few minutes, he and the archers landed.

I could hardly believe it, but he battle was finally over, and we had won.

Chapter 35: Last Things (Tal)

You could probably guess without my telling you, but Dark Me made his escape while the guys were mopping up the last of the ghosts. Apparently, all of the elements of the *tynged* Nicneven had imposed on him related to her: protect her, obey her every command, that sort of thing. Once she was dead, the *tynged* had no force. Dark Me had recovered at least a little of his magic by that time, enough, I guessed, to enable him to slip away—with the lyre of Orpheus, naturally.

"Isn't he going to run out of your blood sooner or later?" asked Gordy.

"Yeah, but by then I'll bet he has figured out how to adapt the magic in Alex's ring to make more," I replied glumly.

"Do we need to go get him?" asked Dan with undisguised weariness.

I laughed despite having a throat raw from ghostly finger-nails. "There are many places he could have gone from Elphame...too many for me to even know where to start. We'll need to work out a spell to find him...or perhaps learn where he is from our resident seer, if she's recovered." With a twinge of guilt, I realized it was the first moment in hours I'd thought specifically of my mom.

"I would not worry too much about him," said Coventina. "He is evil in some ways, of that there can be no doubt. Yet he does not seem to want any of you dead."

"At least not yet," said Carlos nervously.

"I really think he'd rather have us as allies than corpses," I said. "Anyway, there's time to think about him tomorrow or the next day. Right now he has the lyre, but no allies at all, and I doubt even he's so arrogant that he wants to take on the whole world—no, the whole of every world—by himself."

At that point the Dagda lumbered over, looking more or less fully recovered and having retrieved his harp from the dragon's belly.

"Young Taliesin, I thought to have repaid the debt I owed you for saving my granddaughter, and instead I owe you now for saving my own life."

"In truth, you saved us, my lord," I said graciously. "With-out your arrival, we would all have been dead."

"True enough, but you also risked everything to allow the Grail to heal me. You could easily have justified leaving me to die in the name of the greater good, but you did not."

I started to protest, but Gordy muttered, "Just take the praise for a change," and so I did.

"My lord, if I might ask something that is none of my concern—" I began.

"At this point the answer to a question is the least I owe you," replied the Dagda.

"You were trying to keep the fact that you were alive secret. Why did you choose this moment to reveal yourself?"

The Dagda chuckled. "I wish with all my heart I could say I did it to save you, but that would be only half the truth, and you are entitled to the whole truth and more besides. The rest of it is this battle was as good a point as any to declare my claim to be high king, not just of Irish faeries, but of all faeries."

I tried not to betray my disappointment that once again someone's life was dominated by faerie politics, but evidently I didn't do a very good job.

"Do not frown so at me," the Dagda said firmly. "Can you deny the current system of random tribunals to resolve disputes among the faerie rulers has been a failure? Will you argue that faerie society is well governed?"

I sighed. "No, I cannot, but surely such a claim as you wish to make could lead to war."

"Almost anything could lead to war," replied the Dagda, who was clearly becoming annoyed with me. "Yet the time I was high king among the Tuatha de Danaan in Ireland is remembered as a time of peace and plenty. I approached Finvarra before coming here, and he has already pledged his support to my cause...which means, I presume, my ladies, that I can count on your support as well."

"If you have Finvarra's support, then you have mine as well," agreed Mab, though with less than total enthusiasm.

"I will certainly hear out your proposal," said Coventina in as neutral a tone as she could manage. "If nothing else, your bravery today demands that I consider all you have said."

The Dagda looked enormously disappointed at their lukewarm response, and he was not going to let the matter rest. Looking at me, he said, "I would think someone as wise as you would appreciate the advantages that could come from having a faerie high king who has been your comrade-in-arms."

"I do indeed," I replied, deciding that there was no real point in offending him, "but remember…Majesty, I am not universally popular with the faeries. If I side with you too publicly, I may lose you as much support as I gain you."

The Dagda knew I was being evasive, but if he had talked to Doirend much in the past few months, he also knew I spoke the truth. In any case, he simply nodded, clearly deciding that pressing the person who saved his life might be unseemly—at least for a couple days.

He then proceeded to put himself in the middle of picking a new ruler for the Scottish faeries, who seemed oddly willing to accept our judgment. Perhaps Nicneven's long connection with evil witches and demons, neither of which faeries normally got along with, to say nothing of her willingness to rend the veil between life and death, made them ready to accept new leadership.

Actually, the Dagda would probably simply have picked someone, possibly a member of his own large family, but I managed to maneuver him into a meeting involving Coventina, Mab, Eacharn, and me, and from that meeting emerged a surprising consensus choice: Eacharn, pending a meeting of all the faerie rulers to confirm him. I know, that seems counterintuitive, but the Scottish faeries would more easily accept one of their own, and Eacharn seemed to be a man of honor—at least as he defined honor. The Dagda was suddenly won over to the idea when he realized that Eacharn favored the concept of a high king who would be the final word in disputes among faerie rulers.

Soon after the resolution of the Scottish faerie succession, the Dagda said good-bye, doubtless to proclaim his candidacy for high king and make sure everybody knew of the pivotal role he had played in defeating Nicneven. Eacharn, too, took his leave, pointing out that he had much to do. That seemed a good time for Mab to dismiss the men Gwynn had lent her, and after Sir Arilan bid us all farewell an received our thanks, he led the survivors back to Annwn. Mab herself departed next, followed by Coventina, and suddenly we were back to our original group.

"What about the ghosts that got through the portal before Khalid destroyed it?" asked Stan. "Shouldn't we be doing something about them?"

"Oh, I told Tal already, but I guess I should have made a general announcement," said Nurse Florence apologetically. "The first thing I did after the battle was get in touch with Vanora. It seems that after she recovered enough, she lifted the spell on Tal's mother, who fortunately realized a ghost army was going to attack. Vanora contacted Gwynn, who wasn't under any orders not to prevent ghost incursions in the mortal realm, so he used his role as guide of souls to force the stray spirits back where they belong."

"Well, then I guess we should head home," said Carlos. "I feel like I just ran a marathon twice."

"Good idea," I agreed. Turning to Alex, I said, "You can't just show up on your parents' doorstep. I'll hide you out at my place until we arrange your return to them."

"I'm not going back...yet," said Alex slowly. "I need a little work on my...anger issues. Hermes and Asclepius can help me get more control first. Then I'll come back, if you'll still have me."

"There is always a place for you, Alex," I said, smiling. "Just let me know when you're ready."

Alex turned and almost ran right into Shar. "Look, Alex, I think that's a really mature decision—"

"And you don't want me anywhere near Khalid in my present condition anyway, right?" asked Alex bitterly.

"That's not what I meant," said Shar quickly, looking a little embarrassed. "Look, I know I wasn't very accepting at first, but you saved Khalid. You saved all of us. I admit it—I was too hard on you."

Much to my surprise—and Alex's, I'm pretty sure—Shar hugged him, as did Khalid. Pretty soon we had a general hugging session, and more than a few tears.

Now as emotionally drained as we were physically, we were even more ready to go home, and Nurse Florence made preparations to open the portal that would take us back...well, all except Alex, who was about to invoke Hermes and return to Olympus to finish his healing. While Nurse Florence was focusing herself, I noticed a tense conversation between Carla and Eva. I knew I shouldn't have, but I sharpened my hearing just enough so that I could tell what they were saying.

"You've got some nerve criticizing me!" snapped Eva.

"I'm sorry, I'm sorry," said Carla, just a little desperately. "That's not the way I meant it. I just wish...look, I've got to accept that Tal and I will never be together. The only way I'm ever going to be able to move on is if he has. And there's only one person he can move on with."

"That's not fair," said Eva defensively. "I can't just make myself love him. Believe me, I wish I could. It's just not going to happen."

"Why not?" Carla pressed. "He's a great person...and a really hot guy, if you haven't noticed."

"Oh, I've noticed all right, both his hotness and his greatness," said Eva, smiling just a little. "That last part is the problem, though. Maybe he's just too great,"

"Meaning what?" asked Carla, genuinely puzzled.

"Meaning I'd like to be with a guy who needs me, just like I need him. I know," she said, raising a hand to forestall Carla's objection, "Tal thinks he needs me, but in time he'll love somebody else, and he certainly doesn't need me for any other reason."

Carla sighed. "I still don't get what you're saying."

"Tal's life has become one continuous quest to save the world, with maybe a little time off in between," said Eva sadly. "Don't shake your head at me; you know it's true. I don't begrudge him that, but I'm not much help, either. With your loaner bow I was a mediocre archer, and that's it. I'm less useful than anybody else in the group, even people like Alex who started out as total messes. I couldn't take that day in and day out: knowing that Tal has this incredible purpose in life, and I'd be just the dead weight he drags around with him. Being with him would be like dating Jesus."

"That's not the way he sees it," said Carla quietly, "and for the record, dating him is nothing like dating Jesus."

I stopped listening at that point. Dating Jesus, huh? Wow! Could it really be true that good girls liked bad boys? God help me, for a second I found myself being jealous of Dark Me. After what I'd just heard, maybe he'd have more of a chance with Eva than I did.

Then I got the eyeful that really pounded the stake right through my heart and twisted it: Eva was kissing Jimmie. Well, he was definitely someone who needed her in ways I didn't. In fact she was the ideal girl for him, one who knew there was still a frightened nine-year-old inside the hunky sixteen-year-old body, one who would be patient with him as he caught up.

I tried really hard not to hate both of them. I gave myself some credit for almost succeeding.

I felt so bad that for a second I regretting not really loving Carla—at least that's what I thought until I saw the way she and Alex were looking at each other. I resisted the temptation to listen in on them, but it was obvious what was crossing both their minds: each had made a deal with evil that had nearly destroyed everyone else. Who else could either of them be with now without constantly feeling inferior?

Jealousy gnawed at me a little. It wasn't that I suddenly wanted to be with Carla. I knew I didn't love her. Still, there was something about losing the romantic game of musical chairs we'd been playing that irked me far more than it should have.

Fortunately, I was the only one in the group who could truly read minds, and I clamped my emotions down hard enough that neither Nurse Florence or Carla would get even a hint of my feelings. I stayed that way for several days, just to be sure.

***

It was a few days after that I tracked down Merlin's secret letter to me. This is what it said:

***

Taliesin,

There is very little chance that I will survive our upcoming battle, but I ask you not to weep for me, for I should long since have rejoined the cycle of reincarnation. I stayed alive in my prison for centuries because I foresaw the moment of your need, and then I stayed until the battle with Nicneven, knowing that it was what God asked of me. I do not regret that I tarried to play a role in your life, but had I tried to stay longer, I would have done more harm than good. This I see clearly.

I should perhaps not tell you this; call it the foolish whim of a dying old man. But I want you to know this, though the knowledge will bring you pain. I did not stay just so that God's purpose could be achieved. There was a personal edge to my motives.

I was something of a mentor to you when you were the original Taliesin, but that was far from the first time our souls had met. Once you were Heman, son of Joel, son of Samuel. I know this not only because you told me, but because I was Samuel.

Grandson, if I may call you that, though it is too late for me to be your grandfather, you know that Satan planned to make me his Antichrist, that he schemed to have me fathered by a demon for that very purpose. You know my mother baptized me in part to interfere with that plan. What you do not know is that God, too, worked to thwart it. He gave me a strong soul, one that could resist the temptations he knew would face me: the soul of Samuel.

You know from your experiences with David how little ancient Israelites wanted to return to the mortal world. The whole idea was foreign to their world view, yet Samuel made the sacrifice because it was what God knew should happen.

I know this letter brings you comfort colder than Nicneven's heart. I cannot promise what the future may hold for you, but I can tell you this: you and I will meet again, perhaps in this life, perhaps in another. God is not yet done with either of us, or with the bond between us. When again we meet, I pledge not to be the aloof wisdom figure, but the friend and perhaps family member I should have been this time.

With all my heart and soul I will await that day.

Your grandfather,
Merlin

***

I cried for a while, my tears mingling with the snow on the mountaintop. Then I composed myself and headed home.

Afterward I marveled at the intricate way in which the universe was constructed. So many times I could have died. So many times all my friends could have died. Somehow we lived. Somehow we kept one another alive.

Nicneven had the right idea about how to beat us. So did Asmodeus. Separate us. Tear us apart. As individuals without support, we would have been lost. As a group, we had done the impossible more than once.

Part of me was angry with Merlin for making me grieve a grandfather I never knew I had. Yet part of me realized that, too, had a purpose, for Merlin, seer as well as sorcerer, had known the day would come when I would harbor a secret animosity toward Eva and Jimmie, when I would harbor a completely irrational resentment of Carla and Alex. Merlin told me the truth to remind me of the interconnectedness of things…and people.

The people I cared about would be at risk again. I didn't have to be a seer to guess that much.

When that day came I could not be poisoned by my own pettiness.

We had been lucky this time. Either Carla or Jimmie could have doomed us. They didn't, and we endured.

Would it be me next time? Would I be the weakest link?

Not if I could help it. I would love my friends, reminding myself each day that we had all made mistakes and would make plenty more.

***

Over a month later, on Wednesday, March 20, we gathered together at Shar's house to celebrate Nowruz, the spring festival often referred to as Persian New Year. St. Patrick's Day had been only three days earlier, but none of us had gone to the school's dance: too many memories from Valentine's Day, too many figurative ghosts. The band had been offered the chance to perform, but Carla and I turned it down flat.

Actually, Nowruz was the first real celebration we'd had as a group since the return from Elphame. We spent the first few days back readying our defenses against an attack from Dark Me that never came. Maybe he borrowed the Amadan Dubh's idea and went off somewhere to create his own world. Maybe he was biding his time, and his attack would come later. I figured we would prepare as well as we could, and then we'd stop worrying about it. There wasn't much point in living every minute in the shadow of what might happen.

I felt the same way about the continued political uproar in the faerie realms; I couldn't allow it to rule my life. To the Dagda's great surprise, but not mine, his request to be made high king did not receive much immediate support outside Ireland, though the faerie rulers meeting in council had not formally reject the idea yet; some of them doubtless wanted to explore whether having the Dagda as their high king might be politically advantageous—or, if not, whether the continued discussion might move them closer to some other goal. Well, that and the Dagda was more powerful than any one of them. I think some of them were afraid to openly turn down the idea.

Faerie politics being what it was, Titania was still in prison awaiting trial, and Gwynn had been unable to secure me a visit with "Oberon" to see who he really was, though the faerie rulers had promised to formally consider my request…at some unspecified future time. I was going to have to work hard to wring a specific commitment from someone, but not tonight. Tonight I would party, or at least try. I wasn't really in the mood, but I was in one of the act-happy-for-everyone-else's-sake phases of my life.

The celebration was not just for teenagers; the Sassanis invited more or less everyone in town—even Carrie Winn, whom it was fairly well known they didn't really like.

"Spring is a time for new beginnings," said Mrs. Sassani cryptically when Shar asked about Winn's appearance on the guest list. Vanora, playing Carrie Winn to the hilt (and perhaps needing a party herself at this point) came, which meant everybody came. *The Sentinel*, our local newspaper, referred to the upcoming party as "the highlight of the 2013 social season," which made me snicker a little, since it was the first reference I'd ever heard to our relatively small town having a social season.

The venue suited the occasion perfectly. Homes in Santa Brígida were generally opulent, if a little too much alike, but the Sassani residence put most of them to shame. The exterior had the same Spanish colonial revival style everyone else's did, but over the years they had thoroughly remodeled the interior, which, though modern, always somehow reminded me of ancient Persia. The architect couldn't duplicate the typical central courtyard without having to tear down the existing house and start over, but he did manage to work columns, arched doorways, and marble facades into the design whenever possible, and even though the high ceilings downstairs were flat, he had them painted to create the optical illusion of domes. As amazing as that effect was, it was the wall murals that played the biggest role in filling (or haunting, as Shar once said) each room with scenes from Persian history, mythology, and literature. The main room on the first floor, which featured the major events in the *Shahnameh*, the great national epic of Persia, was my favorite, and because of its size, it became the center for the party.

I knew the Sassanis could throw a party, but they outdid themselves this time. The party started late, as I was told Persian parties in Beverly Hills often did, and Mrs. Sassani's explanation of Nowruz, for the benefit of the non-Persian guests (a.k.a. everybody except the Sassanis), was pretty sedate, but after that the party shifted into high gear and kept going until the early hours of the morning. Even the adults didn't remember to remind us it was a school night.

The dining room that adjoined the main room had a buffet of such overwhelming proportions that even my teenage guy appetite was daunted. The Sassanis' enormous dining room table could barely hold the feast, half composed of traditional Persian fare and half of American. I wasn't really hungry, but somehow I ended up with a full plate…just for appearances' sake, I told myself, though I ended up eating everything.

The background music in the main part of the house was an eclectic mix of Persian classical and contemporary American easy listening obviously designed for the adult guests, but in what would have been the basement in most houses, the Sassanis had designed a teenage party spot—very well soundproofed—in which the musical selection was less like the classical sounds upstairs and more like a typical teenage playlist on Spotify or Pandora. We had to go upstairs to get food, which some of us did several times, but for the most part we could stay downstairs, letting current popular songs wash over us. I might have preferred sitting out in the garden, but since the "basement" ceiling had a great painting of the night sky on it, complete with a luminous moon and stars, the room was lined with very realistic-looking plastic palm trees, and the Sassanis had recently added a fountain in the center, I could easily pretend I was outside if I wanted to. In between the palm trees were small tables where we could sit and eat. Around the fountain was a dance floor…for those who had someone to dance with.

Don't start feeling sorry for yourself!

I spent a little while fussing over my *ash-e reshteh* (noodle soup with twisted noodles). The noodles reminded me of Celtic knots, and there was a tradition that someone who could untangle those noodles would have good fortune. Needless to say, mine stubbornly refused to untangle.

I had better luck disentangling Alex from his parents when I ran into them on one of my trips upstairs. Yeah, he was back from Olympus, having been given a clean bill of health by Hermes, and his parents let him come to the party—but they came, too, and they seemed intent on keeping him handcuffed to them. I really couldn't blame them; they thought he'd been in an institution for several weeks following a major breakdown. Maybe if I had a kid who'd just been through something like that, I would want to keep my eyes on him 24-7, too. However, Alex's problem in the first place had been not fitting in, and having to play "Me and My Shadow" with his parents all the time was going to make him look like more of a freak than ever to most of the people at school. I was not about to let that happen.

Shifting into charm-the-adults mode, I said hi to Alex and introduced myself to his parents. Talk about tough crowds! They were actually suspicious of me at first. Wake up, people—your son actually knew a few teenagers who weren't bullies! I was afraid I was going to have to use a little magic on them to pry Alex loose, but Vanora, of all people, came to my rescue.

"Taliesin!" she said warmly, sweeping into our little group like a gentle hurricane. "I was hoping I'd see you tonight. I wanted to thank you for that excellent work you did on that green energy study. Some of your ideas are going to be in the company's future projects."

"I'm glad I could help," I said in my best aw-shucks-ma'am-it-was-nothing tone. "Oh, Ms. Winn, where are my manners? Let me introduce you to Alexandros Stratos, a friend from school, and his parents, Mr. and Mrs. Stratos." Vanora shook hands with Alex and then with each of his parents, who seemed to be having difficulty adjusting to the sudden arrival of the town's number one citizen.

"So, Alexandros...do you go by Alex?" asked Vanora.

"Yeah," he replied, clearly a little flummoxed himself.

"Yes, ma'am," corrected Mrs. Stratos.

Vanora waved a hand dismissively. "I deal with teenagers all the time, Mrs. Stratos, and I never insist they stand on ceremony with me. Anyway, Alex, Tal tells me you're quite the expert on Greek mythology."

Alex blushed a little. "Well, I wouldn't say expert, Ms. Winn, but I read a lot."

"Ah, I wish everyone your age could say that," said Vanora, smiling. "Keep it up." Then she directed her attention to Alex's parents again. "I must say, your son has good taste in friends. He couldn't have a better one than Tal Weaver."

I hadn't seen that coming...and neither, apparently, had anyone else. "Oh," was all Mrs. Stratos could manage.

"He's my intern," continued Vanora, "and frankly, I should be paying him; he does better work than some of my paid employees."

"That's...good to know," said Mr. Stratos, looking at me with somewhat different eyes.

"He's so mature and responsible," said Vanora, I thought maybe overdoing just a bit. "If I had a son Alex's age, I would want him to have someone like Tal."

Yup, definitely overkill—but Alex's parents ate it up. In Santa Brígida Carrie Winn's endorsement might not have been quite as good as if the archangel Raphael had appeared and offered his, but it was pretty close.

After a little more conversation, I said, "If you'll all excuse us, Alex has some friends downstairs I'm sure want to say hello."

Both of Alex's parents looked still looked nervous. "Alex, I'd like to meet your other friends," said his mom after a short pause.

Again Vanora saved us. "Downstairs, as I understand it, is kind of a teenagers-only zone tonight. You know how they are; one look at any of us, and they'll all freeze solid. I'm sure they'll come visit Alex at your place before too long, Mrs. Stratos."

"No chaperones downstairs?" asked Mr. Stratos, trying not to sound as suspicious as he was.

"One of the Sassanis checks in every so often, but honestly, Tal and his group are better than chaperones. Have you met our hosts' son, Shahriyar? He knows what his parents expect, and he's more than capable of keeping his peers in line. You have nothing to worry about."

"Well, in that case, have a good time, dear," said Mrs. Stratos, sounding a little defeated but unable to find a polite way of ignoring Vanora's advice. Besides, Vanora shifted deftly from discussing teenagers to discussing how Winn Industries might be in need of the services of Mr. Stratos's engineering firm, and that was one conversation he did not want to break away from.

"Thanks, Vanora! I don't know what we'd do without you," I thought to her. She seemed a little surprised but nodded as she pulled Alex's parents away from us and toward the other side of the room. I guessed I probably should remember to thank her more often.

"I'm a little nervous," admitted Alex. "I know you and the guys pretty well, but some of the other people—"

"Will not bother you anymore," I finished for him. "We've got your back, buddy. Anyway, have you looked in a mirror lately? Even if none of us were around, I think bullies would think twice before coming after you."

Alex had looked death straight in the eye, but looking his peers in the eye was going to take more work. I nudged him gently down the stairs, and I mentally alerted the whole gang. If I stayed glued to Alex the whole time, that might not be much better than having his parents with him; having different people around him would be more subtle but still give him the backup he needed. Just to make sure he had a good evening and got off to the right start in reintegrating himself with his fellow high schoolers, I amped up his charisma…just a little touch, but enough I hoped. I also cast a little notice-me aura around him, kind of the reverse of the don't-notice-me spells I used when I wanted a discreet way to stay under the radar. The combination of our friendly presence and the magic should keep a steady stream of people saying hello to Alex, talking to him with genuine interest, maybe even complimenting him on how good he looked. Alex was no one's idea of a model, but his new physique—better than Shar's actually, though I'd never point that out—would be good for a few conversations with guys about Alex's workout routine…as well as a few inquisitive glances from girls. Finally, I linked his mind to mine just enough for me to be able to tell if anything was upsetting him. Maybe now *I* was guilty of overkill, and I promised myself I would take the training wheels off in future social occasions, when Alex was surer of himself.

My good for the day done, I settled back at the table with Dan, still single like I was, and a couple of our soccer teammates who were "between girlfriends" and busy most of the time watching the dance floor for prospective new recruits. I pretended to do the same, but what I was really doing was forcing myself to watch Jimmie and Eva dance. They had officially been a couple for at least two weeks, and I was trying to make myself get over wincing when I saw them together. The experience was a little like feeding yourself poison in small doses; you might develop a tolerance, but at the end of the day it was still poison.

When the other guys raced upstairs to get third helpings, Dan noticed where I was looking. He leaned over to me and asked, "You OK with that?"

"Getting there," I lied. What else could I say?

Jimmie had come to me a few days ago to talk about wanting to get together with Eva. He was so mature about the whole thing, and anyway I couldn't love him more if he were really my brother, so I pretended his new relationship didn't bother me. Actually, it didn't bother me in the same sense losing a limb in a car wreck wouldn't bother me, but I couldn't let him know that was how I really felt. I didn't know if he and Eva really loved each other, but I knew he thought he loved her…and I knew she was never going to love me, no matter what. There was nothing to be gained by getting in the way of their relationship. Yeah, for a while I was going to have to be as fake as the night sky painted on the ceiling, but I had spent four years pretending to be someone I wasn't. I could easily do the same for a little while, for the sake of Jimmie…and Eva. Eventually seeing him with her would stop hurting, and my fake facade would become the truth.

I had lived hundreds of lives stretched over thousands of years. I'd written part of the Bible, fought before Troy, served in King Arthur's court—but in this life I still had some growing up to do. Already I thought I'd learned how to forgive people who wronged me. Soon I would learn that loving others sometimes meant letting go of them. Once I understood that, not just intellectually, but emotionally, then I might really be able to call myself an adult.

That would have been a good note on which to end the evening, but at exactly that moment, I heard Dark Me whisper to me from wherever he was, his thoughts oozing arrogance and loaded with contempt. *"Don't get too comfortable, Boy Scout! You and I still have unfinished business."* He shouldn't have been able to reach me in the protected ambience of Shar's home, but we were still having trouble getting the protection spells to distinguish between him and me.

I thought he might have slipped up by contacting me, but he broke the connection so quickly and skillfully I had no time to try to gain a sense of where he was. When my mind tried to follow him, I felt only darkness and emptiness.

I'd had a month's vacation from supernatural menaces, the longest stretch since August. Well, I always knew it wouldn't last forever!

The Adventure Isn't Over!

If you liked this novel, you might also like the other volumes in the Spell Weaver series, also available from Amazon.

"Echoes from My Past Lives" is a short prequel that tells the story of Tal's original transformation. Find out how his past lives first became a part of his present one...and how that process nearly cost him his life.

Living with Your Past Selves, the first book in the series, picks up Tal's life four years after "Echoes from My Past Lives" ends and a short time before *Divided among Yourselves* begins. Having managed to survive the avalanche of past life memories, Tal pulls himself together and makes good use of the lessons learned and skills developed in those previous lives. He still has the ability to work magic, and there is no denying that's cool. No, his life isn't perfect, but he is managing.

However, his best friend, Stan, has begun to suspect his secret, and Stan isn't the only one. Suddenly, Tal is under attack from a mysterious enemy and under the protection of an equally mysterious friend whose agenda Tal can't quite figure out. An apparition predicts his death. A shape shifter disguised as Stan attacks him. An old adversary starts acting like a friend. He and some other students get hurled into Annwn (the Otherworld), face Morgan le Fay, and only just barely get back alive--and that's just during the first month of school!

By now Tal knows he is not the only one who can work magic and certainly not the only one who can remember the past. He realizes there is something that he is not remembering, something that could save his life or end it, some reason for the attacks on him that, as they escalate, threaten not only him but everyone he loves as well. In an effort to save them, he will have to risk not only his life, but even his soul.

Divided against Yourselves, the second novel in the series, picks up Tal's story within days of the end of *Living with Your Past Selves*. Tal thought that he had saved himself and his friends when he defeated the witch Ceridwen. He was wrong.

He always thought of evil as embodied in external threats that he could overcome in combat. Soon he will discover that the worst evil has been inside of him all along....

Tal's girlfriend is in a coma for which he holds himself responsible. A close friend, suffering from a past-life memory trauma similar to Tal's, is getting worse, not better. Morgan le Fay is still lurking around and has an agenda Tal can't figure out. Supernatural interruptions in his life are becoming more frequent, not less so, despite his expectations. In fact, Tal learns that something about his unique nature amplifies otherworldly forces in ways he never imagined were possible, ways that place at risk everyone close to him.

Tal and his allies must face everything from dead armies to dragons. As soon as they overcome one menace, another one is waiting for them. More people are depending on Tal than ever; he carries burdens few adults could face, let alone a sixteen-year-old like himself. Yet somehow Tal at first manages to handle everything the universe throws at him.

What Tal can't handle is the discovery that a best friend, almost a brother, betrayed him, damaging Tal's life beyond repair. For the first time, Tal feels a darkness within him, a darkness which he can only barely control...assuming he wants to. He's no longer sure. Maybe there is something to be said for revenge, and even more to be said for taking what he wants. After all, he has the power...

Hidden among Yourselves, the third novel in the series, picks up shortly after the ending of *Divided among Yourselves*. Tal faces more challenging mysteries than he has ever dealt with before. Unfortunately, solving them means the difference between life and death— and not just for Tal.

He must find out why the spirit of murder is stalking the people of Santa Brigida. He must find out why a war god wants him dead. To keep a powerful enemy from going free, he must find and retrieve an ancient artifact from a realm he did not believe existed, a realm which he cannot enter, and which none of the inhabitants can leave. Along the way he must also try to figure out if one of his friends is really Alexander the Great reincarnated, how someone could be spontaneously resurrected, and whether a madman is really as mad as he seems.

As if these mysteries were not enough, Tal must also confront opponents stronger than ever, armies of them…and this time they aren't going to take prisoners. Not only that, but another one of Tal's friends will betray him, and in a way that will make the earlier betrayal seem like an act of kindness.

"Destiny or Madness" is a paraquel to *Hidden among Yourselves* that looks at the events in Chapter 2 of that work from Alex's point of view.

Alex is on the verge of getting what he always wanted: a chance to escape from his dull life and enter the world of Greek mythology. Unfortunately, he also discovers the truth of the old saying, "Be careful what you wish for, because you might get it!"

Tasked by Ares, the god of war, with killing one of his fellow students, Alex questions his own sanity. That's just the beginning of Alex's problems, though. Now trapped in a struggle between supernatural forces he can't begin to understand and forced to use a weapon that is really using him, Alex's only escape may be to find the love that has eluded him his whole life.

Other short Spell Weaver works, including the short story, "Angel Feather" and the novella, *We Walk in Darkness*, will be released in the next few months, so be sure to watch for them.

If you like to read in other genres, you might enjoy my essay, **"Sea of Dreams,"** available in the anthology, ***Where Dreams and Visions Live***. If you are a parent with a high school age son or daughter and have not always had success interacting with teachers, you might be interested in the booklet, **"A Parent's Guide to Parent-Teacher Communication."**

About the Author

As soon as he learned to read, Bill Hiatt loved reading. Just as kids who are passionate sports fans often want to be athletes, kids who are passionate readers often want to be writers, and so it was with Bill. Though he dreamed of many career paths over the years, two remained while others came and went: teaching and writing. Fortunately for the world, there was no such thing as self-publishing when Bill was in college and writing horrendous love poetry. Luckily, he kept trying other genres, and he kept reading. He also graduated from UCLA with a degree in English and went on to pursue one of his two dreams by teaching English, mostly at the high school level, for thirty-six years.

Teaching was far more than a day job for Bill; it was his life. He had thought originally that he might be able to both teach and write, but the demands of teaching caused him to forget about writing...for a while. Then, one day Bill, trying to write an interesting grammar test, created one in narrative form, a short story about the students in that particular class. He got so wrapped up in it that he stayed up almost all night writing it. The students loved the test, demanded more like it, and scored better in grammar than any group Bill had ever taught. That experience made Bill realized that he hadn't really abandoned being a writer; he had merely postponed it. He found time to publish a little at the end of his teaching career. Now that he is retired, all the stories accumulated somewhere in the back of his mind will finally be able to get out.

If you would like more information about Bill, this novel, and/or his other writing projects, you can visit him at http:// billhiatt.com/, at his author page on Facebook (http://www.facebook.com/#!/pages/Bill-Hiatt/431724706902040/), and on Twitter (https://twitter.com/BillHiatt2). In the first two locations, you can sign up for his mailing list, so that you can be the first to hear about giveaways, new releases, and other cool stuff.

54453479R00261

Made in the USA
Lexington, KY
16 August 2016